INFIDELITY RULES

A MENU FOR DISASTER: THE PERILS OF LOVING FOOD, WINE, AND MARRIED MEN

JOELLE BABULA

Black Rose Writing | Texas

This is a work of fiction. Names, characters, businesses, places, events, and incidents are either the products of the author's imagination or used in a fictitious manner. Any resemblance to actual persons, living or dead, or actual events is purely coincidental.

ISBN: 978-1-68513-630-7
PUBLISHED BY BLACK ROSE WRITING
www.blackrosewriting.com

Printed in the United States of America
Suggested Retail Price (SRP) $23.95

Infidelity Rules is printed in Garamond Premier Pro

*As a planet-friendly publisher, Black Rose Writing does its best to eliminate unnecessary waste to reduce paper usage and energy costs, while never compromising the reading experience. As a result, the final word count vs. page count may not meet common expectations.

PRAISE FOR
INFIDELITY RULES

"Told with humor and heart, *Infidelity Rules* is an honest and open look at the other side of marriage. The story will leave an impression on you and the wine and food pairings will have you swooning."
–Lyn Liao Butler, Amazon bestselling author of *Someone Else's Life*

"Like the perfect wine pairing, Quinn knows how to find the right bottle for every occasion—but when it comes to love, she's always reaching for the wrong glass. As a talented sommelier with a penchant for unavailable men, she's convinced she's better at tasting notes than reading hearts. But when an unexpected romance arrives at the most inconvenient moment, she must decide if she's finally ready to let herself fall. Witty, charming, and brimming with delicious flavors, this is a story to savor."
–Nicole Meier, author of *The Second Chance Supper Club* and *City of Books*

"*Infidelity Rules* is a delicious escape. The complexities of love and wine pair for an emotional journey alongside characters navigating broken hearts and moral dilemmas."
–Audrey Ingram, author of *The River Runs South*

"With smart writing and memorable characters, *Infidelity Rules* is a wild romp through delicious food, wine, and relationships."
–Jenn Bouchard, author of *Considering Us* and *First Course*

For my father. Forever the champion of my boldest dreams.
Thank you for teaching me to always take the big-ass leap.

INFiDELiTY
RULES

CHAPTER 1

Rule #18: The answer is (almost) always YES to Spanx.

"Do you want to be the one who loves the most or the least in a relationship?" I ask my best friend Dezi as I nibble on a hunk of richly veined blue cheese from our shared charcuterie plate.

"That's a doozy of a question, Quinn," she says, turning her barstool toward me. "But I don't think that's the kind of thing you can control. It simply is what it is. You can't control how much you love or who you love."

Watch me.

It's a Sunday afternoon and we snagged bar seats at Facci, a buzzy neighborhood Italian restaurant. We're either indulging in a late brunch a'la the hangover crowd or a grandma-early happy hour, depending on how you look at it.

"But which would you prefer? If you could choose?" I persist, taking a sip of my crisp vermentino.

I watch Dezi frown as I top a fresh fig with a swoosh of goat cheese so supremely funky I know I'll dream about it later.

"Here," I say, handing her the fig and cheese flavor bomb. "While you're thinking, some magic for your mouth."

"The one who loves the most, definitely," she says, setting the fig on her plate. "No question. Isn't that the whole point of falling in love? To really lose yourself?"

I stare at her plate.

"Aren't you going to eat that?"

Dezi rolls her eyes. "Yes, I'm going to eat that. And you never change. It's always about the food."

"Come on now." I give her the wonky eye. "It's not all about the food."

"Sorry, I left out the wine," she says, shaking her head. "Forgive me. It's about the food *and* the wine."

"What else is there, really?" I squeeze fresh lemon juice over a ribbon of prosciutto.

"Well, considering you pretty much drink wine for a living, I get it. But friends, perhaps? Family? Love? Career? Designer shoes?" She crosses her legs, looking pointedly at her feet, clad in the palest of pink leather stilettos, a wisp of a strap magically keeping them in place.

I smile. "Yes, your shoes are gorgeous. And yes to everything you just said. Except for the love part. And honestly, I'm not so sure about the shoe part either."

Dezi cocks her head and trains her vivid blue eyes on mine.

Uh oh. I know that look. She's in therapist mode.

"Now, if we were the same shoe size and I could raid your closet, I might feel differently," I say, aiming to distract and redirect. Although I do wish we were the same size as her closet is a dream—arranged by color, organized by season and large enough to fit a velvet, lip-shaped loveseat. Her closet oozes chic. I bet if I rolled around on the sumptuous carpet for five minutes, some of it would rub off on me. But alas, we are opposites. Dezi is tiny — barely hitting the five-foot mark — with jewel-blue eyes and a pale blonde pixie haircut. She is utterly adorable, like a doll, which belies her scary smarts and unnerving insight. She also dresses as her stylish closet suggests, on trend and sporting sky-high heels, nipped-in waists and all the appropriate accessories.

I, on the other hand, am six-foot-tall in bare feet and have dark, wavy red hair that tumbles down my back and refuses to be tamed. My eyes are as green as hers are blue, and my legs are long enough to render pant shopping a giant pain in my ass. I try to channel Dezi's sense of fashion when I dress for work—as a restaurant sommelier—but otherwise, it's stretchy clothes and no bra for me all the way.

"Quinn, don't you ever want to fall in love again? To really connect with somebody?" Dezi asks, looking at me over the rim of her wineglass.

Here we go.

"No." I shake my head and signal the bartender for a refill on my water. I have to be at Persimmon this evening for my shift, so it's a one drink limit today. "I like my flings. Nothing but freedom and great sex. Love just gets in the way."

I avoid Dezi's gaze and instead eye the baskets of oil-slicked focaccia parading out of the kitchen. The bartender must have sensed my longing as a stack of the warm, freshly salted bread appears before us almost instantly. Cha-ching, his tip just soared.

"You know," Dezi says, folding her cocktail napkin into a tiny fan. "You can have both of those things and still have a genuine relationship. It doesn't have to end up like it did with your exes."

I sigh. I know she's probably right. Dezi is not only my closest friend, but she's also a sex therapist and psychology professor at George Washington University. She likely knows me better than I know myself.

She was there to help keep me afloat when Liam, my fiancé, abruptly discarded me two days before our wedding. At my bachelorette party, no less. And then later, when I divorced after stupidly marrying a different man out of friendship, not love. I had married Chris because he was safe, not because I couldn't fathom a life without him. Both relationships were doomed because somebody loved more, way more. To this day, I honestly don't know what's more agonizing, enduring your own heartbreak or causing someone else's. But I vow to never be in either position again.

"Zero commitment works for me, Dezi. I can't get serious again. I don't know how to pick men for the long haul," I say, biting into a rosemary studded pillow of focaccia. "That and I love my career. I don't want to make time for a commitment."

"Quinn, it's your life," she says, her blue eyes sweeping over my face. "But I worry about you."

"Well, I'm worried about whether I can last the entire evening at the restaurant tonight in these godforsaken Spanx." I squirm in my barstool, trying to release the Lycra pinching at my waist. "One more blob of cheese and I won't be able to breathe."

Dezi rolls her eyes. "Go yank them off. Why are you wearing those horrible things anyway? You're gorgeous without them."

I can feel the heat of a blush creep along my jawline and bloom over my cheeks. I want to free my parts, badly. But I also want my ass to look terrific tonight, equally badly.

"Are you blushing?" Dezi asks, smirking. "Spill it, Quinn."

"Okay, okay," I grumble, pushing the charcuterie board toward her. "Eat some of this, will you? Before I take it down myself."

"Quit stalling."

"I have a whopping crush on a man I've never met, never spoken to, and who probably doesn't even know I exist."

"A love interest, perhaps?" she says, a smile teasing her lips.

"Nice try. A fling interest. A three-months-of-mind-blowing-sex interest."

"And where do the humongous undies fit in here?" she asks, biting into a fig.

"I keep seeing him at Persimmon, but we've never met. And I'm hoping to run into him tonight."

"Ahhhhh. You want to look hot so you can snag this mystery man," she says, still smirking at me.

"That's the idea." I drain the last of my wine. "I need to capture his attention somehow."

"And you hope your ass will do the trick?"

"I figured it's worth a shot. What do I have to lose?"

Dezi laughs. "You're a woman on a mission. And you certainly wouldn't be the first."

"How do I look?" I run my fingers through my tangle of waves and smooth down my pencil skirt. "I have to get to the restaurant soon."

"You're lovely my friend, as always," she says, squeezing my hand. "I hope you run into him, but be careful what you wish for."

I nod. I know exactly what she's thinking.

"I hope he's single," she says, pinning me with that blue-eyed gaze.

I hope he's married.

CHAPTER 2

Daily Special

Ricotta-stuffed meatballs in lemon broth with fried sage
Shaved baby artichoke salad
Bucatini with fresh sardines and wild fennel fronds

I'm pouring the last of the wine for my customers when I overhear a woman sighing with pleasure as she chases a forkful of chef's pasta with a sip of a juicy Sicilian white, my suggested wine pairing.

Yes! A good match. I'm delighted I was able to provide her with this tiny bit of joy.

I love wine. I love food. I love the magic that happens when a great glass of wine pairs perfectly with a dish. It's lusty and romantic, the only goal sheer and immediate pleasure. It's akin to the ideal relationship, fleeting but swoon-worthy, each bringing out the very best in the other. The wine becomes a better version of itself, and the flavors of the food become more vivid, livelier and, if you get a lucky match, the combination will make you moan. I swear it will.

This is what I live for. And it's what I strive to do as a sommelier for my customers at Persimmon.

If only love matches were as easy as pairing food and wine. Stupendous failure would accurately describe all my past relationships, so I don't date single men anymore. I have affairs with married men instead. But I never,

ever play with men in happy marriages. Nor do I mess around with anyone that has children. Either would be like sabotaging the dream food and wine team — barbarian indeed.

I'm smiling at the woman's utter food bliss and daydreaming about my next meal when I feel the heat of a man from across the dining room. Not just any man. My Mystery Man. The one whose mere presence zaps my appetite, flushes my cheeks and makes me want to giggle like a schoolgirl mooning over her first crush. Mentioning him to Dezi this afternoon must have brought me good juju because he doesn't come around that often.

I wonder if he's married.

Tonight, I find out, I think to myself as I watch him stroll toward the bar, all long legs, muscular shoulders and towering, hoop-star height.

I find myself wafting toward this mystery man almost imperceptibly, like a carb-starved dieter trailing after the luscious aroma of freshly baked bread. I bid a hasty goodnight to the last of my diners and pray I'm able to sneak behind him on my blade-thin stilettos to get a peek at his ring finger.

Come on wedding ring. Come on wedding ring. Come on wedding ring, my thoughts flash like a meditative chant in my head.

Okay. Here goes, I think, hoping my colossal, hold-you-in panties are doing their job. I did not, per Dezi's suggestion, wiggle out of them earlier.

Except now Chef is beckoning me from the kitchen. And he's holding out a huge bowl of his steaming meatballs. Mmmmm. These are moan-worthy, make-your-eyes-roll-to-the-back-of-your-head, meatballs.

But I want to catch My Mystery Man before he disappears again, which is what usually happens. I need to find out if he's married. But those meatballs ...

Do I want the man or the meat? Man or meat? Gah! What to do?

Man it is.

I find him alone at the candlelit marble bar nursing what appears to be a whiskey, neat. Our bar is separate from the dining room and manages to be sexy and cozy at the same time. I'd be equally comfortable in a slinky cocktail dress or well-worn jeans and boots. I love the low-lit, old-school crystal chandeliers, deep warm wood tones, candlelight en masse and the crazy-comfortable barstools. If I didn't already spend enough time at Persimmon, I would be a regular here.

I watch Mister Mysterious settle in and sip his drink. He fills out the barstool with his impressive frame, his shoulders dwarfing the deep green high-backed leather chairs. I need to stop staring and start moving. What I should do is be cool and keep my distance, but I can't seem to help myself. I'm sucked into his orbit and am now almost close enough to sit in his lap. Or lick him.

Good grief, Quinn. Get ahold of yourself.

The man swivels his barstool towards me and smiles.

"Join me?" he asks, rising and pulling out the stool next to him. "What can I get you?"

Oh my god, he's even sexier up close. Dark, tousled hair. Orthodontic perfect teeth. And a smile that lights his eyes and carves a single jelly bean dimple into his otherwise chiseled, Hollywood face.

"I can't stay long," I lie, sitting down regardless and smiling at this fabulously tall wall of man in front of me. "I have plans."

I attempt a furtive glance at his ring finger, but no luck. Crap.

"I'll take whatever time I can get," he says playfully. "I've seen you here before. You are most definitely hard to miss."

I cannot help but smile at that.

"I work here," I say, inching closer to him. "I'm the sommelier."

"Ahhhh," he says, drumming his fingers on the bar and revealing — *finally, but damnit* — a naked ring finger. *Sigh.* It appears he's single. Just my luck.

I deflate. I need to exit and fast, but I can't seem to drag myself away. I'm too distracted by his muscular forearms peeking from his partially rolled-up sleeves.

"Clearly that's where I've gone wrong," he says in this hypnotic, radio news voice. "I'm more of a whiskey or beer guy. Something tells me I may have to make an exception here soon."

"Well, perhaps I'm biased, but you're missing out," I say, crossing my bare legs and turning ever so slightly toward him. "I bet I could find a wine you would enjoy."

Shit, I say to myself. *What are you doing? Naked hand! Naked hand! You've been down this road before. No more single men. Walk away.*

"Oh yeah? I'll take that bet. But I'm pretty sure I'd enjoy anything you poured for me," he says, taking a sip of his drink and slowly turning my barstool with his foot so I'm facing him directly.

My brain tells me to run, but my body tells me otherwise. I want to touch his hair. Squeeze his bicep. Stroke, well, just about anything on this man. I briefly entertain the thought of attempting a fling but quickly extinguish it. It won't work, it never does. I've tried the no-strings-attached dating without success. Men are either looking for a one-night-stand or for a girlfriend to play house, there's rarely any middle ground. I want the romance, the seduction and the all-consuming, mind-blowing infatuation that comes with a new crush. With married men, that's exactly what I get—all sizzle with no chance of passion fading into the great big yawn of girlfriend or wifely duties. I get to be pursued. And it's perfect.

No Single men, Quinn. Walk away. Now.

But I can't. I'm acutely aware of his fingertips dangling over the bar and gently grazing my bare leg. My entire body has been condensed to this one tiny spot just above my knee. I swear the electricity generated is zapping my IQ points.

We have slowly closed in on one another and I'm now near enough to smell the smoky, caramel whiskey on his breath. And to see that he's just a few hours past needing a shave. So, so sexy, this one.

"Marcus," he says, taking my hand.

"Quinn," I reply, surprised I even remember my own name.

The universe is torturing me. I'm aware he may indeed be married, despite his ringless finger, but I can't risk it. I'm too attracted to this guy. If he's not married, I'd be in trouble, fast. He's a walking, talking, breathing recipe for hot sex and heartbreak, the latter I'm not willing to gamble on.

"You mentioned you have plans tonight. When do you have to leave?" Marcus asks. He smiles down at me, and I find myself looking up into a pair of Tahoe blue eyes with lashes I would gladly give up wine for. Okay, maybe not wine, but close.

"Soon," I say, glancing at my non-existent watch.

I know I should go. But all I want to do is stay and shamelessly flirt. Marcus is very much my type — tall, broad-shouldered, an easy laugh and just disheveled enough to be squarely in the man category. This is no Lululemon shopping, hair product wearing, man purse carrying metrosexual. No indeed.

HELLO! Quinn! He's NOT MARRIED. He is the exact opposite of your type, I shout to myself. *Do NOT get involved.*

"I'd like to see you again," says Marcus.

Yes! For the love of god, YES, my whole body is screaming. But I don't choose well. I either love too much or not enough.

I slowly stand up, which inches me even closer to him. *I have to get out of here.*

"I'd like that," I say in spite of myself. "You know exactly where to find me."

What are you doing? Stop flirting.

My brain and my body are at war.

As I turn to leave, he stands as well and gently puts a hand on my hip. He leans in, puts his lips next to my ear and whispers, "I do. And I will."

I want to kiss him. I want to press my body against him. I want to take him home. But instead, I smile and head for the door. I know he'll be watching me the entire way and, for once, I'm grateful I chose to wear heels and that I didn't rip off my Spanx per my usual routine. Here's hoping the unyielding Lycra works its derriere-shaping magic and that my ass looks great in my snug pencil skirt.

CHAPTER 3

Rule #8: Choose your confidantes wisely.

I close my eyes and select jars at random, holding the vials just below my nose, my elbows propped on my sun-dappled kitchen table. Hmmm, I get a whiff of juniper berries in one, unripe peaches in another and the slightly pungent, sweet scent of black licorice in a third.

I open my eyes to find I'm correct on all three before moving on to another batch. I have an hour before I'm meeting Dezi for dinner and I'm taking advantage of the time to polish my "sommelier nose" and study my hefty wine bible. It's not just for the restaurant, it's so I can continue to advance as a sommelier. And perhaps, someday, open my own boutique wine shop.

I close my eyes again and open a fourth vial, only to catch a heady mix of caramel and smoke.

Marcus.

Instantly, I'm back in the bar at Persimmon, suppressing the urge to place a finger in his dimple, among other things. It's been two weeks since our brief encounter and the man has invaded my thoughts ever since. My brain finds reminders everywhere and my body buzzes in tandem. A whiskey bottle at Persimmon? Buzz. A tall man on the street? Buzz. A dimpled customer? Buzz. The radio dude with the deep voice? Buzz, buzz, buzz.

Gah. I need to get ahold of myself.

I shake thoughts of Marcus from my head—I am so *not* dating him—and glance at my phone. It's time to meet Dezi. Hallelujah, a much-needed distraction.

•   •   •   •   •

I spot Dezi almost immediately, perched at the bar in Le Petit Cochon, one of our favorite local joints for excellent wine and solid French bistro fare. I'm a sucker for a huge bowl of mussels drowning in wine and butter and this place does a spectacular version, complete with a fresh baguette for dunking.

She doesn't know yet I've met Marcus and I'm hoping she's forgotten about him. I don't want to have to tell her he's single as she'll be thrilled. And she'll no doubt encourage me to date him. Dezi is the only person besides my brother who knows about my penchant for dating married men as few others would understand. She doesn't love it, but she doesn't judge. She's single too, and after listening to countless couples discuss their colorless marriages and sleep-inducing sex lives, she sort of gets it. As a friend and therapist, Dezi probably understands my own motivations for dating married men more than I do.

"Hey there," she says, rising from her barstool to give me a hug. "I swear I just saw your old fling Derek. You just missed him."

"Really? I thought he stopped traveling to D.C."

She shrugged. "Maybe a lookalike then? Or maybe he's just visiting. Who knows?"

Derek was my latest love interest, but we ended our affair for good almost three months ago. I enjoyed him while it lasted — nine months — but he's no longer required to travel to D.C. for work, so our romance naturally burned out. As it turns out, his wife was having her own affair and has since filed for divorce and plans to marry her new love. Good for her.

"I ordered you your usual," says Dezi, gesturing towards a gently fizzing flute filled with Crémant, one of my favorite types of sparkling wine.

"Thanks," I say, clinking my glass with hers.

"So," she says, studying the menu, "did you meet your mysterious man? Is he single? And most importantly, any chance you're ready to try dating single men? You know, the kind who are actually available?"

Sigh. I was stupid to think she'd forget about him. I can always count on Dezi to bring up my dating habits. She rarely pushes too much, but she does like to check in and remind me what I'm doing isn't exactly emotionally healthy. I know she's right, but I'm not about to risk my heart again. Hell no.

"Yes, his name is Marcus. Yes, he's single. And absolutely not," I say, answering her questions. "And you're not allowed to ask me that again for at least a month."

"I just want you to be happy," she says.

"I am. I'm very happy. I'd be even happier if he was married."

Dezi shakes her head and takes a sip of her drink. "Maybe this one is worth it. But you'll never know unless you try. And that's all I'm going to say."

I nod and fiddle with the small flickering lantern adorning the bar, twisting the base to make the light scatter. "I'm not ready, Dezi."

I have terrible judgement.

Shame and guilt sweep through me when I think about how foolish I was with my ex-fiancé, Liam, who strung me—a gullible jackass, apparently—along for five years. And then how much pain I caused my ex-husband, Chris. I put him through an entire wedding and year-long sham of a marriage. I had *wanted* so badly to love him. But wanting something, no matter how desperately, doesn't make it so. I just didn't figure that out until after the big white dress, the vows and the buffet dinner. But I had said yes. So I tried to love and honor Chris, a kind man — my friend — as a husband. But I have since learned, you can't marry the right man, the good man, for all the wrong reasons. Nor can you convince a man to love you who simply doesn't. Nobody thrives, nobody wins.

I shudder at the memory of it all. I'm now glad Liam dumped me. And I know letting Chris go was the absolute right thing to do. But I never should have said yes to either one in the first place.

"Are you okay?" Dezi asks, interrupting my thoughts. Her voice is almost a whisper, barely audible over the restaurant's soft track of French rap music.

"Absolutely, just hungry. Let's order dinner," I say, changing the subject and surveying the menu, although I already know what I'm going to order. I catch the bartender's eye and wave him over. "The frisée salad with extra blue cheese please and the classic mussels for me."

Dezi orders her usual — roasted beets with goat cheese and a plain omelet with fresh herbs.

Dezi and I met almost twenty years ago, shortly after we both graduated from college the first time around. Armed with shiny new degrees, we both found ourselves a bit lost and rather disheartened by the utter uselessness of our generic majors — hers in biology and mine in something called health science, essentially biology for weenies. I briefly considered nursing school until my older sister, a nurse, pointed out that not only would I have to touch people, but they might cough on me. And, I would have to follow gross orders like "drain pus" or "flush catheter" or "insert enema now."

Forget it. She lost me at the word pus.

So, I wound up sitting next to Dezi on our first day of class at the Johns Hopkins Bloomberg School of Public Health in Baltimore. We had both decided that pursuing a master's in public health was the path to our futures.

We were both clearly very wrong.

I made it through one semester before I realized a fascination with weird disease outbreaks (anyone read the Ebola book *The Hot Zone* more than once besides me?) and a fear of vector-borne illness does not an epidemiologist make.

Dezi, however, graduated with honors. Of course. And then she proceeded to plow her way through a Ph.D. program in psychology and currently teaches and works as a much sought-after therapist.

I finally found my way in wine and have never once looked back. It took a while, which seems ridiculous given I grew up in California wine country, but sometimes we're blind to what is smack in front of us.

Needless to say, Dezi and I have been through a lot together. We struggled as we both contemplated career changes, returned to school, moved to D.C. and generally endured the growing pains of our twenties and most of our thirties together. She's like a sister to me.

"So," Dezi says, stabbing a beet with her fork, "what's your game plan for Marcus?"

"No game plan other than to avoid him. And try to stop thinking about him."

"And how is that working out for you?"

I roll my eyes. "Take a wild guess. But enough about Marcus. What about you?" I ask. "Are you still fending off your students?"

Dezi shrugs. "It was only that one time. He was a very sweet kid, just had a bit of a crush."

"A bit?" I laugh. "He brought you a giant, heart-shaped sugar cookie. On Valentine's Day no less."

"I let him down gently," she says, slicing into her omelet. "Thankfully, it doesn't happen very often."

"I wouldn't be too sure." I dip the heel of my baguette into my buttery broth. "I bet plenty of your students are smitten, they're just too wise to act on it."

"Well, let's pray it stays that way. I don't want to deal with that nonsense again. It's hard enough juggling my classes, my clients and my research. I don't need the headache of homesick freshmen with googly eyes."

"What about Alex?" I ask, referring to my younger brother, who I think would be a great match for Dezi.

"Not this again. I'm not getting involved with your brother. Yes, he's cute and smart and funny, but he's your brother. Trust me, it's unwise."

"Okay, okay," I grumble. "But if you're allowed to bug me about dating single men, I'm allowed to bug you about Alex."

"Hmmm, one of these suggestions is healthy, the other is stupid," she says, tapping a finger against her chin. "Doesn't seem like a fair comparison."

"Truce. How about another glass of wine? You're almost empty." I gesture toward her glass.

"Only if you make a recommendation. I didn't love this one."

I throw my hands up in the air. "Um, hello? We have met before, yes? Why didn't you tell me you didn't like your wine?"

Dezi laughs. "Simmer down, my friend. Because I usually don't care that much. But I want something different this time, so go for it. Practice your skills."

"On it," I say, scanning the wine list. "I'll have the bartender set us up with a tasting."

Ten minutes later Dezi and I are each enjoying our own little wine tasting, hers a selection of white Burgundies and mine a trio of Southern French reds.

"To excellent wine and healthy choices," she says as we toast one another.

"Seriously?" I raise one eyebrow at her. "I am so setting you up with Alex."

"Okay, okay," she says. "How about to friendship and designer shoes?"

"Perfect."

Dezi smiles and takes my cue as I guide her through her wines, encouraging her to take note of the scent of crisp green apples in one glass compared to that of crushed flower petals in another.

"What about him?" Dezi whispers, tilting her head toward the sandy-haired bartender sporting a bush of a beard and a Daffy Duck tattoo on his massive forearm. "He keeps looking at you."

I shake my head. "No big beards. No bartenders. And definitely no on the duck."

"Okay, so why not Marcus?" Dezi asks, clearly still pushing. "Not even one date?"

"No," I sigh. "The likelihood of me dating a single man is on par with me asking Daffy over there to see any hidden tattoos."

"So ... give it to me in percentages."

"Zero. Zero percent."

•   •   •   •   •

I didn't plan to start dating married men exclusively. But now I'm terrified of making another mistake—of either losing a man I desperately love or slowly suffocating in a dead marriage. I simply can't ever fall in love again or risk anyone loving me. Married men are safe because it's just a fling. The affairs burn fast and bright, leaving no time for attachment and little chance of anyone getting their heart smashed to smithereens.

The pain of my past outweighs the guilt surrounding these affairs, but not by much. That's why I follow strict rules. Well, some strict—never fall in love, for instance—and some rather bendy—gigantic panties are not *always* the answer, for example. It's the hardline rules that help assuage my heavy heart. First, I don't date anyone with young children as I refuse to take away somebody's dad. I simply do not mess around when kids are involved. And as I said before, I don't meddle in healthy marriages. Besides, strong marriages have a force-field around them and I swear I could shimmy naked in front of a happily married man and he'd excuse himself and go find his wife.

I don't make an effort to turn a married man's head. I am merely available once his gaze is already set to roam.

CHAPTER 4

Rule #5: Never go for the guy who makes you feel unhinged.

I wake up with Marcus on the brain. What *is* it about that man? I barely know him, yet I want to rip his clothes off. But I also want to make him laugh. And feed him. But that's a dangerous place to be. I cannot get involved with a single man. I just can't.

Can I?

I need to go for a long run and clear my head. Dezi's words from our recent dinner are flashing in my head like a damn marquee. Should I think about dating available men?

I quickly pull on a pair of running tights and a T-shirt and stuff my feet into my crazy-colored running shoes. I ditch the earbuds since I don't need any distractions this morning. I need to pay attention to my own thoughts, not drown them out. I gather my hair into a messy ponytail and am out the door before I can change my mind and decide to go for brunch and bloody marys instead.

As I wind my way through the city and towards the Washington Mall, my thoughts keep turning to inane things such as what I want for lunch or whether I should try Latisse to lengthen my eyelashes.

I'm clearly avoiding the topic at hand. I need to decide whether to dip my toe in the dating pool again. With Marcus. For real. Or with anyone for that matter.

It's hard to imagine dating single men again. I've been dating married men exclusively for the past few years and I'm now comfortable and well versed in the whole dance. It seems more complicated than sticking with bachelors, but ultimately, it's much simpler. And, truth be told, it rarely leads to anything more than a few months of shameless flirting and great sex.

What's not to love? It's all the fun without all the heartache. If you play the game right, anyway.

But *Marcus*. He has lust-addled my brain. And he's making me think twice.

So, I keep running, enjoying the sunshine and cool breeze — ideal running weather. Running is how I tend to solve problems. But it's also how I often avoid them. I ran, day after day, until my knees ached and my shoes were bloodied after Liam cracked open my heart. I thought, stupidly, that I could outrun the pain, the empty want in my chest.

And then I did the same while married to Chris. I took crazy-long runs. It was the only time I felt I could breathe freely.

My pace quickens as I remember acutely, physically, what a terrible time that was. I married Chris because he was my best friend and he adored me. At the time, I thought that was enough. So I put on the veil and said I do. What an idiot. I felt doom right after the honeymoon. I would look down at the dazzling diamond wedding ring on my finger and feel like a fraud. The light-throwing, shimmering bauble in no way reflected the dull emptiness in my heart.

I cross the street and continue toward the green expanse of park space at the Mall, passing the Halal cart guys setting up lunch stalls for the day. I can't remember the last time I indulged in shawarma, laced with tahini and stuffed into thick, pillowy pita. That guy on the corner of Constitution and Pennsylvania makes the best version I've ever had.

Keep running. It's too early for lunch. They're not even open yet.

I decide to avoid the route that will take me near my favorite cart. I don't need thoughts of spicy meat and my dating dilemma battling for headspace.

I think back to Chris and how I should have left him right after the honeymoon. But I thought I could fake it. I truly thought I could swallow my despair, tough it out and eventually be the woman he needed. I wanted to give Chris the happy ending I didn't get with Liam. So I tried to be the wife he needed, but our marriage felt loose and flimsy, like a tattered pair of too big shoes. It simply didn't fit. Just like, I suppose, I had never really fit with Liam.

Liam. My head and heart ricochet from Chris, my friend, to Liam, the man I poured myself into. I've never gotten over the shame of getting dumped just hours before my wedding. Or the pain of loving someone so completely, who never really loved me. My stomach flips as I remember how I foolishly ached for him. For months afterward, my heart betrayed me and leapt with each new text message. *Did he change his mind? Did he want me back?* Like any muscle, it had memory and it kicked in out of habit and repetition. I had loved Liam for most of my adult life. But how did I get it so wrong?

And then I got it all wrong again with Chris. It's something I still grapple with today. I made two terrible choices, so how can I possibly trust my own judgement again?

I'm loping along now but break into a sprint so I can whiz past the food trucks without succumbing to the scent of delicious things sizzling on grills or whirling on spits. I really should have eaten breakfast.

I head straight for the middle of the park to stretch and put distance between me and the aroma of lunch. My brain still has work to do. I reach for my toes, allowing my head and arms to hang, my fingertips brushing the grass.

Date Marcus, yes or no, I whisper into the earth, hoping for an answer.

No, my brain screams back at me. *Remember when you lost your shit in Target?*

My gut twists at the memory. I had cried great, gulping sobs in the greeting card aisle while browsing anniversary cards for Chris.

At the time, nothing captured how I felt.

There were no cards that read, "I am tired of playing wife."

"I just can't fake it anymore."

"We made a terrible mistake on our wedding day."

Those cards don't exist.

The very next day, I told my husband of just one year that I had to leave. That I never should have agreed to be his bride. And that I was desperately sorry.

I hated myself for hurting him.

Love sucks. No matter which side you're on.

Somebody always gets their heart cracked open, their world shattered.

Somebody always wants more, loves more, needs more.

How do you find an equal match? You don't.

It was a debacle with Liam and even worse with Chris, the wreckage of our relationship scattered between us.

I had loved the wrong man. I had married the wrong man. And I was never going to do either one again.

Marcus is not an option. Single men are not an option. And that's my final decision, no more internal arguments.

And no more avoiding lunch and my grumbling stomach.

I'm making my way to my favorite cart—the one with the spicy grilled eggplant and preserved lemon pickle—when I get a text from Chef. He's sending me to a wine seminar tomorrow to find some decent bottles of Italian red for the restaurant.

Nice! I love wine seminars. Not only are they great for networking, but I could stand to brush up on my Italian wines. That, and they are often filled with out-of-towners, rendering them fecund ground for finding my next married man, especially if any of them regularly frequent the D.C. area for business.

This couldn't have come at a better time as I desperately need the distraction. And nothing distracts like good wine and, at this very moment, a giant shawarma.

CHAPTER 5

Rule #4: Hands off happily married men.

I'm settled in at the wine seminar, trying to focus on the Italian wine expert carefully explaining the nuances of Chianti wine labels. I'm a whiz with California and Oregon wines, but I swear the Italians like to confuse simply for fun. But I'm determined to learn and crack the code. I'm studying my wine region map when a sommelier from Manhattan stands up to discuss appropriate food pairings with some of these hefty reds. My ears prick up immediately. I hear him say things like "thick tomato ragu," "slow-simmered Bolognese" and "sage brown butter ravioli."

My stomach rumbles. They really should have discussed this part after lunch. I look up from my notes to see the sommelier circling a wine region on a large map. In giant script next to it he writes, "pairs best with a well-marbled, dry aged, thick cut of beef."

Thick cut of beef. Mmmmm. Marcus. Double mmmmmm.

Shit. Bring it back, Quinn. *No. No Marcus, no meat.*

It's too late. Now I'm thinking about Marcus and what I want for dinner.

Marcus with his lone dimple, gusty laugh and well-formed pecs. A thick, juicy, almost mooing rib-eye. Mmmm. It's a 70-30 split. In Marcus's favor.

Pay attention Quinn, I admonish myself. *Quit acting like a jackass. You're on the clock for Persimmon.*

I shake it off and get my head back in the game. Not only would a rich Barolo pair beautifully with the fat steak I'm dreaming of, but I'm also charged with choosing a few new wines to offer at the restaurant. The fact that these seminars are also packed with men is simply a bonus. It would be nice to find myself a married man pronto. Somebody who can yank me back from the gravitational pull of Marcus.

Wine first, Quinn, I promise myself. *Fling, second.*

I scribble notes about Italy's famed Brunello di Montalcino and simultaneously scope out the fellow wine lovers sitting at my table, four men and one woman. Today's event isn't limited to wine professionals, so there are a hodgepodge of attendees. The five seated with me are apparently all out-of-town drug reps playing hooky on their last day of a pharmaceutical seminar.

I glance quickly at the hands of all the men and all but one are wearing gold or silver bands.

It doesn't take long to suss out that at least two of the three husbands at my table are happily married. You can always tell as they bring up their wives rather quickly and will never hold your gaze for long. That, and these two casually positioned themselves between their colleagues, thus avoiding any chance contact with me. I don't know that they did this consciously, but happily married men automatically keep an arm's length — both figuratively and literally — from other women, particularly single women.

I do a quick assessment of the third married man, who catches me looking, scootches his chair over and says, "You here all on your own sweetheart?"

Ewwww.

I nod. "It's business. I'm on the clock."

I'm not into this guy at all, it's just habit now to read the body language and general vibe of married men so I can quickly rule them in or out as potential flings. This particular man, Tim as he introduced himself, doesn't seem to be on the prowl. He's just a big, jovial salesman who clearly loves to chat with new people. I certainly hope he doesn't supply endless commentary throughout this wine seminar.

Thankfully, he shuts up and I start to settle in and focus on the wines at hand, noting interesting vintages, terroir and any bottles I might recommend for Persimmon. The details and labeling of Italian wine can get complicated, so today I try to focus on what's most important to my customers — tasting notes, food pairings and, of course, price. I sip, I swirl, I spit and repeat. I may not be all that lucky in love, but I do feel extremely lucky to be passionate about my work.

I'll never forget the first time a food and wine pairing blew my mind. I wasn't even in the wine business yet, but I knew some kitchen magic was happening when I walked into the dining room at Hier et Aujourd'hui, a tiny little French bistro on the outskirts of Paris. Above the hushed bits of French I could not decipher, there was an unmistakable — in any language — sound. It was a moan. And then another. And another and yet another. All around these miniscule tables, people were swooning with undeniable pleasure. I had never seen or heard anything like it. At that moment, I wouldn't have been surprised if somebody had stood up and clapped.

I had no idea what was rendering these French diners giddy with delight, but I had to have it. It was my first trip to France and neither I nor my husband at the time spoke French, so we simply pointed and did our best to act out, "we'll have what they're having."

We must have succeeded as, 20 minutes later, Chris and I were both moaning ourselves, eyes closed, as we licked thick spoonfuls of a decadent foie gras mousse and chased it with sips of crisp Champagne. On their own, the mousse and the bubbles were delicious, but together, well, it made you flat out moan. There is no other way to put it.

That was my moment. The moment I truly fell in love with wine. I had always loved food, but that experience was the tiny germ that seeded what now serves as both my work and play — the pursuit of good food and wine, preferably together.

I went back to Paris shortly after my divorce, specifically to get lost in the food and wine. I needed a good solid food moan and damn if I wasn't going to get it. So I returned to that tiny French bistro and I moaned along with every other diner in my American accent. Five times in ten days. It was *that* good.

I am sad to say that Hier et Aujourd'hui has since closed, but that hasn't stopped me from trying to find that experience elsewhere or doing my best to deliver it to my diners at Persimmon.

I'm daydreaming about that tiny pot of foie gras mousse when Tim leans over and asks about dinner reservations for his crew tonight at my restaurant. I nod and tell him I'll handle it. At the break I confirm a five-top for Tim's group at Persimmon, and then stand to take stock of the room. There are about 100 people in attendance and it's time for me to mingle.

I shake off any lingering thoughts of Marcus and head into the thick of things.

I'm chatting with a wine shop owner from Baltimore — perfect distance for an affair — when Tim from my table suddenly appears at my elbow.

"Hey sweetheart! I'm looking forward to seeing you tonight," he says, winking at me.

I stare at him, perplexed. Is this man actually *flirting* with me? Married or not, he's seriously not my type.

"Maybe I'll show up early," he winks again, moving in a bit too close.

Seriously buddy? I don't think so. I know married men must be very direct to launch an affair lest we assume they're unavailable, but this guy is too much.

"I'll be busy working, but I hope you enjoy your meal."

I turn away from him and back to my Baltimore wine guy, hoping Tim will scram.

Baltimore wine guy grins at me. "Looks to me like you have yourself a fan there."

This one is very cute. Not quite Marcus cute, but he's piqued my interest. And he's married. *Hallelujah,* I think, catching a glimpse of a platinum band.

"I certainly hope not," I say. "He's at my table with a group and they asked for a reservation at my restaurant ... maybe he's just appreciative."

"I don't know about that," he says, nodding over my shoulder, still grinning. "Looks like he's back for more. Let's see what he has to say."

Oh good grief.

I turn around just a tiny bit and Tim is on me again. *Too close!* I can smell the Brunello on his breath.

"Any chance you might be interested in meeting up for a nightcap later?" he asks, reaching out to touch my hair. "My treat. I'd love to pick your brain a bit about wine."

I duck out of his reach, much to the amusement of Baltimore wine guy. I'm now seriously regretting getting this fool a table at Persimmon tonight.

"Thanks Tim, but I'm not available," I say firmly, turning my attention back to Baltimore wine guy.

"I'm Quinn," by the way, I say, reaching out to shake wine guy's hand.

"Zack," he says, chuckling. "That was fun. I sure do hope he comes back."

"Oh please, no," I shake my head.

I catch Zack spinning his wedding ring on his finger. I can't quite read him. Is he just friendly or flirting?

I think I need to stick around and find out.

"So," Zack says. "You work at a restaurant then? That means you must live in the area. Make your way to Baltimore much?"

"Yes and yes," I reply. "I'm a sommelier at a place called Persimmon and my brother lives in Baltimore, so I do visit regularly. I also happen to like the burgeoning restaurant scene." I smile at Zack and sit on the table next to him, crossing my legs and inching just a bit closer. "And, I'm always looking for a good wine guy, even in Baltimore."

He moves next to me, leaning against the table. This is an excellent sign.

"Oh yeah?" he says, smiling down at me. "Well, lucky me."

Things are looking up around here. I think Zack is interested in something, I'm just not sure what yet. I'm not opposed to a one-nighter by any means, but I prefer a romance to last weeks to months. Just long enough to bask in the glory of a new flame but avoid the boring guts of anything more serious.

"So Zack, you here buying for your shop or just having some fun?"

"A bit of both. I'm here for the weekend," he says, looking straight at me.

Well ding dong! My affair alarm bells are ringing now. Of course, I was way off base with Tim, so maybe my sixth sense is out of tune. But Zack is here for the weekend. What an interesting tidbit of information. That is generally not something a happily married man shares with a virtual stranger. Particularly a single, female, flirtatious, virtual stranger.

"Are you on your own?" I ask, wondering if perhaps his wife tagged along for the weekend.

"I am," he nods. "At least for today. I'm supposed to be meeting up with some D.C. buddies tomorrow."

We are now ever so slightly touching. And it's all his doing. This guy is definitely interested.

"I don't know about you," Zack says with that adorable grin, "but I got what I came here for today. And besides, I've heard the guy lecturing this afternoon before and he's so dull it's impossible to pay attention. There's sound coming out of his mouth but it's like listening to the teacher in a Charlie Brown cartoon, all garbled mumbo jumbo."

I laugh. "What did you have in mind?"

"How about we get outta here and you let me take you to a late lunch? Give me a chance to convince you that I can be your new wine guy."

"You're on. I'm not the kind of girl who says no to lunch."

•   •   •   •   •

Lunch turns into a lovely afternoon of canoodling in a booth side by side, sharing waffles, bacon and huge slabs of avocado toast at a cozy, breakfast-for-dinner spot. Turns out, Zack does sell wine wholesale to restaurants (bonus), he's often in D.C. for business (convenient) and doesn't have any little ones at home (whew). So far, checks all my boxes, so to speak.

And *clearly,* he's interested in an affair.

"How much time do you have?" he asks, dragging a forkful of waffle through maple syrup and offering it to me.

Good god, this man is feeding me waffles!

I take the bite and look up at him, licking syrup from my lips.

"Wait," he says, leaning towards me, his mouth almost brushing mine. "Let me do that." He gently grazes my lips with his and I can taste maple and vanilla and bacony goodness.

Damn what a fine lunch this is turning out to be.

We are now slowly, gently kissing and kissing and kissing. His hand is on my hip and oh boy, we need to stop before we start doing things that are wholly inappropriate at a breakfast-for-dinner place. Or any dining establishment for that matter.

I pull away and smile up at him.

"Wow," he says, letting out a big sigh.

I nod, wanting him to take the lead. I don't know if this is his first extramarital affair so I'm not sure what he's thinking. I know he's enjoying this, but sometimes the guilt kicks in and extinguishes everything before it even starts. That, and neither of us have brought up the obvious yet, THE WIFE, so I'm wondering when that topic will surface.

Zack nuzzles my ear and whispers, "You still haven't answered my question. How much time do you have? Do you want to get out of here?"

Okay, so guilt is not an issue.

I glance at my watch and notice that I'm due at the restaurant in just over an hour.

"Unfortunately, not much at all," I say. "I didn't realize how late it is and I need to get to Persimmon."

Zack nods and calls for the check. "I wasn't expecting this, you," he says. "I'd like to see you again."

"I'd like that too," I say, purposefully looking at his wedding ring. "What did you have in mind?"

"I know. I'm married, obviously. I haven't done this before but, to be honest, I've been thinking about it for a long time. We've both been so unhappy."

"Say no more. It's none of my business."

"So, tomorrow then?" he asks. "Or perhaps even after work tonight?"

"What about your friends? Aren't you supposed to be meeting up with them?"

"I am, but I have time in the morning. I'd love to take you to breakfast or for a walk in the park. Apparently, breakfast food works for us," he grins, gesturing to the empty plates surrounding us.

I arrange to meet Zack tomorrow at a little cafe near the Tidal Basin so we can grab a quick bite and go for a walk if we choose. After a lingering kiss, I'm off to change clothes and get ready for work.

CHAPTER 6

Daily Special

Spring pea soup with fresh mint and feta
Crispy rockfish with charred ramp pistou

At Persimmon the kitchen is humming and I'm in full sommelier mode. Chef has a crispy rockfish special with a charred ramp pistou, a popular dish that makes a menu appearance each spring. It also happens to be one of my favorites. I could eat that ramp pistou with a spoon. And sometimes I do.

I've been busy the last few hours, guiding guests toward either a sauvignon blanc for the rockfish or a barbera for those ordering the seared duck with raspberries, another popular item this evening. We also have several tables doing the five, seven or nine course tasting menus with wine pairings, so that keeps me hopping. I'm so busy I barely have time to think about Zack and our rendezvous tomorrow morning, which is probably a good thing.

Tim and his entourage have come and gone, thankfully. They all seemed to enjoy themselves and I was too busy to linger so I had very little interaction with Tim. I panicked a bit when he tried to get the whole group on board for the nine-course tasting menu, but mercifully, nobody else was interested. That would have meant way too much time for me at their table.

I quickly canvass the room, which is slowly starting to empty for the night. My tables are quiet at the moment, so it's a perfect time to take a quick break. Chef wordlessly hands me a plate of rockfish with extra pistou as I walk into the kitchen and I gratefully dive in. I would never get this kind of treatment as a server or even a cook, but we wine folk seem to have special privileges in the kitchen, something I have never fully understood.

I am hoovering up the last of my late dinner when my favorite bartender, Julian, wanders into the kitchen, looking for me.

"Hey Q. Somebody's asking for you at the bar. A dude."

Shit, I think to myself. *Please do not let this be Tim. He knows I'm sort of trapped here.*

I'm about to ask Julian what this so-called dude looks like when he disappears. Too late. I guess I'll have to go see for myself. Ignoring customers who ask for you by name is frowned upon in the restaurant business.

I slowly make my way to the bar, circling the dining room first to ensure all my wine drinkers are content. I'm dragging my feet.

It shouldn't be too hard to handle Tim, but it's towards the end of my night and I'm tired. The last thing I want to do is fight off advances. I do a quick sweep of the bar but don't notice Tim. Maybe he left? I catch Julian's eye as he flips a cocktail shaker over his shoulder. He nods to an empty barstool with a barely touched drink waiting patiently for its owner.

I stare at it.

Is that a whiskey? Neat? I know, millions of people drink whiskey, but I immediately think of Marcus. Could it be? I just cannot see Tim sipping whiskey. He's more of a beer or Bailey's Irish Cream kind of guy.

I'm about to sit in the stool adjacent to the whiskey glass — may as well face whatever's coming my way — when I feel him. My body vibrates.

Oh boy. There's no way that's Tim. Take a deep breath Quinn.

"Hey gorgeous," says Marcus softly, leaning down to whisper in my ear. "I hear the sommelier here is brilliant. And unbelievably sexy."

I turn to face him and look up into those Tahoe blue eyes again. He's so much taller than me I actually have to look up, which almost never happens.

"I came here to see for myself if the rumors are true."

OMG. What is it about this man? Quinn you are in so much trouble. Why, why, why can't he be married?

"And?" I say, wishing I had freshened up my lipstick and checked my teeth for ramp pistou.

"No arguments here," he says, gently placing his hands on my hips. "Although I'm still testing out the brilliant part. She has yet to wow me with her mad wine skills."

I cannot help laughing. This guy. I mean, Zack is cute and sexy in his own way, but Marcus ...

The man comes near me and I want to get naked.

Simmer down, I say to myself. *Nobody is getting naked.*

"Join me?" Marcus asks in his silky, radio voice, gesturing to the stool next to his.

I glance at Julian who smirks and nods, essentially indicating that my tables are wrapped up and I'm free for the night.

"Sure," I smile. "I just finished up. Good timing."

"I'm known for that," he says, winking and pulling out the chair for me.

I don't know where my head is as I really should be going home and focusing on my date with Zack tomorrow morning. On the early side, I might add. But Marcus is irresistible and what's the harm in just a bit of flirting at the end of a long night?

"So," says Marcus. "I believe you promised to teach me a thing or two about wine."

I point to his glass of whiskey and say, "I hate to tell you this, but you just blew through your palate with that. There's nothing I can give you that you'll truly be able to taste."

"What a shame," he says, pulling my stool closer to him. "I guess that means I'll just have to see you again."

Shit. Shit. Shit. And yes. Yes. Yes. I am losing my mind over here.

I smile. "You are a persistent one. You don't even know me."

"That's very true. But we can change that," he says, leaning towards me, almost putting his forehead to mine.

Julian slides my usual post work Cognac to me and nods to Marcus. "Hey buddy," he says. "Good to see you. Been a while."

"Wait, you two know each other?" I ask.

"Sure," says Julian. "He comes in from time to time. Started to come in a lot more after the boss man hired you."

I look at Marcus and he grins and turns toward me.

"In fact," Julian continues. "I believe his exact words to me were, 'for the record, I fully support hiring six-foot-tall, leggy redheads.'"

I can't help but laugh. I dig this guy.

"Guilty," Marcus says, his blue eyes crinkling at the corners. "I've had my eye on you for a while."

Julian retreats and before I know it, nearly two hours have slipped by and it's well past midnight. We just can't seem to stop talking and laughing and touching. I want to know absolutely everything about this man. Turns out, Marcus is a pilot and although he lives in Manhattan, he also regularly flies out of the local Dulles airport, so he is frequently in D.C. Oh what an ideal arrangement, if only he were married.

Okay Quinn, I say to myself. You HAVE to get out of this. Give Zack a chance.

I finish the last sip of my Cognac and stand up. Marcus immediately does the same and we are so close to one another that I'm pretty sure a feather couldn't slip between us.

He puts his hands on my hips and gently pulls me into him so our bodies are now most definitely in contact.

"I want to see you again," he says. "And I'd like to make sure you get home safe tonight. I've only had the one drink and my car is just around the corner."

"I bet you would," I say, smiling up at him. There is absolutely no way I can let him take me home tonight. "My usual Uber driver is coming to get me," I say, which is sort of true. I do have a usual driver after I wrap up at Persimmon, but I had to text him earlier to say I'd be late.

"If you're sure," says Marcus, tucking a wayward strand of my hair behind my ear.

"I'm sure," I say. "At least for tonight." *Crap Quinn! Why did you add that?*

Marcus grins and puts his arms around me.

OH MY GOD I WANT THIS MAN.

"When can I see you again?" he asks. "I would like to take you to dinner."

Logic vs Lust! Logic vs Lust!

I hesitate. I want him. But I don't want to get involved and I'm not sure how to reconcile this. I would consider a one-night stand but I don't think it's wise. I'm way too smitten. And if he's not married I'd be in trouble. Fast.

Marcus notices my hesitation and leans even closer, his lips almost on mine.

"Are you already seeing somebody?" he asks.

"Sort of," I say. "It's new ..."

"I'm not the sort of man who minds a little competition," he smiles, gently nibbling my lips, his hand cradling the back of my head.

Good god Quinn! Two men in a day! Seriously? Reverse! Reverse!

But I can't. We are now enmeshed in a full-on kiss. It's soft and warm and perfectly sexy and I don't want it to stop. I don't want anything about this man to stop.

I'm utterly lost in this kiss and momentarily forget where I am. Until Julian flashes the lights. Oops. I feel like a teenager caught making out in her bedroom. We pull slightly apart, Marcus still gently brushing my warm lips with his. "I'll see you to your car," he whispers. "And then I will see you very soon after that. You owe me some wine. And, apparently, I have a thing for tall, wine-drinking redheads."

CHAPTER 7

Rule #2: No single men. Ever.

I wake the next morning feeling rather sleepy and very confused. I cannot believe my day yesterday — two men! I've had a dry spell for so long and suddenly I'm overwhelmed. Hands down I would choose Marcus over Zack all else being equal, but I just cannot get back into the dating pool for real. I would love a fling with Marcus but he's single and I fear it would get serious fast. On my end, anyway. At least with Zack, the likelihood of him leaving his wife for me is almost nil. That only happens in movies.

So, I guess it's a good thing I'm meeting up with Zack this morning. And probably an even better thing that I don't know when, or if for that matter, I'm seeing Marcus again, so I have time to think. I may need to call an emergency gal's night with Dezi.

I skip my workout as I'm crunched for time and slowly tackle my morning. Shower. Blow-dry. Makeup. I keep thinking about Marcus and *that kiss*. And his warm, gentle tongue sending electric shocks like pinballs throughout every inch of my body. His rough cheek against mine. His whiskey scent. Those long, muscular arms around me. And his blue, blue eyes.

Stop Quinn. Just stop.

I need to remember that I did have a lovely afternoon with Zack. He fed me waffles for god's sake. He lives close but not too close, he's in the wine business *and* he's married. By all accounts, he's perfect for me.

I get dressed in my favorite, soft snug jeans and a simple white button-down shirt. I add a gauzy, green and yellow spring scarf and tall brown boots and I'm ready to roll.

I wonder if Zack thinks sex is on the menu this morning? Normally it would be, but I'm not sure I can dive into bed with him with Marcus on my mind. Although maybe that's a good way to get Marcus off my mind? *No, Quinn. Absolutely not. Don't make this more complicated than it already is. You hate complicated, remember?*

•   •   •   •   •

Zack is already seated when I arrive at the coffee shop. Like a typical philandering husband, he's chosen a table in the back, away from any windows. Unless his wife is actually in town with him, which would make this whole thing stupid and risky, it's probably overkill. But, I do appreciate that he's trying to keep the drama to a minimum. And, I suppose if he has friends in town and he's keeping mum about this, then he doesn't want to be seen by anyone who knows him.

I'm thinking too hard about this. His wife and friends are his problem, not mine.

"Good morning," he says, standing up to give me a kiss on the cheek. "I ordered a pot of coffee to get us started."

I don't know the man well at all, but I can already tell he's a bit more subdued than yesterday. I'm wondering if he's having second thoughts about all this.

"You okay?" I ask. I sit across from him and look directly at him. He's fiddling with his wedding ring again. "You know," I say, placing my hand gently over his. "It's okay if you don't want to do this."

Zack smiles at me and says, "Why is that? Do you now have the hots for that guy, Tim? Did he show up at your restaurant and make you an offer you can't refuse?" Zack leans across the table and motions me closer. "Did he feed you waffles?" he whispers.

I laugh and roll my eyes. The guy has a sense of humor, I'll give him that.

We part as the waitress stops by to bring our coffee and drop off menus.

"Seriously though," I say. "I get that you're married and you may be having doubts."

Zack nods. "I'm not. I've been thinking about an affair for years, so this isn't anything new. It's just that my wife called on my way here, so I'm feeling guilty about lying. I've never done this before."

I hope he doesn't continue as I don't want to hear anymore. I don't need to know the ins and outs of why my married men stray. Normally, they reveal their reasons throughout the lifespan of the affair, but it's not anything I need to be privy to, especially in the beginning. I just need to know that Zack does not have young children at home.

"Shall we stay and order?" I ask, gently trying to change the subject and give him an out if he'd like to leave.

"Absolutely. Waffles with extra syrup." He grins at me, patting the space in the booth beside him. "Come join me."

I tell him I'm still in sugar overload, so I'll pass on waffles this morning, but I slide in next to him as we peruse the menu together. We're sitting hip to hip, our shoulders and thighs touching. Although it's pleasant and Zack is adorable, it's not that roller-coaster-ride stomach drop I get every time Marcus is near. But it's fun with Zack. And easy. So I am going with it, at least for the moment.

We spend the morning eating bagels and lox, chatting and strolling along the Tidal Basin. I learn that Zack is a born and raised Baltimorean and his family has been in the wine business for decades. He completed a winemaking internship near my hometown in California wine country and aspires to own a winery someday. Although he'd love to set up shop in California, the industry in that area is saturated and the land expensive, so he currently has his eye on property in Virginia.

We continue to talk shop a bit and I find myself thoroughly enjoying our morning together. Zack is smart, interesting and loves to laugh. He's no Marcus, but he's not a bad kisser, either.

"So," says Zack, pulling me under a cherry blossom tree and kissing me gently on the mouth. "I've told you all about my background. What about you?"

"What would you like to know?" I ask, following him to a bench.

"The usual. Where you're from, how'd you get into wine, any brothers and sisters, husbands ..." he trails off.

I know what he's after. Why am I interested in a married man? I don't like to get into this and, thankfully, men rarely push the issue. They get so wrapped up in the dueling emotions of guilt versus sheer pleasure, they tend to forget to pursue that all important question — why would I date a married man? I assume they eventually conclude there's something special about them. And while this is certainly true as I don't date just any married man (remember Tim?), I also don't divulge that it's a particular hobby of mine.

"A younger brother, an older sister and no husbands," I say.

I tell Zack a bit about my brother in Baltimore, my sister who still lives in Sonoma County and my parents who moved to Baltimore after two of their three children did the same. That was before my sister gave them grandkids, however, so who knows how long they'll stick around. I always assumed I'd move back to Northern California, but I fell in love with the East Coast. I do miss California weather at times and the laid-back vibe, but I'm crazy about the four seasons and I love the ability to ditch the car and walk just about everywhere.

And, if I'm honest with myself, California still reminds me of Liam. And the great big Napa Valley winery wedding that never was. And how I drank case after case of my wedding wine with Dezi and my brother, Alex, pouring over every inch of our relationship, trying to analyze what went wrong. When did it go awry? What were the signs before the big pre-wedding dump? And how could I have loved him with such abandon? I still don't have any answers. But I know this—I will never be that vulnerable again.

But I'm not about to divulge any of this to Zack. Too much baggage.

Get your head back in the game, Quinn. This is just a fling. You're not falling in love.

We make it the full two miles around the Tidal Basin, chatting easily, holding hands and making frequent stops to smooch.

"I wish I didn't have to go," Zack says, smiling at me. "I wish I still had my hotel room available ..."

"I'm certainly not taking you home," I say, smiling at him and placing my hands on his chest. *Ooooh, firm.*

"I know, I know," he replies, pulling me to him. "I just wasn't expecting this. You. I want to see you again."

Zack is already behind schedule to meet up with his friends, so we exchange numbers and he promises to reach out soon. Apparently, he travels to D.C. frequently for business, so it shouldn't be too long before he returns. I'm tempted to tell him I'll be in Baltimore tomorrow to see my family, but decide not to push it. It's rather soon for him to want me on his turf and besides, I want to enjoy the chase as long as possible.

Assuming, of course, that I can ignore Marcus.

CHAPTER 8

Daily Special

Chicken braised with shallots, prunes and Armagnac
Roasted new potatoes with caramelized garlic
Baby herb salad with local goat cheese and honey

I show up at Persimmon early as my wine cellar is in dire need of some organization before we get slammed with our weekend crowd. Usually, I tidy up a bit after my shift, but I was preoccupied last night, for obvious reasons. Okay, I'm not being totally honest here. I don't need to organize my cellar as I know where every bottle lives. What I really want to do is corner Julian. And pick his brain about Marcus.

Oh Quinn, you are in so much trouble.

What I should be doing right now is thinking about work and wine pairings tonight. Or, at the very least, mooning over Zack instead of Marcus.

Julian is not behind the bar, so I decide to have a chat with Chef about this evening's menu. He'll be offering spring chickens braised with shallots, prunes and Armagnac. This is exactly the kind of boozy chicken dish I would make for myself at home. A sip of Armagnac for me, a splash for birdie, a sip for me ... oh wait, I suppose that's a great way to never get dinner on the table. Holy crap the kitchen smells incredible — crispy chicken skin, caramelized shallots and soft, silky prunes, all bathing in Armagnac.

Chef gives me a spoonful of the sauce and it's velvety and earthy and sweet. Man oh man do I want to whip up this dish for Marcus at home, with big hunks of crusty warm bread to dunk in that sauce. Or lick it directly from the bowl. Or from his lips.

Stop it Quinn! Focus!

Chef takes one look at my face and smiles smugly. He knows it's delicious.

"I trust you can figure out some wines to pair? I'll save you a plate," he whispers before marching into his kitchen, barking orders.

This dish will be easy to sell and easy to pair. Just about any medium-bodied white or red will do. I usually choose a bottle or two to recommend with each of the daily specials, so for tonight's chicken, it's a pinot noir from the Russian River Valley in Northern California. The particular bottle I have in mind will match beautifully. I open a few bottles to let them breathe and do a quick swirl and sip. It's exactly what I had hoped—fruity, chocolatey, mushroomy, leafy. It's perfect.

•   •   •   •   •

With my wine selection complete, I wander over to the bar to try and get my mitts on Julian before we open. I'm in luck, he's alone and in the middle of bar prep.

"Hey," I say, grabbing a few highball glasses to help him set up. He looks at me sideways, smiling as he fills a tray with olives, lemon slices and brandied cherries.

"Hey," he says. "Tending bar now, are we?"

He's going to make me ask outright. I figured. He's like most excellent bartenders, he keeps his mouth shut and ears open. I've only known Julian since I started at Persimmon a little over a year ago, but we have slowly evolved into friends. We usually help each other wrap up bar service in the evenings, which lends itself to some very interesting conversations. He's not aware of my penchant for dating married men, but he's certainly somebody I would consider trusting with that odd bit of information.

Julian has about 15 years on me, is a long-time, self-confirmed bachelor and, according to my Google search, a former drummer in a pretty darn popular band in the 80s. I know he keeps an eye on his elderly mother who happens to be a rock n' roll loving, still dancing, octogenarian. She's a former Rockette. Once when his mom wasn't feeling well, we called my sister, the nurse, from the bar for medical advice, which proved to be helpful. I think I've grown on him since then and perhaps he sees me as the annoying little sister he never had.

Needless to say, I adore Julian. He's quiet, easy, funny as hell if you pay attention and, he's there when you need him.

"So," I say casually, helping myself to a fat green olive as he expertly snaps my hand away with his bar towel. "How are things?"

"Come on Q," says Julian. "You never come over for a chat just before we open."

"I know," I sigh. "But I should. It's relaxing to talk to you."

Julian nods and continues to press fresh citrus into juice.

I grab another olive and Julian turns to face me and smirks.

"Lemme guess," he says. "Marcus."

"Yes!" I almost shout, which I know Julian hates. "Yes," I whisper fiercely. "Tell me everything. Every. Thing."

Julian shrugs. "Not much to tell. Marcus isn't a big talker and I don't pry."

"Seriously? You've got nothing? Come on."

Apparently, Julian wasn't lying. He doesn't know much more than I do. Marcus is a pilot (yeah, yeah, old news, but, I must admit, still very sexy). He's been a regular at the bar for nearly three years (how have I missed him?). He rarely brings a date (interesting). And he almost always orders the special or just asks Chef to surprise him.

"I think our longest conversation was when he told me he approved of us hiring giant redheads," Julian said.

"Please tell me he didn't actually use the word giant. And why the hell didn't you tell me some hot guy was checking me out? A pilot, no less."

"A former Navy pilot," Julian says.

"WHAT?" I groan. *Can Marcus get any sexier?* "Now you're definitely in trouble."

Julian grins and winks at me. "Maybe I was hoping to keep you all to myself."

•   •   •   •   •

Nearly three hours later, I'm able to take a quick break and hoover up a plate of that crazy good chicken (I was right, totally lick-the-plate worthy). It's been a steady night. I've opened a bottle of Champagne for a couple celebrating an anniversary, I've walked several four-tops through a multi-course tasting menu and I just finished pouring a flight of dessert wines for a party of eight. The Russian River pinot has also been a hit this evening and I think we just may sell out by the end of the night. Thankfully, I've been too busy to even think about Marcus let alone find a reason to peek into the bar area. Okay, maybe I did once. Or twice. Okay, no more than five times. Much to Julian's amusement.

But no Marcus.

I'm disappointed, but I shouldn't be. I need to set my sights on Zack. I like Zack. Zack is handsome. We have chemistry. He suits my needs.

But Marcus makes my heart flutter as if there were wings beating in my chest. He makes my stomach do cartwheels. And he makes me lose my appetite, which is no easy feat.

I poke my head into the bar area one last time to wave goodnight to Julian, but he motions me over. He pours me a Cognac even though I protest as I'm exhausted and just want to go home and get in my PJs. I look up and he's smirking at me.

"I know," I say. "I made a total jackass out of myself tonight."

"You sort of did," he laughs, "but only I knew what you were up to."

"Well," I reply, "I have decided I'm not interested anyway. And besides, I'm kind of seeing somebody else."

"Not interested, huh? Then I suppose I shouldn't pass along the message from Marcus?"

"Wait. What? What message? Marcus was here? Tonight?"

Julian nods. "He had a plane to fly and couldn't wait, but he did leave you this," Julian hands me a note.

And there I go — heart thumping, head whirling, stomach cartwheeling ...

* * * * *

I'm curled up in bed at home with my folded-up square of paper. I feel like a teenager finding a surprise note from a secret crush in my locker. I haven't even read the thing yet. I wanted to get home and get cozy first. Here goes ...

Hey gorgeous. I was hoping to catch you. Sorry I can't wait, I have to fly out tonight. I want to see you.

Coffee? Monkey Roasters Cafe. Thursday. 10 a.m. Coming straight from the airport.

I'll be thinking about you. Impossible not to.

Marcus

CHAPTER 9

Rule #36: Sometimes, two men are better than one.

Thursday. *Thursday*, I think as I wake up the next morning, glimpsing the note on my bedside table. That's four whole days from now. Four days to wrap my head around my next move. Thankfully, I have the next few days off and I'm headed to Baltimore today to see my family for our regular-ish Sunday family dinner habit. It will be good to get out of D.C. and have a long chat with my brother, Alex. He reminds me of a younger version of Julian in that he's a terrific listener. There's not much I can't say to Alex, which is why he's one of only two people who know my affinity for being a mistress.

The morning has gotten away from me and I need to get myself together and off to Baltimore. I'm about to head out when my phone pings. Dezi.

Dezi: What r u up to? Want to order in tonight and watch a movie? In our PJs? With wine?

Me: I wish, but headed to bmore to see the family. Wanna come?

Dezi: No way. You and your mom always try to set me up with Alex. You both think you're sneaky but you're not.

Me: Busted. I still think you two would make a great couple.

Dezi: I'm ignoring that. Have fun. Say hi to all. I still want to hear about this unmarried man …

Me: I'll fill you in. Maybe plan for something later in the week?

Dezi: Yes! Drive safe.

I walk into my parent's condo and, as usual, it smells fantastic, as if my mother has been cooking all day. Which, given that she's Italian, she probably has. The woman does not make fancy food, but she turns out spectacular Italian comfort fare. She's a fan of long-simmered sauces, homemade pasta and ricotta-filled everything. She used to feed us ricotta sandwiches as kids, which is still one of my favorites. Nowadays, fancy foodies would call it "ricotta toast" but back then, it was simply homemade ricotta drizzled with olive oil, sprinkled with sea salt and sandwiched between slices of fresh, warm bread. I often make it at home for lunch or an easy dinner.

"Hey Mom," I shout, sweeping into the condo with three bottles of wine in my arms. "Smells like your red sauce! Glad I brought a couple of Chiantis."

"You know you don't have to do that," she says, throwing her arms around me and planting a kiss on each cheek.

My parents don't like wine. They both hail from wine country and have a sommelier for a daughter, but hey, go figure. They are more gin and vodka connoisseurs. This used to drive me bonkers, but now I like the fact that they prefer cocktails as then I'm truly off duty whenever we're together. I do enough wine pairing and wine chat at Persimmon, so it's a nice break from work.

"You hungry?" my mother asks, gesturing towards a platter of antipasto the size of a long-jump pit. This could easily feed an entire men's basketball team. *After* a particularly grueling game.

"Expecting the Ravens?" I ask, referring to Baltimore's NFL team.

"Funny," she replies, snapping my behind with her dish towel.

There are mounds of marinated vegetables, pillowy piles of prosciutto, wedges of Parmesan cheese, olives, dried figs ... oh, and what appears to be a bucket-sized bowl of her homemade ricotta cheese with hunks of charred bread.

"You have got to be kidding me," I say, spearing a marinated artichoke heart with a toothpick.

My mother, Gemma, is certainly prone to over-feeding, but this is a lot. Even for her and her Italian heart and stomach.

"Your brother is bringing a date," she says.

"What?" I attempt to exclaim over a huge mouthful of ricotta and bread. *OH MY GOD, this ricotta is so good.* "A date? Since when is Alex dating somebody?"

"Since now," says my mother, stirring her tomato sauce and adding just a pinch of her special ingredient — ground cloves.

I'm suspicious. First off, I would know if Alex was dating somebody, especially a woman he's serious enough about to bring home to mama. And secondly, Alex is just too busy and wildly invested in his career to get serious about anyone. At least not yet. He's an investigative newspaper reporter with unbelievable instincts, pit-bull-like aggression when called upon and a firm eye toward moving up the ladder as quickly as possible. The kid has newspaper ink in his veins, I think. He's abandoned dates at restaurants to chase a lead, has missed countless holidays to work a late shift and thinks nothing of spending his time off in tenacious pursuit of a story. Most women don't stick around long enough to become girlfriends. Or, if they do, they soon realize they will always be second to a hot story and make a fast exit. Either that, or they bug him about it so much that he gives them the heave-ho.

So, my brother bringing home a date serious enough to meet mom without my knowledge? No way. I don't buy it.

I'm mulling this over and chewing my way through a pile of finocchiona (fennel salami) when my mother looks at me sideways from her post in front of the stove.

"Is that what you're wearing?" she tries to ask casually.

I do not like where this is going. It's Sunday dinner at home with my family. Since when am I supposed to dress up?

I glance down at my leggings, comfy boots and oversized, plaid flannel shirt. If I was feeling fancy and my stomach felt flat today, I would consider tying the ends of my pink and gray shirt into a cute little bow. But, at the moment, things are hanging loose, a key wardrobe choice for dining at my mother's house. I have learned to arrive in pants that stretch, baggy shirts and no belts. Not much different about today. I'm about to respond and voice my suspicion when my father walks into the room.

"Excited about George, are we?" he asks, folding me into a big hug. My mother is shaking her head furiously at him and my eyebrows shoot up.

"George?" I ask. "Who the hell is George?"

"Uh oh," my father says. "Whoops, I see I let the cat out of the bag."

"What is going on?" I ask, even though I know. They are trying to set me up.

My father quickly shoves a plum-sized hunk of salami in his mouth and points to his stuffed, chipmunk cheeks, shrugging his shoulders. He clearly does not want to get involved in this.

"George works with your father," my mom says. "He's just out of pharmacy school and new to the area. We thought it would be nice to have him here for dinner."

Uh huh. I roll my eyes.

George-the-pharmacist apparently was recently hired by my dad—a seasoned pharmacist— who will be taking Georgie under his wing. The hope here is that George will start picking up more hours so my father can cut back. Oh, and that George and I will fall madly in love, get married and produce three grandbabies in rapid fire succession.

Don't hold your breath, mom.

I'm about to open a bottle of Chianti and just start chugging when I get a text from my brother.

Alex: Almost there. Met your hot date yet?

Me: I'm going to kill you. I haven't even met YOUR date yet.

Alex: Simmer down sis. Mom asked me to just bring anyone. Probably to take the pressure off you and your blind date.

Me: WHY didn't you fill me in?

Alex: She just told me today. Been so busy at work I forgot about bringing a date. Am flying solo. See you soon.

Well, that's just great. I was hoping to talk to Alex about my man dilemma, but it appears I'll be entertaining George-the-pharmacist instead.

My father barely knows him and just figured he's educated, single and has a good job, why not bring him home to meet my daughter?

My gut tells me we will all regret this choice.

George-the-pharmacist has arrived.

George likes to lecture. George is an extremely picky eater — a vegetarian no less! George believes his body is a temple and, as such, he cannot eat, drink, inhale, smell, lick, stand next to or in any way touch anything he deems a pollutant. This extends to my mother's tomato sauce, which, much to my amusement, he's now refusing to eat as it has been "touched" (read, contaminated) by her meatballs.

Alex and I can barely hold it together. This is not going to go well for George.

I see my mother's biceps twitch and I fear she's on the verge of pelting George with a torrent of meatballs. Or beating him over the head with a stick of salami.

I kick Alex under the table and I know we're thinking the same thing. *Please mom. Please, please, please let it start raining meatballs. Hard and fast.*

Alas, my father swoops in smoothly, taking his wife by the elbow and leading her away from the vat of meatballs and sauce.

"I'm so sorry George," says my dad. "I didn't think to ask if you had any dietary restrictions. This is my fault," he says, catching my mother's eye. "I'm sure there's something else we can offer you?"

"Yes, yes, of course," my mother says, regaining her composure.

"I'll be fine with all these vegetables," says George, waving his hand over the massive antipasto tray.

I watch him carefully and I swear he's peering at the tray, trying to see if any meat products are touching the vegetables.

"And just plain pasta will be fine," he says. "I don't need any sauce."

"Would you like butter?" my mother asks.

"Is it from organic and grass-fed cows?" George replies.

My father stifles a laugh as my mother plops a package of cold, straight-from-the-fridge butter on the table.

"See for yourself," she says, shooting eyeball daggers at my dad.

George carefully peers at the butter and frowns.

George-the-pharmacist is frowning at butter.

My mom offers up olive oil. Or cheese. Or egg yolk, which she would then toss in the hot pasta, coating it with a thick, creamy, eggy deliciousness.

I can see George's mind whirring. He'd have to first vet the cheese and the egg, further driving my mom to drink. Or throw meatballs. Probably olive oil is the safest choice.

Olive oil it is!

Wise decision Georgie, I think. *Wise decision.*

• • • • •

With the little problem of dinner for George resolved, I decide it's time to pour some wine. I go to fill George's glass, but he stops me immediately and requests plain water instead.

Oh goodie, this just keeps getting better. He's a teetotaling vegetarian.

I'm waiting for his specifics on the water — filtered, no fluoride, between 50 and 72 degrees for optimal hydration, chipped from an organic glacier, melted at the hands of a vegan virgin ...

But George just smiles at me and accepts a glass straight from the fridge.

Okay, maybe there is some hope for the evening. I'm certainly not going to date this man, but perhaps we can at least have a pleasant time.

I'm making my way through a rather generous second glass of wine and a second helping of meatballs when I notice George eyeing my wine.

"You sure you don't want a glass?" I ask him, taking a sip. "I can open a white or a different wine if you prefer."

"No, but thank you," says George-the-pharmacist. "You do realize that your liver can only metabolize one drink an hour, don't you? So right now, alcohol has saturated your blood and body tissues. Pretty soon, your body will have to store the excess as fat. Even your liver can get fat from too much alcohol," he says matter-of-factly.

Seriously?

The table gets quiet, except for Alex, who is sputtering and trying not to choke on his own mouthful of wine.

I peer at George over the rim of my wineglass as I take yet another sip.

"Do you know what I do for a living George?"

"Um, no, I don't. Your dad never said and, well, um," he starts to trail off. "Perhaps a model?" he says desperately. "Or, um, an artist or something?"

Again. *Seriously?*

Now I'm giggling. This poor guy had no clue what he walked into when he agreed to come to dinner tonight.

"George," I say, as I meticulously wind linguine around my fork. "I'm in the wine business. I'm a sommelier."

•　　•　　•　　•　　•

Dinner wraps up rather quickly after that, much to everyone's relief. Thankfully, George has an early shift at the pharmacy tomorrow so he has an easy out. He may not be socially adept, but he's not an idiot and clearly read the signs — not a match.

Whew.

As soon as George leaves I turn to my father, Sam. "Really Dad?"

"I'm sorry, I'm sorry," he says, throwing his hands up. "He seemed nice enough, and he has a good job. But I won't meddle again."

"I don't buy that, but at least please check with me first, okay?"

"Done," says my father. "You have to admit though, he certainly made the evening interesting."

The four of us settle into clean-up mode and then I convince Alex to join me for a walk. It's a beautiful spring evening and my parents live along the Baltimore waterfront, so there's a lovely path to follow just steps from their condo building.

"So what's up, big sis?" he says, shoving his hands in his pockets. "Usually you'd be stretched out on the couch with a pint of chocolate ice cream, not begging to go for a walk."

"Funny," I say as we stroll by several sailboats slowly rocking in the breeze. I stop to watch a mama duck and her five tiny ducklings swim in a tight little row of feathers and new baby duck fuzz.

"But you're right," I sigh. "I met a man. In fact, I met *TWO* men. And I kissed them both on the same day! I'm a mess."

Alex, who is very much like Julian, remains quiet and simply nods, waiting for me to continue. Sometimes I think he employs his journalism technique with me, which is to shut up and let his sources fill the quiet space.

"One is married," I continue. "One is not."

"Seems to me it's an easy choice then, given your preferences. Unless something has changed?" he asks, looking directly at me.

"I don't know," I say, shaking my head. "I dig the married one, Zack. He's easy and funny and cute and he lives in Baltimore, so it's ideal."

"But?" says Alex.

"But I'm nuts about the single one, Marcus. Totally bonkers about him. I know I barely know him, but we have this wild chemistry. Something I haven't felt in years. If ever," I say with a sigh.

We stroll in silence for a few minutes.

"I should just go for Zack. He's married. It's easy. There's no pressure. And I know we'll have a good time."

My brain is a jumble of thoughts — Zack feeding me waffles, Marcus pulling me in close for a kiss, Zack grinning about the bumbling Tim, Marcus stroking my hair, Marcus writing that note, Marcus and his Tahoe-blue eyes. Marcus. Marcus. Marcus.

I shake my head to clear it, barely noticing Alex leading me to a bench with a water view.

"Zack," I say firmly. "It has to be Zack. Except I cannot stop thinking about Marcus. Ack! I feel like a lunatic."

"No arguments here," says my brother. And then, quietly, "It's been too long Quinn. Maybe it's time."

"Time for what?" I ask, knowing full well what he's talking about. It's been three years since my marriage to Chris crumbled. And longer still since Liam looked me in the eyes and dispassionately told me it was over, discarding me as easily as rotten fruit.

"Come on Quinn," he says, pulling me down to the bench. "You've changed a lot since your divorce. Maybe it's time to at least consider real dating again."

I put my head on Alex's shoulder and watch another duck family, this time out of water and waddling along the path.

"I don't want to make another mistake," I say. "I thought Liam loved me. And Chris, well, I still sometimes wake up at night feeling suffocated and trapped, thinking we're still married. I don't trust myself to pick right."

"I don't think you'll make either mistake again," he says. "Look, I know you didn't get to marry the love of your life. That Chris wasn't Liam. But that doesn't mean you won't get to someday. You'll never know until you get back out there. For real."

"Look who's talking," I say, trying to wriggle out of the conversation. The whole idea of dating single men again makes my skin crawl and I physically shudder. "You rarely date," I point out.

"I'm married to the *Baltimore Independent*," he says, referring to the local newspaper where he works as a reporter. "I date, but apparently women don't like to play second fiddle to work," he says, shrugging. "And I date single women, so there's always the underlying hope that I'll find someone who understands."

I sigh. "I know. I just don't think I even want the possibility of something that might stick. Married men are safe. They're not going to leave their wives and nobody is going to fall in love. I haven't seriously considered real dating for a long time. I'm rattled, Alex."

"I can see that. Look, it's weird, but you've been happy these last few years playing mistress. It surprised me at first, but it does seem to work for you. At least it did. I guess the real question is, how long can you play this game? Are you thinking forever?"

"I don't know. I guess I have a lot to think about."

He nods. "And it's not about either one of these guys, remember that. This is about you and what you want in five years or ten or 20 for that matter."

Oh how I loathe thinking too far ahead. But he's right. I know he's right. But I don't think I can survive another Liam. And I certainly cannot hurt somebody again the way I hurt Chris. Married men are just so much easier.

"Quick," says Alex, launching into a favorite childhood game of ours. "If you were on a desert island and could only take one of these dudes and one type of food, who and what would it be?"

I laugh. "Marcus. No question," I say, rapid fire back. "But just *one* food item? Come on now ... gimme two — a jar of Maranatha peanut butter and a wedge of stinky, funky blue cheese. Now you," I say, happy to be off topic.

"You, of course," says Alex, smiling and putting his arm around my shoulder. "Until I find myself a keeper. And if you're already bringing blue cheese and peanut butter, then I'm in for booze and salami."

CHAPTER 10

Rule #35: Always, always befriend the cheese man.

There's something strange going on with Dezi. I'm at her apartment for our usual Thai takeout night and she's acting weird. Not weird as in she's hula-hooping in a Barbie costume. But weird as in fidgety and flighty. Honestly, it's as if she has ants in her pants.

"Let me pour you a glass of wine," I say, as I watch her pick non-existent lint off the sofa and then start twisting a lock of her pale hair around her finger. "Is everything okay?"

"What?" she says, now fiddling with the Thai takeout menu. "Oh. Yes. Everything's fine. Wine would be great."

I'm not convinced.

I hand her a glass of riesling which she immediately puts down. She goes right back to twisting her hair into spiky little tufts and checking her phone — both very much unlike Dezi. Dezi, who is always so cool and serene, as if she knows all the secrets to life and is just patiently waiting for you to catch on.

I watch and wait. But now she's swilling her wine, another very un-Dezi like trait.

"What's going on?" I ask, peering at her. "Are you okay?"

"Yes, yes," she says, taking a deep breath and sighing. "I'm fine. Really. Now tell me what's going on with you. Are you going to meet up with Marcus or what?"

"Oh no, not so fast. Something's up. Now spill it."

"Okay, okay. I've met someone. His name is Elliot and I'm crazy about him," she blurts out.

"Am I missing something? Who on earth is Elliot? I'm so confused," I say, shaking my head. I look at my best friend and see her cheeks are now hot and flushed as if she just returned from a sweaty spin class. And she cannot stop smiling.

Dezi grins at me and is about to speak when our dinner arrives.

"Hold that thought," I say, jumping up to grab the food. "Okay, go. Tell me everything."

"Wait, food first," she says. "I'm starving."

I quickly dole out chopsticks and containers of our favorites from Basil & Bird — summer rolls, Crying Tiger beef, green papaya salad and drunken noodles. "Two bites. Then you start talking."

"I'm in love," Dezi says, dabbing her summer roll in nam phrik. "At least I think I am," she says, a grin spreading across her delicate, doll-like face.

I nearly spit out a mouthful of wine.

"That's fantastic! But when? How?" I say, firing questions at Dezi. "And why am I just hearing about this now?"

Dezi ignores my last question but starts to fill in the details. The pair met at a cooking class about six months ago. Dezi, a terrible cook, thought it might help motivate her in the kitchen if she had some basic skills (it didn't). Elliot was also participating and since the two of them were the only singles in the class, they were paired up to cook the three-course meal together. Elliot, apparently, is a whiz in the kitchen and he took over as they made homemade mayonnaise, pounded chicken breasts flat, chopped shallots and whisked melted chocolate into fresh cream.

"We just couldn't stop laughing and talking. So much so, we were reprimanded for being disruptive," she says, her whole pixie-like face lighting up at the memory. "I was smitten that very day."

"I remember when you took that class. Why didn't you say anything then?"

"Turns out, he had a girlfriend. A girlfriend who was supposed to be at the class with him but was sick and couldn't make it."

"Well lucky you," I say, grinning and picking up my chopsticks to make a stab at the spicy beef.

"Yes. Although at the time, I was so disappointed. I had finally met somebody I clicked with, and he was taken."

"So," I prompt. "Then what?"

"Elliot broke up with his girlfriend just a few weeks after we met. He then showed up at my office on campus and asked me for a date. He said he couldn't stop thinking about me."

Dezi cannot stop smiling and she has barely touched her food.

"Well, I love this guy already. I haven't seen you this bonkers over a man in ages. If ever. He clearly has excellent taste."

"I'm crazy about him Quinn. I really am."

"So why have you been keeping him a secret?"

Dezi hesitates. "I wish I had a good answer for you, but I just don't know."

I raise my eyebrows at that. "You, the scary smart, wildly successful, insightful therapist? Come on Dez, I don't buy it."

"I haven't been keeping him a secret. It's just so new and it's been so long since I've been in a real relationship. Maybe I just didn't want to jinx anything ..." she trails off.

"Seriously Dez? You can be honest with me. You always are."

"It's your married man habit, Quinn," she says. "You're my best friend and you date married men. I don't know how to explain that."

"So don't. I certainly don't advertise it and you don't have to tell Elliot."

"I know," she says. "It's nobody's business but your own, but what if he finds out? What do I say then?"

"Dezi, you worry too much. He's not going to find out. And even if he does, so what?"

"You're right. It's me he's dating, not you. But I do wish you would at least think about dating single men again. Like Marcus, maybe? For your own sake."

"You'll be the first to know," I say, pouring the last of the wine. "Now, when do I get to meet this mystery boyfriend of yours?"

"Don't be mad," says Dezi, avoiding my gaze.

"What, you don't want me to meet him?"

"It's not that. Oh crap, I'm just going to come out and say it. He's the owner of Barnyard Funk."

Silence.

"Wait. What?" I say, dropping my chopsticks with a clatter.

"I know. I know," says Dezi, covering her head with her hands. "Please don't kill me."

"You're telling me that your boyfriend *OWNS* Barnyard Funk, easily the best cheese shop in D.C?" I say, incredulous.

Dezi nods.

"He is literally *THE CHEESE KING*. He knows everything about cheese. He's a cheese wizard. It's cheese heaven in his shop."

"Okay, okay. Simmer down. I know you're a lunatic about cheese. I promise, I will not only introduce you, but I'll set us up with an entire afternoon of nothing but tasting cheese."

"You're on. Now would you please eat something before I finish all this food by myself? I need to prepare my stomach for this forthcoming cheese."

Dezi digs in, shaking her head and smiling. "You truly are a cheese freak."

"And you, my friend, appear to be very much in love." I engulf her in an enormous hug. "I'm so happy for you."

CHAPTER 11

Daily Special

Spring pea soup with crispy prosciutto
Basil risotto with strawberries, blue cheese and toasted black pepper

It's late afternoon on a lovely spring day so I decide to walk to Persimmon for my shift. Weeknights usually aren't too crazy so I'm looking forward to a relatively low-key evening and hopefully an early night. It's Tuesday. Two more days until I am supposed to be meeting up with Marcus. And I have made a decision. Yes, I will meet with him. No, I'm not going to date him. I just can't. And why put myself through that when there's Zack, a very reasonable and very married choice?

But I do want to tell Marcus face-to-face that I am flattered but that I'm seeing somebody else. He does frequent my bar at Persimmon, so I'm thinking it's wise to show up and be honest rather than ignore his cute note. I don't want things to be awkward.

And it's just coffee after all. I can be an adult about this and ignore the chemistry.

Ha. Who am I kidding?

God help me.

I walk into Persimmon's kitchen and I immediately know Chef is making one of my favorite spring dishes. The air is perfumed with fresh basil and the kitchen is covered in sweet red juice as the line cooks hull and slice through bushel after bushel of early spring strawberries.

Chef grins at me as he hustles by carrying a wedge of blue cheese the size of my head.

"Can you guess tonight's special?" he asks. "It's a little early in the season but the strawberries are gorgeous, so I went for it. We can always bring it back mid-summer."

Ohhhh, heaven. Chef is making his risotto with strawberries, fresh basil, blue cheese and toasted black pepper. He introduced me to this combo last year and I harassed him endlessly afterward until he showed me how to make it myself. It's never quite as good as his — I think he keeps his cooking secrets to himself — but it's so delicious I'll likely make it at home at least a half dozen times this season, as long as the berries are ripe and the basil is sweet.

I start prepping for the evening, searching the cellar for the wines I have in mind for Chef's risotto. This one's a no-brainer, a classic French rosé from Provence and a crisp, off-dry bubbly are both ideal for the dish.

•　　•　　•　　•　　•

I'm two hours into the dinner service and it's been smooth thus far. My guests are low-key and eager to take recommendations, which makes my job easy. There are no Tims leering or boisterous drunks or fighting couples I must tiptoe around. All is calm. I do a lap through the dining room and then make my way to the bar to say hi to Julian. He's putting the finishing touches on a tray of cocktails and looks up just as I walk in.

"Q," he says, nodding.

"What's up Julian? How are things?"

"Can't complain." He gently chars orange zest with a flame. He then swirls the rims of several low-ball glasses with the smoky zest and looks at me. "Sorry, no pilot."

I shake my head and playfully punch Julian in the arm.

"I'm not here for the pilot," I say, although just thinking about him makes my face flush.

"Uh huh," says Julian, noticing my bright pink cheeks. "Right."

"Besides, he's off flying somewhere, doing his pilot thing. So I wouldn't expect him here tonight, anyway."

"Should I expect to see him around more?" Julian asks as he continues to plow through his drink orders, shaking cocktails, zesting fruit and pouring shots.

"I don't think so." I sigh. "At least he won't be coming in for me, anyway."

Julian raises one eyebrow but says nothing. He reminds me of Alex so much.

"Don't you want to know anything? Not even what the note said?"

I see a tiny twitch of a smile on Julian's lips.

"I'm listening," he says, waving vermouth over what is certain to be a very dry martini.

I tell Julian about the note. About our upcoming coffee date. And about how I am NOT going to get romantically involved with this man.

"Let me know how that works out for you," he says.

"You really can't tell me anything more about him?" I ask, stacking Julian's already neat pile of coasters.

Julian shrugs. "I think you know more than I do at this point. He comes in alone. He eats. He has one drink. And he stares at you. But I thought you weren't interested?"

"I'm not. But I am. It's complicated." I run both hands through my hair and blow out a sigh.

"It always is."

"Have you ever had a major crush on someone you knew you shouldn't date?" I ask.

Julian nods. "Yes. But I didn't let it stop me. I don't follow dating rules."

I raise my eyebrows. "And? Plan to give me any details?"

"That's a story for another day," he says, gesturing towards the dining room and Chef beckoning to me. "I think you're needed."

As I turn to leave Julian pipes up and says, "If I don't see you beforehand, have fun on your coffee date."

"It's not a date," I hiss. "It's a non-date."

Julian smirks. "You're the boss."

Chef tells me my tables are fine, but that he only has one portion of risotto left.

"You eat it now, or it's going to table five," he says. "Your call."

"Now. Right now. Are you nuts? I wouldn't give up your strawberry risotto for anything."

Well, except for Marcus, maybe. A married Marcus.

I dive into Chef's risotto with a spoon and it's perfectly creamy and chewy and sweet and peppery. For a moment I'm distracted by this little bowl of pleasure, but then my mind quickly returns to Marcus. How is it that thoughts of him are *infiltrating my food bliss*? That never happens. Ever.

It appears I have a full-blown, high school crush.

•   •   •   •   •

I'm home from Persimmon and cannot get out of my emerald green sheath dress and waist-cinching belt fast enough. Ugh, I don't know how Dezi does it. I now have indigestion from that stupid belt strangling my gut all night like a girdle. I unleash the offensive item, zip out of my dress and get into my soft, cozy, wine-themed pajamas. *Ahhhhhh. Relief.* I'm looking forward to getting into bed with my book and a mug of hot cinnamon tea. I have plans to see Marcus tomorrow morning and restful sleep is key. I don't want unsightly bags under my eyes and I need every ounce of strength going into this so I don't succumb to temptation. I'm suddenly very glad we are just meeting for coffee. I'm pretty sure wine plus Marcus equals me naked.

•   •   •   •   •

I'm heating up my water for tea when my phone pings. It's Zack. Excellent timing, I need a distraction.

Zack: How's my favorite redhead? You home from the restaurant yet?

Me: I am. Just about to get into bed.

Zack: Well that's a lovely picture.

Me: :-) xxx ooo. If only you could see my PJs.

Zack: Been thinking about you. My morning waffles just aren't the same …

Me: YOU are cute.

Zack: Trust me. Not as cute as you. Not even close.

I cannot help smiling to myself. Zack really is adorable.

Me: Hmmm. I can't quite remember. Might need to see you again and assess the cuteness factor.

Zack: So glad you said that. I'm going to be in D.C. on Monday. Wine business. I'd love to take you to dinner. Even a late one if you're working.

Me: I'm not working and I'd love that.

Zack: Great! How do you feel about spicy Thai food?

Me: I feel good about it.

Zack: Perfect. My favorite Thai place lives in D.C. Love to take you. Word of warning though, it's a set menu, so you have to be adventurous.

Me: You're on! Looking forward to it.

Zack: Alright, beautiful. I'm going to let you get your sleep. Although I do wish I was there to tuck you in. Can't wait to see you.

Me: :-) Goodnight.

CHAPTER 12

Rule #20: Wine + Marcus = me naked. Know your own formula.

Tight jeans. Tall boots. Clingy, pale blue shirt.

That's my final decision.

I've been through more than half my closet trying to figure out what to wear to see Marcus and it's starting to get stupid. Dress or skirt? Jeans or pants? Casual or super-casual athleisure wear? Do I even OWN athleisure wear? How is it different from my plain gym clothes?

These are things I don't understand.

But enough already. My bedroom looks like a flea market at day's end with jeans and scarves and bras and blouses flung everywhere.

It's just coffee Quinn, get ahold of yourself.

I take a deep breath, pull on my boots (Heels, no less! There's room for height next to Marcus's six-foot-five frame. Yay!) and give myself a final once over in my full-length mirror.

Butt: not bad. Need to keep after my donkey kicks at the gym though.

Boobs: just a teeny bit of cleavage.

Hair: clean and a bit wild. It is what it is. It has its own personality.

Smile: nothing in my teeth. Tongue thoroughly brushed.

I'm ready. For what, exactly, I don't know.

• • • • •

I walk into Monkey Roasters and see that Marcus has already arrived. He's planted himself in the back of the cafe in the so-called "living room" section, which is outfitted with overstuffed chairs, ottomans and a tangle of wayward plants, spilling out of pots and haphazardly climbing upwards and outwards with abandon. Sort of like my hair, in fact. And sort of like what my gut feels like right this minute — a big jumble of crazy.

Marcus immediately stands as I approach and gives a long, low whistle. All I want to do at this moment is leap into his arms and wrap my legs around his waist. And he's strong enough and tall enough that I could pull it off without toppling us. That would be a first.

"Quinn," he says, grinning and pulling me to his chest for a hug. "Gorgeous as ever."

The man is actually a head taller than me, so I get to lean my cheek against his chest. I inhale that intoxicating man-scent of his and start to automatically categorize the aromas as I would a glass of wine — fresh cut pine, salt, mountain air, black licorice ...

He tips my head up so that I'm looking directly into those merry blue eyes.

I'm a goner.

"YOU," he says, "are in my head. Your voice, your smile, your laugh. Those lips ..."

He wraps his arms around my waist and pulls me even closer.

"Oh yeah?" I say, smiling up at him from underneath my eyelashes.

Stop flirting Quinn! Just stop! What are you doing? Uh oh. There I go. I'm reaching up to kiss him. Yup, that's what I'm doing. Oh boy. It's on.

He meets me halfway and places his hand behind my neck. It's a warm, soft, wet kiss. He gently uses his tongue and I can barely remain standing. Every part of me wants to feel every part of him — skin to skin.

We gently pull back (we are in a coffee shop after all) and Marcus takes my hand and leads me to a private corner table tucked behind the crazy plants. I'm thinking about how much I want to sit on his lap and whether it would be appropriate behind this wall of unruly plants when he pulls me toward him again, placing his hands on my hips.

"Perhaps this secluded table is a bad idea," he says with a smile. "I can't even keep my hands off you in the open. You are a dangerous, dangerous woman."

I smile and lead him toward the table regardless.

"Okay," he grins. "But I can't promise I'll behave."

"I'll take my chances."

Quinn, I shout to myself. *Get a grip. You are not dating this man. You are dating Zack. Nice, cute, married Zack.*

I resist the impulse to sit on Marcus's lap and take the chair he pulls out for me instead.

I desperately need a moment to clear my head and am grateful when a dude with a bushy beard peers around the plants and asks if we want anything to eat or drink.

Marcus and I glance at each other and both nod. "Coffee," we say in unison.

At this, the bearded dude lights up and, with painstaking detail, starts to describe every possible type of coffee drink available in the universe. My eyes glaze over when he starts mentioning flat whites and long blacks and piccolo lattes and the true definition of a perfect macchiato. When he starts launching into milk frothing versus steaming versus scalding, Marcus steps in.

"Well, you are clearly an expert, but I think I'm going to sorely disappoint," he says, eyes twinkling. "Just a plain black coffee for me."

I smile gratefully at Marcus for halting the coffee dissertation and ask for the same, but with cream and sugar. I like coffee but I'm not into the fancy drinks. I'm already looney enough about wine, I don't need another intense beverage habit.

Bushy beard dude shrugs and turns to fetch our boring drinks, clearly labeling us as misguided coffee imbeciles, the kind who buy pre-ground supermarket coffee, shove beans in the freezer and occasionally enjoy a cup from a fast-food window. As we wait for our drinks, Marcus excuses himself briefly to take a work phone call and I use the few moments alone to gather my thoughts and steel myself for what's to come. I can't date a single man. No-strings-attached dating never works, even if that's the goal at the outset. Somebody always winds up wanting more.

Except for married men.

I have to tell him I'm seeing somebody else. I take a few deep breaths, think about Zack and try to calm my nerves. I'm so jumpy that I'm not sure caffeine right now is wise.

My heart is slamming against my rib cage, my stomach feels on the verge of turning inside out and I'm starting to sweat. I don't think I can do this.

I don't think I can let Marcus go.

Marcus returns just as our coffee arrives and we sit in silence for a few moments, grinning stupidly at each other.

He pulls my chair closer to him, taking both my hands in his.

Uh oh, I think. He looks serious.

"Quinn," he says, "I asked you to meet me here today not just because I wanted to see you, but because I have something I need to tell you."

I look right into his blue, blue eyes and I have no idea what to think. Do I want him to say something creepy — like he's already in love with me and wants to be my husband — that makes it easy to let him go? Or something wonderfully sweet and charming that will render me senseless and unable to do anything but give in?

Stop thinking Quinn. Pay attention. Let him speak.

"Quinn, I am married."

Did I just hear him right? Did he just say that he's *married*? Oh thank you Jesus! I start to feel tears well — tears of relief and pure joy — but Marcus sees them differently.

"I am so, so sorry," he says, still holding my hands. "I wanted to tell you before things got too far. I wanted to be honest with you."

I stare at him, speechless.

"I understand if you want to end this," he whispers. "But please know that I don't. I am in this. And I'm crazy about you."

•　　•　　•　　•　　•

Marcus throws money on the table and we race to the door so fast the coffee dude's beard blows in the ensuing breeze. We dash across the street and into the park where Marcus takes me in his arms and we start feverishly kissing and kissing and kissing. I'm now backed up against a tree with my arms around his neck and my body pressed against his, my hip bones pushing into the tops of his delightfully muscular thighs.

He picks me up and pulls my legs around his waist.

OH. MY. GOD. We are violating a tree. What are we, teenagers?

I giggle and Marcus joins in with a deep laugh, spinning me around and gently placing me back on the ground.

"I'm sorry," he says, as our bodies press up against each other yet again. "I just cannot keep my hands off you."

"And I like it," I say.

"You know," he says, brushing my hair back from my face and kissing my lips. "My hotel is just a few blocks away ..."

And we are off.

My old track coach (who not-so-kindly referred to my running speed as so slow I appeared to be a statue) would be amazed at how fast I can move. Apparently, it just takes the right kind of motivation. Motivation that comes in the shape of a six-foot-five-inch, muscular wall of man.

•   •   •   •   •

We get to his hotel suite and Marcus picks me up and carries me directly into the bedroom. This should be cheesy as all get out. It really should. But I'm enchanted. It's as if some crafty, stay-at-home-mom came into my world and literally bedazzled it with sequins and glitter and jewels. Everything is brighter, shinier, more alive around Marcus.

I am buzzing. I fear if I touch my own skin I'll get an electric shock.

He lays me down on the king-sized bed as I will my body to stop trembling.

What is it about this man?

My nerve endings are at military attention.

I can't decide if I want to tear all his clothes off and straddle him or slow things down and savor it.

Get naked? Slow it down? Naked? Slow?

I don't know why I bother. Marcus is clearly in control.

He lifts both my legs in the air and slowly unzips my knee-high boots. He tosses them to the side, pulls me up off the bed and directly into his chest as we start kissing again. It's gentle at first but quickly accelerates into a frenzy of touching and tongues and his hands on my ass, pulling me tightly against him.

His shirt is suddenly off (when did that happen?) and I'm mesmerized by his broad, smooth, well-defined chest. I wrap my legs around his waist as he backs me up against the dresser, still clutching me to him, his lips on mine.

And then I hear a loud, incessant beeping. What *is* that?

"Oh no no no," Marcus groans, mid-kiss. He swats his phone off the dresser and starts to kiss his way down my neck, to my collarbone, now at the tops of my breasts — oh yes!

Oh no! That beeping is back.

"Ah. Quinn," Marcus says, taking my face in his hands. "That's work paging me. Earlier in the coffee shop, they called to give me a heads-up they might need me to fill in for another pilot."

He gently puts me down. "I have to take this."

I nod, trying to get myself together. Whoo whee that was seriously fun. And I am seriously turned on.

Marcus looks at his phone and shakes his head. "Quinn, I have to go. That pilot owes me BIG TIME."

He takes me in his arms and nuzzles my neck. "You have no idea how sorry I am," he groans.

"It's okay," I say, smiling and trying to tame my wild hair with my fingers.

"Don't," he says, grabbing my hands. "I love the way you look right now."

I grin and give him a kiss. "Go fly your plane. You know where to find me."

"I do, but I don't want to leave until I know when I'm seeing you again."

Oh thank goodness he's married. I am utterly smitten with this man.

Marcus tells me he'll be back in town soon and wants to take me to dinner.

Done.

"Dinner, among other things," he says, grinning and pulling me up against him. "Clear your schedule."

•   •   •   •   •

I'm at home, grinning like an idiot and recovering from the best foreplay of my life when I get a text from Dezi.

Dezi: You at Persimmon tonight?

Me: I am.

Dezi: Great! I'm bringing Elliot by for a drink. Give you two a chance to meet.

Me: YES! Cannot wait to meet the Cheese King. Dinner too? Can set you up with a reservation.

Dezi: I'd love that but Elliot has a date night planned, so we'll be stopping by late just for a drink.

Me: See u tonight.

CHAPTER 13

Daily Special

African spice-rubbed ahi tuna steaks
Avocado salsa with roasted piquillo peppers and charred finger limes
Cucumber salad with Champagne vinaigrette

Tonight's special sounds divine and this is a new one for me. And since I have no real idea of the flavor profile (African spice rub?), I will need a taste or two before I can find a good wine match.

"Hey Chef," I say, finding him in the kitchen, dumping spices into a grinder. "The special sounds fantastic. Can you give me a rundown on the spice rub?"

Chef holds up one finger, advising me to wait and then blasts the grinder for several seconds. "Twelve different spices," he says, holding the bowl to my nose. "Tell me what you can pick out."

"Hmmmm. I'm getting coriander, turmeric, ginger and ... is that nutmeg in there?"

Chef nods. "Yup. Also dry mustard, cayenne and orange peel, among other things."

Chef whacks off a small chunk of fresh fish, sprinkles it with the spice rub and sears it quickly in peanut oil. He lays it on a few fresh slices of marinated cucumber and tops it with a dollop of avocado and pepper salsa.

"Viola," he says, handing me the plate. "I trust you have something up your sleeve for this."

He disappears into the walk-in pantry, leaving me to do my job.

The tuna is delicious on its own, but the combination of the soft fish, crunchy cucumbers and creamy avocado really elevates the dish. It's a riot of texture and flavor — spicy chiles, warm ginger, sweet, dried orange and tart lime.

My red drinkers will likely enjoy a new world zinfandel or Spanish Rioja to amp up the sweetness and combat the heat. Personally, I would choose a white for this dish and I have just the wine in mind—an unoaked chardonnay with enough body to handle the richness of the plate, but plenty of crispness to slash the spice.

Ah, my work here is done.

•   •   •   •   •

The dinner service is winding down so I check on my last table and then wander to the bar to see Julian and let him know to keep an eye out for Dezi. Simply the sight of the bar with all the whiskey bottles makes me think of Marcus. Who am I kidding? *Everything* makes me think of Marcus. I'm grateful for work and for Dezi's presence later tonight as I'm whirring inside and need some distraction. I also need to figure out what to do about Zack on Monday as he's supposed to be taking me to dinner.

I find Julian behind the bar, as usual, expertly making drinks and nodding thoughtfully as a regular customer spills the most recent details of his life. I hear snippets about a fight with a brother-in-law and how the ole' wife brought home yet another cat when Julian catches my eye and gestures over my shoulder.

I turn to see my tiny, blue-eyed and beaming friend make her way towards me, her high heels clacking on the hardwood floors. I duck out from behind the bar and give her a hug.

"Where's Elliot?" I ask, looking around for this new boyfriend of hers.

"Parking the car." Dezi jumps up on a stool and smiles at Julian. "It's been awhile. Do you remember my usual?"

"Already on it," says Julian, dumping briny olive juice and gin into a silver cocktail shaker. "How dirty do you want your martini this evening Dezi?"

"Positively filthy," she says, grinning. "And extra olives please."

Julian slides the murky cocktail towards Dezi and she takes a long sip and sighs. "I needed that. I am wiped. And thirsty. We've been dancing for the past few hours."

"Club Central?" I ask, referring to one of the few dance clubs I've been to. "Did you take the lesson?"

"We did. A salsa lesson, but Elliot was doing it just for me. He genuinely knows how to dance. Old-school, lead and follow type dancing."

"Nice. He knows cheese AND he can dance. You have found yourself quite the man my friend."

Dezi nods and looks over her shoulder towards the door. "Quinn, before he gets here, there's something I need to tell you."

"I'm listening."

She takes a deep, yoga-like breath and looks at me. She's about to speak when Elliot (I assume) swoops in and puts his arms around her shoulders, planting a kiss on her head.

"I'm so sorry my love, parking was a bit crazy. Glad to see you found your favorite drink. You must be Quinn," he says, turning to me. "I've heard so much about you."

Elliot is small but sturdy, sort of like a tall gymnast, if there is such a thing. With his longish, sandy brown hair, big brown eyes and dimples, it's easy to see Dezi's attraction.

"It's so nice to finally meet you," I say, holding out my hand for a shake.

"None of that." He waves my hand away and pulls me in for a bear hug. "I feel like I already know you. And I'm sorry, I know I've been taking up all of Dezi's time. I can't help it, I'm nuts about her," he says, wrapping an arm around Dezi's impossibly small waist.

"Well, that certainly shows you have excellent taste," I say. "That, and YOUR CHEESE. Holy crap you know your cheese. I love your shop. I have dreams about your cheese." I glance sheepishly at Dezi and shrug. "Sorry, you knew I was going to have to talk about cheese."

"It's okay," she says, rolling her eyes. "I warned him."

•   •   •   •   •

An hour later I have thoroughly picked Elliot's brain about everything and anything to do with cheese. And now I want nothing more than to dive into a cheese plate. Or into Marcus's perfectly form-fitting jeans. I'm dreaming about gooey goat cheese and Marcus's sweet ass when Dezi returns from chatting with Julian and sits next to me.

"Quick, Elliot is occupied and I need to tell you something," she says, gesturing to where her boyfriend and Julian are deep in some dude conversation.

"Shoot," I say.

"We ran into Elliot's brother-in-law tonight. At Club Central. I thought Elliot was going to kill him. I've never seen him so angry."

"What happened?"

"His brother-in-law, Greg, has been cheating on Elliot's sister. He essentially blew up the family. It's been a nightmare for his sister and two young nieces. Greg broke their hearts and now Elliot is pissed."

I nod, although I'm not sure exactly why she's telling me this.

She goes on to say that Elliot regrets not beating him to a pulp but has held back because Greg and his sister, Emma, are trying to work things out for their daughters. And yet, Greg was cavorting at a nightclub when he should have been home with his family.

"I'm sorry, that's terrible," I say.

"Quinn, he's enraged over this. He's so protective of his sister and his nieces. He can't fathom why his brother-in-law sabotaged his perfectly good family," says Dezi.

"I agree. He should be angry. I can't imagine how those kids feel."

"Quinn," says Dezi, piercing me with her gaze. "You're not getting it. He called the other woman a slew of choice words. And then he said, and I'm quoting here, '"That fucking homewrecker. How does she live with herself? I can only hope karma is a real bitch."'

I suck in a breath. Okay. I'm getting it now.

"I know you have your rules and you don't mess around with men with little kids, but Elliot won't appreciate the nuance," says Dezi. "His heart has really been battered by this."

I don't know what to say. Except that my dating life is really none of Elliot's business. So I stay quiet.

"He can never find out, Quinn," she says. "You know I love you and I understand your motivations for dating married men, but Elliot will never accept it."

"Never accept what?" asks Elliot, surprising us mid-chat.

"Never accept my offer to provide a dessert cheese cart at Persimmon," I blurt. "It's something I've always wanted to put together."

Dezi mouths thank you at me as Elliot grins and nods. "I'd be happy to work with you on that," he says, delighted. "It would be great for business."

We say our goodbyes and I engulf Dezi in a hug.

"Relax my friend," I whisper in her ear. "I'll never tell him. And besides, he's dating you not me. Why should he care that I date married men?"

CHAPTER 14

Daily Special

Watermelon and peach gazpacho with blue cheese and fresh tarragon
Crunchy, cornmeal-crusted Maryland soft-shell crabs
Arugula and candied lemon salad

I walk into Persimmon's kitchen and inhale the scent of the ocean and all its fresh, sweet and briny glory. There are live soft-shell crabs quietly napping in two human-sized bushels as the line cooks clean and prep them for tonight's special.

Welcome to soft-shell season. I wasn't always a fan, but done well, soft-shell crabs are a treat this time of year. I prefer them deep fried and slapped between a soft roll, crispy legs akimbo and resembling a big, scary insect. However, I know Chef's lighter and more elegant version will be equally delicious and much less freaky on the plate. Nothing but bubbles will do with this dish, so that's what I'll be offering — a selection of Champagne, Crémant and Prosecco.

The soft-shell crabs come flying out of the kitchen as patron after patron order the evening special. Marylanders (we get a lot of guests from our neighboring state) are nuts for their soft-shells and Chef's version is exceptional. Many diners take my wine recommendations, but I also suggest beers and pour still wines for those who prefer something besides bubbly. It's a relief to be busy as although I do need to make a decision about dinner with Zack, I'm just too jazzed about Marcus and our upcoming date to think about much else.

I'm also excited for Dezi as Elliot seems kind and sweet and he clearly adores her. I do love a man with good taste. Which reminds me, now that I already asked Elliot, I need to pitch my dessert cheese cart idea to Chef. I know we've toyed with the idea before, but now we have a real in with a knock-out cheese purveyor. If not now, then when? I'm pretty sure he cannot turn this down — think of all the free cheese tastings. *Oh boy. Cheese tastings.* Surely I'll need to sample frequently so I can suggest the appropriate wine pairings. Good lord. I'll need to make better use of my gym membership.

Chef is currently yelling at a new line cook, something about NOT poking the live crabs, so I'll approach him later, when he's calm and the kitchen is winding down for the night.

I do my usual dining room sweep and see all my patrons are happily crunching their way through soft-shells and sipping wine. I have a few minutes, so I'm off for a quick chat with Julian.

He's doing his usual thing behind the bar, shaking, pouring and snapping off bottle caps as he quickly sets up a row of eight beer bottles.

He smirks as soon as he sees me. "Q," he says, wiping down the bar with a towel.

"Hey," I say, putting my elbows on the bar. "Busy night?"

He shrugs. "Steady."

"What do you do when you're not here tending bar?"

He raises his eyebrows and looks at me. "Eat. Sleep. The usual stuff."

I shake my head and laugh. "There is absolutely *nothing* usual about you."

"Goes both ways," he says, measuring out a splash of amaro with a practiced eye.

"Come on, give me something," I say, ignoring his comment. "And what are you making there?" I ask, watching him create a beautiful, sunset-colored cocktail.

"Paper plane," he responds. "I play my drums. Box. Check in on my mom," he says. "Will that do?"

"Yes," I say, grinning. "For now, anyway." I start folding his cocktail napkins into teeny tiny planes.

"Q," he says. "Spill it."

"Oh alright," I say, smoothing out a mangled napkin. "I had my date with Marcus and we hit it off. I mean *REALLY* hit it off. I'm on track for a serious, full-on crush."

"Wasn't this the non-date?" Julian asks. "So, what's the problem? You like him. He likes you. Not complicated."

I throw my head back and sigh. I'm tempted to tell Julian that Marcus is married, but something in my gut stops me. Although I don't think Julian would harshly judge, I do think I'd lose some of his respect and I'm not prepared for that.

"But it is complicated," I say. "I'm afraid I'll get too attached. That, and there's somebody else I'm already sort of seeing. Somebody I do like, but..." I hesitate, not sure of my own thoughts, exactly.

Julian remains quiet as he shakes up yet another drink.

"I feel sort of out of control with Marcus and it freaks me out," I say. *SHIT. Did I just say that out loud?* I didn't mean to. "I like this other guy, Zack. But it's not the same. I don't feel unhinged around him."

Julian nods as he stuffs green olives with chunks of blue cheese.

"Have you ever felt that way about somebody?" I ask. "Unhinged?"

Julian nods again and hands me a freshly stuffed olive.

"What did you do?" I pop the olive into my mouth.

"I rode it out. What else is there?"

Julian stops stuffing olives and looks at me. "Quinn. Decide who you want to be. The one who loves the most. Or the one who loves the least."

I chew on that for a moment, recalling the time I asked Dezi that very same question. I don't want to be either. Either side tears you up. I felt gutted alive like a fish in the aftermath of both Liam and Chris. A violent emptying of my insides.

"Can't it be equal?" I ask, ever hopeful.

"Nope," he says. "Somebody always loves more."

"I hate that," I say, frowning. "What am I supposed to do with that?"

"It's life, Q. It's okay if you don't know yet."

"I can't even decide between these two men," I say, sighing yet again.

"Who says you have to? You're not married."

Well, that is certainly true. I'm not, but they both are. Which, technically means they're not exclusive with me. So why do I have to be with them?

The answer is I don't. At least not right now. If I'm a bit of a distraction for Zack from his wearisome marriage, then he can be a distraction for me from falling too hard and too fast for Marcus.

I smile at Julian before heading back into the dining room. Immediate problem solved.

"I dig our chats," I say, grabbing one more olive.

He nods and shoos me out of his bar. "Anytime Q. Anytime."

•   •   •   •   •

Back in the dining room I check on my tables and see that things are winding down. I uncork and pour what will likely be the last bottle of wine this evening and head into the kitchen in search of Chef. I find him standing by the sauté station, overseeing the final order of soft-shells.

"Are we all out?" I ask.

Chef shakes his head at me and then proceeds to shout at the sauté cook. "Not yet! Not yet!" he yells at the sweaty young man who was just about to pull the crabs off the heat. "Crunchy! We want crunchy! Those are NOT DONE."

"We have a few left," says Chef, turning back to me. "Thought I'd cook them up myself. No sense letting them go to waste. You in?"

"Hell yes," I say, as he starts to dredge the crabs in cornmeal. I don't think I've ever turned down his food. And I'm not about to start.

I take a bite of the shatteringly crisp soft-shell sandwich slathered in homemade lemon mayonnaise and my eyes roll back in my head. "Mmmmm, delicious," I say between mouthfuls.

Chef just nods and plows through his own sandwich. He knows it.

I savor my last bit of crispy crab leg and lick the mayo from my fingers. Chef offers to make me another but I decline. I want to look good naked — no particular reason, of course — so a second sandwich is unwise.

"So Chef," I say, as he fries himself up another critter. "I have an in with the owner of Barnyard Funk. What do you think? Cheese cart time?"

Chef flips his crab and nods. "You arrange for it and I'll give him a shot. Let him wow me."

YES! I try to refrain from jumping up and doing a little cheese dance. *YES! YES! YES!* The only thing I enjoy perhaps even more than wine is cheese. I won't lie, I'm most looking forward to the chance to regularly sample unbelievable cheese, but I'm also eager to take on the challenge of pairing wines with a rotating selection.

"Thanks Chef," I say, in disbelief. *That was so easy.* "I'm on it."

"Don't I know it," he says. "Now get out of here and go enjoy the rest of your weekend."

•   •   •   •   •

As I climb into bed, I think about my productive day. I sorted out my pressing man woes AND I am getting my dessert cheese cart. Not bad for a day's work. I have much to be grateful for, my blossoming friendship with Julian at the top of the list. I sink back into my pillows and tell myself that I will NOT feel guilty about dating both men. Surely they cannot expect exclusivity when they can't give it in return.

Can they?

I can hear Dezi in my head. *Funny how you feel guilty about dating both men, Quinn, but not a trace of remorse for trampling on their wives' territory.*

I suppose she has a point, in theory. But she's right, I don't feel guilty. I didn't make any vows. And I guarantee both marriages were dying long before I ever came into the picture. For all I know, the wives are involved in their own illicit affairs.

I really don't want to know. Marriages can often float along for years on a subterranean river of resentment, guilt and god only knows what else.

It's too complicated. And I don't want my life to be.

CHAPTER 15

Rule #24: Know your own kryptonite.

Zack has found my weak spot. I wasn't expecting it, but the man knows food. He's as looney tunes about food, flavors and ingredients as he is about wine. And I find that terribly attractive. If Marcus wasn't buzzing around in my head, I would have been keen to take Zack home last night. Yup, that's how good our dinner was.

Zack took me to a restaurant called Little Serow.

The place doesn't accept reservations. There are no menu choices. And the restaurant doesn't cater to picky eaters — you eat what you get and that's that. And for all this, we had to stand in line for over an hour, dine at the ridiculous time of 5:30 and shell out $50 for a multi-course, Thai tasting menu.

I must admit, I found the whole bit a little jackassy at first, but the food more than made up for the pomp and circumstance.

Thankfully, Zack had been many times and knew we had to line up early. We were the second couple to arrive, but by the time Little Serow opened almost 90 minutes later, the line outside the unmarked door was at least 80 people deep and snaked down the sidewalk and around the corner.

Once inside the Tiffany-blue restaurant, I knew I was in for a food thrill. The aromas — both exotic and familiar — were heady and intoxicating, much like Marcus's masculine scent. Or his lips brushing my neck. Or his hands on my hips. Or my ass.

But I digress. *Bring it back Quinn, bring it back.*

The warm scent of spices mingling with the fresh scent of citrus and herbs promised the delicate flavor balance that makes Thai and Vietnamese cuisine so appealing — spicy, salty, sour and sweet.

We were not disappointed.

Zack and I munched our way through house-made fried pork rinds that we dabbed in a deep red, flamingly hot spice paste made of catfish, tamarind and fresh chilies.

We fought over our bowl of rich coconut soup.

We used bits of sticky rice to scoop up every last chunk of meat, pool of sauce or lone herb from the parade of dishes that followed the pork rinds and soup.

"This is my favorite dish," Zack would say, while I nodded in agreement, our mouths full of that heavenly spicy/salty/sour/sweet combo.

But then the next dish would appear.

"No, THIS one is my favorite."

"No, it's THIS one." And so it went.

We enjoyed snakehead fish with kaffir lime, chicken livers with hot peppers, sour pork with peanuts and crispy rice balls and beautifully charred ribs doused with Mekong whiskey.

The dishes on their own were utterly delicious. Delicious as in, yes, I would wait in line all over again. But what elevated every bite and truly made the meal spectacular were the piles of fresh herbs and vegetables that arrived at the table, along with friendly recommendations from staff as to when and how to eat them.

Grab a leaf of Thai basil or mint to cut through the rich, unctuous liver-based dish.

Crunch a sliver of Thai eggplant or radish to temper a spice or enhance a flavor.

Try a fresh cucumber slice to quell the peppery flames.

The combinations of flavors and textures were endless.

So endless, I wound up unbuttoning my jeans by the end of the meal.

The date was most definitely a win. We laughed, we canoodled, we fed one another spoonfuls of coconut pudding and we avoided all talk of his wife.

It was easy. It was comfortable. And certainly a distraction. For both of us, I think.

I still don't know yet how far Zack wants to take this affair, but I'm good with that. It's effortless and uncomplicated, which is exactly what I need.

·　　·　　·　　·　　·

After a long make-out session in Zack's car (so retro, I know) and a promise to call soon, we parted ways. I'm now back home in full stretchy clothes mode — barefoot, ponytail and face scrubbed clean of makeup.

It was a relief that Zack didn't bring up sex tonight. I'm content with our teenager-like foreplay for now and Zack is clearly still just dipping his toes into the waters of adultery. It's not a surprise. New cheaters are often hesitant to seal the deal, so to speak. If they haven't yet crossed the threshold into full-on sex, they still think of themselves as faithful to their vows. Ah, the power of denial. But who the hell am I to judge?

I'm not quite ready for bed yet, so I text Alex.

Me: You around?

Alex: I am. What's up?

Me: Just got home from a date.

Alex: Oh yeah? Which one was this?

Me: Zack. The one I like, but not totally bonkers over.

Alex: Married or not married?

Me: As it turns out, they are both married.

Alex: I'm shaking my head right now. How do you find these men?

Me: Don't know. It's a gift. :-)

Alex: So, what's the problem here?

Me: None really. Dating both for now.

Alex: Why both?

Me: I need the one to keep me sane about the other.

Alex: Sounds like you're afraid of falling for this guy.

Me: Yup.

Alex: Why not find somebody single you can fall for?

Me: Sigh. You know why little brother. At least with him, there's a clear boundary. He's married. And he's not going to leave his wife.

Alex: What if he does?

Me: What? No. That never happens.

Alex: Just saying.

Me: Ack. I can't think about that. Okay. Enough. What are you up to?

Alex: Working on a story.

Me: Big shock. About?

Alex: Philandering husbands and the women who date them.

Me: Ha ha. Very funny.

Alex: What? I could be.

Me: You make me laugh, little brother.

Alex: You make me crazy. Don't get in over your head.

Me: It's sweet that you worry. I'll be okay. When are you coming to D.C.?

Alex: Soon. Night sis, gotta put this story to bed.

CHAPTER 16

Rule #34: Beware of the man scorned.

My mouth is full of buttery, warm lobster chunks when Elliot asks me if I'm dating anyone.

"A double date would be fun," he says, grinning at Dezi, whose blue eyes widen as she takes a bite of her own lobster roll.

The three of us are having an outdoor lunch at Claw, my favorite food truck specializing in all things lobster and crab.

Oh boy, I think to myself. Double dating is tricky with married men. One, we already have limited time together. Two, our dates are often secretive. And, in the end, it seems sort of pointless and somewhat mean to parade about as if we were a normal, healthy couple, forging friendships and hosting dinner parties.

That's just not how it works.

"I'm sort of in between men right now," I say, side-stepping the question as best I can. "But sure. As soon as I get serious about someone."

I'm pretty sure Dezi wouldn't want me to offer up a double date with Zack or Marcus. *Two* married men? Elliot would freak out. According to Dezi, anyway.

"We're going dancing again soon," he says. "You should join us. Maybe you'll meet somebody."

"Yes, Quinn," says Dezi, her eyes boring into mine. "Maybe you *will* meet someone."

I shoot eyeball daggers at Dezi as I take another bite of lobster roll. "This is insanely good," I say, licking butter off my fingers. "But I'm a mess."

I wander away to fetch more napkins and avoid any further talk of double dating. The last thing I need is for Elliot to try and set me up with anyone. I return to our picnic table just in time to see Elliot's face darken and hear him mention his sister's, "cheating jackass of a husband."

Uh oh.

"Should I leave you two alone?"

"Absolutely not," says Elliot, shaking his head. "I was just talking about my sister's worthless prick of a husband. Don't leave on his account."

Dezi and I watch as Elliot grinds bits of his toasted roll to dust.

"Hey," says Dezi softly, putting a hand on his arm. "It's going to be okay. They're trying to work things out, right?"

Elliot nods. "As far as I know. But then we saw him out at Club Central doing god knows what. I just hope Emma knows what she's doing."

"It's her life," Dezi says carefully. "I'm sure she has her reasons."

"Any chance they can come see you for counseling?" he asks Dezi. "If anyone can get them back on track, it's you."

"I'm sorry, but no," says Dezi firmly. "One of the cardinal professional rules, we don't treat friends or family. It can get sticky very fast. Otherwise, I would have fixed Quinn years ago," she says, looking at me with a wry smile.

I give Dezi my best wonky eye and pray Elliot will stop talking.

"That's probably wise," Elliot says. "Honestly, I don't care about him, it's my nieces I'm worried about. I don't want them to lose their dad, even if he's a jerk to Emma. He's always been good to them."

"I can see this still upsets you," says Dezi quietly as the two of us exchange looks.

This entire conversation is making me twitchy. I wish I had another lobster roll to focus on.

"I want to kick his ass," says Elliot. "For Emma. For those girls. Why did he have to be one of those guys?"

"I see a lot of this in my practice," Dezi says, taking his hand and gently unclenching his fist.

"And? Is there any hope?"

"Almost always," she says. "It depends on the underlying problem. Most people are married to basically decent people, but stuff happens. People stop trying, affection wanes, sex slides and that opens the door to a crush. It's hard to judge unless you know both sides."

Elliot blows out a sigh and looks at Dezi. "Are you suggesting this is Emma's fault? Do you think that too?" he asks, turning his attention to me.

I give Dezi my bug-eyed, please get him to shut up look. She ignores me and plows ahead.

"I'm not saying that," she says, treading carefully. "But nobody really knows what goes on inside a marriage. I dig around in marriages every day and people still surprise me."

"How do you mean?" he asks.

"It's easy to blame the cheating spouse. But often, cheating husbands and wives do so because they're missing something at home. Not because they're evil."

Geez. I hate this conversation. It's making me feel like married man bait.

Elliot is quiet, nodding. "So it's about finding that missing piece."

"Exactly. And that's where I come in," Dezi continues. "I try to tease out the underlying reason and gently suggest that both parties carry some responsibility. Sometimes, not so gently. It depends on the couple."

"So there's hope," says Elliot, more to himself as a statement than a question.

Dezi nods. "Yep, there usually is after an affair. As long as the cheating spouse isn't simply a genuine selfish ass. Then all bets are off."

"What a mess," Elliot says. "I wish Greg had never met that homewrecker."

I feel Dezi's eyes on me. I return her gaze and shrug. I don't know what she wants from me.

"You have to let this go," Dezi says quietly. "It's your sister's life. And she's choosing to work it out."

"You're right. I know you're right. But answer me this," he says, looking from me to Dezi. "What kind of woman even wants a man who would cheat on his wife and kids? And what kind of woman tries to fuck with another woman's family?"

CHAPTER 17

Rule #9: No regrets.

I wake up starving. Stress, I think. My metabolism is still all jacked up from that annoying conversation I had with Dezi and Elliot at lunch a few days ago. He's very opinionated that one. I really don't care what he thinks, but I do very much care about Dezi and don't want to do anything to hurt her. I just hope the mess with his sister gets resolved soon. I climb out of bed and take my time making my way into the kitchen. I have nowhere I need to be today which is a glorious break. I get my coffee going and decide to make what I call SFAT for breakfast. San Francisco Avocado Toast. I had it at a tiny cafe in San Francisco right before attending a wine seminar a couple of years ago and it's been one of my favorite breakfasts ever since.

Avocado, lemon, zaatar and Aleppo pepper. Mash it up, spread on thick slices of toast and top with jammy, barely set eggs and a hit of olive oil and sea salt. So satisfying.

It's also now my brother's favorite, so I make it for him whenever he comes to visit.

I'm finishing the last bite of toast and reading Alex's most recent story in the newspaper when my phone pings at me.

It's Julian. He never texts me.

Julian: Q. You are not working today?

Me: I'm not. Everything okay?

Julian: Yup. I think you should stop by if you can.

Me: Okay. Do you need me to fill in or something?
Julian: Nope. All good.
Me: Okaaay. Plan to expand on that?
Julian: You have a message.
Me: Wait. WHAT? WHAT? Did Marcus stop by again???

I put my phone down for a second and try to collect myself. I'm so excited I might hurl. My stomach cannot handle the stress of the SFAT and my utter hysteria.

Julian: Stop by. He dropped off a note late last night.
Me: When? When will you be in?
Julian: Noon-ish. Training a newbie bartender.
Me: Can't you just tell me what it says???
Julian: Not opening it, Q. Patience.

Noon cannot come fast enough. I wonder why Marcus didn't just text or call? Perhaps he's trying to avoid any type of communication his wife can intercept. Okay Quinn, you need a distraction. I attempt to continue reading the newspaper but fail miserably. I keep staring at the same headline and can't even make sense of that. *Okay. Enough.* I need to get moving. I throw on a pair of stretchy gym pants and a tank top, strap on my sneakers and head outside. I figure I can walk for an hour then walk right on over to Persimmon. I debate heading toward Dezi's office to see if she's free to grab coffee, but I don't think I need the extra stimulant. That, and I think she's teaching a class at this moment, anyway. Maybe I should walk over to Barnyard Funk. I'm a wee bit annoyed with Elliot, but I do need to talk to him about arranging a cheese tasting for Chef. Might as well knock that out. And, bonus, cheese will be an excellent distraction.

•　　•　　•　　•　　•

Barnyard Funk smells just like its namesake. And just as it should — all goat hoof and grass and animal musk. I walk through the doors and take a deep breath, inhaling all that moldy, pungent goodness. I'm dazzled by the array of cheeses arranged by type of milk. There are goat and sheep cheeses, cow's milk, buffalo milk and plenty of mixed milk cheeses. Fresh, aged, blue, washed rind ... oh my! I look around the shop but don't see Elliot, so I inquire with the nice young man behind the cheese counter. He offers me a hauntingly goaty glob of oozing cheese and says he'll be right back.

I'm swooning over the hoofy goo when Elliot comes over and gives me a hug.

"I thought I might see you in here eventually," he says with a grin. "What do you think of that cheese?"

"Heaven," I say, closing my eyes and savoring its perfect funk. "That is a spectacular cheese." *Okay. He's forgiven.*

"It's one of my new favorites. A raw goat's milk from the Pyrenees."

Elliot guides me through several more samples from all over the world. Some are sweet and taste just like fresh cream. Others are redolent of mushrooms, hay or lavender. One hard cheese in particular tastes just like buttered toast of all things. Toast!

"How do you feel about stinky cheese?" he asks.

"I feel great about it."

"Figured as much. Close your eyes and have a whiff. This bad boy here was the inspiration behind the name of my shop."

I don't even have to get close. I can easily smell that thing three feet away. It's barnyard alright, but also the dueling odors of ripe feet and armpit. *Mmmmmmmm. My kind of cheese.*

"It's a Trou du cru from France," he says happily. "I'm working Dezi up to this one. Baby steps."

"You two seem so happy together," I say.

"I know I sure am. I cannot believe my luck." He grins.

He's adorable when he talks about Dezi and I can't help but be utterly delighted for my friend.

I thank Elliot for the cheese education and tell him Chef wants a sample cheese platter before officially teaming up.

"Absolutely," he says. "I already have some thoughts."

"I warn you, Chef can be a bit rough around the edges and his exact words were, 'let him wow me.' Just so you know."

"I love a challenge," says Elliot, rubbing his hands together. "I'm in."

I thank him again and promise to get in touch soon with dates to woo Chef.

And now it's past noon and I'm on a mission to get to Persimmon as fast as possible.

•   •   •   •   •

I unlock one of the many dockless scooters lying around the city and zoom my way to the restaurant. Ten minutes later I'm outside Persimmon, trying to calm my heart rate and simmer down a bit before Julian can see how nuts I am. I'm so excited it's difficult to even take a deep breath. *Relax Quinn,* I say to myself. *Breathe in, breathe out. Breathe in, breathe out.*

This stupid yoga breathing is so not working. Whatever. I'm going in.

I burst through the front doors and head straight to the bar where I find Julian setting up for the evening.

"What happened to your newbie?" I ask.

Julian shrugs. "Apparently a no-show. His loss," he says, as he slides a white envelope across the bar towards me.

I stare at it. My name is written in a messy half-cursive, half-print across the top.

"Another hand-delivered note from your non-date," says Julian with a smirk.

I smack him with the envelope. "Should I open it now? Would that be weird?"

"Your call. I'll be in the back checking our bottle supply if you need me," he says, disappearing to give me some privacy.

I stare at the envelope, wondering if I should feel swept off my feet by this old-school wooing or totally creeped out. Definitely the former, I think as I slide my finger underneath the flap.

Hey gorgeous.

I wake up thinking about you. I fall asleep dreaming about you. And I simply cannot wait any longer. I have to fly to Paris. Can you get away and meet me? Hotel suite booked. Two nights. Plane tickets enclosed.

Please say yes. I don't want to wait another week to see you.

Marcus

Screw yoga breathing. I need a drink. I jump behind the bar and am just pouring myself a shot of gin when Julian returns.

"That bad, huh?" he asks.

I knock back my drink and wordlessly hand the note to Julian.

He scans it, eyebrows raising. "The dude has balls, that's for sure," he says, handing it back to me. "He goes after what he wants."

"Is this crazy? Am I totally nuts to consider this?"

"A little," he says.

I let out a big sigh. "I want to do this," I say. "I really, really want to do this."

"So do it," Julian says. "Life is short. No regrets."

I shake my head in disbelief and stare at the plane tickets. I cannot believe I'm meeting Marcus in Paris. If this isn't a rendezvous, I don't know what is.

"No regrets," I say, grinning. "Oh my god. What am I going to wear? When am I going to pack? What about work?"

Julian hands me another small glass of gin. "Relax, Q. I'll handle your schedule. Now go pack. Just text me your hotel information."

"Worried about me?" I ask, teasing.

"Not really," he shrugs. "I have a good feeling about the guy, but be smart about it. No regrets works both ways."

•   •   •   •   •

I race home to start packing. This whole thing sounds crazy in my head, but utterly perfect in my heart. Yes, I followed my heart with Liam, but that was different. We had potential to grow. With Marcus, our fling has a built-in end, otherwise known as his wife and marriage, so it feels much safer. So yes, I'm going with my heart again. Or, more accurately, my raging Marcus lust. I followed my head with Chris and look where that got me. A big fat divorce and a weird hang-up about dating unavailable men. Yup, I am doing this.

But Julian is right, I will make sure both Dezi and Alex also know the details. Alex is not going to like this, but he has a reporter's sensibilities — to him everything leads to mayhem, disaster or an untimely death.

CHAPTER 18

Rule #21: Sometimes, gigantic panties are NOT the answer.

I arrive in Paris a couple hours ahead of Marcus (his own flight was booked) and make my way to the hotel suite he's arranged for us on the Ile Saint-Louis. I can't believe I'm here. I dump my carry-on bag to the floor and scan the opulent, all-white room complete with crystal chandeliers and a king-sized bed. There's a beautiful cut crystal glass vase filled with fresh lilies and irises, perfuming the air with the scent of spring.

I take a deep breath and sit on the plush bed. I know this whole thing is a bit looney tunes. Okay, maybe *a lot* looney tunes. But I also know this — my cheeks ache from smiling and my stomach won't stop somersaulting. That, and Marcus and I spent an hour on the phone last night, giggling and flirting and acting like a couple of ridiculous teenagers in the first throes of love.

I never felt this way about my ex-husband, Chris. Not ever. Maybe a smidge like this over my 9th grade health teacher who was fresh out of college and sported a five o'clock shadow and faded rock concert T-shirts.

But certainly not with Chris.

Not even with Liam, if I'm honest. *Oh man am I in trouble. Serious trouble.*

I shake away the thought and am about to check out the bathroom when a simple, matte black gift bag catches my eye. I pull out the pale cream tissue paper and find an exquisite, emerald green and midnight blue silk scarf. It's very French. And very chic. It's utterly gorgeous.

There is, of course, a note.

For you, the lovely, leggy redhead who swept into my life.
It matches your eyes.
Meet me at 6 p.m. The bar at Chez Ami Jean across the street. Bring your appetite.
Marcus

Ooooh. He's taking me to dinner first. Wise man. I know we're getting naked tonight. He knows we're getting naked tonight. But we get to continue the tease and the foreplay for just a bit longer. I love this. I soooo love this.

But now my big conundrum. Not just *what* to wear, but what kind of underwear? Do I go with the industrial version that makes my ass look high and perky? Or the wee kind that look great on their own but do nothing under clothing? Gah! Sometimes being a woman sucks.

I'm going with itty-bitty. I'll be sitting during dinner anyway, so why scare him away later with colossal panties? It's also a veritable circus act to watch me remove them. I fell over once trying to yank them off in a rush — yes, a man was involved. Sort of like one of those fainting goats, I just crashed to the floor.

Not my best moment.

Red lace thong it is.

I stare at the thong I've tossed on the bed. Clearly, I need more to my dinner outfit. Why is getting dressed for Marcus so paralyzing? Thankfully, I've packed light and have limited options. It's unfortunate I had zippo time for Dezi to help me choose an outfit prior to throwing things into a bag and running to the airport.

Come on Quinn. Get it together. Nobody cares what you wear.

I decide on my snug black skinny jeans paired with a nude-colored off-the-shoulder lace top. I slide my feet into strappy, high-heeled flesh-toned sandals and take my new scarf downstairs in search of fashion assistance.

I wander over to the concierge desk and approach the stunning French woman behind the counter, tapping her perfectly manicured pale pink fingernails on the computer keys.

"Bonsoir," I say, wondering if it's too early to say good evening and whether I should have said bonjour instead.

"Bonjour mademoiselle," she says, glancing up at me from her computer screen. "May I help you?" she asks, in perfect English.

"Please," I say, showing her my new silk scarf. "I need some fashion advice. How should I wear this?"

"You wish to wear theez scarf?" she asks, raising her eyebrows.

I nod, wondering why she's looking at me as if I just handed her a bag full of monkey turds.

"With theez outfit?" she says, eyeing my clothes and looking me up and down.

I nod again.

"Non," she says fiercely, shaking her head and waving me away. "Does not go. No scarf."

Well alrighty then. I suppose that was helpful. Somewhat.

"Merci," I grumble under my breath and slink away to my room for a final once over. I fluff my hair, slick on some lip gloss and grab my small purse. I'm as ready as I'll ever be.

•　　•　　•　　•　　•

I'm sitting at the bar at Chez Ami Jean and fiddling with my new scarf, which is now knotted around my neck. Yeah, that's right, I'm wearing it anyway. I snuck it out of the hotel in my purse so the fashion police wouldn't see. I'm scoping out the cozy, candle-lit bar and restaurant when I notice the bartender approaching. He's holding a spectacular bottle of Champagne (I recognize the label) and pours the pale golden liquid into a coupe glass directly in front of me.

"Mademoiselle Quinn, yes?" he inquires, still pouring.

I smile and nod.

"From your gentleman friend." He hands me the glass. "He'll be here soon. Enjoy."

•   •   •   •   •

I can feel Marcus in the room before I even see him. My pulse quickens. My stomach churns. The tiny hairs on my arms stand up like meerkats, sensing a change in the environment.

If only I had paid attention in chemistry class instead of wriggling out of most of the work by flirting wildly with my nerdy partner. There must be a fancy name for this. Frisson? Covalent bond? Wild rumpus?

Whatever.

What I do know is this: Marcus transforms the molecules in my air space. And he makes them dance.

"Hey gorgeous. How's my favorite redhead?" says Marcus, pulling my hair to one side and whispering in my ear.

He spins my barstool towards him and sweeps me up and into his arms in one magic motion. How does he *do* that?

"Man have I missed you," he says, nuzzling my neck. "I'm so glad you made it. Welcome to Paris."

I sigh with pure pleasure at the feel of his arms around me and his lips so close to mine.

"Paris," I say, rolling my eyes. "Such a hardship."

I smile up at him just as he leans down to plant a soft kiss on my lips.

Ah Quinn, I think to myself as I sink into his kiss, *you are doomed.*

Once again, it appears we cannot stop kissing. But we are in France and nobody cares.

We eventually break apart and Marcus takes my hand and leads me to an intimate table for two. "You look absolutely beautiful," he says, pulling out my chair. "And I was right, the scarf does match your green eyes."

"I love it. Thank you," I say as my hand flies to my neck. I had totally forgotten I was even wearing it. "The woman at the concierge desk didn't seem to think it went with my outfit at all. She just shooed me away and provided no details."

Marcus laughs. "Ah, that must be Claudette. She has rather specific opinions. And she's not one for sugar coating."

"So I gather," I say as Marcus reaches across the table to take my hands.

"I'm happy to see you wore it regardless," he grins. "Not many a woman would cross Claudette."

"Full disclosure," I whisper, looking around furtively. "I snuck it out of the hotel in my purse. Remind me to take it off before we head back."

Marcus bursts out laughing. "I like you," he says, shaking his head. "You're a bit nuts, but in the best way possible."

A waiter stops by and pours more Champagne as another brings a thick slice of country pâté along with a baguette, Dijon mustard and crunchy cornichons.

"It's their house-made pâté and it's delicious," he says, spreading a bit on a hunk of bread and topping it with mustard and a tiny pickle. "Here," he says, feeding it to me. "See for yourself."

"Mmmmm," I sigh, crunching through the perfect combo of rich meat, spicy mustard and tart pickle. "I could attack that whole thing with a spoon."

Marcus has taken the liberty of ordering everything in advance, including the wine, which is absolute bliss for me. I don't have to do a thing except eat, drink and shamelessly flirt with this unbelievably sexy man.

This is yet another reason why I date married men. I can't bring myself to get off the ride. It's too good. And when it's just a fling, the ride never ends. There's no opportunity for somebody to fall out of love. Or for passion to wane. It's all sizzle, no boring guts.

The restaurant's sommelier brings a bottle of Chateau La Conseillante from the Pomerol region of Bordeaux. I stare at the bottle, then look at Marcus. Then stare at the bottle again.

"How did you know? How could you possibly have known this is my absolute favorite wine in the world?"

"I have my ways," he says, winking at me and grinning. "Do the honors?" he says, gesturing towards my glass as the sommelier pours a taste.

I slowly swirl the wine and gently breathe in that classic nose of violets, licorice and truffles indicative of the chateau's terroir. It is a perfect, perfect Bordeaux. And he chose an excellent year, I might add.

"Please tell me we're having beef with this," I say, raising my glass to Marcus and taking a small sip. "And have a taste, tell me what you think."

"Anything that makes you this happy, makes me happy," he says. "And yes, meat is on the way."

The waiter approaches and hands us each a small menu. "Viola," he says. "The chef has prepared for you a special menu."

Le Menu

Whole roasted artichokes with lemon aioli

Cote de boeuf for two with rosemary butter,
Bordeaux jus and white asparagus

Morel mushroom risotto

Assorted French cheeses

Apricot and fresh fig clafoutis with cream

"You expect to see me naked after all this?" I say, raising one eyebrow just as our waiter delivers warm bread with pots of sea salt and creamy, golden butter.

"Expect? No. Want? Yes," says Marcus, slowly running a hand up my thigh and looking at me intently with those blue, blue eyes.

Oh boy. It's wild rumpus time.

"I'm going to need a solid walk after all this," I say, feeling my cheeks burn and my pulse quicken.

"I can think of other, more interesting ways to burn calories," says Marcus slowly, his eyes never leaving my face.

"Oh yeah? How, pray tell, do you expect to accomplish that?"

"Come a little closer and I'll whisper it to you," he says, pulling my chair towards him as his fingers gently graze the tops of my thighs. "You see. It involves me, slowly driving this gorgeous, green-eyed redhead wild. For as long as she'll let me."

Oh. My. God. What beef? What wine? My brain is addled. But I'm so glad I nixed the jumbo, elephant panties.

Two hours and several orgasms later — sorry, lost count — we are tangled together, naked, feeding each other strips of cold, rosemary-scented beef, nibbling hunks of cheese and sipping my favorite red wine straight from the bottle. My cheeks are flushed, my body feels as if I've had the best massage of my life and I'm nestled in Marcus's strong arms.

Does it get any better than this?

The answer to that is emphatically NO. It does not.

•   •   •   •   •

The next morning, after an equally sublime and significantly slower-paced round two, we are sipping tiny cups of room service coffee and sharing a trio of utterly perfect croissants.

"Why are these soooo good?" I moan, as I lick the buttery pastry flakes off my fingers.

"Because they are the real deal," says Marcus, smiling at me. "Let me do that," he says, gently taking my hand and slowly sucking my fingers. "Are you thinking what I'm thinking?" he asks, as his hands stroke my nipples through my diaphanous white gown.

I laugh as I fling the croissants aside and straddle him. "Okay," I say, slowly grinding my hips against him. "But if we're going for round three, you're going to have to seriously feed me after this."

"Done," he says, grabbing my waist and pulling me closer. "So done."

Me too, I think, closing my eyes and sinking into Marcus. *I am so done.*

CHAPTER 19

Rule #12: Never be the first one to bring up the wife.

Several hours later we are finally dressed and finishing up a leisurely lunch at an outdoor cafe — oysters and salad Niçoise for me, steak tartare and frites for Marcus. Things are so easy with him that I forget we have only known each other for a handful of weeks. The conversation flows, the banter continues and I genuinely feel like I can be myself. It's as if I'm talking to Alex or Dezi, or even Julian for that matter. Except, of course, unlike those three, Marcus makes my heart race and my head dance. That, and I want to rip his clothes off.

But I digress.

So far, we've discussed our childhoods and our families. I even confided in him about my ex-husband, Chris, which is unusual for me. Marcus grew up in upstate New York with three older sisters, a father who still works as a veterinarian and his mother, a stay-at-home mom and part-time librarian. Oh, and two cats, Boogie Nights and Disco Biscuit. Don't ask.

The only topic we have yet to broach is his wife. And I am not bringing her up. That's almost certainly sudden death for a new affair. Or, at the very least, it would seriously kill the mood. And I'm not about to extinguish my wild rumpus ride.

What I do know about his current family is this — no children. Whew. I have yet to break that cardinal rule of infidelity and I certainly don't want to start now.

•   •   •   •   •

We wrap up with lunch and Marcus stands to take my hand and guides me around the crowded outdoor tables. He pulls a plain brown paper bag out of his inside coat pocket and grins at me. "Come on gorgeous, we have a fun little errand to run."

I look at the bag suspiciously as he opens the top to show me what's inside.

"Twinkies? What the hell? Please tell me that's not dessert."

"What?" he says straight-faced. "I hear they go great with wine."

I raise my eyebrows. He cannot be serious. Can he?

Marcus laughs and kisses me on the lips. "You should see the look on your face right now. Don't worry, I won't force you to eat these," he says, stowing away the bag and leading me down the sidewalk. "You're gonna love this."

"Marcus, why on earth did you haul a package of Twinkies with you to Paris?"

"I'll show you," he says, as we approach what appears to be a bit of a line outside a cheese shop. We queue up as Marcus whispers to me that he's hoping his favorite "cheese dude" is working today.

I'm quite smitten over the fact that Marcus even *has* a cheese dude.

Apparently, said cheese dude is a cheerful Brit who guides any non-French speaking, naive cheese cretins through the hushed halls of cheese at this award-winning fromagerie. And, as Marcus tells me, there's even a procedure for procuring cheese at this place:

Step quietly but quickly up to the entrance.

Do not speak to the cheese. Do not look at the cheese. Do not wave at the cheese. And most certainly DO NOT touch the cheese.

I giggle as we wait patiently for assistance.

I notice a very tall, very French, dark-haired cheese monger surveying the shop. He's wearing what I come to find out is the signature neck scarf for the award-winning elite who make and age their own cheeses. Marcus tells me he's the owner and doesn't speak any English, hence the jovial British man assisting all the English speakers in the shop.

It's times like these I really wish I would have kept up with my Rosetta Stone French lessons. Although, even if I had been diligent in my practice, I have a feeling I would crumple under the pressure of attempting the language in the presence of an actual French cheese king.

We are next in line and the cheese king is free, so he begins his approach. It's obvious, however, that we do not speak French, so he graciously delivers us to his British mentee. Then, satisfied we are in excellent, cheese-choosing hands, he turns to help an elderly woman who is clearly French and knows to whisper amongst the cheeses lest she disturb their delicate slumber.

Enter the saucy Brit, who practically prances right up to us, bouncing lightly on his toes and tapping his fingers together. His joyful energy is infectious. I have to quell the urge to link my arm through his and go skipping through the cheese shop and hippity hopping right out the door.

"So, Americans are we, eh?" says the bouncing blond man, still grinning. "Don't mind The Master, he doesn't speak any English. What can I get you? A fresh milky chevre, perhaps? A Comté aged right here in our caves? Or if you enjoy a blue now and again, then maybe a Fourme d'Ambert?"

Just as I was about to say, "all of it. Get me all of it," Marcus pipes up with, "pssst, we have Twinkies."

The Brit stops. The cheese he was holding, drops. He grins so wide I can count the silver crowns on his molars.

"It's you," he whispers and claps his hands together. "You're the American who promised to bring me a Twinkie. A real American Twinkie. From America."

"It is. And I didn't forget," says Marcus.

"Let me see," he says eagerly. "Let me see."

Marcus pulls out his brown paper bag and surreptitiously opens it to reveal the quintessential, bright yellow, tube-shaped American snack cake.

The Brit gasps, keeping a close eye on The Master to ensure he is otherwise occupied and then gleefully claps Marcus on the back.

He grins and opens the bag, staring at the yellow treat as if the presence of a Twinkie among the hallowed cheese luminaries is akin to him sitting on the Queen's lap.

"I cannot wait to show these to The Master," he says, rubbing his hands together. "He just won't believe it's supposed to be food."

Ahhhh. Now I understand. This wisecracking, jovial man was not going to actually eat these. Oh no. The strange, weirdly shaped, preservative-laden, immortal Twinkie was destined to be a gag gift. He was going to use it to tease the hell out of his boss, The. Great. Cheese. Master.

I start laughing. "I cannot believe you actually brought a Twinkie to Paris to scare a French cheese monger," I say to Marcus, loving every minute of this quirky side to him.

He shrugs, grinning. "I said I would and I did."

"Shhhh. We have to pipe down," says the Brit, choking back a chuckle and hiding the bag in a nearby drawer.

He straightens up, throws his shoulders back and says, "okay, anything else for you two today?"

"Absolutely," I say. "Cheese, please."

Marcus and I tumble out of the shop, laughing. We have lost two twinkies but gained four pounds of cheese.

"You're a bit of a nut," I say, delighted with Marcus and his antics.

He smiles down at me. "I'm pretty certain I'm nowhere near as crazy as you," he says, planting a kiss on my lips. "I've seen the telltale signs."

"Oh yeah?" I ask. "And they are …"

"Well for one, you're dating me," he says between kisses. "That automatically makes you a bit of a lunatic."

"No arguments here," I say, putting my arms around his neck. "Is that what we're doing? Dating?" I ask, instantly regretting the words as they come out of my mouth. *No, Quinn. No. No. No.* This path will lead directly to talk of his wife. And I really don't want to know anything about her. This is most definitely not dating. It's an illicit affair and now I'm wondering how many of these he's had? *GAH! Stop thinking like this. Do NOT ruin this lovely Parisian rendezvous.*

Before Marcus can even answer, I distract us both by sliding my hands underneath his jacket and pressing my breasts up against his chest.

"Quinn," he groans, wrapping his arms around me. "I cannot get enough of you."

"Then it's a good thing you have me for the next 24 hours," I say, running my hands down his stomach.

Once again, we're grinning and staring at each other like total asses. I can only imagine what we must look like to any passersby. We seem incapable of untangling from one another when we're forced to by my phone, blowing up with texts. Uh oh. I've been ignoring everything and everyone except Marcus.

My phone is pinging like mad with texts from both Alex and Dezi.

Alex: What the hell? You okay? Get back to me asap! You are seriously in trouble.

Dezi: Is your brain addled from too much sex or are you floating in the Seine? What's going on???

Alex: Don't make me get on a plane. Where are you?

Dezi: I'm worried. I'm about to call your brother.

I group text them back immediately.

Me: SORRY. Having the time of my life! Marcus is a doll and I'm over the moon. Plus, I'm in Paris, so there's that … again, so sorry to worry you both. I'm in excellent hands.

Dezi: I bet …

Alex: Okay, I'm out of this conversation. Quinn, I'm glad you're okay. Text me the moment you land.

Dezi: Details my friend, details!

Me: Ha! Of course. I'll be back late tomorrow but then a gal's night? How's Elliot?

Dezi: YES! He's great. We have a date tonight.

Me: Have fun. Tell him hello. Hugs and kisses to you!

"Sorry about that," I say to Marcus, putting my phone away. "My best friend and brother were worried ..."

"Afraid I might whisk you away and turn you into my French fancy woman?" he asks, putting his jacket over my shoulders as a chilly breeze starts to pick up.

"Wait, isn't that EXACTLY what you did?" I laugh and snuggle into his jacket.

"I suppose it is." He lifts my hand to his lips. "Well my French fancy woman, how do you feel about heading back to the hotel for a nap?"

"I feel good about it."

CHAPTER 20

Rule #28: Things can always be worse.

What the fuck? Seriously? I cannot be trapped in a porta-potty. This cannot be happening.

I'm in Paris, trapped in a public toilet. What the hell?

Marcus is waiting for me on a picnic blanket laden with fresh baguettes, fruit and cheese. And I'm trapped.

Why won't the freaking door open?

And now the lights are going out. Oh my god. It's pitch black and I cannot even see my hand in front of my face.

Can this possibly get any worse?

Yes. Yes it can.

Because now what appears to be toilet water is spraying everywhere and I'm getting soaked. In the dark. In a filthy public toilet.

This is utterly disgusting.

I'm on the verge of panic and start banging on the walls when the lights finally turn on and the door automatically opens.

I rush out of the bathroom, my pants soaked from the knee down and my shoes and socks sloshing with water, the source of which I never want to know.

I'm trudging back to the park, utterly contaminated with toilet water, when Marcus spots me.

"Hey," he says, taking in my wet feet and stained pant legs. "Looks like you got yourself a free shower." He grins and wraps me up in a tight hug.

"Not funny," I say, as I melt into him.

"I'm so sorry," he says, stifling a laugh. "Those public toilets are known for trapping people during the automatic cleaning cycle."

"Of course," I say, rolling my eyes and grumbling. "You can go ahead and laugh. But you're now covered in toilet water too," I say, pressing my legs against him.

Marcus just smiles and gives me a long, soft kiss. He strokes my face and nibbles on my ear. With a whisper, he says, "come on, let's get you cleaned up. We can finish this picnic in our room."

What toilet water? What wet shoes? I have forgotten everything except the fact that soon I'll be naked in the shower with Marcus.

It's wild rumpus time.

•　　•　　•　　•　　•

Several hours later we are flushed, spent and STARVING. It's now well past 10 p.m. and Marcus has one more surprise, so he's gathering up the picnic supplies and simultaneously feeding me bits of cheese and saucisson to keep my grumbling stomach happy.

It's a gorgeous spring night, so, with picnic basket in hand, we head outside for our final night together. Marcus takes me to a huge, grassy area stretching out from the base of the Eiffel Tower. Dozens and dozens of people are lounging in the grass with piles of food and bottles of wine. I hear a mix of French chatter along with English and several other languages I don't quite recognize.

Marcus sets up the blanket and lays out a spread of cheeses, meats, honey, fruit and fresh bread. I snuggle up against his chest as we sip red wine and look up at the Eiffel Tower.

"Not half bad, huh?" he says, stroking my hair and pulling me tighter against him.

I'm tempted to ask how many women he's been here with but decide I'd rather not know.

"It's spectacular," I say. "But what is this?" I gesture to the fast-growing group of people setting up on the lawn. "Have you been here before?"

"I haven't," he says, looking down at me. "But I've been hearing about it for years. It never seemed appealing to come on my own. And now I have you," he says, nuzzling my neck.

Is it possible this is Marcus's first affair? I'm not naive enough to think that, but maybe it is.

"Just wait until midnight," he says, his jewel-blue eyes twinkling, even in the dark.

Ah yes, I think to myself, the Eiffel Tower always gets lit up at midnight, much to the dismay of French locals, I understand.

"What time is it now?" I ask, simultaneously excited to see the show but also wishing midnight would never come.

We apparently have just under an hour until showtime. We spend it talking and touching and kissing. I learn more about Marcus's family, his time spent in the Navy and what drove him to become a pilot.

"My grandfather was a pilot and I grew up hearing his flight stories and making model planes with him. We spent a lot of time together. It was an escape from a house with three older sisters."

I laugh. "That's a lot of estrogen in one household."

"What about you?" he asks as we gaze up at the stars. "What drove you to wine?"

"Besides my ex-husband?" I smirk. I can feel him smile next to me. I tell him about my lame degree, my fleeting thoughts of becoming a nurse like my older sister and my aborted attempt at the school of public health in Baltimore.

"Nothing felt right until I figured out I could make a living drinking and studying wine. It was a dinner I had here in Paris that inspired me. The wine pairings blew my mind and I knew I wanted to learn how to recreate that experience."

"Speaking of wine," Marcus says, pulling out a bottle of chilled Champagne. "It's just about showtime."

It certainly is. Marcus pours bubbly as the night sky explodes into what can only be described as a razzle-dazzle display of shimmering, twinkling, racing white lights. It sort of looks the way my insides feel whenever Marcus is around.

"To you," says Marcus as we clink glasses. "My wildly beautiful redhead. You have rocked my world."

I cannot stop smiling.

He called me his. And I rocked his world.

He has done the same to me.

CHAPTER 21

Daily Special

Seared scallops with hazelnut vinaigrette
White bean puree with crispy bacon
Radicchio with honey and roasted feta

Shit! Shit, shit, shit. I explode through the doors at Persimmon, 15 minutes late and looking like I just got off an insane roller- coaster ride. I am jet lagged and was zonked out on my sofa until just a few minutes ago, waking only to the sound of my phone pinging at me with texts from Alex. Thankfully, I heard them.

I head straight to the ladies' room to make an attempt to look presentable. I only have a few minutes before I need to check my tables, so I take a quick look at my reflection in the mirror and prioritize.

Wait, is that bacon I smell? Never mind. Focus, Quinn, focus. You need to not look like a dead person.

I stare into the mirror.

A white, pasty face stares back. I have red eyes and wild, electrified hair. Even my eyebrows are sticking out every which way. I must have slept on my face.

I toss drops in my eyes, sweep my hair up into a messy bun and dab red cherry Chapstick onto my cheeks and mouth for some color.

It's the best I can do. At least my clothes are clean and unwrinkled. I tuck in my shirt, smooth my eyebrows and head into the kitchen.

Chef is busy helping the new cooks shuck fresh scallops, so he doesn't seem to notice I'm late. Or he pretends not to. Either way, I'm grateful.

He looks up as I approach and gives me a taste of the silky white bean puree with a drizzle of vinaigrette.

"Hmmmm, bacon," I say, savoring the creamy, smoky bite.

"Scallops on top, radicchio scattered around the plate, all topped with a hazelnut balsamic dressing," he says with a flourish.

"I'm on it," I say. "I have both a red and a white in mind." And I do. I thought of both as soon as I walked through the door and smelled bacon and briny shellfish. I'm all about French wines tonight, so I'll suggest either a red Sancerre or a crisp Chablis. Bubbles would be good here too. *Ahhh bubbles*, I think, as my mind wanders back to my last night in Paris with Marcus, under the Eiffel Tower.

•　　•　　•　　•　　•

I am dying to talk to Julian but need to pay a visit to my tables first. I make my rounds, offering wine suggestions for the regular menu items, special bottles for birthdays and anniversaries and, of course, my top picks for the scallop special. There's a boisterous after-work crowd in the bar area and I can see that Julian is whizzing through his orders at top speed. The restaurant is hopping and I am grateful for the distraction.

A group of four just sits down but I need to let them get settled and have a chance to peruse the menu before I make an appearance. I have a couple of minutes and sneak away to check my phone. I said goodbye to Marcus less than 24 hours ago and shouldn't expect anything. But I am hoping.

I have a text!

Oh. It's from Dezi. I shouldn't be disappointed to hear from my best friend, but there it is. I want to hear from my man.

Dezi: Aerosmith?

Me: Huh? What about it?

Dezi: Want to join me and Elliot at a concert?

Me: Uh. I think I'll pass. Are they still alive?

Dezi: Oh come on, it would be fun!

Me: Steven Tyler gives me the heebie jeebies.

Dezi: Ha! I get it. But this could be a good, non-coupley way to all get together.

Me: Hard pass. Sorry my friend. Not even for you.

Dezi: Eye-roll emoji. Elliot keeps asking about a double date ...

Me: I'm not dating anyone.

Dezi: So you say. Okay. Okay. I get it.

Me: We'll figure out something else. I'm at work. Wine calls! Can't wait to catch up.

Dezi: Me too. And welcome home!

That was weird. I've never known Dezi to be an Aerosmith fan. Or a concert goer for that matter. But she's clearly sipping out of the love fountain.

I'm about to get back to the dining room when my phone pings again. Ooooh yay! Marcus! My stomach cartwheels, my heart rockets around, my intestines whirl. All this for just a text? I, too, am sipping out of the love fountain.

Well, the infatuation fountain at least. I don't fall in love.

Marcus: Hello there gorgeous. I miss you already. Did you get some rest?

I summon every ounce of restraint and put my phone away. I will ride this high and respond later. I have to play the game at least a little bit. That, and I most definitely do need to get back to work.

I poke my head into the dining room and take a quick look around. I imagine that last table of four needs my attention, so I make my way over. There is something oddly familiar about one of the men sitting there. The one with his back to me.

Oh no. Not tonight. I don't have the energy for this buffoon. It's that fool from the wine seminar, Tim. At least he's with a group and not alone at the bar, waiting for me.

"Good evening," I say, all smiles. I do a quick debate in my head about whether I should pretend not to recognize him but decide to be a grown-up instead. "Welcome back Tim," I say. "I see you brought some friends tonight." I glance around the table. All men this evening, which is unfortunate. At least with his wife or other women in tow, he's more likely to behave.

Tim grins at me, puffing up in front of his friends because he "knows" somebody at the restaurant. "Quinny," he says. "The Quinster. The Queen of wine."

Really? I think to myself, trying hard to keep my eyes from rolling round and round in their sockets like the exorcist baby.

"You'll take good care of me and my buddies tonight, won't ya?" he says, trying to pat my waist with his huge, thick paws.

"Of course," I say, turning on the professional charm and smiling at all the men individually. "You're my favorite table already," I say, leaning over and whispering. "Now, tell me what you're in the mood for this evening. I can make recommendations and set you up with tastings if you're not sure."

"Don't you just love this woman," says Tim, rubbing his hands together.

I again suppress an eye roll and step just far enough away so Tim can't accidentally touch me. I just want to get through the night, talk to Julian and keep Tim's hands away from the vicinity of my ass.

And maybe get a decent tip.

It's an IPA for the quiet blond. A Sazerac for the dude with a beard. And a bottle each of the recommended Chablis and red Sancerre. Four glasses all around.

I get Tim's group settled and circle the room, checking on other tables, filling glasses and chatting with customers. I'm holding up well despite my jet lag. Drunk on adrenaline and desire, I suppose. Things that most definitely disappear in a marriage.

I wander over to the bar and see that Julian is out of the weeds. The post-work cocktail crowd has thinned out and he's tending to just a handful of folks nursing drinks.

He looks up at me and smirks.

"Q," he says. "Back safely I see."

I'm grinning. Grinning and blushing. I just want to run over and hug him. Julian, after all, is sort of the one who brought me and Marcus together.

"You're looking a bit crazy. But happy," he says, pouring brandy over a bowl of dark cherries.

I can't stop smiling. My cheeks ache. *Jesus Quinn, knock it off. You're scaring him.*

I know Julian isn't a hugger, but I can't stop myself. I run over and engulf him.

I'm surprised I notice he smells like apples and lemon and Christmas trees. Although I do sniff things for a living, so I suppose it's not too shocking.

"Thank you," I whisper, squeezing him. "Thank you."

"I didn't do anything, but I'm glad you had a good time," he says, untangling himself from me.

"But you did," I say. "You've been the go-between and you helped me deal with work so I could jet off to Paris."

Julian just shrugs and starts to muddle the cherries, splashing a bit of brandy around in the process. "Happy to help Q. Marcus seems like a good guy."

"I think so," I say, still grinning stupidly. "No red flags yet."

"So he's not hiding a wife and ten kids off somewhere then," Julian says, smiling.

The comment startles me. I wonder if there's any chance Julian knows he's married. Marcus has been coming to the bar for months now. Maybe he mentioned a wife? No. Can't be. There's no way Julian would let me unwittingly date a married man. Let alone run off to Paris with him.

Do I tell him? Oh god. This is so awkward.

Julian looks at me strangely.

Do I lie? Do I tell the truth? What the hell do I do here?

I move to whack Julian with a towel in the hopes of deflecting the whole thing when Tim saunters over to the bar. *YES.* I never thought I'd be happy to see Tim, but his timing is perfect. I get to weasel out of the moment.

Julian nods his head in the direction of Tim. "You have a visitor," he whispers.

Tim puts his forearms on the bar and leans as far over as he can, his soft, round belly somewhat hampering his trajectory. "Hey there, lovely lady," he says, clasping his hands together. "You took such great care of us all tonight. We loved the wine."

"I'm so glad. Are you all wrapping up? Is there anything else I can get you? I was about to head in your direction."

"No, no, we're good," he says. "The guys are heading out and I thought I'd come say hello and have myself an after-dinner drink," he says, winking at me. "Any chance you might be getting off soon?"

I hear Julian cough. More like stifle a laugh.

"Tim," I shake my head. "I'm working until close." I look at him and stare pointedly at his wedding ring, hoping he gets the hint.

"I heard you don't mind," Tim says in a loud whisper, looking directly at me and slowly turning his wedding ring round and round his sausage finger.

Oh for fuck's sake, I think to myself. This guy is a real jerk. And I know Julian is hearing all of this.

"I don't mind what, exactly?" I ask, feigning total ignorance. How could he possibly be privy to my dating preferences?

"You know," he says, grinning and cutting his eyes to his wedding band.

"Tim," I say firmly. "I have no idea what you're talking about, but I'm involved with somebody. And you're married. And now I must get back to work."

"Okay, okay," he says, putting his hands up and shrugging his shoulders. "Message received my little wine queen. Message received."

I've had enough.

"The name is Quinn. Enjoy your beverage. Julian will take care of you."

As much as I want to march Tim to the door, I can't. But he's no longer on my service in the bar area so at least I can walk away.

I shoot Julian an apologetic look and return to my tables in the dining room. Less than two minutes later I see Tim hustling out of the restaurant without even looking up. He didn't even bother to put on his jacket.

Julian, I think to myself and smile.

I seriously owe that man.

•　　•　　•　　•　　•

Two hours later I am home, showered and in my comfy stretchy clothes. I scroll through my phone to find Marcus's text from earlier today. I can't stop thinking about him.

Marcus: Hello there gorgeous. I miss you already. Did you get some rest?

I think about what to say and then start typing.

Me: Not enough. But it was all so worth it. Thank you for the incredible trip. Good food, good wine, great company ...

I'm certain he's home with his wife after the Paris trip, so I don't really know when to expect a reply. I don't even know when I'm going to see him again, but I'm confident he'll reach out. We have too good a thing going. Oh look! Those three little dots ...

Marcus: Happy you thought it was all worth it. I know I'd do it all over again.

Me: Me too. (smiley face, kissy face emoji)

Marcus: Wish we were back in our hotel room now. I cannot stop thinking about you.

Me: Me too. Quite possibly my favorite trip to Paris. Ever.

Marcus: What do you mean possibly??? Possibly my ass.

Me: Well, I think I need a little reminder. You know, just to be sure ...

Marcus: Oh I am happy to remind you. And soon.

Me: I'd love that.

Marcus: Should have my flight and D.C. schedule soon, so I'll get back to you ASAP. Would next week be too soon? Or even this weekend?

Me: Never.

Marcus: Glad to hear it. Good night gorgeous. I will see you soon. In the meantime, I am thinking about you. Always.

I blow out a big sigh and clutch my phone to my chest. Could things possibly get any better between us? He is my perfect man. My perfect, perfect man. If I don't tread carefully here, I could be in real trouble.

I think I already am.

CHAPTER 22

Rule #7: It's always wise to choose a man from a different state.

I tuck myself into a cozy booth and wait for Dezi. We're meeting up for brunch at Dough, which, incidentally, is where Zack and I shared waffles and syrupy kisses. I did get a few texts from Zack while I was in Paris, but I haven't responded yet. I don't want to ghost him, but I'm not sure yet what to do about him either.

As usual, I make my life more complicated than necessary. Which, I am certain, Dezi will point out today.

I order a pot of French press coffee for us to share and peruse the menu. I'm not in a waffle mood, but I'm thinking about an omelet with a side of extra crispy bacon. Oooh, and a couple of slices of their homemade, perfectly chewy rye bread. I'm mulling over whether to get cheddar or Swiss cheese in my omelet when my phone pings with a text.

Dezi: So sorry. Am running late. Will be there soon. Order us a pot of coffee?

Me: No problem. Already sipping our French press. Take your time. I'm in a booth by the window.

I'm in no rush as I'm not due at Persimmon for hours. I turn my face toward the sunlit window and close my eyes, letting the sun warm my cheeks. I feel the booth shake a bit and open my eyes to find a small brunette with a pert nose and a smattering of freckles sliding in across from me. She fixes me with her large, round navy-blue eyes.

I have no idea who this is.

She leans across the table and says, "You don't know me. But I know you."

Well, I guess that explains it, I think to myself. *Persimmon maybe? But I don't think I've ever seen this woman before.*

The waitress stops by to see if this strange woman wants anything, but she just waves her away.

"Can I help you?" I ask.

"Yes," she says. "Tell me how you did it."

I look at her questioningly. I'm baffled. *What is she talking about? Does she have the right person?*

She sets her phone on the table and slides it toward me. She starts slowly scrolling through photos.

I see myself kissing Zack.

Then Zack is kissing me, his wedding-ring-clad hand cupping my cheek.

The next is a close-up of Zack feeding me waffles.

Then of me licking syrup off his fingers.

Oh boy, I think to myself. *Shit.*

Shit, shit, shit!

I certainly cannot pass this off as just a platonic friendship. I can feel my face heating up as if I'm huddled over a campfire.

I take a deep breath and prepare myself for a scene. Yelling. Name-calling. Crying. Hell, she may even try to punch me for all I know. I've never been caught before.

"How did you ..."

She cuts me off. "It doesn't matter," she says, snatching her phone and dumping it into her purse. "What matters is how you did it."

"I'm not sure I understand," I say, still baffled by the whole thing. And rattled by those zoomed-in photographs.

She holds my gaze with those dark blue eyes and blinks at me slowly. Like one of those old-school dolls with the creepy, blinking eyelids.

This is so weird.

"How. Did. You. Turn. His. Head?" she asks, haltingly, as if I were a child. Or stupid.

Just then Dezi slides into the booth next to me, eyebrows raised and looking at me questioningly. "What's up?" she says, looking pointedly at me, then at who I assume to be Zack's wife. "Did I miss something?"

"Your friend here fucked my husband," says Ms. Blue Eyes matter-of-factly. "And I want to know how she did it."

Dezi's own blue eyes widen as I quickly correct this woman's assumption.

"I never slept with Zack," I say quietly. "It never got that far. It was just that one day."

"Whatever," she says, rolling her eyes. "As if I'm going to believe YOU," she says, her voice starting to wobble.

I look up at Zack's wife and notice her eyes are shimmering and filling fast with tears. She is no longer stoic.

"He's been different for a while," she says, looking down at her hands. "He looks at me differently. I can tell he's less interested. And he looks at other women now, too. He never used to," she says, tears dropping onto the table.

I look at Dezi who mouths, "Your bed." I look at this woman across from me who is now sobbing quietly, head in her hands. I feel terrible. Zack was not worth this.

"I love my husband," she says, lifting her head and locking her eyes on mine. "And I want to keep him. Will you help me do that?"

It's so quiet and still in our booth, I can hear the faint sound of a bike bell outside the window. I can hear my stomach gurgle, the acid of the coffee churning with the stress of this weird encounter.

"I'll stop dating him," I say quickly. "I planned to anyway. I'm seeing somebody else," the words come tumbling out of my mouth so fast I almost choke on them.

"That's not what I meant," says Zack's wife, her eyes still glued to mine.

I look at Dezi for help, but she just shakes her head and starts to get up. I grab her leg under the table and give it an urgent squeeze. I need her to stay.

I return the woman's gaze and say, "I honestly don't know what you are asking. Do you *want* me to keep dating your husband?"

"Of course not, that would be absurd," she says, cocking her head and looking at me oddly, as if she's working out why on earth Zack would pick me. "I know he's not going to be seeing you anymore because I found out. And he's been trying to text you to end it."

I nod, thinking of the unread texts from Zack on my phone.

"But I want to know that he'll never stray again," she says, any trace of tears now gone. "I want to know that, even if you were to tap dance naked on a crate of his favorite wine, he would still ignore you and come home to me."

"Well, that's a lot to ask of a man," I say, trying to stifle a nervous laugh. "But I promise you this, I will never, ever tap dance naked on top of anything. Let alone a crate of wine."

Dezi smacks me under the table.

I know this situation is anything but funny, but I don't know how to handle it. I am officially floundering.

Zack's wife just continues to stare at me. I can feel her eyes tracking mine like laser beams. It's unnerving. And I want her to stop. I want her to just go away.

"Zack is not a bad guy," I say. "And he doesn't love me. Maybe you just need some marriage counseling?" I ask, hopefully, looking at Dezi for help. She shakes her head at me. I can tell she's not going to come to my rescue.

I sigh and look directly at this woman.

"Look. I am sorry about all of this. I really am. I promise to stay away from Zack, but otherwise, I don't think I can help you," I say, almost wishing she would just yell and scream and make a scene.

"Well, I think you can," she says quietly, reaching for her phone. "Zack never did anything like this with me," she says, pulling up her photo app again.

"No, no, no, please not again," I say, waving my hands. "I do not want to see those pictures ever again."

"YOU don't want to see those photos ever again?" she says, incredulous. "Did you just say that to me? Did you just imply that seeing photos of MY HUSBAND kissing syrup off YOUR lips makes YOU uncomfortable?"

People are staring at us.

I feel like such an ass. A huge, Godzilla-sized ass.

"You're right," I say. "I'm sorry. That was ridiculous of me. I just don't know how I can help you."

"Zack was not your first affair," she says to me. It's not even a question.

"No," I whisper, shaking my head and once again feeling like a humongous ass. The biggest ass possible. If there's a bigger ass on the planet right at this moment, I'd like to know about it.

"You know exactly what you're doing," she says. "You know who and how and when to strike."

I nod slightly, chewing on my bottom lip. *I suppose I do,* I think. *Can this day get any weirder?*

"I want to get inside your head. I want to know how you knew Zack was available. I want to know why you chose him. And how you captured his attention."

"Now?" I ask, still thinking to myself, *No way. No fucking way!*

"Of course not," she sighs, rolling her eyes and looking at me sideways as if I had my finger stuffed up my nose. "You need time to figure out a plan and break it all down for me."

"What?" I say, staring at her as she quickly gathers her purse and stands to leave.

She places her palms flat on the table, leans so close to my face I can smell her Jo Malone Pear and Freesia perfume and says, "I'll be in touch. Don't worry. I know where to find you."

And with that, she's gone.

"What the fuck just happened?" I say, whirling around to stare at my friend.

"Wow. You just signed yourself up to teach dating lessons. Or seduction lessons. Or whatever the hell that woman thinks she wants," says Dezi. "That's what just happened."

"Well it's absurd and I'm not doing it."

"I'm pretty sure she thinks you are," says Dezi, starting to giggle. "I'm sorry, that poor woman. I know it's not funny, but the look on your face is priceless. And you kind of deserve this," she says. "You had better get on it. I think she's expecting a lesson plan. And a syllabus. And maybe even homework." Dezi grins.

I rake my fingers through my hair.

"I need my omelet. And a freakin' bloody mary. Extra vodka."

"Count me in," says Dezi, still chuckling over my utter discomfort.

As we wait for our food, I put my head in my hands and sigh. "What am I going to do?"

"Don't worry about it," Dezi says, shrugging. "I think this will all blow over. The important thing is that you stop seeing Zack. You WILL stop seeing him, right?"

"Of course, of course. No question there."

"In all honesty, this was bound to happen eventually," says Dezi. "At some point, you were going to get caught. And this won't be the last time. I guarantee it."

I blow out a sigh. "You're right. I know you're right."

I'm grateful to see our waitress placing two thick, red bloody marys brimming with celery, cucumbers and fat green olives in front of us.

I take a long, slow pull of the spicy drink from my straw. "Now I'm going to be looking over my shoulder, worried she's lurking around, waiting to demand her lessons," I say, crunching on a stick of celery.

I look up and see Dezi looking right at me. I know exactly what she's thinking.

"You're right. I deserve this, don't I?" I ask.

She nods. "You do, my friend. You most definitely do."

CHAPTER 23

Rule #16: Avoid double-dating.

I'm at Club Central watching Dezi and Elliot on the dance floor, but I can't take my eyes off Todd, their utterly charming dance instructor. He is most definitely commanding the room. I've never seen anyone move their hips that way. Sporting shiny pleather pants and a leopard print vest, I watch him saunter over to the DJ booth and put on salsa music.

"Gentlemen," Todd booms at his students. "DO YOU KNOW WHERE YOUR HIPS ARE?"

He stops the music and turns to the couples on the floor, all in various stages of salsa-ing.

"The salsa. Cannot be danced. Without the hips," he says, striding over to one poor guy who was stiff-legging his way through the basic steps, barely bending his knees.

"Ladies — bless you all — you know where your hips reside and what they do. Go twirl and let me introduce these gentlemen to their hips. And, apparently, their knees."

I smile. Todd is hilarious and so good with his students. I now wish I had arrived on time for the lesson. Goodness knows I could use it.

"I think I'm finally getting it," Dezi says to me as the lesson wraps up and Elliot twirls her around three times in rapid succession, tossing her into a deep dip.

"I'll say. You two look great out there. You make it look so easy."

"It's all him," Dezi says, grinning and tapping Elliot on the chest.

"Absolutely not true," replies Elliot. "She makes me look good."

"Well get back out there and boogie." I shoo them away. "You're fun to watch."

"We will. We will. But I need a break. And I'm thirsty," says Dezi.

"Well, that's my cue to get you ladies some drinks," says Elliot. "What will it be?"

"Gin and tonic," we both say in unison as Elliot heads off in search of a bar.

"Thanks for coming out, Quinn. I'm glad you and Elliot are getting to know each other a bit better."

"I'm happy to," I say. "I like Elliot. And I need to make sure he's good enough for you. That, and it's always wise to make friends with the guy who keeps you in cheese."

Dezi rolls her eyes at me. But then she gives me a funny look.

"What? Do I have something on my face? Why are you looking at me like that?"

"Quinn, your eyes are all shiny and weird. What's going on with you? Did you just see Marcus or something? It's like you physically change whenever you're around him."

"What? No," I say quickly, trying to swallow my smile. "But he's stopping by here later," I rattle on as Dezi's eyes widen. "Just briefly on his way to the airport. I haven't seen him in over a week and this is our only chance."

"Quinn." Dezi blows out a sigh, ruffling her pixie cut. "Elliot thinks you don't have a boyfriend. That's why we haven't been double dating ... what am I supposed to tell him?"

"Don't worry about it. Marcus will keep his mouth shut. I keyed him in. And besides, we'll say we're just friends."

Dezi snorts at this. "Friends? You and Marcus? Just friends?" she says, shaking her head. "The instant you two are in a room it's like the rest of us are caught in the middle of a magic wand war between Harry Potter and his nemesis. Electricity just flies out of you both at warp speed."

Frisson. Wild rumpus, I think to myself. *Oh yeah.*

"Just friends my ass," says Dezi, grumbling. "Do not mess this up for me Quinn. I am not going to lie for you."

"I would never ask you to. We'll say we're newly dating, which is true."

"You need to get your romantic life together," says Dezi, shaking her head and sighing. "You know I love you, but you are making this very awkward."

"I'm sorry Dez. I know I can be a royal pain in the ass, but I don't see how my love life is any of his business. And I don't have a problem if you tell Elliot the truth about me and Marcus. Or about my preference for dating married men. I really don't."

"No way. I'm not ready to drop that bomb on him. Trust me, he would not react well at all."

I shrug. "It's your call. He's your boyfriend. How long have you two been dating now?"

"Almost nine months. It's hard to believe," she says, her face lighting up. "I have never felt this way about anyone."

"Well I, for one, am delighted to hear that," says Elliot as he approaches with our drinks. "At least, I am if you were talking about me." He hands Dezi her gin and tonic and pulls her tightly to his chest.

Dezi's doll-like cheeks turn the most beautiful shade of petal pink.

"That's the exact color your cheeks turned when I found you hiding in my pantry the other night," says Elliot, laughing.

"What?" I say. "Do you two need a moment here?"

"No, no, no, we're fine," says Dezi, rolling her eyes at Elliot. "I was not HIDING in your pantry. I was eating Wasa crackers and didn't want to wake you up. They are loud and crunchy. And I needed a midnight snack."

"Well, I noticed you were gone and followed the sounds of crunching. It looked to me like you were hiding in my pantry."

I watch this adorable exchange and smile.

"I was just eating crackers," says Dezi. "And counting your spices. I have about six. You have over a hundred different spices. ONE HUNDRED. I got tired just trying to count them all."

"I love to cook," says Elliot, shrugging. "In fact, I think we need to throw a dinner party soon. Quinn, what do you think? You in?"

"Sure," I say, searching Dezi's face for confirmation. "As long as you're the one doing the cooking, I'm game. And I'll bring the wine."

"Done," says Elliot. "And now if you'll excuse us for a few minutes, I need to get this one out on the dance floor."

"Go, please," I say, sipping my cocktail. "I'm fine here and I'd love to watch."

Three songs later I'm still watching them dance when I feel him. *Marcus.* It never fails. The tiny hairs on my arms stand at attention and I can feel the heat of him, marching towards me.

Sure enough, there he is.

"Hello gorgeous," he leans down and plants a kiss on my neck, then scoops me up into his arms. "I have missed you," he says, burying his head in my hair. "You smell just like an orange creamsicle."

"So much for pretending we're just friends," I say, laughing and kissing his face.

"Yeah. That was never very likely," says Marcus, gently nibbling my ear. "Why can't we just tell him the truth?"

"Which is what, exactly?"

"Which is that we're dating," he says, putting his arms around me. "And that we're nuts about each other. And that we're about to get the hell out of here and go get naked."

I smirk and raise one eyebrow. "You're serious, aren't you?"

Marcus just nods and pulls me into him, hands on my hips. "Very," he says, grazing my lips with his. "I never joke about getting naked."

"Okay you two, break it up," says Dezi, flicking cold water at us from the dregs of her drink.

"Oh hey," I say. "I didn't even notice you were back. Where's Elliot?"

"Getting us another round," says Dezi, shaking her head at me. "Just friends. Uh huh. Right. I knew you two couldn't pull that off."

"Of course not," says Marcus, putting his arm around me. "Now, where is this man of yours?"

"He's coming. But he has no clue about YOU," Dezi looks at Marcus pointedly.

"I'm happy to make us both disappear," says Marcus, winking at me.

"Absolutely not," says Dezi. "You two stay right here and keep it PG. Well, PG13 at least. I suppose you were going to meet Elliot eventually, so we may as well get this over with."

"You're the boss," says Marcus, as he leaves in search of bottled water.

"It's going to be fine," I say, reaching over to squeeze Dezi's hand. "What are you so worried about?"

Dezi looks at me, fiddling with the gold necklace at her throat.

"Quinn. You date married men. On purpose. How am I supposed to explain that? You know I don't care, I never have. But I'm afraid Elliot's judgment is clouded by what happened to his sister. You heard him when we were having lobster rolls. I just don't know how he's going to feel about it..." she trails off. "I don't know how he's going to feel about me."

"Oh Dezi. Elliot loves you. And there's nothing I can do to change that. But I don't want to make things complicated for you. I really don't. We can leave."

"No, I don't want you to go," she says. "You're my best friend. Elliot's my boyfriend. I can't keep trying to separate you. It is what it is at this point, right?"

"I'm sorry," I whisper, wishing I could simply dump Marcus and make everything better for Dezi. But I can't do that.

"And besides, I have to admit, you and Marcus are adorable," she says, as if reading my mind. "I know I've only hung out with you two a few times, but he seems perfect for you, married or not."

·   ·   ·   ·   ·

Marcus returns with bottles of water and pulls me onto his lap. I'm melting into his firm chest when Elliot finally makes his way back with cocktails.

"Hey, I'm Elliot," he says, striding right up to Marcus with a smile. "I didn't know you were bringing somebody," he says to me, shaking Marcus's hand. "Unless, wait, you two didn't just meet right now, did you?"

"We did," says Marcus. "Just now. Couldn't take my eyes off this one." He gazes down at me.

"Oh, don't listen to him," says Dezi, playfully swatting Marcus on the shoulder. "Quinn just told me a moment ago that Marcus was going to stop by for a bit before he catches his flight."

"Where are you off to?" asks Elliot. "Business or pleasure?"

"Definitely business," says Marcus. "Especially since I'm the one flying the plane."

At that, the two men start talking aviation and military and airplanes — a common insta-bond among men, it seems. That, and sports, of course.

"Look at that," I say, grinning and nodding towards the men. "Those two have hit it off."

"Well of course they have," says Dezi. "But to what end? What's going to happen between you and Marcus?"

"I have no idea, but you need to stop worrying so much. I'm sure Marcus and I will run our course as per my usual affairs."

"But it's different this time, for both of us," Dezi replies. "I'm serious about Elliot. And you seem totally smitten with Marcus. Who has a *wife*, a fact you seem to conveniently ignore."

"I've been dating married men a long time, Dezi. I'm used to this whole dance. I can handle this."

"I'm worried about you this time," she says, squeezing my hand. "You spend a lot of time together. It looks to me like you're falling in love."

Love. I'm about to speak but my throat feels too dry. I'll admit, I have a whopper of a crush on Marcus. But love? But Dezi's right, there is something different about us. Marcus just *gets* me and accepts me. All of me. The good, the bad. All of it. He's like the male version of Dezi. But *love*?

My phone blows up with text messages, interrupting my thoughts.

"You'd better check that," says Dezi, nodding toward the phone as it continues to ping wildly.

I glance at the screen, then up at Dezi. "Zack," I whisper.

Zack: Hey. Are you around? You haven't been answering my texts.

Zack: I'd really like to talk to you. I promise it won't take long. I want to apologize.

Zack: Is this what ghosting is?

Me: Hey. It's okay. Really. I'm not ghosting you. Just trying to bow out and keep you out of trouble.

Zack: Too late for that. But it's not your fault. I just wanted to make sure you're okay. And I'm sorry. I really am.

Me: Seriously, no worries. Stuff happens. I hope you two can work it out.

Zack: Really? That's not what I want. Is that really what you want? Can I see you? Talk in person at least?

Me: I don't think you're supposed to be talking to me at all.

Zack: I know. It's just … I need to see you.

Me: Zack. You're married. And your wife knows. There's nothing left to say.

"Hey gorgeous, are you talking to your other boyfriend again?" says Marcus, coming up behind me, his eyes twinkling. "And here I thought I was the only one," he says, wrapping his arms around me, nibbling my neck.

"Very funny," I say, quickly dropping my phone into my small bag. "You know full well you're in competition," I tease. "I haven't decided quite yet who the front runner is."

Elliot raises his eyebrows and looks at Dezi. Then at me.

"Have you been hiding not just one, but two boyfriends from us?" he asks.

"Actually, three," I say with a smirk. "But who's counting?"

"I am. I am most definitely counting," replies Marcus as he lifts my hand to his lips. "I need to step up my game, apparently," he says, winking at Elliot.

"Just ignore them," says Dezi, shaking her head. "Come on, let's dance."

•   •   •   •   •

A half-hour later Marcus says his goodbyes to Dezi and Elliot and gives me a long, lingering kiss. "Three days," he says gruffly in my ear. "I'll be back in three days and we're going to my hotel. And then I'm buying you dinner. In that order."

CHAPTER 24

Daily Special

Beef tenderloin with rhubarb and red wine
Crushed baby potatoes with rosemary and horseradish cream
Charred broccoli rabe with lemon and pine-nuts

I dressed for work this evening fully channeling Dezi. Tight sheath dress, cinched in belted waist and high, high heels.

Ugh. Now I wished I hadn't. I will have to hold in my stomach all night. I don't know why I do this to myself. I buy all these tight-fitting dresses and heels and think to myself, *yes, I will wear this!* Never mind that in my closet live seven identical and equally uncomfortable items. *But THIS dress is different. THESE ridiculous shoes are somehow magically comfortable.*

Yeah right. It never seems to work that way.

I don't even know if I can bend over to pick up wine bottles in this dress. I probably should have tested that out.

Sigh. I wish I were impervious to the desire to dress sexy for my man. But alas, I am not.

I'm wearing this get-up tonight because of Marcus. Who else?

There's a chance. A teeny, tiny chance I might get to see Marcus tonight. Although it's unlikely, he might stop by if his flight gets in early. Before he heads home to The Wife.

The last time I saw him was briefly at Club Central with Dezi and Elliot, so I'm eager to get my hands on him again, so to speak. Even for just a few minutes.

Half-way through my shift we have almost sold out of tonight's tenderloin special and my recommended Alexander Valley pinot noir, so I'm in the wine cellar, looking for bottles within reach. Because no, as it turns out, I cannot bend down in this dress. Or twist, for that matter.

"WHAT IN GOD'S NAME ARE YOU DOING?" booms Chef, finding me in the cellar, awkwardly folding myself around the constraints of my stupid dress, trying to maneuver into a position to get at the wine.

"What does it look like I'm doing?" I snap back, starting to sweat with the effort.

"It LOOKS like you are doing some kind of new-fangled and preposterous exercise routine. In MY cellar. That's the appearance you give, anyhow," he fires right back.

I stand up, tugging down the hem of my dress as it had hiked up, nearly revealing my mammoth, hold-you-in panties.

"Sorry Chef," I grumble. "We are almost out of the wine I've been recommending, so I'm getting a backup," I say, holding up a bottle of cabernet franc.

"Ah. Excellent choice," he says, peering at the label. "I've been to this winery myself."

Chef helps me collect a case of the wine, asking me my thoughts about his rhubarb sauce.

"Are you kidding?" I say. "I love rhubarb, but who knew it belonged anywhere but pie? It's delicious with the beef. You're lucky I can barely breathe in this dress, otherwise I would have hoovered up more."

Chef grins, apparently appeased and wanders back into his kitchen.

I survey my dining room and make my rounds, walking carefully on my stilt-like heels. The last thing I need is to take a tumble carrying wine and glasses.

"Wow, you are tall," says one of my diners, looking up at me as I display the bottle of cab franc to the table. "Do you mind me asking how tall?"

Here it comes ... "Do you play basketball?"

And. Wait for it ... "It's just so rare to see a woman this tall," he says.

I smile. It's always the same three.

"I'm just over six-feet barefoot," I say, delicately kicking up a high-heeled clad foot. "But probably closer to six-foot-four inches today with the shoes. And if by basketball, you mean flinging that big orange ball through a big orange hoop with big people chasing me all the while? Then no, I do not play and never have. Much to the chagrin of my high school basketball coach."

The man laughs, nodding appreciatively. "I get it," he says. "I coach boy's basketball and I'm always looking for the tall kids. Well, you wear it well. It's nice to see."

"Thank you. Now, who wants to taste the wine?"

•　　•　　•　　•　　•

It has been a busy evening and my feet are killing me. Note to self, no more sky-high heels. At least not at work. What a stupid choice. Especially since I know Marcus doesn't care what I wear. In fact, I'm pretty sure he'd rather I just be naked all the time. But we are still so new and it's still soooo good. I want to dress up for him. I'm not about to start revealing my wild-haired, stretchy clothed, dingy underwear self. Once I'm on that precipice, it's time to start a new affair. Time to start looking for my next married man.

I quickly check my phone, but nothing from Marcus. That probably means he's still in the air and likely will have to go straight home. Sigh. I know I wanted a married man, but it's times like these that I'm jealous of the wife. His wife, in particular. She gets first dibs. I'm trying to ignore her. And I'm trying to squash that nagging feeling in my gut that I'm getting too involved. That my lust is evolving into something more. Something I may not be able to easily shimmy out of.

Damn that Marcus. Damn that wild rumpus.

I glance around the dining room and see that most of my tables are wrapping up, so I head to the bar to say hello to Julian. I haven't seen him all night.

I walk into the bar and Julian looks up, giving me a long, slow whistle. "Well don't you look great tonight," he says, grinning. "Dressing up for somebody special, are we?"

"Thanks," I say, feeling a bit sheepish. "I was hoping, but I don't think he's going to make it."

"Ah. Too busy flying planes?"

"Something like that," I say, sighing and eyeing Julian's tray of cocktail condiments. Glistening, fat cherries. Pickled onions. Crisp, tart tomatillos. Candied bits of citrus peel. And green olives, oozing with creamy blue cheese.

"Don't even think about getting your hands in there," he says, handing me a napkin with a couple of olives and a tomatillo. "Just point if you want anything else."

"These tiny morsels are all I can manage in this dress," I say, looking down at my pinched waist. "That's it," I say, unleashing the tight, unforgiving belt and dropping it directly into the trash can behind the bar. "Ahhhhhhhhh. So much better," I say, as my stomach expands to its natural resting state. It's mostly flat (thank you mom for the flat abs gene), but certainly not concave.

Julian laughs and shakes his head. "Women. I will never understand you."

"Speaking of women," I say, tapping my fingers on the bar.

Julian looks at me, one eyebrow raised. "Yes?"

"Oh, come on. Are you dating anyone? Do you have a girlfriend you're hiding? Are you even looking?"

"No. No. And yes. Always looking."

"Okay then. When was your last date? Last girlfriend? Longest relationship?"

"So many questions," he says, handing me another napkin with a stick of olives and onions.

"Well, you never give me any answers," I say, my mouth full of cocktail onions. "So I ask them all at once."

"One question," he says. "Shoot."

"What's your type?"

"Clever," he says. "That's several questions in one."

"Well?" I persist.

"Tall. Redhead. Athletic. Throws bits of her clothes in the trash," he says with a wink.

"Funny guy," I say, swatting him in the arm and shaking my head.

"Quinn," Julian says, nodding over my shoulder and towards the entrance of the bar. "I think you have a visitor."

Marcus, I think, my heart starting to thump. Although, oddly, no wild rumpus.

"NOT your pilot," Julian whispers in my ear.

I turn around and see a familiar petite brunette, her round, navy blue eyes piercing mine. No wonder there was no wild rumpus.

Shit.

Zack's wife is marching towards me. Her eyes tracking my face with military precision.

Oh boy. This is not going to go well.

Maybe I could run.

If I wasn't wearing these ridiculous shoes. And this tight-ass dress.

"She's coming right for you. And she looks pretty pissed off," says Julian. "Is everything okay?"

"I don't know," I whisper back. "It's complicated. It could get weird."

"Let me know if I can help."

"Well, well, well," says Zack's wife, pulling up a barstool and plopping down next to me. "If it isn't my favorite home-wrecking twit."

I cringe. Oh boy. I'm certain Julian heard that.

"Can we please take this outside? Or meet after my shift," I whisper urgently. "This isn't the appropriate place."

"Oh really?" she says, her voice rising above a whisper. "NOW you're worried about being appropriate? But not when, say, you were screwing my husband?"

"Jesus," I say, glancing at Julian, who quickly looks away. "Look, I have already apologized. I'm not seeing Zack anymore. And I never slept with him."

Zack's wife looks at me with those huge, round, navy-blue eyes.

I hold her gaze and repeat myself, slowly. "I. Never. Slept. With. Zack. I promise you that."

She blows out a sigh and bows her head. She sure comes out feisty, but thankfully, that seems to quickly fizzle. "I just cannot get those photos of the two of you out of my head," she whispers.

I have nothing to say to this. It's terrible. And I cannot even imagine.

"I'm sorry," I say lamely. "But I don't know what I can do to help you."

"I want my lessons, like we talked about," she says, squaring her shoulders and lifting her chin.

I can see Julian out of the corner of my eye, his eyebrows shoot up so far they almost disappear into his hairline.

I shake my head. "I'm not going to give you lessons. It's absurd. I wouldn't even know where to start."

"You can start by telling me why you zoned in on my husband. And exactly what you did to make him put his hands all over you. In a restaurant. While eating waffles."

I slowly close and then open my eyes, hoping she might just go away.

Nope. She's still there.

"That would be an excellent place to start," she says, standing up. "I'm not going to ask again nicely. I'll be in touch."

•   •   •   •   •

"Do I even want to know what that was all about?" asks Julian, looking at me seriously.

The playful twinkle in his eyes from just a few minutes ago is gone. He almost looks like a stranger.

I sigh and put my head in my hands. "I have found myself in a bit of a pickle. And I don't know what to do."

Julian is quiet, calmly polishing glassware.

"I know it's my fault, but ..." I trail off, not sure what to say. Not exactly sure what Julian even overheard.

"But what?" Julian asks. "Seems pretty simple to me. Am I correct in that, for whatever reason, you screwed with another woman's marriage?"

Geez. Once again, I feel like a giant ass.

"Yes," I whisper, unable to look Julian in the eye.

He sighs. "Oh Q. Shit happens. It's not like you knew he was married and did it on purpose."

My insides turn to ice. I literally feel as if a tiny, invisible creature is coloring my veins with an icicle, carefully tracing all the branches and vessels.

I can't breathe. I am shivering.

"Hey," says Julian softly. "It's okay Q. It sounds as if she's giving you the chance to fix things," he says, rubbing my shoulders. "Seems like a gift if you ask me."

CHAPTER 25

Rule #32: Grab every opportunity to fill your tank with good juju.

I hurl the axe towards the wooden target and WHAMMO, bullseye on my very first try.

I bust out a little bullseye dance and turn to my brother, Alex. "Take that!" I say. "I love this game."

Alex grins and hands me a beer.

"Axes *and* beer? Does it get any better?"

"I thought you might like this," he says, picking up his own axe. "Once you get past the initial shock of it all, it's actually very safe. And weirdly soothing."

I'm visiting Alex in Baltimore and he surprised me by taking me axe throwing. Apparently it's a thing now. People drink alcohol and toss axes for sport, akin to bowling, I suppose. Except instead of huge, heavy balls and disgusting rental shoes, there are dull hand-held axes and you get to wear your own footwear, albeit no open toes.

"So, how did you even hear about this place?" I ask, gesturing around the old warehouse, now outfitted with multiple throwing lanes, picnic tables and a bar. Groups of all sizes are milling about the different lanes, all in various stages of gameplay and imbibing.

"A friend of mine threw a party here a couple of months ago," he says, nailing a bullseye with a satisfying thwack. "Been coming here about once a week ever since."

"I can see why." I line myself up for another throw. "What a great stress reliever."

"Yup," he says, taking a swig of his beer. "I sometimes come from work, right after I make deadline."

Alex picks up his axe and boom, boom, boom. He hits three in a row, dead center.

A high, sing-songy, female voice comes from behind me. "I see somebody's been practicing. Wow Alex, you are getting really good at this," says the voice, practically cooing.

I turn to see a woman wearing short, fraying jean shorts and black cowboy boots. Her blonde hair is in two braids, fanning down her shoulders and she's tied the ends of her pink and purple flannel shirt into a cutesy little bow.

I raise my eyebrows at Alex. *Oh man, I'm going to have so much fun with this.*

"Hey Fantasia," he says, nodding in her direction. "What's up?"

Fantasia? Fantasia? Who is this 20-something making googly eyes at my brother? And taking this whole lumberjack thing just a tad too far?

Fantasia practically prances over, flipping one ribboned braid over her shoulder. It looks like she's about to launch herself into Alex's arms when she notices me.

"Oh, hey," she says, stopping mid-prance and just short of Alex. She looks me up and down and it's clear she's trying to work out who I am and whether I'm competition. She bites her lower lip and hops from one foot to the other, twirling a braid.

Seriously? Who is this child?

Alex puts her out of her misery.

"Fantasia, this is my sister, Quinn," he says. "Quinn. Fantasia."

"Oooooh, I love your name," she squeals. "Quinn! I just love it!"

"Fantasia works in the bar area, so she keeps me supplied in my post work beer," Alex says to me.

Ah. I suppose that explains the outfit and pigtails. Sort of.

I bite back the urge to ask if she's even old enough to drink.

"Nice," I say. "Seems like a fun place to work. And I imagine you're now pretty good at the axe throwing."

"Nah. I don't throw. I spend way too much time at the salon to ruin my nails," she says, displaying a hand for us to admire her watermelon taffy-hued manicure. "But working the bar is pretty fun. And I get to meet handsome men like your brother here," she says, touching his arm and flicking her eyes toward him.

I smirk at Alex, who shrugs his shoulders at me as if to say, *what am I supposed to do about this? It's not as if I encourage it.*

"Can I get anything for either of you?" asks Fantasia, smiling stupidly at my brother.

"I think we're good at the moment," he says. "But I know where to find you if we need anything."

Fantasia scurries back to the bar and I start singing.

"Fantasia and Alex sitting in a tree, k-i-s-s-i-n-g ..."

"Real mature, Quinn. Real mature," Alex says, rolling his eyes.

"No kidding," I say, full on laughing now.

Alex just shakes his head, but I can see him trying to hide a smile.

"You know I love you little brother," I say, as I watch Fantasia sneaking looks at Alex from the bar.

"I do," he says. "Now quit yacking," he hands me my axe. "You're up."

•   •   •   •   •

A couple of hours later we are strolling along the Baltimore waterfront, working off those beers and a rather large lunch — a crab cake sandwich for me and a fried oyster po' boy for Alex. I am crisscrossing my arms in front of my chest, trying to stretch out my sore shoulder muscles. I'm not used to all that axe throwing, apparently.

"Quick. Name three people you would absolutely NOT want with you on a desert island," I say as we walk.

"George-the-pharmacist. My OCD editor Donald Mann. And Fantasia," Alex says.

"What, no Fantasia?" I ask, laughing. "Why on earth not?"

Alex just rolls his eyes at me.

"Please, please tell me you are not dating her, little brother."

"Of course not. She's much too young and she's not my type."

"Well, she most certainly has her eye on you."

"I know. It's starting to be a bit much. I may have to find a different axe place. Or at least try to avoid the hours she works."

"Or you could bring an actual date. You know, somebody you might be interested in. That might discourage her."

Alex ignores me entirely and instead fires the desert island question back at me.

"Hmmm. I agree with you about George-the-pharmacist. And maybe this guy Tim I met at a wine seminar who keeps showing up at the restaurant. Can I also say Fantasia?"

"No. You cannot. What about Chris, your ex-husband?"

"Nah, I wouldn't ban Chris. We got along beautifully. That was never our problem."

I think for a moment. "Okay, I've got it. Zack's wife."

Alex's eyebrows shoot up.

"Did you just say Zack's wife? Isn't he one of the husbands you're currently dating?"

"Yes. And no. I'm not dating him anymore, for obvious reasons."

"What happened? Spill it Quinn."

I fill Alex in on the whole saga of Zack's wife and her recent second appearance at Persimmon.

"That's weird Quinn. Very weird. But I suppose it could be worse."

"Like what? She slashes my tires and boils my pet bunny rabbit?"

"Well, yeah," says Alex. "Something like that. Do you think she would get dangerous if you say no?"

"No. I don't think so. She genuinely seems kind and sweet. And smart, even. I sort of feel like we could be friends. Under different circumstances."

Alex and I keep walking in silence. I'm always reminded of how much I love Baltimore whenever I visit. It's not as frantic and busy as D.C. It's not as crowded. And people look you in the eye and say hello. It's like the favorite, comfy sofa of cities. The more glamorous ones are lovely to look at, but you never want to sit in them. And you always wind up wondering how you got suckered into the purchase in the first place.

We wind our way along the waterfront, passing joggers, walkers and families with strollers.

"So, what are you going to do?" Alex asks.

"Do? Nothing. I'm certainly not giving her lessons of any sort. I don't even know what that means."

Alex just nods, quiet.

"You think I should do it," I say, astounded.

He shrugs and sticks his hands in his pockets. "I don't know. But it seems harmless enough. And it's a way for you to even out the bad karma. Maybe make up a little bit for stealing her husband."

"I was not the one who took vows," I remind him. "He came on *to me*. He was clearly *looking*."

"I know. I know. You have your rules and your playbook. But you had a role in this too, Quinn."

"So you think I should agree to her demands to earn myself some good juju?"

Alex starts laughing at that. "You are ridiculous sometimes, big sister," he says. "But sure. Yes. If that's how you want to look at it. Maybe you should consider it."

I frown. I really hadn't even considered the possibility.

"It's absurd," I say. "What would I even teach?"

Alex shrugs. "I don't know, exactly, but you've been dating married men now for years. You seem to know who's open to an affair."

We keep walking.

"Whether you like it or not, you are the other woman, Quinn. And clearly you have some insight she thinks is valuable. Honestly, she's probably right."

I nod, grumbling. "I suppose, but I'm still not doing it. Good juju my ass."

•   •   •   •   •

We end our walk at the entrance to my parent's condo. I have time for a quick visit, so we head on up to say hello. I'm not about to sneak into Charm City without stopping by. My mother would never forgive me and I'd be cut off from her homemade ricotta forever. Not a risk I am willing to take.

"Hey," Alex and I say in unison as we tumble into the foyer. "We're home!"

We find them playing Scrabble at the breakfast table, which has a spectacular view of the harbor through floor-to-ceiling windows. I can see the waterfront pathway Alex and I were just walking on ten stories below.

"I thought I saw you kids down there," says my mother, jumping up to give us both hugs. "Your father said it was impossible to tell, but I just knew it."

My dad peers at my mother over his wire-rimmed glasses. "That, and Alex did call this morning saying they would stop by," he says. "Right around this time."

My mother ignores my dad and says, like clockwork, "Who's hungry? What can I get you two to eat?"

She jumps up and starts pulling things out of the refrigerator. There's an endless parade of containers and cartons and Tupperware.

"Stop. We ate. We aren't hungry," I say, helping her put everything back.

She, of course, wants to know exactly what we had for lunch. And where.

"We ate fried seafood sandwiches at that axe throwing place I was telling you about," says Alex. "I'll be hungry in about an hour."

"Ugh. Not me," I say. "I'm stuffed. But happy to take anything home you might have lying around. Preferably homemade."

With that, out comes the parade of food again — ravioli, thick slices of porchetta, lemon ricotta cheesecake, eggplant parmigiana, a square of taleggio and leftover linguine with clam sauce, one of my favorites.

"How's this?" My mother gestures to the array of food on the counter.

"Absolutely perfect, thank you," I say, kissing her on the cheek and envisioning the delicious picnic Marcus and I will enjoy. On my bed.

"So," says my mother as she starts packing up all the food for its journey with me to D.C. "I hear you have yourself a boyfriend."

"What?" I say, then shoot eyeball daggers at Alex.

He just shrugs and silently mouths, "Not me."

"When were you planning to tell us?" asks my mom again.

"Gemma, leave the poor girl alone. These are all rumors," says my father. He looks at me. "Apparently, George was at Persimmon and saw you at some point. With a man."

"Canoodling with a man," my mother interrupts. "He says you were at the bar, practically sitting in a man's lap."

George. Son of a bitch.

"First of all, it's none of George's business. And second of all, I do not have a boyfriend," I say firmly.

"So you don't know who he's talking about, Quinn?" my mother asks, one eyebrow raised.

"I don't. I work at a restaurant. Clients come in to say hi all the time. It could have been any one of them."

"Are you suggesting that you make it a habit of sitting on the laps of your dining patrons? At your restaurant?" my mother asks, aghast.

"Of course not, mom. That would be absurd." I throw my hands up in the air. "God only knows what George thought he saw. You've met him. Can you trust a man who doesn't eat meat? Or drink wine?"

My mother considers this.

"I suppose you make a good point," she says, eyeing me sideways. "But you would tell us if you had a boyfriend, wouldn't you?"

"Of course," I say, relieved. "You know I would."

But Marcus is not my boyfriend. He's my married lover. I'm pretty sure my mother's head would explode. She would never recover. It would be worse than offering her a can of Chef Boyardee beefaroni for lunch.

I see Alex looking at me from across the room.

Positive juju, I think to myself. *Maybe I do need some.*

CHAPTER 26

Rule #30: A slightly buzzed hostess makes for an excellent dinner party.

Elliot's house smells fantastic. Like rosemary and garlic and red wine. And meat.

I inhale deeply as I watch Elliot and Dezi together.

They swoop around his townhouse, putting the finishing touches on appetizer trays and setting his old farm-house dining table with navy linen napkins, huge steak knives and a slew of candles.

I'm early per their request as they prepare to throw their first dinner party together. They are going old-school with a menu of deviled eggs, shrimp cocktail, prime rib and a baked potato bar, complete with all the fixings.

"Where would you like me to set up the cocktail bar?" I ask, as I watch Dezi fiddle with the creamy strand of pearls around her neck. "I love the idea of a make-your-own martini bar, by the way," I say, as I set out coupe glasses, shots of olive brine and lemon peel twists. "Leaves you free to enjoy your own party."

"Hmmm, how about in that corner across from all the food," says Dezi, piling grated cheese and heaping mounds of sour cream into bowls. "That way, people have to move around a bit and mingle."

They are expecting a party of ten tonight, including Elliot's sister, Emma and her husband, Greg. Apparently, they are making a go of their marriage and Elliot is starting to make peace with the whole thing. He at least is no longer referring to Greg as that cocksucking, jerk-face ass-wipe, so says Dezi. Progress.

"Everything looks beautiful, Dezi," I say. "And you look gorgeous." And she does. She's wearing a cream strapless A-line dress splashed with pale pink and yellow flowers. Her hair is freshly blown out and with minimal makeup, she looks like an enviable advertisement for spring.

"Thanks." She smiles at me. "I'm so glad you could make it. And thanks for coming early."

"Of course. I wouldn't miss this. You aren't nervous about Marcus coming, are you?"

Dezi sighs. "I adore Marcus, you know that. And I love having you here. And Elliot is so excited to host you both. But I won't lie, Quinn, the two of you around Elliot make me nervous. Just promise me you will never, ever, mention he's married."

"Of course not," I say. "We'll never say anything. You're in charge of what you want to divulge to your boyfriend. Always."

"I could use a drink," she says, smoothing out her dress.

"Lucky for you my friend, I have just the thing." I hand her an icy gin martini, murky with olive brine.

"Am I allowed to drink before my guests arrive?" she asks, accepting the drink and taking a delicate sip.

"Absolutely. In fact, it's a rule. A slightly buzzed hostess makes for an excellent party."

"Well far be it for me to ignore the rules," she says, biting into an olive.

She's the only person I know who bites an olive in half, rather than plopping the whole thing in her mouth in one go. Same thing with cherry tomatoes. And almonds of all things.

I'm mixing up a second drink for Elliot — orange bitters and a twist — when I feel that familiar buzz in the air. *Marcus,* I think as my stomach flips and somersaults. Here comes that roller-coaster-ride whoosh.

Every. Time.

"You know your wine AND your martinis. You are a very, very fancy woman," says Marcus, taking the glass out of my hand and pulling me in for a long, soft kiss. "I have missed you," he says, putting his forehead against mine and fixing me with those jewel-blue eyes. "I do not get to see you nearly enough."

"Well, I, for one, couldn't agree more." I wrap my arms around him. "But you're here now. And I don't plan to let you out of my sight. Well, except of course when I'm eating. Or drinking. Or defending my cheese plate. Or otherwise doing lady things." I smile up at him. *UP! I get to look up!* I still get such a kick out of that.

"What's this about not getting to see enough of each other?" asks Elliot, coming over to say hi to Marcus. "Hey buddy, so glad you could make it," he says, clapping Marcus on the back, dude-style. "And I agree. We rarely get to see you."

"Pilot life," says Marcus, handing Elliot a bottle of whiskey as a host gift. "And I live in New York City, which probably doesn't help much. But I see this one every chance I get," he says, putting his arm around my waist.

"Well, we should get a double date on the calendar soon," says Elliot. "Maybe I can even get you two on the dance floor. Oh, I know, we can all do a long weekend in New York," he says excitedly. "I love the city and I'm due for a reconnaissance mission to Murray's Cheese Shop."

My eyebrows raise at this. I'm pretty sure a group outing to New York, where my married lover lives, *with his wife*, is out of the question. I don't really even know much about Marcus's home life. I know he owns an apartment somewhere in Manhattan and that he and his wife have two cats, Zulu and Bogey. I also know he's a regular at a gym within walking distance where he plays racquetball and throws weights around. But that's about it. I don't even know his wife's name or what she does, and I think we both like it that way.

I nod at Elliot, non-committal, and quickly change the subject. "So, tell me what we're having tonight so I know which wines to open now and get decanted," I say, pointing to the four bottles of wine I brought. "I heard something about prime rib …?"

• • • • •

I slice into my slab of steak and it cuts just like butter. It's that perfect, ruddy medium rare with a fabulous peppercorn crust. Mmmmm. The bite melts on my tongue, all crunchy salt and beefy, bloody goodness.

I'm about to tell Elliot and Dezi how delicious it is when I feel Marcus's hand gently stroking my inner thigh. Time-out. My brain is addled.

Meat. Wine. Marcus. This is a delicious combination. Bite of meat. Stroke. Sip of wine. Caress. Another sip of wine. Stroke, stroke, stroke.

I am woozy with desire. This cannot continue, not if we want to remain dignified and at this dinner party.

I turn to Marcus with a forkful of baked potato and offer it up as a distraction. Mine is a beautiful vessel for melted butter, whereas Marcus's version is simply adorned with salt and pepper.

"Come on," I say, holding up the fluffy, buttery pile. "You know you want some."

"I very much want some," says Marcus, his eyes twinkling. His hands, stroking, stroking, stroking.

Uh oh. Bad choice of words on my part.

He pulls my chair closer to him and plants a kiss on my neck. I'm grateful Dezi is seated on the other side of me so she cannot see my rapidly flushing face.

"Hey, you two love birdies. You need to cool it," says Elliot's sister, Emma, slightly slurring her speech and sloshing around what is most certainly not her first martini. She pounds her palms on the table, spilling her drink. "I said cool it," she says again, her words starting to bleed together. "Or I'm gonna comeoverthere and sit between you all."

Emma is most definitely in her cups, so to speak. We had the chance to chat briefly during the cocktail hour, before she was several drinks in, and she seemed nice enough, but definitely cranky. Her eyes tracked her husband all over the room, almost as if she were hunting him. And every time Elliot and Dezi got close together, she would insert herself in between, laughing gaily and saying syrupy things like, "Aren't they the *sweetest* couple? Isn't Elliot so *lucky* to have found Dezi. I am just soooo happy for them."

I know her history with Greg so perhaps I'm projecting, but the woman did not seem happy about anything.

She complained about the shrimp — cocktail sauce was too spicy. She complained about the fresh baguettes — not as crusty and authentic as what she buys. She even complained about her brother's cheese selection — why can't you ever have just plain, normal cheese? Why does it always have to stink up the place?

"Is she always like this?" I had asked Dezi when we had a moment alone before sitting down to dinner.

She rolled her eyes. "Elliot says no. That she's normally sweet and joyful and lights up a room. His words, not mine," she told me. "I've never seen that side of her exactly, but she's always been thoughtful and kind in the past. Nothing like tonight."

"So what gives?" I asked. "She seems so angry."

Dezi sighed. "From what Elliot says, she's having a hard time with Greg's affair. And she doesn't even believe it's over. It's been a bumpy road and honestly, he doesn't seem all that remorseful. It doesn't help that she overhead Greg telling Elliot tonight that all the women here are hot."

Marcus smiles at Emma but does not remove his hand from my thigh. "Sorry about that," he says. "I haven't seen this one in a while and I can't seem to keep my hands off her."

"Yeah, well, you aren't the only one with that problem," she says, turning sloppily to her husband and patting him on the arm. "This one here, he likes the laaaadiiees."

At that, Elliot swoops in, whisking away Emma's drink and replacing it with a glass of sparkling water. He also hustles her into the kitchen under the guise of helping him carve more beef.

Dezi, ever the therapist, expertly steers the conversation elsewhere as Elliot tends to Emma in the kitchen. Before we know it, we are all clinking glasses and going back for seconds as if nothing ever happened. They are a good team, I think, happy they have found each other. And very glad Elliot manages to bring a more subdued Emma back to the table.

"Maybe it was too soon to have those two at a dinner party together," whispers Dezi in my ear. I watch her take a tiny bite of her potato, loaded with bacon, sour cream and cheddar cheese.

"Ya think?" I ask. "But you and Elliot did a great job of handling it. And besides, what's a dinner party without somebody getting a little sloppy drunk?"

"Drunk I don't mind," she says. "It's the fighting with her husband at my dinner table I'm trying to avoid."

"Well, she seems to have simmered down," I say, nodding towards Emma, who is now quietly tucking into her food. "And at least she's eating something. That will help."

•　　•　　•　　•　　•

Elliot announces it's time for coffee and dessert, so we all make our way over to the living room to sprawl out a bit. He presents a gorgeous, wedding cake-esque coconut layer cake. *Ohhhhh, that is absolutely one of my favorite desserts.* Right up there with soft-serve ice cream and no-bake cheesecake.

"Why didn't you tell me there would be coconut cake?" I say, chiding Dezi. "I would have saved some room."

I tell Elliot that Marcus and I will share a piece as he pulls me into his lap. "Meaning I'll get one bite," says Marcus, wrapping his arms tightly around me as we sink into the chair together.

I am thoroughly enjoying the feel of Marcus's muscular chest against my back when I notice Emma sitting across from us, staring. She's holding a glass of clear liquid that looks suspiciously like gin or vodka and staring at us. *Man, she really doesn't like to see cozy couples,* I think, as Marcus feeds me a bite of cake.

"Oh wow, that is good cake." I take another bite. "I think that cake just made it on my death row menu."

Elliot laughs and tells me that he ordered it from his favorite pastry shop in D.C. He's about to tell me the name and neighborhood when I interrupt him. "Oh god, please no. Do not tell me," I say, putting my hand up to stop him. "I need to forget this place even exists. If you tell me, I will never fit into my jeans again."

"Well by all means, help yourself to more cake," he says, diving into a healthy slab of his own. "There's a ton of it in the kitchen."

I can see Emma is still staring at us. And she has no cake.

I grudgingly disentangle myself from Marcus and say to Emma, "I'm going back for seconds. Can I bring you a piece?"

Emma cocks her head and looks at me oddly, as if I just asked her if she'd like to join me in the backyard for a hootenanny. She keeps staring.

"Emma," I say gently, so as not to startle her. "Cake?"

"What?" she says, shaking her head as if trying to dislodge a memory. "Oh no thanks. No cake."

I shrug and think, *suit yourself.*

"Anybody else?" I ask, looking around the room. Everyone is otherwise engaged in their own cake or conversations or after-dinner drinks. I am the only oinker. But to be fair, I did share my slice with Marcus, so really I've only had half a piece. Three-quarters, tops. I'll go for a long, long run tomorrow.

I am rationalizing as I make my way to the kitchen. I snoop around a bit on my way and notice that Elliot's place is lovely and stylish, with beautifully restored hardwood floors and a stunning, not-quite-Emerald green accent wall in another room. He likes big, hulking furniture but it's sparse and tastefully arranged, so the rooms still appear open and airy. The man has excellent taste.

I wander into the kitchen and find the cake, resplendent and formal under its glass dome. The man has a cake stand! I don't even own a cake stand. I put my glass of bubbly on the kitchen island — cake and Champagne are magic together — and help myself to another wedge. To share of course. I'm licking a bit of frosting off my fingers when Emma comes tumbling into the kitchen.

"Oh hey," I say. "Did you change your mind? Shall I cut you a piece?"

Emma comes right up to me and points a finger in my face. "I know you," she slurs, her eyes now just slits.

Wow, she's short, I think, as I look down at her. *And very, very tipsy.*

"Well, yes, you do," I say, pulling out a barstool for her to sit down so she doesn't take a tumble. "And I know you." I eat a forkful of cake.

"Noooooo," she says, refusing to sit down. "I know who you are. You're the one giving fuck me lessons."

Whaaaaat …? I think as a hunk of cake falls out of my mouth.

"I recognize you from the pictures Cindy showed me," she says, peering closely at my face.

Cindy. Zack's wife. Holy shit.

Just then Elliot and Dezi breeze into the kitchen, Dezi searching my face and Elliot trying to steady his tottering sister.

"Everything okay in here?" asks Elliot.

"It's her," says Emma, spitting the words out. "She's the one who ruined Cindy's marriage. She's the one who had an affair with Zack."

Elliot frowns and looks from me to Emma, clearly confused.

"Emma," he says, taking her gently by the elbow. "You can't be serious. You've had a lot to drink. You must be mistaken." Elliot looks at me and mouths, "I'm so sorry," as he tries to calm Emma.

"No!" she shouts, thrusting her phone in his face. "It's HER."

Uh oh. Those can only be waffle-feeding photos. Syrupy kiss photos. *Oh boy. This is bad.*

"You have got to be kidding me," says Elliot, studying the photos. "It *is* you. What's going on?"

Fuck. Fuck. Fuckity fuck!

Elliot keeps staring at the phone, scrolling through the photos. "I don't understand. He's married. And you're," he gestures toward me, "you're practically licking the wedding ring right off his finger."

It's so quiet I swear I can hear the creamy frosting nestling into the coconut cake. I'd like to do the same, frankly.

"Elliot, I dated Zack briefly," I say, breaking the silence.

He suddenly snaps his head toward Dezi. "Did you know about this?"

I glance at Dezi, who looks, well, gobsmacked.

"Dezi had nothing to do with this," I say quickly. "And it wasn't an affair. I never slept with him."

Elliot holds up a hand to stop my excuses. "Please," he says quietly. "Just don't say anything. Do me that favor, okay? I don't want to hear from you right now."

He looks again at Dezi, who seems frozen, her eyes wide and barely blinking.

"Come on," I say, ignoring him. I'm not about to let him badger Dezi. "This is stupid, it was nothing."

"Nothing?" he says, incredulous. "Is that how Cindy feels do you think? What about my sister? Who still sometimes shows up at my house in tears. Do you think it's nothing to her that Greg had an affair? That he broke their vows?"

"Yeah! Yeah," pipes up Emma, still tottering about and slurring her words. "You tell her big brother. It's not nothin!"

Okay. Now I feel stupid. Maybe I will shut up.

"Zack was a mistake, Elliot," says Dezi, finally emerging from her stupor. "People make mistakes."

"But you knew," he says. "You *knew*."

"She's my best friend Elliot. Yes, I knew, but it didn't get far. She had two dates and then ended it. But honestly, it's not any of your business. And it's not like I was cheering her on," Dezi says.

Elliot sighs and rakes his fingers through his hair. "I know. Of course you weren't," he says. "I'm just shocked by all of this. Emma. Cindy. Quinn. Those pictures."

Damn those pictures.

"Look, I know shit happens and people do stupid stuff," says Elliot. "But I'm just still pissed about Emma's nightmare and now this. I've had my fill of homewreckers for the moment."

Ouch. I suppose I deserve that.

"Elliot," says Dezi gently. "Quinn didn't break up their marriage. In fact, she's helping. Aren't you?" she asks, her eyes piercing mine.

What the hell? Is she referring to those absurd lessons? No way!

"But why did you have to go and mess with Cindy's husband in the first place?" he asks, looking pointedly at me. "Why did you have to go and mess with anybody's husband? Don't you get the pain it causes?"

I'm about to answer when he cuts me off.

"You know what, never mind," he says, shaking his head. "I don't think I even want to know. But it's over, right?"

I nod.

It's quiet in the kitchen, all of us looking at each other. Emma frowns and collapses in a chair, the booze finally catching up with her. And then I watch with relief as Elliot pulls Dezi into a hug and rests his chin on her head, his eyes closed. I'm about to slink out of the room when Marcus swoops in.

"Everything okay in here?" he asks. "I seemed to have lost a gorgeous, green-eyed redhead."

Emma whips her head around and says, "Marcus baybeee! It's all good. We're just talking about how your girlie friend here screwed my friend's husband. And now she's giving fuck me lessons," Emma says, cackling.

Oh boy.

"I'll explain later," I say, pushing Marcus out the door.

"I want some of those lessons too," shouts Emma. "Heck yeah!"

I hustle Marcus out of the kitchen and into the living room, but now what? Do we leave? Do we continue with the party? Normally I'd stay until the end and help with dishes, but I'm not super eager to walk back into that hot mess of a kitchen. I glance over at Marcus and he's grinning at me.

"I can't wait to hear about these lessons," he says, his eyes twinkling. "You are just so much fun."

I roll my eyes at him. "I promise to fill you in." *What else can I do?* "But I should check on Dezi," I say, steeling myself for more crazy. "You go mingle with the remaining guests so it doesn't look weird."

"I'm on it. Take your time," he says, still smiling. "But for the record, I think you'd make an outstanding teacher."

I slip back into the kitchen just in time to see Emma slide down a stool and stretch out on the floor. "Marcus is hot," she says, talking to the ceiling. "Like, smokin' hot."

I am starting to wonder about Greg, her husband. Why isn't he in here checking on his wife?

"I betcha he's married too," she says, giggling to herself. "The hotties always are."

Dezi and I lock eyes in an instant. It's just a flash. A mutual *oh shit* current of electricity passing between us, but Elliot notices.

"I don't know what's fact or fiction around here," he says, sighing. "Dezi, please tell me Marcus is not married. That you didn't invite a philandering husband into my home. Not after everything we've been through with Emma."

"Marcus is married, Elliot," Dezi says quietly. "I'm sorry. Believe me. I know this is a really sensitive topic for you."

"What is wrong with you?" Elliot says to me. "And you," he says to Dezi. "You're a therapist. How could you go along with this?"

"I am a therapist. And a damn good one," Dezi says. "But that requires patience and compassion and understanding. Yes, Quinn sometimes drives me crazy, but people are complicated. Marriages even more so."

"But they don't just get a pass," Elliot fires back.

"Of course not," Dezi says. "But you don't know Quinn's history. Our history together. Or even Marcus's history. Nothing is as simple as it seems. And I'm not going to dump my friend just because I don't agree with her personal choices. And Quinn doesn't need to explain herself to you. Or anyone else for that matter."

Okay. I've had enough. My romantic life has nothing to do with Dezi. But I'm grateful she's standing up for me.

"Elliot," I say. "Dezi isn't the boss of my love life. So if you have a problem, it's with me. And frankly, my love life is none of your business."

"You're absolutely right. It's not," says Elliot. "But my sister is my business. And my girlfriend is my business. And this is all just too much for one night."

I look at Dezi. "I am so sorry," I whisper. "I never meant to put you in the middle."

"I know. You never do," she says, raking a hand through her pale blonde hair, making it stand on end. "Quinn," she says, with a big, exhausted sigh. "The party's over."

CHAPTER 27

Daily Special

Bone-in grilled pork chops with rosemary and fennel pollen
Caramelized fennel & charred lemon
Crispy polenta with Sambuca butter

I'm hiding in Persimmon's wine cellar with a note from Marcus clasped to my chest. I need to read it again. The heavy cream paper is already creased and soft like a favorite T-shirt thanks to the number of times I've read and re-read his latest note. I savor the scent of Marcus lingering on the paper — salty sea air, citrus and Scotch — and sink down to my knees to read.

Hello my gorgeous redhead,
I can't get enough of you. And yet, it feels as if I have known you a lifetime.
I am beyond smitten.
I have, unequivocally, fallen in love with you Quinn. And I need you in my life.
Always.
You are the one I have been looking for.
Marcus

I stare at his words. "You are the one I've been looking for, too," I whisper, tracing the penned words with my fingers. My heart feels too big for my chest. I swear my ribcage cannot contain it. I have read this note over and over and over again and each time it brings me to my knees. Literally. Which is why I started there this time. Saves me the trouble. I'm about to read the note one last time before heading back to my tables when Julian walks in and finds me, hidden in the wine cellar, on my knees. I must look like a total nutcase.

"Whoa, Q. You okay?" he asks, helping me up. "I didn't even know you were here. Haven't seen you all night."

"I'm fine," I say, brushing off my pants and standing up as I blow out a sigh.

"What's going on?" he asks.

I wordlessly hand him the note. Julian has been with me for this whole wild ride, may as well continue with it.

He quickly reads the words and hands it back to me, eyebrows raised.

"And this is a bad thing? I thought you two were nuts about each other. You certainly act like it," he says, smirking.

"Yes and no," I say, my face-splitting grin betraying my conflicted heart. "It just makes things more complicated is all."

"Love always does Q. It always does."

•   •   •   •   •

Julian is right. Love does complicate things. But I knew it was headed in this direction. We have spent the last few months doing nothing but flirting and texting and talking on the phone just about every night. It's as if he's not even married. We see each other almost weekly — even if it's just for a quick kiss at Persimmon before he heads to the airport. Or sometimes we meet for long, meandering walks around the city when he returns from a flight. I've never been this involved with any of my other married men. And I'm both delighted and terrified. It depends on the day. Sometimes the hour.

Things really started to pick up speed with us after Elliot's dinner party and the fiasco with Emma in the kitchen. In fact, that whole dinner party blow up didn't even seem to faze him. He actually laughed his ass off afterward, his blue eyes dancing at the thought of me tutoring women in the ways of feminine wiles.

"Don't get me wrong, I think you'd be a sensational tutor," he had said at the time, when we were safely back at his hotel after the party. "It's just the look on your face in that kitchen, when Emma howled about wanting lessons, killed me."

"You're not upset with me?" I had asked, after explaining about Zack and then Cindy's surprise visit and demented request while Dezi and I were having brunch.

"I'm not. I know you were dating other men," he said. "But ..." he trailed off.

"But what?" I asked.

"I don't have the right to ask, but I'm going to anyway," he said, pulling me in close and gently kissing my cheeks and then my lips. "No more other men. I want it to just be me."

•   •   •   •   •

I fold up the note and Julian holds the cellar door open for me as we both head back to our customers.

"It's a slow night," he says to me. "You know where to find me if you need an ear."

"I do. Thank you, Julian," I say gratefully, giving him a hug. We are finally on hugging terms. Well, I hug and he allows it. But still. I am so thankful for him. He's been my rock these last several months and he doesn't pry, which is priceless.

I make my usual rounds, pouring several selections of Italian red wines to accompany what is a very Italian specialty menu. People are sighing with pleasure all over the dining room thanks to Chef's crispy polenta with just a hint of sweet anise.

"How did the chef make this?" asks one woman, swiping a heel of bread across her plate, wiping up every last, buttery bit. "It's crispy on the outside but like custard on the inside," she marvels to her friends at the table. "I must have this recipe," she says to me.

"I'll see what I can do." I smile and top off her wineglass.

"Thank you," she says, clasping my arm and peering up at me. "Pardon my asking, but are you single?"

"I'm not." I blush and feel for Marcus's note in my pocket. "I have a boyfriend." *Boyfriend*, I think. I'm still getting used to saying that aloud. I do know that, by any normal frame of reference, I'm actually single. A married boyfriend doesn't count for most people.

But I am not most people. And it counts for me.

"Shame," says the woman. "Because you're so tall. And my nephew is so tall. It would be a perfect match."

I smile and internally roll my eyes. That's like saying, well, you have brown hair and my nephew has brown hair so .... I mean, really? Don't people get that?

I finish pouring their wine and head into the kitchen to see how many more special plates are available to order this evening.

"Quinn," booms Chef as he plates an order of Coq au Vin, sprinkling fresh chopped parsley and lemon zest over the shallow bowl of chicken stew. "What is happening with our cheese cart? I'm not in love with the cheese."

Uh oh, I think, as Chef drizzles the chicken with olive oil.

"I was in love with the cheese. But I am no longer in love with the cheese," he says, looking at me, hands now on his generous hips.

"Yeah. I sort of had a falling out with the owner of Barnyard Funk," I say, sighing. "I was trying a different cheese shop for now."

Chef raises an eyebrow at me. "This pains me greatly," he says. "FIX. IT."

I nod as Chef storms out of the kitchen. *I'm trying*, I think. And believe me, this pains me greatly too. I have attempted to reach out to Elliot multiple times with no luck. He's still cranky with me and yanking his cheese is his way of showing his solidarity to Emma, according to Dezi, anyway. He tolerates me now as Dezi's friend, but, thus far, doesn't want a relationship beyond that. Even a business one.

"What a night," I say to Julian, as I finally wrap up my shift and make my way to the bar.

"Nightcap?" he asks, already pouring me my favorite Cognac.

"Please." I gratefully take the glass and wrap my hands around the bowl.

"No pilot tonight?"

I shake my head but don't offer up that the pilot is with his wife. I hate these nights.

We are comfortably silent for a few minutes. Julian sets up for tomorrow while I slowly sip my drink, letting the heat of the alcohol seep through my veins, blurring the vivid slide show in my head of Marcus at home with his wife. A wife I still know nothing about.

"So, what's new with you?" I ask Julian, breaking the quiet. "How's life outside the bar?"

"There is such a thing?" he replies.

"Come on. You know the story of my life. I jog the Tidal Basin, eat way too much cheese and date a pilot. Hell, you even know all about my family in Baltimore."

"You, Q, are much more interesting than I am," he says, tossing a bar mop over his shoulder and smiling at me. "But you can ask me anything."

"As if I ever get a real answer," I say, throwing a crumpled napkin at his head.

"But before you ask, let me save you the trouble," he says, dodging and blocking the napkin balls I keep hurling at him. "No. I am not dating anybody."

I sigh. "Okay then, we're going to play the Alex and Quinn game."

Julian looks at me sideways.

"If you were on a desert island, what three items would you take? And at least one of them has to be a person."

"My drums. My motorcycle. And you," he says with a grin.

"I knew you were going to do that," I exclaim. "You can't say me. OR your mother."

"So many rules, Q. So many rules."

I shake my head. "You are impossible."

"Violet," Julian says quietly.

I look up at him from my drink, willing him to say more. I decide to keep my mouth shut.

"Violet," he says again. "Definitely."

"And she is ...?" I prompt, clearly unable to remain silent — how does Alex *do* that?

"The one that got away," he says simply.

Well, that is a doozy. But I know Julian well enough to know that I'm not getting anything more out of him tonight.

We are back to comfortable silence when Julian glances over my shoulder and says, "Hey, your friend is here. Haven't seen her for a while."

Dezi, I think, delighted. I know that Elliot isn't thrilled with me, but Dezi and I are fine, thankfully. I just don't get to see her as much anymore. Things were a little rough right after "Cake Night," as we like to call it now, but we're okay. In fact, I think we are even closer now if that's possible. We're still navigating the rocky road between me and Elliot, but with time, I'm hopeful we'll come to a detente. We have to, right? Apparently, Elliot equates befriending me with betraying Emma. And, according to Dezi, he's still annoyed with himself for not kicking Greg's ass to begin with. And then for upsetting Emma on "Cake Night" by inadvertently inviting a philandering husband and his mistress. I get it, I suppose. And I still feel terrible for causing Emma any pain. What a mess.

I shudder thinking of that embarrassing night. Especially when Emma shoved the waffle-feeding photos in Elliot's face. I mean seriously, what's the likelihood of running into a friend of Zack's wife, at my best friend's boyfriend's home? It still boggles my mind.

But if I think too hard, I know I deserved it. The total nightmare of a scene. And I wonder now, had I not already fallen in love with Marcus, if I would have changed my dating ways.

•   •   •   •   •

I turn around just in time to see my tiny blonde friend marching towards me, her gorgeous, high-heeled shoes a lyrical staccato on the hardwood floors. She stands fiercely in front of me, arms crossed and feet planted wide, as if she's staring down her boxing opponent before entering the ring.

"Hey, hey, hey," I say. "Dez, are you okay? What's going on?"

She's not her usual calm, serene self. She looks pretty pissed off.

"What's happening?" I ask, wondering if I should go in for our usual hug.

I glance over at Julian just as he slides another Cognac in front of Dezi. I mouth, "Thank you," as he nods and turns his back to us.

Dezi takes a deep breath. Then another. I swear she's radiating steam.

"You know I love you Quinn, but you have to fix this," she says. "I don't know how to be your friend and Elliot's girlfriend. This just sucks."

"What happened?"

"Are you kidding me?" she says, her blue eyes pools of dark ink. "Zack. Zack happened. And now Marcus. No. Wait. Actually, first it was James. Then Derek was it? Or was Nathan next?"

I don't know what to say. She's right.

"They were married, Quinn. All of them. And now I feel like a jerk for standing by. Marcus is married. You need to face that reality."

Her words are a punch in the gut, like when I was a kid and got nailed in the stomach during dodgeball games. Ooof.

"You don't think I know that?" I whisper to Dezi, running my fingers through my already crazy, untamed hair. "You don't think I feel totally out of control here?"

Dezi sighs and shakes her head. "Quinn. We barely see each other because Elliot just can't wrap his head around you and Marcus. I'm trying to smooth things over, but it feels ridiculous when you two are still sneaking around and lying to Marcus's wife. You're making it impossible for me."

"He's not punishing you for my choices, is he?" I ask.

"No, but he's upset. He's trying to balance my feelings and Emma's. And he genuinely liked you and Marcus, so he feels blindsided. Look Quinn, I want you all in my life, but I can't keep defending you. Not when you refuse to make any changes. I'm starting to feel foolish. And totally caught in the middle."

I stare at her.

"You *have to* fix this," she says. "I need you both in my life."

I watch my best friend turn and leave and then put my head in my hands. I don't know whether to cry or be angry. My life, however screwed up it is, is none of Elliot's fucking business. And Marcus's life is none of Elliot's fucking business. And if he takes it out on Dezi so help me I will open up a can of whoop ass on that short little dude. Who does he think he is? He knows nothing about me. *Nothing.*

A strong, gentle hand on my shoulder interrupts my internal psychotic rant.

Julian.

"Hey. Q. You okay?"

"Not really. I have made a mess of things. And I don't know how to fix it."

Julian hands me a bowl of nuts. "So I heard."

"Oh boy. And you still want to talk to me?"

Julian sighs. "You definitely surprised me Quinn. Which rarely happens."

"And ..." I prompt.

"I'm still here," he says matter-of-factly.

Oh thank god, I think, relieved. I feel myself start to unclench a bit.

"Marcus is really married?" Julian asks.

I nod.

"When did you find out?"

I fight the urge to avoid Julian's gaze and instead look directly at him.

"Before Paris?" he asks, his eyebrows raised.

"From the very beginning," I whisper, nodding. "I knew from the very beginning."

CHAPTER 28

Rule #27: The wife winds up being your problem, never his.

I'm in the middle of teaching a fuck me lesson when Cindy starts to cry. *Oh for Pete's sake*, I think, exasperated by Zack's wife and these ludicrous lessons.

And I really need to stop thinking of them as fuck me lessons. Damn that Emma.

"Cindy. I did not sleep with your husband," I say, trying to hide my annoyance. "We've been over this."

I am trying to be sensitive, but I'm in no mood for tears today.

I woke up this morning with my head pounding. I barely slept as I was so worried about Dezi and the whole rotten situation. She left Persimmon last night before we had the chance to really talk it out. Is Elliot angry with her? Can we remain friends? How am I supposed to fix all this? I have so many questions and no answers. But what I do know is this, I would erase James and Nathan and Derek and Zack if I could. I really would. But not Marcus.

I just can't. I won't.

I didn't even get the opportunity to tell Dezi about these dumb lessons. Not that it would help her situation much, I suppose, but there's a chance. I agreed, on a trial basis mind you, to give Cindy what she wants and start these "lessons" a few weeks ago. I haven't mentioned it to a soul because, well, it feels so hokey. But I'm here, trying to teach lesson #3. I'm not exactly sure why I agreed to this trite nonsense, but I'm certain it's a combination of things — those disturbing photos, the horror of "Cake Night," the fear of Cindy-the-stalker and just plain old guilt.

Oh, and my sincere lack of excellent juju.

So here I am, trying to take this seriously.

"Cindy, things seem to be going much better with you and Zack, yes? So let's not get hung up on the past."

Cindy just nods and sniffs and takes a sip of her tea. "It's true," she says. "Just last week he brought home flowers and cooked me dinner."

"Well there you go," I say, encouragingly.

"It's a step in the right direction," she replies. "But it's still nowhere like with you and the waffles."

I'm not a magician, I want to shout. *I have no control over the level of romance in your relationship. Nada. Zippo. Zero.*

"I'm sorry Cindy, I just don't think I'm any good at this." I sigh. "I don't seem to be helping you at all."

"No, you are," she says. "You really are. Things are better and Zack is paying a lot more attention to me."

"Don't you think that maybe, just maybe, it's because of you? And this has nothing to do with me? Or these lessons?" I ask hopefully.

She shakes her head. "Absolutely not. He didn't want me before you. He didn't want me after you. But he wants me now," she says, smiling.

I'm glad she's happy, but I think she's wrong. Clearly, however, I'm still on the hook for this tutoring nonsense.

"So, what's next?" Cindy asks me eagerly.

I'm exhausted and I've run out of little nuggets of womanly wisdom. At least for today. I'm about to tell her we need to wrap up early when she gets a text. And it's from Zack, apparently.

"It's soooo working," she squeals, clutching the phone to her chest. "Look," she says, showing me the text screen:

Zack: Surprise dinner. 8 p.m. Wear a cocktail dress. I'll text you the address.

"That's great," I say, smiling. And I really mean it. "Does Zack know about these lessons, by the way?"

"Of course not. Are you nuts? He would royally flip out."

I shrug my shoulders. "Okay. Are you sure you want to hide them from him?" I wish I could take back the words as soon as I say them. They sound preposterous given the situation.

Cindy just gives me her navy-blue-eyed stare. "Seriously? Anyway, the last thing I need is for him to know we're hanging out. I don't want him to think about you at all."

"Fair enough," I say, hoping to usher her out of my apartment soon so I can take a long nap and unscramble my brain. It appears a bit of good juju is with me as she stands and collects her purse and jacket. *Hallelujah*!

"I'm heading out," she says. "I have a new dress to buy."

I smile. I'm happy today is over, but also genuinely happy for her and Zack. I do think deep down he's a good guy and I really like Cindy. I hope they find their way back to each other.

"Sexy," I shout from my open door as she makes her way down the communal stairs. "Sexy dress!"

She turns to look at me and rolls her eyes so hard I fear her blue irises will spin around to the back of her head and never return. Which would be such a shame.

"Again, seriously?" she asks. "THAT much I do know. It's a good thing I'm not paying you."

I laugh and wave goodbye. She's a hoot, that one.

•   •   •   •   •

I need a snack before my nap and pop a piece of bread in my toaster. I slather it with peanut butter, thinly sliced green apple and a scatter of raisins. Comfort food. I pour myself a glass of milk and sit down to turn my phone back on in the hopes that Dezi reached out. I take a big bite of my toast and, yay, a text!

Zack: Surprise dinner. 8 p.m. Wear a cocktail dress. I'll text you the address.

What the hell? A wad of half-chewed toast falls out of my mouth. I really need to stop getting surprised while I'm eating. I text him back immediately.

Me: You accidentally sent me this.

Zack: No accident. I miss u. Please don't say no.

You have got to be kidding me, I think, crunching through the last of my toast while trying to think fast. *What in the world is happening?*

Me: Zack. U sent this same message to your wife.

Zack: What? No I didn't.

Me: Yes, you did. Check your phone.

Zack: Holy shit! I did! Wait, how do you know?

I ignore his question entirely. Frankly, I'd like to know how he managed to send the same suggestive text to both his wife and his former fling, but I'm not about to prolong this conversation.

Me: It's over Zack. You know that. I am very much in love with somebody else. Please, please, go on this date with your wife. She loves you.

Me: Cindy LOVES you.

So much for my crack juju. Or my nap. I need Dezi.

CHAPTER 29

Rule #29: Yes, a Pilates ass would be nice. Good luck.

I'm standing outside Dezi's apartment, afraid to knock on the door. Dezi is family to me. She's been the one solid fixture in my life for years. I can't lose her. It would tear me up more than losing Liam did.

I take a deep breath and gently knock on her door.

No answer, but I hear voices. I think she's watching an exercise video. I can faintly hear a woman saying something about squeezing your buns.

I knock again. And now I hear footsteps.

"Hey," I say as Dezi opens the door. "You haven't been answering my texts. I'm worried."

Dezi engulfs me in a hug. "I'm so glad you're here," she says, her voice muffled against my shoulder.

"Me too," I say, as my limbs go weak with relief.

We stand in her living room, staring at the Pilates instructor on TV.

"Pull your belly button toward your spine and engage the glutes," says the perfectly sculpted woman, wearing impossibly tight yoga pants and a sports bra. "Ribs in, neck long, squeeze your inner thighs together," she says, breathing in and out with a whooshing sound.

We both watch the woman for a few minutes, marveling at her abs, which are flat with a distinct looking number eleven carved into them.

"I was trying to do a Pilates class," says Dezi, gesturing toward the television. "I got as far as a few lazy leg lifts and a couple of butt squeezes."

"Don't let me stop you, squeeze away."

"I'm done. Pilates ass be damned," she says, turning off the TV. "I'm so glad you came. But you're not totally off the hook. We need to figure this out."

"I know, I know. That's why I'm here."

"Sit," she says. "I'm going to make some tea."

"Wait. You have to tell me first, is Elliot being a jerk to you? Be honest."

"Of course not. Do you really believe I'd stick around for that? Obviously, he was upset and initially confused. And wondering about my involvement in your affairs."

"I hope you've made it clear you're not involved. In fact, you're the one who is always trying to therapize me out of my wanton ways."

"Yes," Dezi nods. "He gets that, but it's not as if it's just Marcus. Or Zack. You've been playing mistress for years now and that would be hard to explain."

"So don't. My past is not up for discussion. And honestly Dezi, I still don't understand why he gets to be the judge and jury regarding my love life. It's none of his business."

"You're absolutely right, it's not any of his business. But who he associates with and who he socializes with and who he surrounds himself with *is* his business."

I nod, running my fingers through my hair, electrifying it.

"I am now his business," says Dezi softly.

"Jesus Dezi. I'm sorry. I don't want to come between you two."

"I won't allow that," she says firmly. "I love him Quinn and I do think he'll come around, but not if you continue as is."

"What can I do?"

"Figure out Marcus. Stop sneaking around. And please, no more married men."

"When you say figure out Marcus ...?"

"Quinn. Forget about Elliot. What do *you* want going forward? Where is it going with Marcus? Is he worth it? How long do you plan to play second fiddle to his wife?"

"Wow. Are you suggesting I try to break up their marriage?"

"I'm just asking you to think ahead. Understand your actions reverberate and have real consequences. This isn't just about you."

"You're right," I say with a sigh. "It feels very different this time. And if I could take back all my married men, I would."

"Would you?" asks Dezi.

I nod. "In a heartbeat. Except Marcus. But I'm scared. I'm scared of how I feel about him. I'm scared to think he'll leave his wife. And I'm scared to think he won't."

We sit in heavy silence. I know Dezi is treading carefully as she never wants to crossover from friend to therapist. She's always been in my corner. On my side. And I've been a giant ass. I've been acting like a giant ass for years. And now it's hurting my best friend.

•   •   •   •   •

"I'm giving those lessons," I blurt out suddenly, breaking the silence. "It's stupid and I hate it, but I felt like I owed it to Cindy."

Dezi jerks her head up. "Are you serious?" she says, grinning. "I love it!"

"Really? It's just so corny. And I'm terrible at it."

"I think it's great you're at least trying to help. And what makes you say that? You clearly knew how to snag Zack."

I tell her about the twin texts.

Dezi starts laughing so hard she doubles over. She's in the midst of a full-blown belly laugh.

"Gee, thanks," I say, as Dezi continues to cackle.

"I'm sorry," she says, wiping tears from underneath her eyes. "But that is just too good."

"Are you done?" I ask, cracking a small smile. "It is pretty crazy, isn't it?"

Dezi nods, still chuckling. "Oh, thanks for the laugh. Whew. I needed that. My life would be so dull without you."

"Yeah, yeah, yeah," I grumble.

"You did a good thing," says Dezi, hugging me. "I bet you Zack will show up for the date."

"I'm certain I'll find out all about it at our next lesson," I say, rolling my eyes.

"Can I come?" asks Dezi eagerly, starting to laugh again. "Oh please, let me sit in."

"When hell freezes over. Unless, of course, you'd like to be a guest lecturer?"

"Absolutely," says Dezi. "The moment I get my growth spurt and shoot up to your height. Or when my abs look like the woman in the Pilates video. Whichever comes first."

CHAPTER 30

Rule #13: Trust me, you don't REALLY want to know her name.

I pull on a pair of snug-fitting yoga pants and a stretchy top that knots and twists in the front, exposing just a teeny glimpse of belly. Now you see it, now you don't, kind of thing. This is not my usual exercise get-up. This is my pricey, Lululemon, I-wouldn't-dream-of-actually-sweating-in, athletic gear. I know, ridiculous, right? But I prefer to work out in old, ratty stuff that I don't have to worry about hand washing. Or stinking up on my long runs.

So why the fussy, expensive yoga pants? Marcus. He's taking me on a leisurely bike ride today along the Potomac River. Picnic included! I haven't seen him since his love note and I cannot wait to throw myself at him. He's going to be in town for the next two days and I'm hoping to spend every possible moment with him.

Hence the cute workout clothes.

Marcus isn't due to pick me up for another half hour, so I start throwing clothes and toiletries into an overnight bag. I'm staying at his hotel with him tonight, per his request. We've stayed at my place a few times, but honestly, nothing beats room service pancakes. Or somebody else making the bed and providing fresh, fluffy towels.

I'm rifling through my underwear drawer looking for a clean pair of sexy panties when I glimpse a framed photo of Dezi and me on my dresser.

We're posing in New York City's Central Park on a gorgeous fall day, with the iconic Bow Bridge in the background. That was one of our last trips together, just us girls. Before both Elliot and Marcus. Before things got so complicated.

I sigh thinking about Dezi beseeching me to figure out Marcus. I know she's right, but I'm certainly not going to be the first to bring up his wife. I've never broken any of my cardinal rules. And I don't plan to start now.

"Ah ha," I say aloud, finding a beautiful black lace thong tucked in the back of my drawer. And there's a matching bra! "Where have you two been hiding?" I really need to go lingerie shopping again. Oooh, maybe Marcus would want to join me. I smile at the thought. But as I continue packing, my mind wanders away from lingerie shopping and I simply envision us strolling, sharing Sunday brunch, grocery shopping, folding laundry—all the day-to-day things regular couples do. This is decidedly not my usual daydream. Not even close. And it makes my stomach feel weird. Thankfully, my odd reverie is interrupted by a soft rap at my door.

I throw open the door and there stands my 6' 5" hunk of man. He opens his arms and grins as I jump into them, wrapping my legs around his waist and burying my face in his neck. He carries me into my living room easily, as if I'm the size of a cat or a lap dog rather than a basketball player.

"Quinn," he breathes into my hair as he wraps his arms tightly around me. "Have I missed you."

I find his face and look into those startling blue eyes and smile. "Oh yeah?" I ask playfully. "How much have you missed me?"

Marcus starts backing me up toward the kitchen island, kissing me gently as he talks. "Well, my gorgeous redhead," he says, punctuating each word with a kiss. "Why don't you let me show you?" he asks, putting me down on the counter, his hands on my hips.

"Come on now," I say, teasing. "I was promised a bike adventure. And a picnic."

"Oh I'll give you an adventure," he says, sliding his hands under my shirt. "And your picnic."

•   •   •   •   •

"Well, you were right. That was an adventure," I say, snuggling up in the sheets next to Marcus. I put my head on his chest. "We should definitely go bike riding more often."

Marcus laughs and rolls me over, pinning my arms above my head with one hand. "I couldn't agree more," he says, his free hand doing delightfully unspeakable things to my body.

After round two, we are both spent and sated and lounging in my bed, my carefully chosen Lululemon outfit discarded in a heap on the floor. Who cares? It served its purpose. Well worth the price tag, I think.

I cannot stop smiling. I look up at Marcus, his eyes are closed and he's smiling too. *Maybe he'll leave his wife,* I think.

Wait. Did I just say that aloud? I glance at Marcus quickly. Whew. I did not. But I thought it. And that surprises me. I have never thought that. I have never, ever wanted that.

Oh boy, maybe this is the first step in "figuring out Marcus" per Dezi's request.

I'm trying to get a handle on my thick stew of emotions — love, lust, terror and dread — all under the sheen of post-coital bliss, when Marcus stirs.

He puts an arm around me and nuzzles my neck. "Hungry?" he asks. "Somebody I know was promised a picnic. And I like to keep my promises."

"Yes, I'm starving," I say, grateful for the distraction of food. But I am indeed wildly famished, as if we had actually gone on a long bike ride.

We bag the biking and decide to head to his hotel for the remainder of the afternoon. The plan is to order an early room service picnic dinner and cuddle up with movies. Perfect.

"Grab a couple bottles of that red wine for our picnic," I say to Marcus, pointing to a case I purchased but have yet to unload. "No sense ordering wine at the hotel. I'll go finish packing my bag."

"Please tell me you're packing for two," he says, pulling on his shirt.

"For two?" I ask, somewhat confused.

Marcus comes to me and cups his hands around my face. "Two nights," he whispers. "I want you to stay both nights."

I smile. "Shall I pack for another crack at a bike ride?"

"Always," he says, his eyes twinkling. "Always pack for a bike ride."

•   •   •   •   •

We finally make it to his hotel room and I'm now officially ravenous. I scan the room service menu as Marcus opens the wine and pours me a glass. I'm so hungry that absolutely everything sounds delicious. Club sandwich? Yes! Salmon Caesar salad? Yes! Meatloaf and mashed potatoes? Yes! Yes! Yes!

"Get us whatever you want," says Marcus, handing me a soft, cozy hotel robe. "Let's get comfy."

"How do you feel about French dip sandwiches? I can't remember the last time I had one of those. Oooh, with fries. And coleslaw."

Marcus smiles. "Sure, sounds like perfect rainy-day food," he says, peering out the windows as rain starts to smack the glass. "And don't forget the coconut cake for dessert."

"Gah!" I whack him with a pillow. "I don't think I can ever eat coconut cake again."

Marcus grins at me as he picks up the hotel phone and places our dinner order. Including a slice of coconut cake.

"You had better eat your share of that cake," I say, shaking my head at him.

"I promise." He pulls me toward him, tipping my face up toward his. "But you have to promise me one thing in exchange."

"Hmmmm, I'm not sure I can do that carte blanche. Even for you," I say, kissing him gently on the lips. "But let's hear it. Shoot."

"You have to tell me all about those lessons you're giving," he says, still grinning.

"Hell no. And why did you have to remind me? You really are spoiling for a fight, aren't you?" I laugh and pummel him with a huge, king-sized down pillow. I'm about to whack him again when there's a knock at our door. "Dinner," I say gratefully. "Yay!"

•   •   •   •   •

We're lounging in bed, drinking wine and finishing our sandwiches, when Marcus's phone starts going berserk. I see him glance at the screen and then frown. Uh oh, I think. It's either work or the wife. I'm not sure which I would prefer. Work usually means he has to leave. The wife, well, I don't know. I've never been around when she's reached out. I still don't even know her name.

"It's okay if you need to get that," I say, pointing to his phone. "I can give you some privacy."

"It's fine," he says, tossing the phone in the bedside drawer. "It can wait." He puts down my wineglass and takes me in his arms. "Now, let's see about our dessert, shall we?"

"You cannot be serious. I'm spent. And full. And just a wee bit tipsy."

"I am always serious about dessert," he says, lazily nuzzling my neck and lightly grazing my stomach and hips with his fingers. "Especially when coconut frosting is involved."

Just when I start to feel as if I may be up for some "dessert," Marcus's phone starts acting up again.

"Don't move," he says to me, planting a kiss on my belly. "I'll be right back."

There's pretty much no chance of me moving. I'm deliciously drowsy and quite content in this huge, ridiculously comfortable bed. I flip over on my stomach and start doodling on the hotel stationary as I wait for

Marcus, who disappeared into the other room with his phone. It's his wife, I am certain, but I'm trying not to think about it.

My brain feels a bit woozy from too much red wine as I draw human faces with extra-large doe-eyes and big, goofy smiles. I'm no artist, so I try for a poem instead:

Lake Tahoe is blue.
Your eyes are blue.
I like cheese.
Your eyes are still blue.
Cheese.

Wow. That is a terrible poem. I blame the wine. And my sex-addled brain.

I return to doodling human heads, now with ponytails and big ears, when I hear Marcus's voice coming from the other room. He's not yelling or anything, but his voice is now definitely above a whisper.

"I can't do this right now," I hear him say. "Juliette, please be reasonable. I'm about to fly a plane."

Juliette. Huh. Her name is Juliette. It's a very pretty name.

"It's my job. I'm a pilot," Marcus says. "This is nothing new."

Juliette. Juliette. Juliette, I think. I have no idea what she's saying on the other end. I really shouldn't be listening to any of this at all.

I doodle in earrings on my human head and try to block out his voice. Although I admit, I'm not trying too hard.

"Okay sweetheart. I'll be back home in a couple of days," says Marcus. "Uh huh. Yep. Yep. Okay, gotta run. You too."

My stomach drops at the "sweetheart" and the "you too." That was clearly an "I love you too," moment.

Huh.

I keep doodling. *Do NOT bring up the wife, Quinn. Whatever you say, whatever you do next, do NOT bring up Juliette. Just. Don't.*

"Now then," says Marcus, striding back into the room, his blue eyes twinkling. "Where were we?"

He's not going to say anything? Really? I suppose this shouldn't surprise me. He hasn't mentioned his wife since the day he told me he was married and we irked that bearded barista. And practically violated a tree in the park.

But it's out there. Hanging thick in the air like bad perfume.

Juliette.

"Hey," he says softly, curling up next to me on the bed and putting my head on his chest. He gently starts playing with my hair.

I will myself to stay quiet. The ball is so in his court.

"Well, well, well," he says, picking up the hotel stationary. "You, my love, are a very talented poet."

"Oh shut up," I say, trying to grab the pad from him as he reads the absurd piece aloud.

Wait. Did he just say love?

"... Your eyes are still blue. Cheese," reads Marcus with a flourish, laughing and kissing the top of my head.

He called me his love.

His. Love. He's written it, yes, but he's never actually said it.

Tears spring to my eyes as my heart soars. There is no other way to describe it.

"You are certifiably nuts," says Marcus. "And damn it woman, I love you."

●   ●   ●   ●   ●

Forty-eight hours later, I'm standing at my front door, saying goodbye to Marcus. His "trip" complete, he must head home to The Wife. I've stopped thinking of her as Juliette. It's just easier.

We cannot stop kissing. We cannot stop touching. Each time we separate he pulls me back to him for one last embrace. Which is stupid because I'll see him next week.

We are love-struck jackasses.

"Never, ever stop writing poetry." He smiles and crushes me to his chest.

"You are never going to let me forget that, are you?" I ask, relishing my last few moments with him.

"Not on your life," he whispers, leaning back to take my face in his hands. "Quinn. My Quinn. I love you," he says, his blue eyes soft. "I love you like no other."

"Me too. I love you too."

•   •   •   •   •

I finally walk into my apartment, drop my bag on the floor and look around. Funny how I feel totally different — somehow lighter and at peace and well, beautiful. Even my apartment looks brighter and feels airier, yet everything is exactly the same. But my world has changed. Love, I assume? It's not what I wanted, but it's here and I may as well face it. I am in love with Marcus. *Shit, shit, shit*. How did I let this happen? Do I enjoy the ride and brace for the inevitable crash? Or run?

Now.

I don't know what to do with myself, so I text Alex.

Me: Hey little brother, I'm in love!

Alex: Oh boy. Marcus?

Me: Yes, Marcus! Who else?

Alex: So now what?

Me: Not sure exactly. But we had a good talk.

Alex: And?????

Me: Too much for text.

Alex: Is he leaving his wife?

Me: And there's the reporter in you …

Alex: Well?

Me: I'll tell you in person soon. I promise.

Alex: Okay. I'm happy for you big sister. It's been a long time coming. But you had better have a plan. For your own sanity.

Yikes. That's a tall order, and one I will likely ignore. Marcus and I did have a good talk, but I really don't know what lies ahead for us. And, quite frankly, neither does he. We spent the last two days in bed, snuggling, talking for hours and falling madly in love. All of which can gum up the wheels of logic, much like kindergarten paste in curly hair.

Marcus did finally address his wife though, which felt like a big step for us. I'm just not sure in which direction.

Here is what I learned about said wife:

1. They married young. Too young, according to Marcus.
2. She teaches piano and illustrates children's books (geez, really?).
3. They have sex just a few times a year, on special occasions.
4. She checked out of the marriage years ago, hence the limited anniversary and birthday sex.
5. She is content with the status quo.
6. I am his second affair.
7. He never loved the first woman.
8. And he no longer loves his wife.

That's about the extent of my knowledge. Marcus didn't expound much nor did he mention divorce and I did not pry. I wouldn't dream of asking him to leave his wife. I'm in love, yes, but I feel safest with Marcus married. I don't want anything to change. When I'm with him, it's easy to pretend I'm not scared out of my mind. It's easy to strangle that persistent whisper in my head — what if, in the end, he's like Liam?

So for the moment, I still have a very married boyfriend. And there is no simple answer here. The simple truth, however, is that Marcus and I are in love. And we want to spend as much time as we can together.

But, for better or worse, we are both excellent at ignoring Juliette.

CHAPTER 31

Daily Special

Pan seared veal chops with fried caper berries and lemon
Brown butter sage gnocchi
Shaved radish and celery salad

Chef gives me the wonky eye as I walk into the kitchen. He's been giving me that crazy eye ever since I lost Barnyard Funk.

"I know, I know," I say, sighing. "The cheese cart. Yes, I'm still working on it, I promise."

If he only knew.

"Yes, Chef, I am delighted to report that the cheese cart is now appropriately stocked from that most excellent of dairy purveyors," says Chef, as he supervises the saucier and eyes me sideways. "These are the words I wish to hear, Quinn."

I nod. "We'll get there," I say. "I promise."

"When? When will I get my promised cart of cheese? The excellent cheese. The cheese I love?"

"Soon," I reply, hoping I'm right. "It's a bit of a delicate situation."

Chef turns to face me, his shoulders square and his arms crossed in front of his white coat. He looks at me expectantly. Blinking his eyes.

Well Chef. Here's the thing. My best friend's boyfriend's sister's husband cheated on her. And that made him very, very angry. The boyfriend is the owner of Barnyard Funk (the excellent cheese purveyor). He found out that I had an affair with his sister's friend's husband. And then he found out that I'm currently sleeping with a different married man. A man I've been parading about much as I would a boyfriend, rather than an illicit lover. And then I brought said married man to a dinner party, at the Cheese Man's home no less. So you see, he's not super thrilled with me at the moment. As I said, a delicate situation.

Yeah right. There's no way I'm saying all that. It sounds crazy making even to my own ears.

"I will fix it," I say firmly to Chef. "I just need a little bit more time."

•   •   •   •   •

The restaurant is bustling tonight. I've got three birthday celebrations, an anniversary, a girl's night out and several six- tops, along with the usual Friday night dinner crowd. Orders for Chef's special are flying out of the kitchen and I'm trying to stay a step ahead. Empty wineglasses when food arrives is a huge pet peeve of mine. I personally want my wine before my food and so I try to do the same for my diners. I don't want any of my customers searching for me, empty glass in hand, while their meals cool in front of them. Not on my watch.

So this evening, I am hustling.

Champagne for table one. Two bottles of gamay for table two. Wine pairings for the six-tops at tables three and four. A Spanish tempranillo for table five. And a "red wine that doesn't taste like dirt" at table six.

I approach a recently seated couple and ask if I can be of service. They are wearing wedding rings, appear to be in their early 50s and look bored out of their minds. It's like she's suffering through a Star Wars marathon and he's enduring the movie Dirty Dancing for the tenth time.

His eyes roam around the room as she fiddles with the menu and examines her cuticles. Everything is more interesting to them than each other.

Why are they even here? I wonder. They are a perfect example of why I don't want to get married again. Here they are, at this lovely restaurant on a Friday night, with absolutely nothing to say to each other. The woman is now biting off a hangnail and he's staring out the window, picking at a scab on his chin.

They can't even hide their misery.

"May I interest you in wine this evening?" I ask pleasantly. "Or a cocktail perhaps?"

The man looks surprised to see me. He looks surprised that he's even here, at a restaurant. I bet you anything she whined for a date night and he finally, grudgingly, agreed.

Marriage killed these two. Or they didn't choose right to begin with. Which I understand all too well.

I am so happy I'm not married. And that I have Marcus.

But do I? Do I have Marcus? And is that even what I want?

I shake the thoughts from my head and focus on the pair in front of me.

The woman puts her hands in her lap and looks up at me. "Oh yes, wine would be nice, wouldn't it Phillip?" she says, nodding eagerly, trying to get her husband's attention.

"What?" he says. "Fine. Whatever you want." He takes the wine menu from me and glances at it. "Something in this range," he says to me, gesturing towards the lower end of the price points.

"Of course sir," I say, continuing to smile at this sad couple. "Red? White? Sparkling, perhaps?" I ask, all the while wanting to kick Phillip in the shin. *Buy your wife a god damn nice glass of wine you ass,* I scream inside my head. *Hold her hand! At least LOOK at her for crying out loud!*

"Oooh, Champagne would be lovely," the woman says, clapping her hands together. "Oh Phillip, we haven't had Champagne in ages."

This crushes me. One should *always* be able to recall the last time one had Champagne. Sort of like sex. If you cannot remember the last time you indulged, it's been too long.

"We have a wonderful selection of sparkling wines, including Champagne," I say, willing Phillip to say yes so this poor woman can enjoy a glass of bubbly.

He looks at his wife dully over the top of his menu and again mumbles, "Fine. Whatever you want."

The man is about as exciting as an umbrella.

I hurry off to get their Champagne, grateful to get away from the suffocating whirlpool of their life. What happened to them? He looks at her the way I used to look at my ex-husband, Chris, with a mixture of sadness and marvel. And marvel not in the good — wow, how did I get so lucky — way. I mean marvel in the — how did I miscalculate my feelings and throw the trajectory of my life so far off that I cannot even figure out a way back — kind of way.

It's a weird feeling. A trap of your own making. Sort of like digging your own grave, I would imagine.

Anyhow, I recognize Phillip's look. And his attitude. And I'm glad I let Chris go. It wasn't a purely selfless act, obviously, but I'm glad I got out when I did rather than put him through a slow, painful relationship death. He deserves a woman who really loves him. And that just wasn't me.

I'm aware not all marriages are doomed. My parents, for instance, are still happy and very much in love after nearly 50 years. And I do believe Dezi and Elliot can go the distance if they so choose, but I think a lot of marriages crash and burn out, eventually.

All of my married men are a testament to that.

I present the bottle of Champagne to Phillip and he just grunts and nods. He scrutinizes the gorgeous, pale liquid, sparkling in the glass like tiny diamonds. And then he asks for a beer.

"Right away, sir," I say, as his wife sighs into her glass. *Well, more Champagne for her. At least there's that.*

•　　•　　•　　•　　•

The next few hours go by quickly and before I know it, I'm done. Thankfully, I had no more run-ins with Chef and, after the Champagne and beer were distributed, limited contact with the pained married couple. Now it's time for my usual end-of-night chat with Julian, one of my favorite aspects of working at Persimmon.

I wander into the bar and find him doing his usual post-shift wipe down and set up. I hope things aren't weird between us as I haven't seen him since he found out Marcus is married.

"Q," he says, looking up at me with a smile and handing me a plate of pickled tomatillos.

Whew. Things appear normal.

"Am I going to find out anything else about your life tonight that's going to make my head explode?" he asks.

Okay. Maybe not.

I look at Julian and cannot think of anything to say.

"I disappointed you," I say, looking down at my hands.

Julian sighs and leans on the bar with his elbows, so his head is level with mine.

"Q. Look at me."

My eyeballs feel suctioned to the floor. I don't want to see the look in his eyes.

"Q," he says again. "Please look at me."

I drag my eyes upward and can almost hear the suction release in my head — pop, pop.

I look at Julian. I don't think our faces have ever been this close before. All I see is kindness.

"I'm no saint and I don't expect you or anyone else to be either," he says. "You just surprised me. Marcus, not so much. But you ..."

"I know," I say, nodding. "I wanted to tell you but at the same time, didn't want you to know."

"I get it. But for the life of me, I don't get why such a beautiful, funny, smart woman would settle for a married man."

"It's complicated, Julian."

"More complicated than the current mess you're in?"

"Wow. What happened to my silent Julian who says nothing and lets me yap at him?" I ask, attempting to lighten the mood.

Julian cracks a smile at that.

"I just don't want to see you get hurt Q," he says. "You showed me that note from Marcus, remember? Seems pretty serious."

Ah yes. The love note, I think, the memory making me smile in spite of everything.

We are quiet for a few minutes. I have no idea what he's thinking. But I'm thinking of Marcus. And then, suddenly, Juliette.

"His wife's name is Juliette," I blurt out. "Juliette. I wish I didn't know."

Julian sits next to me and just nods.

"Do you love him, Q?"

"Yes," I say simply.

"Is that enough?" Julian asks.

"I don't know. Enough for what?"

"Enough to break up their marriage. Enough to let him go and know you had this great love once. Enough to forever be the other woman. There are a lot of ways to answer that question."

"What would you do?"

"Ah Q. You know I can't answer that for you. Nobody can."

"What would you do about Violet? If you had to do it all over again?" I ask, referring to the woman who stole his heart. "Has it been enough for you to know you had this one, great love?"

"Yes and no," he says.

"Geez, and you think I'm complicated," I say, poking him in the ribs.

He smiles. "Yes, because it's enough now for me to know I once had that kind of love."

"And no ..." I prompt.

"No, because I'll forever wonder what could have been. What kind of love it could have become. What kind of man I'd be today."

"No regrets," I whisper.

Julian nods. "I should have asked her to marry me."

CHAPTER 32

Rule #23: You are not the one breaking vows.

It's a chilly afternoon and I'm curled up at home, making my way through a late lunch of grilled cheese and tomato soup. I went for a long run earlier to clear my head and am now enjoying the warmth of my kitchen and the comfort of gooey cheese and a can of old-school Campbell's tomato.

I'm back at Persimmon tonight, which I have mixed feelings about. On the one hand, I will have to endure more cheese cart questions and the wonky eye from Chef, but on the other, I get to ask Julian more questions about Violet.

That was another doozy he laid on me last night and I didn't get the chance to follow up.

I'm not letting him off so easily tonight.

Julian also gave me a lot to think about in terms of Marcus and how I would play this all out if I had my way. I was hoping the run this morning would help. It did not. I wanted a fling, I wasn't expecting to fall in love. I also wasn't expecting to rope Dezi into my crazy romantic life. I want to help her, I really do, but I'm just not ready to make any big decisions. For now, I want things to stay the same. I love where we are, suspended in this blissful romantic cocoon. I don't want to poke holes in it and I don't think it's my job to poke holes in it. If there are any moves to make, they really need to come from Marcus. He made the vows. And he's the one breaking them. My love for him does not blind me to the fact that he is, in fact, cheating on his wife.

I'm slurping the last of my soup just as my phone pings. *Marcus,* I think, my heart soaring. Nope, Cindy. Sigh.

Cindy: Our date was wonderful! One of the best we've had in years!

Zack showed up! Hallelujah!

Me: I'm so happy to hear that. What did you wear?

Cindy: Clingy blue dress. His favorite color.

Me: Matches your eyes. Excellent choice.

I see those three little dots moving and I know she's responding. Maybe she's firing me! Oh please, please, please tell me the date was so good we are now done with these dumb lessons.

Cindy: Can't wait for our next session. I'll be in touch.

Sigh. Wishful thinking. I'm glad Zack showed up though. And here's hoping he forgets about me. I like Cindy and I can see how they ended up together. Maybe they'll find their way back.

CHAPTER 33

Daily Special

Veal tartare
Cacio e Pepe
Roasted cauliflower with golden raisins and pine-nuts

Oh my. Chef has put together another of my favorite menus. I know I'll be spending much of my time this evening explaining cacio e pepe to guests, but I don't care. As long as Chef saves me some. I'll happily endure his hairy eyeball for a plate of this pasta — bucatini, tons of toasted black pepper, even more tons of grated Pecorino Romano, all doused with olive oil so delicious you could drink it on its own. It's simple but, when done well, it's lick-the-plate perfection. When I make it at home, I have to stick to tiny portions, otherwise I'll down an entire pound of pasta in one sitting. I know because I've done it.

And yes, cacio e pepe is most definitely a part of my death row meal plan.

"I might curl up and die if you don't save me a plate," I say to Chef as I rush past the kitchen and to the wine cellar, trying to avoid close contact. He's distracted and busy with cheffy things so I am in luck, for now at least.

I choose both a red and a white for my wine pairings. A white vermentino for those who want to cool the warmth of the black pepper and a Chianti Classico to help cut the richness of the cheese. Either would be delicious, so it really depends on the diner's mood and wine preferences.

I need to reign in my cacio e pepe enthusiasm as the special is flying out of the kitchen faster than I can pour wine. If I don't stop gushing about it, I fear there won't even be a forkful left for me.

Chef waves me into the kitchen.

Uh oh.

"God forbid you curl up and die," he says, handing me a warm plate of pasta. "Not in my kitchen."

I smile.

"Eat," he points. "While it's still perfect."

Who am I to argue with that?

I'm grateful for the delightfully toothsome bucatini AND for the fact that Chef is currently not in my face about Barnyard Funk. I realize I need to address the situation, but right now, I need to eat.

Twirl, eat, sigh with pleasure. Repeat.

•   •   •   •   •

I manage to avoid Chef the rest of the night. I'm not sure how much longer I can hold him off. Chef is many, many things, but patient is not one of them.

I sneak a bit of the bucatini into a coffee mug to bring to Julian. Not that Chef would mind, necessarily, but he does have odd proclivities and the last thing I need right now is to further rile him up. So I pile some noodles into a mug and head to the bar.

Julian is doing his Julian thing. I watch him for a moment as he finishes making his final round of drinks, garnishing glasses and expertly eyeballing liquor amounts. He skewers a black cherry and an orange peel and then sprinkles a different glass with what looks like lime-colored dust. Turns out, it is, in fact, lime dust.

"Making up your own drinks these days?" I ask, smiling at my friend.

"Always," he says, handing me a specialty cocktail list.

"These are all your creations?" I ask, reading through the list of concoctions.

"More or less," he says, shrugging.

"J's Juice?" I laugh, raising an eyebrow at him. "How come I've never seen this list before?"

"You prefer classics. You don't need a list for those."

"True. But I work here. Providing alcohol, so …"

"This is strictly for the bar-goers." He winks at me. "It's where the real fun happens."

"Is that so? Does Chef know about this hidden little gem of a menu?"

Julian points to a cocktail several items down on the list. He named it "Toque Blanche."

I shake my head. "You are always full of surprises."

I peruse the menu and see drink names such as, "Daddy's Riff" and "Groove Me" and "Naked with Shoes On."

"What, no Quinn?" I ask, teasing.

"Keep going," he says.

And there it is. "Q." The final drink on the list. Champagne, gin, tart cherry juice and a splash of simple syrup.

I smile. "Dare I ask?"

"Well, Champagne was obvious. You dig gin. And, well, you're a redhead."

"Now I have to try one."

"Done," says Julian, grabbing a coupe glass.

"Oh, I almost forgot," I say, passing the mug of pasta to Julian. "You must try this. It was Chef's special tonight."

Julian glances at the mug and says, "No thanks, I'll pass."

"What do you mean you'll pass? Do you have any idea what this is?"

He shrugs. "Some sort of spaghetti."

"Some sorta spaghetti," I grumble. "Typical dude. Some sorta spaghetti my ass."

I meticulously explain cacio e pepe to Julian.

"And that," I say with a little bow, "is why the dish reigns supreme."

He stares at me as if I'm, well, naked with shoes on.

"You cannot be serious," he says, laughing. "Are you sure you're normal?"

"You're not even going to have a bite?" I ask, ignoring his comment.

"Well, after that lengthy presentation, how can I refuse?"

I peer down into the mug only to find it empty. "Oops," I say sheepishly. "I think I ate it. While you were making my drink. Which is excellent, by the way."

Julian starts laughing and I fear he won't ever stop.

I sip my pink-hued, namesake cocktail, roll my eyes and wait patiently for him to get a grip. "It's not *that* funny. Let me see if there's more in the kitchen."

"No, please, I'm fine," Julian says, still chuckling. "Next time, okay? I promise never to refuse you again."

This makes me smile. I fiddle with his cocktail menu and notice there's a drink called "Love, Violet."

"That's an interesting choice," I say, pointing to the menu as Julian washes the empty cacio e pepe mug. "What's it mean?"

Julian dries the mug and looks right at me. "Wishful thinking."

I'm about to inquire further when he grins at me and points over my shoulder.

"I love it when you have visitors," he says, smirking.

Oh no, I think. *Oh no, no, no.* I don't even want to turn around and find out.

"Who is it?" I ask. "Man? Woman?"

"Both, actually. This looks like it could be fun."

I spin around, not sure who to expect. If it's Alex and Fantasia I might faint. Nope, it's Elliot and his sister, Emma.

Oh boy.

I haven't seen Emma since "Cake Night," which was several months ago now. She looks exactly the same — medium height, medium straight brown hair, pale golden eyes and perfect, peachy skin — except this time she's not tottering about, drunk.

Elliot I've seen a few times in passing with Dezi. He hasn't spoken more than a couple of words to me since "Cake Night." One of which was the word "no" when I inquired about ordering cheese for our dessert cart at Persimmon. But he recently allowed me to apologize, which is new, so I think we're moving in the right direction.

"Hi Quinn. I was hoping to catch you," says Elliot.

"What can I do for you, Elliot?" I ask with a tentative smile. I nod at Emma and say, "It's good to see you."

Emma's peachy cheeks turn sunset orange. She touches my arm and says, "I am so sorry about that night. I was upset. And drunk. And now I am so embarrassed."

"No need to apologize at all," I say. "Really, I'm the one who needs to apologize. To both of you." I turn to face Elliot. "Elliot, again, I'm sorry for causing a scene at your dinner party. Emma, it's okay. I know you were hurt and just protecting your friend."

I gesture to them both to sit as Julian approaches to see if they'd like anything to drink.

Elliot asks for a gin and tonic and then swivels his stool toward me. Emma, interestingly, points to the "Love, Violet" cocktail.

"Look Quinn, it's no secret I'm not thrilled with your choices. And I don't get it. But we both love Dezi," he says. "I just want to move forward as best we can. For her sake if nothing else."

Oh thank god, I think.

"Is that why you came all the way down here?" I ask, mentally keeping my fingers crossed that maybe, just maybe, I can also get back into his Barnyard Funk good graces.

"Well, yes, but I also have a favor to ask," he says, glancing at Emma. "We have a favor to ask."

"Yes. Anything," I say. "Anything at all."

"Emma wants to sign up for your, um, you know ... your lessons."

CHAPTER 34

Rule #26: Not all cheaters are asses.

WTF? WTF? Nooooooo. I couldn't be more stunned if Emma whipped down her pants, bent over and mooned us all right then and there at the bar.

I can see Julian out of the corner of my eye, a smile playing at his lips. I know he's roaring with laughter on the inside.

"Will you excuse me for just one minute?" I ask, smiling sweetly. I make good use of my long legs and get to the ladies' room in just a few strides. I'm about to have a meltdown.

The world has gone crazy. Berserk. Looney tunes.

I squeeze my eyes shut and take a few deep, yoga-like breaths.

I have no business teaching these lessons. How did I get into this?

I just want my wild rumpus.

I just want Marcus.

I open my eyes and collect myself. I can't say no. Not if I want to keep Dezi in my life. And not if I want to keep the peace with Chef.

I suppose it's not a high price to pay.

And it may just buy me more time to figure out Marcus.

•   •   •   •   •

"Okay Emma," I say, returning to the bar. "I'll do it."

Emma smiles. "Thank you. I know you don't have to do this, but I was hoping. It seems to be working so well for Cindy and Zack."

Except for the double text, I think. But whatever.

Emma goes on to describe how Cindy was just thrilled with their recent date night. And that Zack brought home flowers and her favorite bath bombs from Lush and that he's more attentive than ever, blah, blah, blah. I look over at Elliot and he just shrugs.

"It's like he's trying to win her over all over again," Emma says, starting to get animated and way too excited.

I need to put the kibosh on this right quick.

"I can't make any promises, you know that, right?" I ask. "And honestly, I think Cindy and Zack are working because of Cindy and Zack. Not because of me."

"But you'll still do it?" Emma asks.

"Yes. I just want to set expectations. I'm not a magician or a witch."

Emma nods. "I understand."

"We are talking about your husband, Greg, yes?" I ask, mentally recalling that jerk-face who was with Emma on "Cake Night." I didn't interact with him too much, but I do remember him ogling Dezi's cleavage. And staring at my butt (per Marcus). And rolling his eyes whenever Emma spoke. In fact, I even remember him flinging a forkful of potato at Emma like a bored child, willing her to call him out on it. She just simply brushed the food off her chest and gave him a wan smile.

What a turd. And yet, she still wants him.

"Yes, Greg," says Emma, interrupting my thoughts. "We have two young daughters."

Ah yes, the little girls, I think. It's as if she read my mind. I suppose she has good reason to want to keep him around. But he's no Zack, who, in my opinion, really is a decent guy at heart. He just lost his way.

But Greg? I can't get his smarmy face out of my head. And then there are all those stories Dezi told me about his philandering ways — multiple one-night stands, sneaking home at dawn, flirting with her friends, gawking at other women in Emma's presence. And once, apparently, he felt up Emma's favorite yoga teacher. Emma was so embarrassed she never returned to class. GAH! This is so going to be a waste of Emma's time. Not to mention mine.

Emma drains her drink, the "Love, Violet," and looks at me. "When can we start?" She stands up to leave.

"How about now?" I ask suddenly, looking from Emma to Elliot. "This first one is a quickie."

"Okay," says Emma, looking at Elliot for confirmation. He just nods and shrugs and sits back down.

I can see Julian shuffle a little closer, his back still to us. I can't see his expression, but I can imagine his eyebrows rocketing skyward.

I take a sip of my "Q" cocktail and beckon Emma to sit.

"Emma. There are nice guys out there who veer off the path. They just need a little coaxing to get back on track. A little sweetness, if you will. Like Zack."

Emma nods.

"And then there are jackasses, pure and simple. Greg is the Titanic of asses. Herculean. He is, if you will, a super-duper ass."

I wait a beat to let this sink in.

"And, sometimes," I continue, "an ass is just an ass."

Emma looks at me strangely. "What are you saying?"

I can see Julian's shoulders shaking. And Elliot looks amused.

"Emma. You don't need me. You need a good lawyer."

·   ·   ·   ·   ·

Julian and I watch as Elliot escorts his stunned speechless sister out of the restaurant. He is steering her by the shoulders when he turns to give me a quick nod. "Thank you," he says quietly. "I couldn't agree more."

I smile and nod. "Happy I could help."

As they walk out the door, Elliot turns one last time to look at me. He points to the cheese cart. "I'll set you up. No sense wasting good business," he says as the door swings closed behind them.

"Oh, that is very, very good news," I say to Julian as I sigh and collapse onto a barstool.

"Which part? The cheese or the fact that you just wrangled yourself out of having to give love lessons?"

"Both. Definitely both."

Julian hands me a glass of sparkling water with lime and a plate of creamy green olives. He always seems to know exactly what I need.

"I do love it when you have visitors," Julian says with a grin. "I always learn so much."

"Yeah, yeah, yeah." I pop an olive into my mouth. "If only I could say the same about you."

I sip my water as Julian cleans up the bar.

"It sounds as if you are giving *somebody* lessons?" asks Julian. "Would this be that other woman who came storming into the bar a few months ago?"

I roll my eyes and sigh. "I was hoping you didn't overhear that."

"Oh Q." He smiles. "I hear everything."

I shake my head. "It's ridiculous. The whole thing is nuts."

"If I recall, I thought it was a pretty good idea," he says. "Still do."

"And Emma?" I ask. "What about her?"

"Seems to me you were spot on with that one." He grins. "Sounds as if her husband, and if I may quote you here Q, is a 'super-duper ass.'"

CHAPTER 35

Rule #25: Never introduce family.

I'm rocking out at home to 90's dance music, which is my exercise of choice today. I don't feel like gearing up for a run. And besides, I'm so happy to be tiptoeing back into Elliot's (and by association, Chef and Dezi's) good graces that I just need to dance it out. Plus, I dodged the student Emma bullet AND I'm seeing Marcus today. These are all the makings of an excellent day.

I'm in the middle of an extremely poor attempt at the Running Man when my phone pings. My dancing is about as good as my drawing skills. Perhaps I should take Dezi up on joining her for lessons.

Speak of the devil, I think, glancing at my phone.

Dezi: Hey. I hear Elliot paid you a visit. He's coming around.

Me: Seems that way! I'm so happy I'm dancing. Literally right this minute. The Running Man to be precise.

Dezi: Ha! I also hear you're getting your cheese cart back. And he's thrilled with your no-nonsense approach to Emma.

Me: Glad to hear it. Hope she wasn't too offended.

Dezi: I don't think so. I think it was just the sort of wake-up call she needed. We'll see what happens.

Me: Keep me posted. Double date soon?

Dezi: I don't think so. You and Elliot really need to be solid before we try to push Marcus on him. Cake Night really threw him.

I text her a thumbs up, a frowny face, a kissy face and a disco dancer emoji and leave it at that.

•   •   •   •   •

An hour later I'm wrapping up my dance jam when there's a knock at my door. I'm not expecting anyone, so a package, maybe? Or perhaps a neighbor annoyed by my leaping about? I look down at my outfit. Crazy-old black leotard. Weirdly shiny electric blue tights and rainbow sherbet-colored leg warmers. I sort of got a little carried away. Okay, *a lot* carried away.

I open the door only to find Marcus, holding two cups of coffee and fresh bagels.

"Oh, this is good," he says, smiling and looking me up and down. "This is better than good. I really need to make surprise visits more often."

I'm in his arms in an instant, leg warmers be damned. "Shut up," I say, burying my face in his neck.

"That is quite an outfit," he says, his blue eyes crinkling at the corners. "I dare say I've never seen anything like it."

"It's a long story." I usher him inside. "Mmmm, bagels and coffee. To what do I owe this pleasure?"

"Leotard story first," he says with a grin, kissing me and setting out a spread of bagels, lox and cream cheese.

"Well, it's not really a long story." I dive into a pumpernickel bagel, slathering it with cream cheese. "I was rocking out to dance music while weeding out my closet and found this," I say, gesturing to my aerobics get-up.

"And ...?" He prompts.

"And I thought it would be fun to put it on and dance. There is something about leg warmers that really gets me in the mood."

"There is something about leg warmers that really gets me in the mood, too," he says, taking the bagel out of my hands and planting a long, soft kiss on my lips.

"Coffee, bagels and nookie. This is turning out to be an excellent morning."

"I'll say," says Marcus as he scoops me up and carries me into the bedroom.

• • • • •

We're snuggling and enjoying a bagel picnic in my bed when I remember to ask Marcus why he's even here. Not that I mind, but we were supposed to have a date tonight. Somehow, I think this is now the date.

Marcus must have read my mind because he pulls me towards him and tells me that his work schedule changed and he needs to fly out in a few hours. He won't be back tonight.

"I'm sorry," he says, nuzzling my neck. "I meant to tell you as soon as I walked in but, well, there was the leotard. And the leg warmers."

I nod earnestly. "It can be very distracting."

"You, my love, can be very distracting," he says. "I hope it's okay that I dropped by. I wanted to see you."

"Of course." I feed him a bite of bagel. "Wait until you see what I'm wearing next time."

Marcus's eyebrows shoot up and he smiles. "I look forward to it. When can I see you again? I'm free tomorrow when I get back from my trip."

"I'd love that." I'm past the point of playing games. I will see him every chance I get. "Oh no! I can't," I say, remembering I'm seeing Alex. "I already made plans with my brother."

"Would this be Alex? I'd love to meet him."

"You would?" I ask, feeling my heart skip a few beats. "Since when are we meeting family?"

"Since now," says Marcus. "And yes, I would. I would very much like to meet him."

• • • • •

Two hours later, Marcus leaves for the airport after we solidify plans to drive to Baltimore tomorrow to see Alex. Alex, of course, has no idea. *How am I going to pull this off? Do I surprise Alex? Do I give him the heads-up? What in god's name did I just agree to?* I am brimming with nervous energy. I see my shiny tights and leotard in a heap on the floor and wonder if I should dance this all off.

No, no, no, Quinn, I tell myself. *You need to figure this out. Now.*

I decide to call Alex. We're supposed to go axe throwing again tomorrow and I cannot just show up with Marcus.

He answers on the first ring.

"Hey. What's up? You never call."

I get right to the point.

"Marcus is coming with me tomorrow. He wants to meet you."

Silence.

More silence.

I can hear Alex breathing, but that's it.

"Alex? Are you there?"

"I'm here, Quinn."

"Are you okay with this? I know it's weird. It just sort of happened and I didn't want to spring it on you tomorrow."

"Well, I appreciate the heads-up. It's fine, I guess. Weird, but fine."

"Why don't you bring a date?" I ask him. "Take some of the pressure off."

"Quinn. First of all, I'm not dating anyone. And even if I was, I certainly wouldn't bring her to meet my sister and her married boyfriend. I would look like a jerk."

"Since when do you care what people think?"

I hear Alex sigh.

"I love you Quinn, you know that, but you must see how crazy-making this is."

"I'm nodding," I say. "I know. I know. I am figuring this out."

"And you don't think Marcus meeting your family is going to muddy the waters and make everything harder?"

"I honestly didn't think that far ahead," I say. "We never discussed meeting family and then your name came up and suddenly he asked to meet you and I said yes. This was literally just a few hours ago."

"Okay," says Alex. "I'm cool with it."

"Thanks. I'm hoping maybe after you meet him, you can help me figure it out."

"I wouldn't count on it. You won't like my answer."

I sigh. "Just wait until you meet him, okay?"

"Okay. Just promise me you won't bring him around to mom and dad's tomorrow."

"Of course not. That would be suicidal."

"Honestly," says Alex, "I don't know that you'll ever be able to bring him home. Not unless he's divorced."

"No comment. See you tomorrow."

•   •   •   •   •

Marcus hits a bullseye on his very first try. Then another. Then another. And another.

"Impressive," Alex says to me as we watch Marcus throw. "Are you sure he hasn't done this before?"

I shake my head. "First time. Must be that pilot eyesight."

I am thoroughly enjoying my view of Marcus. Normally we're in such close proximity I don't get the chance to really look at him. He's at least a head taller than anyone else around with broad shoulders, sculpted arms and a gorgeous, statue-of-David ass. And he's clearly athletic, too. I watch him focus on the task at hand and continue to tally up points with every throw.

I sigh with pleasure as I drink him in.

"Wow, you're nuts about this guy, aren't you?" asks Alex, interrupting my mooning session.

"Is it that obvious?"

"About as obvious as Fantasia," he says with a grin, nodding over my shoulder. "Looks like she's coming over to say hello."

I hear her sing-songy voice behind me.

"Alex," she squeals. "I haven't seen you in a while. And Quinn, so good to see you again."

She flips her hair so that it brushes Alex's shoulder and positions herself as close to him as possible without actually touching him.

"Hey Fantasia," I say, as Alex nods at her and attempts to brush her hair out of his face. I can see it's tickling his nose.

"Ooooh, I see you brought someone," Fantasia says to me as she ogles Marcus. "And he's a hottie, too. Just look at him throw. Oh wow. He's really good at this."

Alex rolls his eyes at me as he mutters, "Women" and "Damn Navy pilot" under his breath.

"So, what can I get y'all to drink? Alex, you want your usual?" asks Fantasia, lightly touching my brother on the forearm and looking up at him with her big brown cow eyes. They are cartoonish, framed with absurdly long eyelashes — extensions no doubt.

"We'll do a Monument pilsner and two 51 ryes," says Alex, looking dubiously at Fantasia with her huge lashes, so stupidly thick and long we can hear them smack together when she blinks. Which is often.

Fantasia turns to get our drinks just as Marcus finishes his final throw with a satisfying thwack. "You're up," he says to me, pulling me in for a quick kiss. "For good luck," he says.

"I'll need it after you. I'm hoping that was just beginner's luck."

I head towards the throwing area but then turn around and look at Marcus and Alex, already involved in conversation. "Hey, you two, behave," I say.

"I wouldn't count on it," Marcus says with a wink. "When have you ever known me to behave?"

Two hours and two beers later, my brother and I are getting our asses handed to us by Marcus.

"He's impossibly good at this," Alex says with a sigh as Marcus leaves to find the men's room.

"Quick," I say to Alex, as it's our first opportunity to chat alone for a moment. "What do you think?"

"Besides the fact that he's making me look bad? And that he opened up a can of whoop ass on us?"

"Come on, come on, spill it before he gets back," I say, trying to hurry him along.

"You want the good or the bad first?"

"Whatever, just say it already."

"He's great, Quinn," says Alex. "I like him. I really do. In spite of the fact that he's seriously messing up my axe game AND he's got bigger biceps than I do."

I laugh and give Alex a friendly punch in the arm. "Yours aren't half-bad."

"Gee. Thanks," he says. "Soooo ..."

"Don't bother telling me the bad." I interrupt him. "I already know it."

Alex just simply nods, but he scrutinizes my face. It's as if he's searching for Waldo in a Where's Waldo poster. *What is he expecting to find?*

"You're the boss," he says matter-of-factly.

"That she most definitely is," says Marcus, coming up behind us and wrapping his arms around me. I sink back into his chest as he rests his chin on my head. I feel myself soaking him up — his scent, his voice, the feel of his forearms and the tickle of his five o'clock shadow. I simultaneously want to feed him and nurture him and straddle him naked.

I have never known a love like this.

"So. Marcus," says Alex. "What's up with your wife?"

"Alex!" I say, glaring at him and mouthing, "Are you crazy?"

But I can see my brother is in full reporter mode. And there's no stopping him.

"It's okay," says Marcus softly in my ear. "It's a fair question." He returns Alex's gaze. "What would you like to know?"

Alex doesn't say anything. He just lets the silence hang in the air until it almost becomes palpable, like a thick haze of smog. I know exactly what he's doing. He's employing his journalism skills, trying to get Marcus to jump in and fill the uncomfortable silence.

Marcus does not comply and I find this weirdly attractive.

The two men in my life are staring at each other.

"Marcus," I say, unwinding myself from his arms. "You don't have to answer."

"I think I do," he says quietly.

CHAPTER 36

Rule #33: Love sucks. Even in the best of times.

"I never meant to start cheating on my wife," Marcus says to Alex.

Alex continues to just look at him. I can read his thoughts. *Tired excuse. Boring. Cliché.*

"She checked out of the marriage a long time ago," he says. "Long before I did."

"So why not get a divorce?" asks Alex, never one to mince words. "Why are you still married?"

Marcus sighs and runs his fingers through his thick, wavy hair. "Believe me, I've thought about it. I even contacted a lawyer. And this was before I met your sister."

Both Alex and I are quiet. This is all news to me. I'm not sure how much I want to know. Damn that brother of mine.

"Have you ever been married, Alex?" Marcus asks.

Alex shakes his head.

"Marriage can be very, very complicated. Especially when you've been together a long time. Quinn, you can attest to this. You were married."

I nod, recalling the life-sucking quagmire of my marriage to Chris. When I was in it, I couldn't see. It wasn't until I got out that everything became clear.

But I got out. I didn't have an affair.

"Yeah, sure, I get that," says Alex. "But now you're having an affair. With my sister. And I don't like it."

"Alex. I am in love with your sister. I didn't expect that," says Marcus, taking my hand.

My heart flutters and swells at his use of the word love. Here we are, discussing my married lover's wife, and I can't help my delight. I'm such a goon.

Alex does not appear at all impressed with Marcus and his professions of love.

"I don't claim to know what it's like to be married, but I've had a front row seat to Quinn's failed marriage," says Alex. "She got out, though. She never broke her vows."

It's like he's reading my mind.

Marcus just nods.

"Who knows what would have happened if I had met Marcus in the middle of my mess with Chris?" I say, jumping to Marcus's defense. "I might very well have cheated on him."

Alex just looks at me, eyebrows raised. "But you didn't."

"But I could have, just as easily," I say. "If I had met Marcus then, I'm almost certain I would have."

I put my head in my hands as Marcus wraps his arms around me. "How did we get into this mess?" I whisper. "I love him," I say to Alex. "I love you," I say, looking up at Marcus.

"I love you too, sweetheart," he says, pushing the hair back from my face.

"This is insane," Alex says, exasperated. "Marcus. I like you, I really do, but you have a wife. And you are carrying on with my sister as though you're single. Have some balls, man. Do the right thing."

Marcus is quiet. I don't know what to say.

What is the right thing? Leaving his wife? Or leaving me?

My brother stands with his arms crossed, watching us.

"Marcus, you still haven't answered my questions," says Alex. "I get that you love my sister. I can see that. But what's up with your wife? Why are you still married?"

Marcus slowly pulls a small square of black and white paper out of his wallet and carefully unfolds it.

"I was going to tell you eventually," he says to me. "Privately."

"Is that an ultrasound picture?" I ask. "Is that ... is that your baby?"

"Yes," he says, gently folding the picture and placing it back in his wallet. "That was my son."

I put my hand over my mouth as my eyes swim with tears for this man that I love and his lost baby boy. "Oh Marcus, I am so, so sorry. I didn't know ..."

"Shhh, it's okay," he says to me. "Really, it's okay. And of course you didn't know. How could you?"

"I'm sorry man," says Alex. "I can't even imagine that kind of pain."

Marcus sighs. "I know this still doesn't explain things."

Alex holds up a hand. "It's okay. You don't have to go on."

"No, I do," Marcus says. "My wife, Juliette, always wanted to be a mom. Always. She got pregnant soon after we were married but lost the baby. No real reason, the doctors said. Just told us to keep trying."

My eyes are glued to Marcus's face as I watch his Tahoe blue eyes mist over.

"So we did keep trying, but she never got pregnant again. Something inside Juliette died the day we lost him. And with each negative pregnancy test, well, it was like I lost another little piece of her."

"Oh Marcus," I say, reaching for his hand.

"I begged for counseling. I begged to stop trying for a while as it broke me to see her so crushed. But she was like a robot — intent on the task and yet so frighteningly detached. She wouldn't touch me unless she was ovulating. And even then it was like she was cringing her way through it."

I look over at Alex who is just listening, quietly.

"She's not the same person I married," says Marcus. "I lost her a long, long time ago."

Marcus grips my hand and turns his gaze to me. "I haven't felt married for years. But I just could never bring myself to push for a divorce. To hurt her even more."

Marcus looks at Alex. "And then I met Quinn and I fell in love and well, here we are."

Alex nods. "Thanks for being honest. Sorry for the grilling."

"No problem," says Marcus. "I would have done the same for my sister."

We all take a sip of our now lukewarm beers.

"I don't promise to have all the answers yet, but any other questions?" Marcus asks.

Alex shakes his head.

"What was his name?" I whisper, looking up at Marcus. "The baby. What was his name?"

"Jett. His name was Jett."

•   •   •   •   •

A couple hours later, after an emotional goodbye to Marcus at the train station, I'm now strolling along the Baltimore waterfront with Alex, per our usual routine. Today's revelations exhausted me, but Marcus assured me we would figure things out. And then he boarded a train homebound to Manhattan.

To his wife.

"What a day," I say to my brother. "I am wiped out."

"Quick, if you were on a desert island and could only bring three games to play, what would they be?" asks Alex, trying to lighten the mood. "Assume you have somebody to play them with, of course."

I sigh. "Alex, I have no idea. I can't think straight right now."

"Come on Quinn," he says, jabbing me in the ribs. "That's the beauty of this game, no thinking allowed. Just go."

"Scrabble. Bocce ball. And Twister," I say triumphantly.

"Twister?" asks Alex, laughing. "Seriously, Twister?"

"What? It's my island. My games."

"But Twister? What are you, four?"

"Hey little brother, no more giving me a hard time today." I give him a swat. "You have reached your quota for the day. The year, in fact."

"Okay, okay. Truce."

We walk in silence for a while, our long strides mirroring one another. My head is spinning. Marcus, Chris, Liam, vows, marriage, divorce, love, sex, Jett and Juliette, all are whipping inside my mind like laundry during a spin cycle. I can't tease it out. I can't see what's what.

Where does my heart begin and Juliette's end?

"What am I going to do, Alex? What on earth am I going to do?"

I feel sliced in two, punctured and cleanly slit by a surgeon's scalpel. I am half delirious with joy and half wild with fear. *What if Marcus stops loving me? What if our delight in each other suffocates under the slop of daily routine? What if he breaks Juliette's heart?*

What if he breaks mine?

"Try and be patient, Quinn," Alex says. "Let your subconscious chew on this for a bit."

"You're the one who's been pushing me to figure this all out," I exclaim. "And now you want me to be patient?"

"You were hit with a tsunami of information today," he says. "You need to let it sink in. And talk to Marcus."

I sigh and plop down onto a bench, beckoning Alex to join me.

"You're right," I say. "I know you're right. I can't possibly think clearly at the moment."

"And you don't have to figure it all out right now, anyway. At least you have some clarity."

"I suppose," I say, stretching my arms upward to the sky, trying to release some tension. "So, what do you think of Marcus now?"

"I told you, I like him. I like the way he seems to adore you. And I'm sorry he lost a child. I just wish he wasn't married."

"You and me both," I say quietly.

"Really?" asks Alex. "Do you mean that?"

I sigh and roll my neck from side to side, working out the kinks. *I'm not sure what I want anymore.*

"Quinn. Look at me. Do you genuinely mean that?"

"I think I do," I say, returning his gaze.

"That's good to hear. Because I think he's going to leave his wife."

My mouth falls open. Thankfully, there's no food in it.

"Does that mean I have to marry him?"

"Of course not," says Alex.

"Then what does that mean?"

"It means you are very, very serious about him. And that he's very serious about you."

"And ...?" I prompt.

"And that you have to learn to trust your own judgement again. And to get over this notion that marriage strangles romance and kills love."

"You are just full of doozies today, aren't you?" I ask.

"What it really means, Quinn, is that you're finished dating married men," says Alex. "That you are ready for the real deal. And everything that comes along with it."

CHAPTER 37

Rule #19: You will be judged.

"Well, that about wraps it up for today," I say to Cindy, thankful another lesson is behind us. I still think this whole thing is nuts, and it's not as if I have any earth-shattering gems to share, but Cindy seems pleased with the results and I suppose it's the least I can do. Especially given those waffle photos that are now forever out there, floating in space. And forever branded in my memory.

"Already?" she asks, glancing at her watch. "I was hoping you'd tell me more about how you and Zack met. And how you knew he'd be open to an affair."

I sigh. I was hoping to avoid this. I want her to move forward, not backward. But I suppose having some insight into how, exactly, your husband strayed and why he was lured into another woman's arms is the crux of these so-called lessons.

"Are you sure you want that kind of detail? You and Zack seem to be doing so well."

"We are," she says, smiling at me. "He actually pulled me onto his lap the other day which he hasn't done in years. Years!"

"So why regress?"

Cindy furrows her brow and wrinkles her freckled nose. I can tell she's considering this.

"I don't want to be blindsided again," she says, quietly. "I want to examine this from every angle, otherwise, what's the point?"

"Okay," I say. "If you're sure."

Cindy nods. "Remember what I said about tap dancing naked on a case of wine?"

I laugh. "How could I possibly forget? You want to know, in your bones, that a woman could dance naked in front of Zack and he'd turn her away and head straight home to you. That was the gist, yes?"

"Yes," she says. "But we're not there yet. I'm not ready to put him through that test yet."

"Wait," I say, starting to freak out a little. "You're not thinking of staging that experiment, are you?"

Cindy shrugs and says casually, "Maybe. We'll see how things go."

I don't know whether to laugh or wig out.

"That is bananas." I shake my head. "And for the record, I want zero part of that caper. I want to know nothing about it."

"Until it's done," she says, matter-of-factly. "I would imagine you'd want a full report afterwards. Think of it as an end-of-semester review."

I stare at Cindy. She cannot be serious, can she? I'm not sure I even want to know. One minute she's swooning over Zack and the next she's scheming ways to test his devotion. And given his somewhat recent double texting incident, I'm not so sure it's a hot idea.

It is most definitely time to wrap things up.

"We are out of time for today," I say. "We can pick up where we left off next time, okay? I'm meeting up with my friend Dezi soon."

"Dezi. That's the woman who was with you at Dough?" asks Cindy, referring to when she first stormed into my life, demanding lessons. "Elliot's girlfriend, right?"

I nod. "Yes and yes."

"I heard what happened at his dinner party. Emma told me."

Cake Night, I think, shuddering at the memory.

"I'd tell you I'm sorry but I'm not," says Cindy. "You sort of deserved it."

"Cindy, I admire your honesty," I say. And I really do. The woman has chutzpah.

Cindy smiles at me. "I love what you told Emma about Greg, too. He is a jackass and I wish she'd leave him."

"Is she going to, do you think?" I ask, curious as to how that's going to play out. Although I'm certain Dezi will keep me in the loop.

"I don't know. But you sure did give her a lot to think about. She even contacted a lawyer."

"Wow," I say, surprised. "I didn't really expect her to listen."

"Hard not to when somebody calls your spouse a super-duper ass," Cindy says, laughing.

"Geez. I probably shouldn't have said that." I shake my head.

"No. I'm glad you did. You just told her what she's been thinking all along. What we've all been thinking, really. But you said it aloud," says Cindy, gathering her things to leave. "You're much better at this than you think you are, Quinn."

•   •   •   •   •

An hour later, I'm settled at an outdoor sidewalk table with Dezi at Mamacita's, one of our favorite places for casual Mexican fare. I've had tacos on the brain for days and Dezi mentioned margaritas, so here we are. It's a lovely evening for people watching and we have a pile of hot, salty tortilla chips, salsa and a bowl full of chunky guacamole in front of us. Mexican food heaven.

"So," says Dezi, dunking a chip in salsa. "What's new? How are those lessons panning out?"

"Very funny," I say, sipping my extra sour margarita. "They'd be going much better if you'd agree to be a guest lecturer."

"No way in hell."

I fill her in briefly on today's lesson with Cindy, including her crazy idea to "test" Zack.

"I think she might actually be serious."

Dezi grins at me. "These lessons are so much fun."

"Yeah, yeah, yeah," I grumble. "For you, apparently. I wonder when Cindy will cut me loose?"

"Probably when Zack passes the test," says Dezi, her blue eyes dancing.

"I need to get out way before then," I say, eyeballing the taco menu. "Anyway, I want to hear about you. How are things? How is Elliot?"

Dezi's face lights up at the mention of her boyfriend. "He's great. We're great. Even better now that you two are on better terms." She smiles. "Your advice to Emma was priceless. You got on his good side with that."

"Well, I'm glad I could do something right. And Chef is beyond pleased to have his cheese cart back. I have strict orders not to piss off Elliot ever again."

"Well *that* I can get behind," says Dezi, crunching through a handful of chips. "We had better order before I inhale the rest of these." She pushes the basket towards me.

We place our taco orders — a grilled fish and an al pastor for me, a shrimp and a gringo-style for Dezi — and request another side of extra hot salsa.

Dezi tells me that she and Elliot now see each other nearly every night. They take dance lessons together and often meet for lunch as he can easily bike from Barnyard Funk to her office.

"Yesterday he put together a picnic lunch from a selection of cheeses and charcuterie from his shop," she says. "I'm starting to understand the cheese freak in you."

"It's about time. I knew you'd come around. You can't date Elliot and not fall in love with all things cheese."

Dezi nods. "Even the blues and the stinky ones now."

"Wow, you two *are* serious," I say, smiling at her. "I'm so happy for you Dezi. He's a good guy."

"He is," she nods. "And we are. Which begs the question, Quinn ..." Dezi says, looking at me expectantly, one eyebrow raised.

I know she's asking about Marcus. She still doesn't know about Alex and the inquisition the other day.

"Marcus is not Liam or Chris," she says quietly, putting her hand over mine. "You must see that. But he has a wife, Quinn. A wife. How long do you plan to hide from that?"

"Look, saved by the food," I say, as our server places platters of tacos and several bowls of hot sauce on the table. The sun has just set, so she takes down the umbrella and leaves us to enjoy our dinners.

"Briefly saved," says Dezi, delicately biting into her gringo taco. *How does she do that?* It's as if she's biting through a carrot rather than a messy, saucy, ground beef taco.

I am not that talented, I think, as I top up my fish taco with a pile of pickled red onions and a squeeze of lime. I take a big bite just as I start to feel an electric charge in the air, as if it's going to storm. Lightning and all.

Marcus.

It can't be. It simply cannot be.

But it is.

That is Marcus. My Marcus. Walking by. With whom I can only imagine is Juliette.

My mouth drops open. Taco falls out.

Dezi whips around to see what I'm staring at.

"Is that ... Marcus?" she asks, slowly.

I nod. "Yes. Yes it is."

"Did he see you?"

"I don't think so." I shake my head and attempt to wipe bits of taco and lime juice off my chin.

We watch as Marcus and Juliette disappear down the sidewalk. I'm relieved to see they aren't holding hands. I didn't get a good look at Juliette, but I saw enough to know she's lovely. She's willowy and in the tall-ish category — probably hovering around five-foot-seven or so. She has long, honey-colored hair that hangs in a glossy sheet down her back. It swings perfectly with every step. I'm mesmerized by the hypnotic sway across her shoulders as they walk away. I'm certain she just wakes up with hair that perfect.

Bitch, I think, then chastise myself. I'm the one sleeping with her husband.

"Who is that with him?" asks Dezi.

"That, my friend, is Juliette. His wife," I say, sighing and taking a huge glug of my margarita.

Dezi's blue eyes widen as she looks at me, taking a swig of her own drink.

"Spill it," she says, signaling our waitress for another round. "We clearly have some catching up to do."

I tell Dezi about my day with Alex and Marcus. And Juliette. And the ultrasound picture of Jett.

Dezi's eyes don't leave my face as I recount the whole hoopla from that afternoon of axe throwing.

"Wow," says Dezi. "That is quite a bit to take in. And so, so sad about the baby."

I nod, my eyes welling with tears again at the thought of Marcus in all that pain.

"Hey," says Dezi, squeezing my hand. "I know it's overwhelming, but this is a good thing. Your brother stepped up and forced his hand a bit."

"I'll say," I reply. "I wanted to kill him at the time."

"But now you're armed with information, which may help you make a decision down the line. You are not the only one with a choice here."

"I don't know that I have a lot of say in the matter. My only real choice at this point is to stop seeing him."

"That's not the only choice," she says, looking at me with what I can only describe as her therapist gaze. "But it may be the wisest choice."

"But their marriage is over, Dezi," I say, eyeing my tacos warily. I'd like a bite, but fear this conversation is leading toward my mouth flopping open again. I'm tired of food falling out of my face.

"Quinn, they all say that. Plus, he was out tonight. With his wife."

I nod, look around furtively to ensure no surprises lurk within my sightline, and take a hasty bite of my taco. "I knew you were going to say that. It has to work out for some people."

"How, Quinn? How do you foresee this working out for you? Do you want to marry him?"

I sigh and push away my food. "I can't answer that yet. I don't know if I ever want to get married again. I think the first question I have to answer is whether I want him to leave his wife."

Dezi fixes me with her blue-eyed gaze and waits. She reminds me of Alex in this moment. And Julian.

"I like things the way they are," I say quietly. I put my hand up as I see Dezi gearing up to respond. "I know that's not possible. But Dezi, I wasn't supposed to fall in love. It never gets this far with married men. I don't know what the hell happened."

Dezi nods and tells me to eat my tacos. "Brain food," she says. "You have a lot of thinking to do."

We pick at the last of our tacos and sip our second round of margaritas.

"Are you going to tell Marcus you saw him tonight?" asks Dezi, folding her napkin into a little hat.

"Probably," I nod. "Now that I know more about his wife and their marriage, I feel comfortable asking him about it. I'd sort of like to know what they were doing in D.C."

"Oh that's right, they live in New York," says Dezi, now unfolding her little napkin hat and fanning it out on the table. "Are you certain that was his wife?"

CHAPTER 38

Rule #31: The past is never truly behind you.

Anniversary sex! I think suddenly as I struggle to pull up a pair of too tight Spanx. The thought rankles me so much that I practically topple over mid-panty heave. *Did Marcus and Juliette have their usual anniversary sex?* This shouldn't bother me. It's never bothered me with my other affairs, but it does with Marcus.

I am angry. And sad. And desperate to both know and not know.

Ugh! I think, yanking off the unyielding spandex. I am not wearing this nonsense tonight. I'm just going to Persimmon after all. No need to mechanically suck in my gut all night.

I wish I didn't have to go to work. I'm in no mood to deal with customers and their proclivities tonight. I was doing okay today, until the thought of those two having anniversary sex creeped into my head. That and I just don't know what I want. It's easy to love Marcus in the moment. So much harder when left to my own tornado of conflicting thoughts. I'm scared of staying. But I'm terrified of letting go.

Oh Quinn. What did you get yourself into?

I pick up my phone to re-read the text exchange I had with Marcus late last night after what is now forever known as "Taco Night." I had to ping him after Dezi suggested that perhaps the lovely blonde was indeed *not* Juliette.

Me: Hey. Were you in D.C. tonight? Thought I saw you walking down the sidewalk …

Marcus: Hey beautiful. Yes, I was. You probably saw me with a blonde woman then?

Me: Yup.

Marcus: Juliette. It was our anniversary and I had to fly out, so it made sense to grab dinner in D.C. I'm sorry you had to see that. I should have told you.

Me: No, it's okay. I was just surprised to see you. I know you have a life. And a wife.

Marcus: Just going through the motions. I love YOU Quinn. You do know that, right?

Me: I know you do. Me too.

Marcus: I want to see you as soon as I get back from my trip. I miss you.

I scrutinize that text chain but there's no hint as to whether those two "celebrated" their wedding date by getting naked. Perhaps it's better I don't know. At least he was honest with me about being in D.C. and I do believe him about Juliette and their anniversary. I just wish I hadn't seen them together. Damn that "Taco Night."

CHAPTER 39

Daily Special

Baby lamb chops with olive oil and oregano
Israeli couscous with preserved lemon
Beet and goat cheese salad with pistachios and dill

I arrive at Persimmon rather cranky, but tonight's menu helps cheer me up. There's nothing about this menu I don't love — lamb! Beets! Preserved lemon! And Chef makes his own couscous by hand, so it's an absolute treat whenever he decides to make it. And now that I'm back in Chef's good graces, I know he'll save me a plate.

Hmmmm, now for the wine pairings. I choose a Sonoma County old vine zinfandel and a Spanish Rioja, both of which will complement the lamb and the pungent preserved lemon.

I'm about to wander into the kitchen to say a quick hello to Chef when my phone pings.

My brother.

Alex: How are you holding up?

Me: Okay. A lot to think about.

Alex: Yup. That's why I'm checking in. Any decisions?

Me: Nope.

Alex: If you don't make one, a decision will be made for you.

Me: Gee, thanks for that brilliant tidbit. At work, gotta run. Talk more later.

"Quinn," I hear Chef boom at me as I quickly tuck my phone away and head into the kitchen. "Your cheese man tells me he's coming tonight and bringing a date."

He is? Dezi didn't mention it, but perhaps she doesn't even know.

"Treat him like a king. Bottle of wine is on the house," he says.

"You got it Chef. Great menu tonight, by the way."

"Yes," he says, nodding. "I'll save you a plate."

Nice, Dezi and Elliot will be a good distraction for me tonight. And I'm delighted he chose Persimmon. I'm going to view this as yet another olive branch. I peer into the dining room but it's still early and our first patrons are just being seated.

I ask our hostess to save our best two-top for Dezi and Elliot and then venture into the wine cellar to take stock and collect my bottles for tonight.

An hour later the restaurant is humming. I've got five tables settled with bottles of wine, two with a variety of glasses to sip, two doing the wine pairings and several more indulging in cocktails and beer. Chef's lamb special, his roast chicken and the Baltimore-style crab cakes are the popular menu items this evening.

I'm busy and almost forget about Elliot and Dezi until I look up and see Dezi waving at me. They are just now being seated at a romantic two-top by the windows.

I hustle over and swoop my friend into a hug. I look at Elliot tentatively as I'm not sure if we're on hugging terms again, but he just nods and gives me a small smile. "I wanted to surprise Dezi," he says. "I've never eaten here and she always raves about it. And I know she misses you."

Yes! Olive branch!

"Well, I'm delighted to see you both," I say, smiling. "And I'm under strict orders from Chef to provide the royal treatment."

I give them some time to settle in and select a rather nice bottle of Champagne for them, on the house. I notice Elliot has just excused himself from the table, so I head over to chat with Dezi for a few minutes.

"I'm so glad you're here," I say.

"Me too. Hey, have you recovered from 'Taco Night?' And did you find out if that was Juliette?"

"No and yes. I'm still reeling a bit from everything but yes, that was Juliette. They were out celebrating their anniversary."

Dezi's eyebrows shoot up at that.

"I know, I know," I say, shaking my head.

"Quinn."

"Not now," I say, relieved as Elliot approaches. "You, my friend, are to enjoy your date."

I pour Champagne, make some menu recommendations and leave them to it. "I'll be back to check on you. But take your time and enjoy."

•   •   •   •   •

The night turned out much better than expected considering the rough start with *Anniversary Sex* muddying my brain. But there's power in good friends, good food and work that I love. I feel better and I don't need to know. Really, I don't.

My tables are all wrapped up for the evening, so I make my way to the bar to pay Julian a visit and wait for Dezi and Elliot to join me.

It's quiet and Julian doesn't look up right away as he's watching something on his phone, which he has propped up on the bar.

"Watcha looking at there?" I ask, trying to sneak a peek.

"Q," he says, looking up at me and smiling, all the while trying to subtly block his phone from view. "I didn't hear you come in."

"Are those hedgehogs?" I ask, nodding towards his phone. "Why are you watching a video with hedgehogs?"

Julian shrugs. "My mom wants one. I'm doing some research."

I start laughing. "Did you just say your mom wants a hedgehog? Isn't she, like, a hundred years old?"

"Very funny. Eighty-two to be exact. The woman is eighty-two. If she wants a hedgehog, she should have a hedgehog."

"Fair enough," I say, still laughing. "But please, stop saying the word hedgehog."

"What's this about a hedgehog?" asks Elliot as he and Dezi plop down on barstools.

I nod towards Julian. "I'll let him explain."

"My mom wants a hedgehog, so I'm getting her one," he says, matter-of-factly.

"Sounds reasonable," says Elliot, nodding. "My cousin had a hedgehog. His name was Funyun."

"Funyun?" Dezi and I say in unison.

"As in the fried snack?" she asks.

We both giggle helplessly. I don't know why it's so funny, but it just simply is. Funyun the hedgehog!

Julian rolls his eyes and tells Elliot to ignore us.

"Oh, that was fun," I say, wiping tears of laughter from my eyes. "Thanks for the laugh, both of you. I needed that."

"Happy to help," says Julian, shaking his head. "Now, what can I get all of you to drink?"

It's Cognac all around.

We sip our drinks as Elliot and Julian start talking drums and motorcycles and guy stuff. I am just delighted that Elliot is actually speaking to me. In full sentences.

"So," says Dezi, crossing her legs and spinning her barstool closer to mine. "Have you ever considered him, you know, as a possibility?" She nods toward Julian.

"What? No. Absolutely not. We are friends and that's all. Plus, he's way older than me."

"Well, he certainly doesn't look it. He's awfully handsome and you two seem to get along great. Just saying."

"We do get along great. As FRIENDS."

"Okay, okay," Dezi says. "I'll back off, but there is definitely some chemistry there."

I raise my eyebrows at her and say nothing.

I suppose she's right. There may very well be some chemistry there, but I've never really thought about it. And even if there is, it's nothing compared to what I have with Marcus. The man comes near me and it's as if somebody just plugged me in. I light up like a 100-watt bulb.

I'm lost in thoughts of Marcus when Juliette starts creeping into my head. *Gah!*

"Dezi, do you think his wife knows something is up?" I can't seem to bring myself to say her name.

I watch as Dezi's brow furrows, clearly contemplating Juliette.

"That's a tough question. In my experience with clients, they almost always fess up that they knew something was wrong. But from what you've told me about Juliette, she's likely depressed, which changes everything."

"How so?"

"If she's truly depressed, she's going to be less receptive to any external or internal warnings, so to speak. And, even if she thought something was wrong, she may very well be too depressed to care. Quinn, why are you asking me this?"

"I don't know," I whisper. "I guess she's been on my mind since we saw her."

"Are you afraid she's going to find out?"

"Yes. No. I don't know," I say, running my fingers through my hair. "What do you think I should do?"

"Quinn, honey, I can't tell you that. You have to decide if you want him. And how far you're willing to go to get him."

"This wasn't supposed to get complicated. I hate complicated."

"The choice is simple, but I know it's excruciating for you. Do you want Marcus enough to ask him to leave his wife? Or do you bow out and let him go?"

"Are you suggesting an ultimatum?"

"If it comes to that, yes," says Dezi. "It's an option."

"Jesus. I'm not ready to do that."

We sit in silence, sipping our Cognac. I have no idea what to say or where to go from here. Marcus has shaken up my life, in the best way possible, but I am rattled. My brain refuses to step forward. But my heart won't let me step back.

"You ready to get out of here, Dez?" asks Elliot, halting the emotional battle in my head.

She nods and gently squeezes my hand. "You're going to be okay," she whispers in my ear. "You'll figure this out. And I'll be here, every step of the way."

As the pair moves to leave, Elliot turns to me. "I know we've had our differences Quinn, but I want to thank you for what you said to Emma. She actually kicked her husband out of the house."

My eyebrows shoot up at this.

"I'm so glad you called him a giant ass. It was not what I was expecting, but it was perfect. And exactly what I wanted to say."

With Dezi and Elliot gone, I stick around to keep Julian company. He sets out a plate of bar snacks for me and then grins as I see him glance over my shoulder. Uh oh. I know that look.

"Looks to me like you have another visitor."

"You have got to be kidding me. I'm afraid to look. This never goes well. Can you give me a hint?"

"Well, it's a man, but it's not Marcus. Never seen this one before."

I take a deep breath and turn around.

Zack. Fuuuuck. This cannot be good.

"Zack? What are you doing here?" I haven't seen Zack in months. Not since we had that Thai food dinner, which was ages ago. Before Paris. Before I fell in love with Marcus. He's as adorable as ever in an eggplant-colored V-neck sweater and dark jeans. But, I am pleased to note, I don't feel remotely romantic towards him. I feel irritated. He should be home, with Cindy. His wife. The woman who keeps making me give her these preposterous lessons.

"Quinn," he says with a tentative smile. "It's been a long time. I was hoping to catch you here tonight."

"Zack," I whisper. "You really shouldn't be here. You shouldn't be talking to me."

"I know," he says, reaching to touch my arm. "But I need to talk to you."

I glance up and see Julian looking directly at me, eyebrows raised. There's a clear question in his eyes — *want me to take care of this punk for you*?

I gently shake my head and mouth, "It's okay." I turn to Zack.

"You should be home with your wife. Why are you here, Zack?"

He blows out a sigh. "I'm not here to hit on you, I promise. I know it's over and Cindy and I are in a good place."

I look at him warily. "You recently tried to get me to meet you for a date, Zack."

"I know, I know. And that was a mistake. Look, I wanted to apologize. I shouldn't have texted you and I shouldn't have continued to try to pursue you."

"And you came all the way here to tell me this?"

"Yes," he says simply. "Things felt unfinished between us and I felt like such a jerk after that text. I wanted to apologize. In person."

"Okay. Well, apology accepted but there's no need. We're good. And I'm glad you and your wife are doing well."

Zack nods. "We are. She's trying and now I'm trying. I do love her. I think I was just bored and well, distracted there for a while."

"It happens Zack. To the best of us."

Zack hesitates. He starts fiddling with the hem of his sweater.

"What?" I ask. "What's really going on?"

"How did you know that I accidentally sent that dinner date text to my wife?"

I shake my head. "Nope. Not happening. I'm not getting involved. You need to talk to her."

"But I can't. I can't tell her that text was meant for you and you called me out on it."

I sigh. "I suppose not. Why does it matter?"

"Because something funny is going on," he says. "It's driving me crazy. It feels as if she's hiding something and I can't quite figure it out. And then suddenly you, my ex-lover or whatever, know what I've texted to my wife? It doesn't make any sense."

I'm quiet. I'm not sure how to reply. So I employ the Alex technique and say nothing.

"Look. I want my wife back," he says. "But I need to know what's going on. I need to be able to trust her."

"You can," I say, looking him directly in the eyes. "I promise you. You can trust Cindy."

I truly believe he can. Until I think of her mischievous navy-blue eyes twinkling while scheming a harebrained "test" for him that involves a naked woman. Oh boy. I cannot get in the middle of this. And I know Cindy does not want him to know about the lessons.

"You can," I say firmly. "Trust me on this."

"Okay," Zack says dubiously. "For now."

"Zack, things are going well, yes?"

He nods.

"Then why are you picking it all apart? Why are you looking for problems when there aren't any?"

"Because I screwed up. I almost blew up our marriage," he says, looking pained, as if he's about to have diarrhea. "I never thought of myself as the kind of guy who could have an affair."

"Nobody ever does, Zack."

"Well, if I can, then she can too," he says softly.

"Is that what you're worried about?"

He nods. "I never was before. But now ... I feel as if I opened the door for her."

"Oh Zack. You didn't. Really, Cindy is not having an affair."

"How could you possibly know that? She's acting so different. In a great way, don't get me wrong. She's sweet and well, happy for once."

"Have you ever thought that maybe, just maybe, it's because of you?"

Zack nods and stands to give me a hug goodbye. "I hope you're right, Quinn."

"I am," I say. "I know I am."

"Thank you for everything. For not being weird about any of this."

Zack leaves and I flop back onto a barstool.

"Some night, Q," says Julian. "You okay?"

"I am. As long as nobody else shows up for a visit."

Julian smiles. "You handled that well. You're pretty good at this, you know?"

I give him the wonky eye. "Good at what, exactly?"

"Love lessons," he says with a grin.

"Jesus Christ," I say, tossing a paper napkin at him. "I am helping one woman. ONE. Out of sheer guilt for making out with her husband. I do not *give* love lessons."

Julian tosses the napkin right back at me. "Oh, but I think you do."

CHAPTER 40

Daily Special

Frisée salad with blue cheese crumbles, crisp bacon and poached egg
Beouf Bourguignon
Parsley butter mashed potatoes

Tonight's wine pairing is a breeze. Beef Bourguignon is literally beef cooked in red Burgundy, so there really is no other wine to serve with this dish. In fact, I won't even allow it. It would be criminal to drink anything else. I hope my guests feel the same.

It's a chilly winter evening so Chef could not have picked a better night to serve this hearty, rich stew. It's one of my many favorite cold weather dishes and Chef's version rivals those I've had in France. In fact, his is one of my favorites. He doesn't take any shortcuts, so the long-simmered meat falls apart with a simple nudge of a fork. He marries it with the requisite browned pearl onions and mushrooms, rendering it all into a luscious, beefy, winey stew. It never fails to remind me why I am not and could never be, a vegetarian.

We're not packed tonight as I think a lot of people stayed home due to the cold. It's definitely a good night for pajamas and take-out in front of the fire, which is exactly what Marcus and I did a few nights ago at his hotel. Pizza, red wine and PJ's. My face starts to feel hot and flushed just thinking about it. We followed up the night with blueberry pancakes and bacon in bed the next morning while watching the season's first snowfall. Sometimes I feel as if everything I have with Marcus is simply too good to be true. I'm waiting for it to all come crashing down around me. But then I remember, it actually *is* too good to be true. He's married. And I'm his mistress. And I'm still not sure if I want to be anything more than that.

Sigh. We didn't discuss Juliette at all during our pizza and wine night. An unspoken, mutual decision, I think. Avoiding the subject keeps things so peaceful. In fact, her name hasn't come up since "Taco Night."

I am jolted back to reality by Chef grabbing me by the shoulders and marching me into the kitchen. "Sit. Eat," he says, handing me a small bowl of the beef stew. "You look peaked."

"Gee, thanks," I say, gratefully diving into the steaming bowl of beef and vegetables. "Oh wow. Oh wow. Oh wow. This is so good." And it is. Comforting, too.

Chef beams and nods, handing me the heel of a baguette. "To wipe up the sauce. I can't have you licking the bowl."

"You know I would, too," I say, taking the crusty hunk of bread.

"Yes," Chef nods, sighing and shaking his head. "I'm well aware you were apparently raised in a barn," he says, turning back into the thick of his kitchen.

I laugh. I know he's just pretending to be exasperated. He loves it when anyone adores his food. And what's more flattering than somebody licking the plate it was so good?

I soak up the last bit of sauce and then do a quick table check in the dining room.

My guests seem settled and happy, most of them enjoying the stew and good red wine.

One couple appears to be arguing over what to order, so I give them a few minutes to settle down. I get a few more tables squared away with wine pairings and finish pouring the last of the wine for a six-top before making a quick stop to see Julian.

"Q," he says, nodding at me as he looks up from behind the bar. "Slow night."

I nod. "It's the weather. This is the kind of night you want to be cuddled up at home with the person you love."

Julian nods again. "You haven't wrapped up already, have you?"

"No. I wish. I'm ready to go home and get cozy myself," I say, yawning. "I've had a few too many late nights."

"Let me guess, the pilot?" he asks, smirking.

"Is there anyone else?"

"I never know with you." He winks at me. "But I always seem to find out more fun stuff whenever you stop by at the end of the night."

"Very funny," I say, rolling my eyes. "I suppose it's true though. Maybe I ought to skip the after-work chat tonight."

"Your call. But I recommend stopping by even for just a minute."

I look up and he's holding an envelope with my name scrawled across in a familiar script.

Marcus.

"Wait, when did you get that? When was he here?"

Julian just smiles and shrugs. "I have strict orders not to give you this until the end of your shift tonight."

I shake my head and grumble, "Men," as I return to check on my tables. "I'll be back," I say over my shoulder.

"Don't I know it," he says with a grin.

I wish all these people would hurry up and finish their food and chug their wine. My brain has officially departed. I haven't seen Marcus since our pizza and wine night at his hotel, so when did he stop by? I know he's flying tonight, perhaps he caught Julian when he first arrived to set up the bar.

I jet around the dining room and see that most of my tables are wrapping up — hallelujah! The couple that was arguing apparently left in a snit, so that's one less table I need to worry about. Although I do feel sort of bad I never had the chance to stop by and offer booze. A bit of distraction and a little wine may have saved their evening.

I watch my tables in pumped anticipation of the moment they all clear out. It's like I'm hunkered down in the racing blocks on the track before the starting gun fires. I'm coiled and ready to sprint to Julian. And my love note.

My sheer delight in Marcus just seems to know no bounds. It hasn't dimmed at all. Even now, my pulse is practically skipping over itself just thinking about him sitting down to pen me a letter.

Finally. Finally my tables clear out and I'm in front of Julian in what feels like an instant. I flop breathlessly onto a barstool and start tapping my fingers impatiently.

Julian just smirks and continues polishing glasses and bar tools.

"A little excited, are we Q?"

"Come on, man. You cannot be serious."

"Simmer down, Q, simmer down," he says, pouring me my after-dinner Cognac and setting me up with a bowl of olives and nuts.

Julian hands me the note.

"Did Marcus say whether he wanted me to open it here or at home?" I ask, now wondering if I should wait.

Julian shakes his head. "Only instructions were to give it to you at the end of the night."

"What should I do?"

"Your call. I can give you some privacy if you like."

I eyeball my glass of Cognac and the bowl of olives and nuts and decide to stay and read. I'm both hungry and thirsty and there's no way my body can handle the excitement of waiting any longer.

"You're good," I say to Julian, beckoning him to continue with his evening wrap up. "There's nothing you don't know about us at this point."

I'm about to open the envelope when Julian tells me that Dezi just walked in.

"What?" I ask, putting the note aside and turning to see that, sure enough, Dezi is practically skipping towards me, stilettos and all.

"I'm engaged," she sings, thrusting her blinding, diamond-clad hand at me. "Elliot asked me to marry him."

"Oh Dezi," I say, jumping up and pulling her in for a tight hug. "Congratulations! That is such great news! I am beyond excited for you." I look up to signal Julian for some Champagne and I see he's already on it.

Dezi is beaming and I couldn't be happier for my friend.

"Now let me see that rock," I say, grabbing Dezi's hand. "Holy crap that is gorgeous. Wow. Elliot knocked it out of the park with this one."

"He did," says Dezi, gazing at her dazzling new ring. "I'm still in shock, I think, but I wanted you to be the first to know."

"Did he propose while you were in Virginia doing the wine country thing?"

Dezi nods. "At the Inn at Little Washington. He surprised me with an overnight stay. And dinner!"

I'm utterly speechless for a moment.

"Did you just say the Inn at Little Washington?" I ask, referring to the well-known historical inn with its world-class, award-winning restaurant and chef. "Do you have any idea how hard it is to get a reservation at that hotel? Let alone the restaurant?"

Dezi nods, her face exploding in a smile.

"He's a keeper, my friend," I say, smiling at her.

Julian pours us each a glass of bubbly, tells Dezi congratulations and then makes himself scarce.

"Now sit," I say, pulling out a stool for Dezi. "And tell me everything. Every. Last. Thing. From the beginning."

Dezi happily obliges, clearly delighted to pour over the details and relive the experience. She fills me in on the day of wine tastings, the surprise detour to the inn and the proposal on bended knee at sunset.

"He had everything perfectly planned out. A beautiful room, a roaring fire and the most fabulous sunset walk in the gardens. I thought we were just doing a day trip, so he even packed a bag for me."

I shake my head in awe. "Could he be any more romantic?"

"I know, right? It was so perfect it still feels unreal. He told me he wanted to spend the rest of his life loving me and putting a smile on my face."

"Did you have any clue?" I ask, curious if she had any inkling that something was up. I've always found it interesting that most women I know had some idea that a proposal was looming because the guy starts acting weird. And, of course, there are the women who know it's coming soon because they badger their live-in boyfriends with ultimatums and drop ridiculous "hints" like circling engagement rings in magazines and leaving the pages open. Or "accidentally" sending links to Blue Nile's engagement ring website. For the record, I had no clue that my ex-husband, Chris, was going to propose. Looking back, I think it's just because I didn't feel that kind of chemistry with him so it never occurred to me that he might ask me to marry him.

Boy was I stupid.

But, for the most part, it seems like a tremendous feat to pull off a true surprise proposal and I think Elliot just nailed it.

Dezi shakes her head. "I was blown away," she says. "I had no idea it was coming. I mean, we had discussed marriage, obviously, but nothing else. He never even asked what kind of ring I'd like."

"Seems like he chose perfectly."

"He did. It's exactly what I would have picked out myself. I still cannot believe it's mine. And that Elliot is going to be mine," she says, grinning at me.

I smile right back at her. I look at her ring again and shake my head. "It's absolutely stunning. Which is fitting, as you are going to make a gorgeous bride."

"Oh god, don't remind me. Wedding planning seems so daunting."

"Well, I am at your service," I say, giving her a little bow. "And just think of all the dress shopping you get to do. And shoes!"

"Shoes! Wedding stilettos! You sure do know the way to my heart," she says, her sapphire blue eyes lighting up.

"You know you must have a cheese station at your wedding, right? That's non-negotiable. People are going to expect some seriously good cheese."

"Oh boy, maybe we'll just elope," Dezi says. "Maybe I'm too old for a big, white wedding."

"Nonsense. You can have any kind of wedding you want. Wear a red gown. Or just a bikini and heels on the beach. Or go to Jamaica or Florence or Paris. Just don't run off and do it in secret."

Dezi laughs. "I wouldn't do that. Although a very small destination wedding is enticing."

"Just promise me that I'll be there. You are not allowed to get married without me."

"I promise," she says, squeezing my hand. Dezi hesitates for a moment and then looks right at me. I know that look. She's gearing up to tell me something I'm not going to like.

"Spill it. What's going on?"

"Quinn. Elliot has made peace with the fact that you are in my life. And right now, that also includes Marcus to some extent."

"But?"

"But it's our wedding day," she says, her eyes meeting mine. "We'll be taking *vows*. And you've made it rather clear you don't respect them."

I stare at her.

"Those are Elliot's words, Quinn, but I have to say I sort of agree with him."

"Okay. So what are you trying to tell me, exactly?"

"Elliot doesn't want you in the wedding," she says with a sigh. "He's pretty adamant about that. If we decide to have a wedding party at all, he wants people up there with us who honor marriage vows. It's hard to argue with that."

I'm quiet. I can see Elliot's point, unfortunately. I can see how hard I've made things for Dezi. I can't change my past, but what I can do now is make life easier for my friend, no matter my disappointment.

But I am sad.

"You're my best friend, Dezi. I wouldn't get married without you at my side."

"Believe me, I know. I'm wrestling with this. But Elliot's going to be my husband. We're going to be a team. And I can't simply ignore him."

"What's *your* opinion?" I ask.

"That you're my family. That you have a giant heart. And I love you. I stand by you Quinn, but your actions do have consequences," she says softly. "They reverberate outside our friendship."

I don't know what to say. But she's right. I am hurting the people I love the most.

"Quinn, I've always been honest with you. I think I agree with Elliot on this one. He makes a very valid point."

I can swallow my hurt. I can. I have to. I'm the one who put Dezi in the middle.

"Can I still help you pick out a dress?" I ask.

"Of course," she says, engulfing me in a hug. "I wouldn't dream of choosing a dress without you."

"I'm still at your service for anything else you need," I say, tightly hugging her back. "I don't need a title."

"Thank you, Quinn."

I smile as I watch her face split into a grin.

"I'm getting married," she says softly.

"You're getting married," I echo. "It's huge."

We drain our Champagne flutes and Dezi gives me a final goodnight hug.

"I'm so glad you stopped by. You made my night."

She smiles and waves goodbye to Julian.

"You know," Dezi says to me, "Not making a choice is, in fact, making a choice."

"You're getting married!" I say, ignoring her comment and hugging her back.

• • • • •

I watch Dezi leave. Elliot irks me, but I also feel somewhat guilty. Mostly though, I'm delighted for Dezi. She and Elliot are a great match and it's clear they adore each other, which is key. In fact, I'm not sure who loves the other more, which also bodes well for a life-long marriage. That, and Dezi knows how to choose well, a skill I most certainly lack. I am so wrapped up in Dezi's news I almost forget about Marcus's note.

Almost.

As if on cue, Julian returns with the note I had hastily cast aside.

I open the envelope.

My beautiful redhead,

Emeralds are green
Your eyes are green
I, too, like cheese
I've left my wife
Your eyes are still green
Cheese
It's true. I have left Juliette. You are the one for me. The only one.
I love you Quinn.

Marcus

I am lightheaded. I am dizzy. I think I might throw up. But I also feel like I might want to try on wedding veils. *OH MY GOD.*

I put my forehead down against the cool marble of the bar.

"Hey, Q, everything okay?" Julian asks softly.

I hear Julian but it's muffled, as if he's talking to me underwater. My body feels as if it's peacefully floating and yet my heart and lungs are pounding and expanding as if I'm sprinting. I am conflicted in every possible way. I want to jump up and down like a kid receiving her first big-girl bike on Christmas morning. I want to run as fast and furiously as possible to burn off the sizzle of energy emanating from my skin. I want to wrap my arms around Marcus and never let go. I want to dance. I want to throw myself into the ocean and get pummeled by the waves. I want to hurl. I want to slap Juliette for ever marrying my man.

And I want to slap myself for ever getting this involved.

I feel a pair of strong hands on my shoulders. "Q. What's going on?"

Julian's touch pulls me out of my fugue.

I look up into his concerned face and whisper, "Marcus has left his wife."

Julian's eyebrows shoot skyward as my cheeks split open uncontrollably. I am beaming.

He looks at my face, a soft smile on his lips. "Well, I was going to ask how you feel about it, but it's pretty clear by the look on your face."

"I'm not sure how I feel," I say, feeling my cheeks flush.

"That's not what it looks like to me," he says, gently. "I'd say you know precisely how you feel. Your brain just hasn't caught up yet."

He's right. For an instant, I felt nothing but joy. But as we sit in silence, my heart stills and I can hear the cacophony of alarm bells clanging in my head. I feel the cold creep of fear, like ice water down my back. I am spooked.

"It's a lot," I say, starting to tremble.

He nods. "Yes."

"I just broke up a marriage," I whisper.

"Doesn't sound as if there was much left to break up. And remember, you're not the one who took vows."

We are quiet for a moment.

"Fuuuuck. Julian. I don't think I can do this," I say, feeling a tidal wave of panic rapidly rising and choking off my airway. "I wasn't supposed to fall in love," I say, barely squeaking out the words. "He wasn't supposed to leave his wife."

"Q. What are you so afraid of?"

I can't speak. I can only shake my head and take in what feels like small sips of air. I am seriously *FREAKING OUT* here.

Okay Quinn, snap out of this, I say to myself, trying to suck in oxygen. *Marcus is not Liam. He's not. And he's not Chris.*

"I'm afraid of destroying what we have," I say slowly. "Of making yet another horrific mistake. Of hurting each other so deeply the wounds will never heal."

Julian wraps me in his arms. "Quinn," he says softly. "What you should fear most is missing out. Missing out on your Violet. Don't suffer through that kind of pain."

"Oh Julian." I pull back and look up at him.

"Hey, I'm good. But I'll always be a little tormented by the big What If. Don't sign up for that if you don't have to."

I nod. "You loved her."

"I did," he says simply. "Still do. But it's just a quiet hum of pain now. And more of regret than anything. Quinn, you love Marcus. Don't let fear hold you back. That's not living."

"No regrets," I say, feeling my heart rate slow, the frenzied panic almost leaking from my skin. My bones sag with the emotional exhaustion of it all. But I feel better. Calmer. Julian's words and presence a soothing balm.

"Q. You are smiling again," Julian says with a grin.

"I guess I am," I say, my cheeks starting to ache. "My heart knows what it wants, I suppose."

"It usually does. The real question is, will you listen?"

CHAPTER 41

Rule #22: Enjoy the ride, it never lasts long.

I'm standing outside my parent's condo, stamping my feet in the cold. There's no way I can go in until I see Alex. So I text him.

Me: Alex. Meet me outside ASAP. Don't tell mom and dad I'm here yet.

I get a response back almost immediately, thankfully, as I can't feel my toes.

Alex: I'm not even there yet. Running late. Will be there in a few minutes.

Me: Park out front and leave the heater running. I'm going to jump in when you get here. I need to talk to you. And It's freezing out!

I'm in Baltimore for our usual Sunday family dinner, but I have to talk to Alex before facing my mom and dad. It's been a few weeks since Marcus left Juliette and the only person who knows is Julian. It seems too huge to do over text, so I wanted to wait until I saw Alex in person. Same with the bride-to-be. Our schedules just haven't matched up what with all the wedding planning on her end and all the Marcus canoodling on mine.

Marcus.

I still cannot believe he's left his wife. I'm an emotional smorgasbord, ricocheting from heart soaring joy to sheer, sweat soaked panic. *Do I really want this?* I know he's technically still married, but he's told her it's over and he's moved out. To D.C. no less! I want Marcus, but I don't know if I can stomach everything that comes with a real relationship. Thankfully, we aren't discussing the future yet, just loving the fact that he no longer has to answer to Juliette. And I no longer have to think about anniversary sex. Or any other kind of intimacy between them. He's made it clear that it's over between them, regardless of me, which takes some of the pressure off. I don't know what our future holds, but I'm slowly starting to warm to the idea of having a real boyfriend. And I find that the moments of bliss seem to surpass the times of hysteria. But ask me again in an hour.

·   ·   ·   ·   ·

I shove my gloved hands into my pockets and look up in time to see Alex in his blue Honda CRV slide into a parking spot along the street. I jump in, grateful for the heat.

"What's up?" he says, putting the car in park and turning to face me. "What's with that lunatic grin on your face?"

I get straight to the point.

"Marcus left Juliette," I blurt out. "He's rented an apartment in D.C."

Alex just looks at me, the expression on his face reminding me so much of Julian.

"What?" I say, punching him in the arm. "Why are you looking at me like that? Say something."

"This is big, Quinn," he says, a smile slowly emerging. "You're free. You're finally free."

"What the heck does that mean?" I ask, happy to see him smiling at the news.

"You broke out of your married men only habit. You're free of Chris. And Liam."

I shrug. "Maybe. But we haven't discussed anything further. I don't even know yet if he's planning on a divorce. And I still don't even know if that's what I want."

"I'm just happy you stuck around," Alex says, leaning over to give me a hug. "I'm happy you didn't run the moment he moved out."

"It's funny, he never even mentioned he was seriously thinking about leaving Juliette. He just moved out and told me after the fact. I never really had a say in the matter."

"So, by default, you ended up with an almost single man in spite of yourself. Is that what you're saying?" Alex asks, laughing.

"I suppose."

"Well, I'm not surprised by Marcus at all. From what little I know of him, the man goes after what he wants. And I have a feeling he often gets it."

I smile at that. "You better believe it. But you like Marcus, don't you?"

"Absolutely. Even more now."

"Good. Because he's coming to dinner tonight," I say, as I open the car door.

"You're bringing him home to meet mom and dad? Tonight?" Alex asks, incredulous. "Do they know?"

"Yes, he'll be here soon and no, they have no idea. That's why I wanted to fill you in first. I'd like not to reveal that he's still married at this point."

Alex just shakes his head. "This should be interesting. Are you sure you're ready to introduce him?"

"I can't keep hiding him. We're sort of a couple now, whatever that means. And I'm in love," I say simply. "Besides, he's going to be my plus-one at Dezi's wedding, so they need to meet him eventually."

"You're the boss," says Alex. "I just pray he files for divorce soon."

•　•　•　•　•

We walk into my parent's condo and I can tell immediately what my mom is making for dinner. I inhale the warm, yeasty aroma of her sausage bread and homemade minestrone soup. Yum. What a perfect, cold weather combination — hot soup and big slabs of cheesy sausage bread slathered with spicy mustard. I adore her sausage bread so much I almost forget that Marcus is on his way.

Almost.

"Smells fantastic mom," I say, shedding my coat, hat and gloves and handing over four bottles of simple Italian red wine.

"Don't you look nice," says my dad, coming over to kiss my cheeks and give me a hug.

"Thanks." I smile. I suppose I am dressed a bit nicer than usual, for obvious reasons. Just because Marcus is separated doesn't mean I can start slobbing around in fleece and flannel all the time.

"What's new?" my mother asks, turning away from her pot of minestrone soup and eyeing me suspiciously. She knows something is up. I never dress in snug jeans, sexy, over-the-knee boots and tight sweaters for Sunday dinners at home.

May as well get right to it.

"Dezi is engaged," I say excitedly. "Oh, and my boyfriend is coming tonight."

A chunk of Parmesan cheese falls out of my mother's mouth. Now I see where I get it from.

"Great," says my dad, pulling out an extra wineglass and table setting. "On both counts."

"That explains the outfit," my mother says. "But since when do you have a boyfriend?"

"It's pretty new, so don't give him the third degree, okay?" I ask, mentally crossing my fingers that she behaves. "Alex has already given him the thumbs up."

Alex shoots eyeball daggers at me from across the room.

"Alex," my mother says. "Is this true? You've met your sister's young man?"

Alex nods. "Yup. He's a good guy. You'll like him."

My mother quickly gets over the fact that she was the last to know and simply beams. "We are just so glad that you're finally dating again. Aren't we Samuel?" she says, turning toward my father.

My father nods and winks at me. "Don't worry, we'll be good. Now get in here and have a glass of wine."

I'm sipping my wine and enjoying a few chunks of cheese with dried figs when I feel the atmosphere shift. It's an almost indescribable sensation, as if Marcus is invisible but hovering so close I could lean in and give him butterfly kisses. It's what I have come to know as the Marcus Phenomenon.

He is in the air.

And sure enough. Marcus is now at the door.

I fling it open and Marcus scoops me up and into his arms. Our usual greeting often includes some fun in the bedroom. Or kitchen. Or on the living room sofa. Or in the shower. But, alas, not today.

Marcus shakes my father's hand, says hello to Alex and then completely wins over my mother by pulling her in for a hug and a kiss on the cheek. "It's so great to finally meet you," he says, training his twinkling, Tahoe-blue eyes on her face. "I've heard so much about you," he smiles and looks around. "All of you."

My mother is pink faced and swooning. I totally get it. Marcus is tall and chiseled and charming with his vivid, laughing eyes and disarming smile. He also is currently sporting a five o'clock shadow, which certainly doesn't tamp down the sexiness factor.

"My, my," says my mother, looking up at him and fanning herself with a dish towel. "You are so tall. And so handsome," she says, glancing at me, eyebrows raised.

What? I've never brought home a cute guy before? Sheesh. But she's right, Marcus is unequivocally, over-the-top, hot.

Marcus just smiles, hands her a bouquet of winter lilies and tells her everything smells delicious. Then he asks what he can do to help. The man is winning big, which I am very grateful for. The more they love him, the less they'll pick over his history.

"Nonsense," says my mother, shooing him out of her kitchen. "You can help by enjoying a glass of wine and some snacks before dinner."

"Well that I can most definitely do," he says, taking me by the hand. "Alright gorgeous," he says to me. "Take me to your wine and food. Your mother's orders."

My mom cannot stop grinning. Marcus won her over in an instant. Either that, or she's just so deliriously happy that I'm dating again that she can't help herself. Regardless, it's an excellent outcome.

I settle Marcus with a glass of wine and a plate of cheese, figs and prosciutto with lemon. We join my father and Alex at the bar as my mother slides a tray of her sausage bread into the oven. The three of them converse easily, Marcus inquiring about Alex's latest news story and then asking my father about a new medication his mother just started and its potential side effects. Another win-win for Marcus. Saying my brother loves discussing the top news stories of the day is an understatement. It's like proclaiming that Michael Jordan enjoys basketball.

As for my father, well, he loves nothing more than discussing all things pharmaceutical. Once you get him started, he rarely stops of his own accord.

My brain starts to flame out as I hear my dad mention things like vasoconstriction and hypertension and skin sloughing. I glance at Marcus, but he seems genuinely interested and is now asking follow-up questions, much to my father's delight.

The evening continues to go smoothly. My parents ask Marcus all the normal questions — where do you live, how did you two meet, where are you from, what do you do for a living — but don't pry, thank goodness. Of course, why would they have any reason to ask if he's married?

I didn't think the evening could get any better until my father finds out Marcus was a Navy pilot. His eyes light up and now both Alex and my dad are peppering him with all sorts of military and pilot questions. *What is it with men and airplanes?*

But hey, whatever works. I'm just so relieved the night has been a success. Marcus charmed the pants off my parents, so to speak, and he and Alex bonded a bit more, so I am happy. Sort of, anyway. If I'm being totally honest here, I'm trying to ignore a tiny voice in my head and heart telling me I should have waited. For what, exactly, I'm not sure. For him to file for divorce? For me to know for sure that's what I want? I sigh inwardly. I guess it really doesn't matter as it's too late now. I have unleashed Marcus. And, more importantly, I have unleashed my mother and all her dreams of marrying me off for good this time.

What have I done?

I shake it off. It's already done. I look over at Marcus and he's eyeing me questioningly while giving my knee a gentle squeeze. I can't help but smile, the man knows me well. He leans in close to me. "You okay?" he whispers into my ear.

I nod. "Just tired. And full."

"That I understand," he says, patting his absurdly flat, six-pack abs. "I'm stuffed."

"Don't let my mother hear you say that." As if on cue, my mom comes to the table with a tray of dessert. I'm grateful to see it's just espresso and her homemade anise biscotti, so nothing over the top. Even so, I cannot eat another bite.

Apparently, this is not the case for Alex and Marcus, who both start crunching through cookies.

"Quick," says Alex, employing our desert island game as my mom and dad head into the kitchen to make more espresso. "If you could only take two people with you to a desert island, who would you take? And it cannot be anyone here."

"Seriously, Alex?" I groan. "Too many rules."

"Go," he says, looking at me.

I think for a moment. "Well, if I cannot take any of you hoo-hahs, then it's Dezi and Julian."

"Julian, huh?" says Marcus, eyeing me sideways. "Your bartender, Julian?"

"Yes." I smile at Marcus. "Jealous, are we?"

Marcus laughs. "Not in the least. I think I'd take Julian myself." He winks at me. "Always good to have an excellent bartender around. Especially on an island."

"And who else?" I ask.

"You," he says, nuzzling my neck. "Sorry Alex. I don't play by the rules."

"I've noticed." Alex shakes his head and tosses a cookie at Marcus.

"Who doesn't play by the rules?" asks my mother, returning to the table. "And Alex, did you just throw a biscotti at our guest?"

Marcus, Alex and I all burst out laughing.

"I can see you three are going to be a real handful," says my mother, feigning exasperation.

A few minutes later, we say our goodbyes and collect our winter coats and hats. My mother hands us bags of leftover sausage bread and biscotti and kisses us both on the cheeks.

"Now Marcus, when do we get to see you again? Don't go hiding him from us," she says, looking pointedly at me.

"I'm already looking forward to it," Marcus says, thanking my parents for the evening and the leftovers.

"Soon, I promise," I say, giving my mom a big hug.

I wave goodbye to Alex, who gives me a grin and the thumbs up sign. He obviously thinks the evening went well, too.

The door is just closing behind us when I overhear my mother say, "He's such a catch. I wonder why he's not married?"

Marcus and I look at each other, eyebrows raised.

"Dodged that bullet," I say.

"You know, I soon won't be," he says, holding my gaze.

"Won't be what?"

"Married," he whispers. "I soon won't be married."

CHAPTER 42

Rule #14: Be prepared. You will test the patience of those you love the most.

Dezi emerges from the bridal salon dressing room looking like a princess cupcake decorated with too much frosting. The kind that looks much too sweet to eat.

The look on her face says, "Kill me now."

"Don't you dare laugh," she says, heaving herself and the dress over to a platform facing a three-way mirror.

"Oh Dezi, that is terrible," I say, giggling.

"I know. I'm too small for a ballgown. I tried to tell my mother this, but she insisted I at least try one on and take pictures. So here it is."

"Due diligence," I say, snapping a bunch of photos with my phone. "I can't even see you under all that fluff. All I see is dress."

"Exactly. It would be lovely on somebody tall, like you. But I can barely move in this mess."

"Take it off. It's hideous. Let's get to the real stuff. Something you might actually wear."

One bridal attendant helps Dezi out of the acres and acres of white froth, while another brings a selection more suited to Dezi's slight frame and personal style.

I fully intend to enjoy the forthcoming fashion show as I relax on a pale pink velvet sofa with a glass of Champagne. I have yet to tell Dezi about Marcus leaving Juliette and moving to D.C., but hopefully, I will find the opportunity today. I wanted to see her well before the dress shopping started, but our schedules just never lined up. Perhaps later this afternoon I can broach the subject, but right now, the woman needs to focus on finding her wedding dress. And it's my job to help her do just that.

The bridal attendant knows her stuff because every gown that follows Big Froth looks beautiful on Dezi. They are all simple, sleek and form-fitting gowns in different shades of ivory, white or cream. Some have bits of crystals or beading, others lace and others still are unadorned, allowing Dezi to shine as the jewel. It's a parade of gowns, one more lovely than the next.

I shake my head and grin as she emerges in yet another winner. This one is cream-colored silk with long lace sleeves as the only embellishment.

"What?" asks Dezi, as she turns around on the pedestal to get a look at the back of the gown.

"I don't know how you're going to choose," I say, taking a sip of my Champagne. "You are beautiful in all of them."

"You are sweet, thank you," she sighs. "I think I need a break."

At that, the bridal attendant sweeps over, gives Dezi a cozy robe to change into and sets her up next to me on the sofa with a glass of bubbly and a stack of bridal magazines to peruse.

"Wow, now that's what I call service," I say. "You need to go wedding dress shopping more often."

"It's exhausting," she says, sinking into the plush sofa. "But definitely fun. I'm so glad you're here."

"I wouldn't miss this for anything. And I got a ton of photos so you can send as many as you'd like to your mom."

Dezi nods as she flips through the magazines. "I think just a picture of the poof ball dress will be enough. At least she'll know I tried."

"Okay." I know Dezi and her mom are not exceptionally close. She vanished when Dezi was sixteen and resurfaced in Florida a year later, leaving Dezi and her father to fend for themselves. She remarried at some point and popped out a few more kids and has tried to reconnect with Dezi with little success. Dezi is cordial with her and manages a weekly dutiful phone call, but that's about the extent of it. I don't think Dezi has ever forgiven her for walking out on them when she was a teenager. I can't even remember when Dezi last saw her mom. And I have only met her once, when she crashed Dezi's grad school graduation day.

"So, do you have any wedding plans yet or are you just focusing on the dress?" I ask.

"Just the dress. No date. No venue. Nothing. We are both so overwhelmed by all the choices I figured I'd start with the dress and maybe work backwards."

"Not a bad idea. A few of these dresses would work at the beach or outdoors, the rest scream fancy. You have all your options."

Dezi tosses the magazine she was flipping through onto the sofa. "Come on, let's get out of here. My dress doesn't live here."

"Wait. Are you serious? We're just getting started."

Dezi's face splits open into what I now deem her "Elliot Grin" as she pulls me up off the sofa. Quite a feat for such a tiny person.

"I've tried on enough. I know the dress I want," she says, her blue eyes sparkling like sunshine on water. "Follow me."

We leave the bridal salon and burst out into the icy but brilliant sunny afternoon.

"Lunch first," she says, leading me to a small cafe around the corner. "And then we'll visit my dress."

I am torn between food and really, really wanting to see this dress. Like now. But the bride-to-be wants lunch, so that's what we're doing.

"No questions about the dress," says Dezi as we slide into a booth. "You'll see it soon enough."

"Okay, okay. I'm very excited to see this thing. But why did we bother with that bridal shop?"

"Because you can't just buy the first dress you see. Who does that? I wanted to make sure," she says, still grinning at me. "And now I am."

Our waitress stops by and we both order steaming bowls of soup — beef and barley for me, chicken noodle for Dezi.

"You must know what type of wedding you're shooting for then, right?" I ask, nibbling on a sourdough roll.

"Ah. No questions. No hints. But yes, at least I have an idea now. Sort of."

"What does Elliot want?"

"He wants whatever I want. Isn't that what they always say? It's sweet, of course, but not super helpful."

"Well, you have me. Just tell me what you need and I'm on it."

"I'm sorry you can't be my maid of honor," Dezi says quietly. "You're the only one I want."

Tears spring to my eyes. I have let down my dearest friend. How did I get so off track? I am the opposite of honor and integrity. I am not the kind of person you'd want as part of your wedding ceremony. I have been the enemy to married women everywhere.

"Hey, Quinn, don't cry," says Dezi, noticing my tears. "It's just a stupid title."

"It's not that. I'm just so sorry for disappointing you. For putting you in the middle. And for not being the kind of friend you need. I'm sorry for it all, Dezi."

"I know," she says, squeezing my hand. "It's okay. And I'm sorry for not doing more to help you address your past and your pain."

"Oh Dezi. That was never your job. And you did do that for me. Gently, which I appreciate."

"Quinn, you *have* been a good friend. You bring me joy and laughter. And I know, no matter what, you have my back. Your love life may be screwy, but you lift me up in a way that's rare in female friendships. There's no competition. No jealousy."

I slide over to Dezi's side of the booth and envelop her in a hug.

"Thank you for that," I whisper.

We sit in companionable silence for a beat.

"I do have some news," I say. "About Marcus."

Dezi raises her eyebrows and waits.

I tell her that Marcus left Juliette and moved near me. That I've been wanting to tell her in person and just haven't had the chance. That he's met my parents who adore him. And that he wants to file for divorce.

I even showed her the note with the poem, which I've been carrying around with me ever since.

I watch Dezi's blue eyes grow wider and wider with each confession. She now almost looks like a cartoon version of herself.

"So that's my news," I say, blowing out a sigh. "I didn't want to spoil your wedding dress day."

It's Dezi's turn now to squeal with delight.

"Are you kidding me? This is great news. On so many levels."

I nod. "That's essentially what Alex said."

"You are finally dating an available man. You are opening yourself up again to the possibility of a genuine relationship. Real love, Quinn. This is good. So good."

"I'm happy," I say, smiling at Dezi. "Terrified at times, but mostly happy."

"Just take it one day at a time, Quinn. Remember, you're just dating right now. You're not signing up for a lifetime commitment."

I nod. "You're right. You are absolutely right. But you are. So, take me to your dress."

·   ·   ·   ·   ·

Dezi emerges in what is clearly HER wedding gown and I am speechless. Now, my friend is a beautiful woman. But in this dress, she is breathtaking. I put my hands over my mouth and just stare. Several other women in the store come over and just stare.

That's all we can do. She is stunning.

Dezi is wearing a curve-hugging, floor-length, silky mermaid gown. It's the exact color of the deep, deep ocean. It's the blue of the waves that roll by when you're on a ship with no land in sight.

"Oh Dezi," I say, my eyes pricking with tears.

"Do you like it? I know it's an unusual color choice," she says, looking down at the silky satin that skims over her curves in a way that's somehow both elegant and sexy.

I nod. "You are stunning. I have never seen anything like it. Elliot may faint before you make it down the aisle."

She beams at me and then turns to step onto the pedestal.

"Wow, you are going to make quite the entrance and the exit," I say, now staring at the back of the dress. The gown is sleeveless with a draping, cowl neck back. There's a back slit up the skirt that's lined with deep blue tulle embellished with rows of tiny, shimmering crystals. It looks like twinkling stars against a midnight sky when she walks.

"What do you think of the back?" Dezi asks, peering at the dusting of sparkle peeking out. "Too much?"

"Are you kidding? The back is gorgeous and the sparkle is incredibly subtle. You sort of have to look for it."

"Good," she says, smiling.

"It's a knock-out. It's so simple and clean in the front and just a hint of a party in the back. It's perfect, Dezi. Just perfect."

"I'm glad you like it. I knew it was my dress the moment I saw it."

"Veil?" I ask.

Dezi shakes her head. "No, I don't think so. But I am considering opera-length gloves and maybe something in my hair."

A bridal attendant comes bustling over and helps Dezi slide on a pair of matching blue satin gloves. She then tucks the tiniest of tiaras into Dezi's pale blonde hair. Once again, it's subtle and gently catches the light when she turns her head.

"Well?" asks Dezi, turning around to give me the full view.

I smile at her and nod, tears starting to roll. Other people in the salon actually start to cheer and clap.

"You're done," I say. "You've found the magic combination. I don't think a more beautiful bride exists."

CHAPTER 43

Daily Special

Endive with green apple dressing, gorgonzola and toasted walnuts
Double-cut pork chops with charred orange-caramel sauce
Crispy olive oil freekeh cakes

I'm at Persimmon early today because I need the chance to assess our wine inventory before we open for dinner. My brain has been everywhere but work lately and my cellar is in desperate need of some organization and attention. Life has been good, but busy. I see a lot more of Marcus now that he's left Juliette and lives near me. I'm helping Dezi plan her wedding. I need to squeeze in Alex from time to time. Cindy is still stopping by for her lessons, unfortunately. And now, I've got my mother hounding me to bring Marcus back for another family dinner. Plus, of course, all the usual detritus of life — work, exercise, laundry, dental appointments, eyebrow plucking — piles up with zero regard for my love life or best friend duties. I'm getting the hang of juggling everything, though. Marcus I see every chance I get. Dezi genuinely needs my help. Cindy is well, Cindy, so I've been keeping our bi-weekly appointments. So basically, my mother, my brother and my wine cellar are getting the short shrift.

Time to take care of the wine cellar. And I'm hoping to see Alex later this week. Progress.

I have more than an hour before I need to think about tonight's patrons, so I hunker down in the cellar to get organized. While I stack bottles and review inventory, I also keep an eye out for wines to pair with Chef's special tonight. I can hazard a few good guesses, but I think I may need a spoonful of that charred orange sauce before narrowing down the selection. I'm certain Chef will oblige.

I'm putting a few bottles of bubbly in the coldest section of the wine refrigerator when my phone pings.

Marcus. Just seeing his name light up my screen brings on the butterflies and the roller-coaster rush. I'm coming to terms with the fact that I'm crazy for this man. I want this man. And I'm pretty sure it's too late to turn back now anyway. I'm too far gone.

Marcus: Hey gorgeous. I know you're at work, but I wanted to say hi. I miss you already.

I can feel my cheeks crack into a smile. Marcus left for a trip yesterday morning. We took forever saying goodbye and he ended up having to rush to the airport. This is the longest stretch we'll be apart since he left his wife.

Me: Hey handsome. I miss you too. Sorry you were almost late for your flight.

Marcus: I'm not sorry at all. It was so worth it.

Me: I couldn't agree more. Trip going okay?

Marcus: Yup. Status quo. But I cannot wait to come back to you.

Me: Yes!

Marcus: Dinner and slumber party at my place when I get back. I'm cooking.

Me: You're on! And you're cooking! What did I do to deserve this?

Marcus: Hell if I know. (wink emoji) But you're under my skin. And in my head. And I love you.

Me: Me too.

I sigh with pleasure as my cheeks stretch to accommodate an even bigger grin. I do love that man. So much it still scares me because I can feel myself spinning out of control. And I miss him when he's gone. But now he's given me something to look forward to. Dinner *and* a slumber party.

• • • • •

A few minutes later I'm in the kitchen licking a spoon coated with a burnt orange caramel sauce. It's delicious and different — silky, pleasantly bitter and both citrusy and sweet.

"Mmmmm," I say, as Chef stands impatiently in front of me, tapping his foot. "This is really good." I smack my lips. "And I know just the wine."

"I should hope so," says Chef. "That's what we pay you for."

He makes an abrupt about-face to resume his cheffy things when he suddenly turns back to me.

"I hear our cheese purveyor is getting married, yes?"

I nod. "He is. Just proposed to my best friend."

"I shall congratulate him then. Any wedding plans yet?"

"They're thinking a very small, intimate, evening wedding at this point."

"Excellent choice," says Chef, nodding his approval. "Small and elegant. Always the way to go."

I'm about to burst out and tell him the bride is wearing blue, but catch myself. That little tidbit is supposed to be a secret, to everyone except me. I love that she's wearing blue. It's sassy and spunky and surprising, just like my friend. That and the shade she chose is a dead ringer for the color of her eyes. Elliot is going to lose his mind.

• • • • •

It's time for me to get to work. I whiz through my tables, offering tastings, pouring wine and making menu recommendations. I'm also fielding quite a few menu questions tonight, which makes me wonder if our new server isn't up to speed yet. But I don't mind. I love chatting with our guests.

Yes, the pork chop is wonderfully different and not overly sweet. No, the short ribs aren't fatty and greasy. Yes, we can remove the head from the whole fish if you'd prefer, although I don't recommend it, those cheeks are delicious. No, freekeh is not a bean, it's a chewy, nutty grain. And no, I'm sorry, we do not have any vegan cashew cheese.

Seriously? Vegan cashew cheese? More like nut goo. Why even bother at that point?

I get my tables settled and take a brief break to grab a snack and sit for a moment. I'm dipping carrots through a swoosh of hummus when my phone pings. It's Alex.

Alex: Hey Quinn, what's new? You engaged yet?

Me: Ha ha. Very funny little brother. And NO. NOT READY.

Alex: Well, you better tell mom that. She's gone berserk over Marcus. I think she likes him more than she likes the rest of us.

Me: (eye roll emoji) Tell me about it. She can't wait to see him again. I think I need to wait a bit though. Let her cool down some.

Alex: Good call. We still getting together?

Me: Absolutely! Axe throwing????

Alex: How about something else? I'm tired of Fantasia. She's exhausting.

Me: Ha ha ha! She has a whopping crush on you.

Alex: She asked me out. I said no. Now it's weird.

Me: Of course she did. That little minx. No worries, we'll figure something out.

I tell Alex that I need to get back to work and then do just that, all the while chuckling about Fantasia. She is just way too young and cutesy and sticky-sweet for him, but I do admire her chutzpah. He needs somebody wise, witty and with a bit of an edge. I had always hoped he and Dezi would get together, but I suppose it's much too late for that. At least Alex said no to Fantasia. I'm not sure I could stomach that one for very long.

I make my rounds and see that everyone is wrapping up and the checks are all paid. That is my signal to duck into the restroom and unleash any uncomfortable clothing — snug belt be gone — and visit Julian. But not before I also take off my bra, which is poking me with its underwire. I stuff both into my bag and do a quick check in the mirror to make sure it's not obvious the girls are swinging free. Nope, all good here — one of the perks of small breasts and winter clothing. I really should go sans bra more often.

I find Julian setting up the bar for tomorrow and organizing his tools.

"Hey Julian," I say, plunking down on my usual stool. "How's life? What's new? Dating anyone yet?"

Julian smirks and shakes his head at me. "So many questions, Q."

"Well? You never really give me any answers."

"What will it be tonight? Usual Cognac?"

"See. There you go again. Mister Mysterious. I want to try that Love, Violet cocktail."

Julian cocks his head at me, raising just one eyebrow. "Interesting choice," he says, grabbing a coupe glass.

"So," I say, drumming my fingers on the bar. "You going to give me any answers?"

"I don't remember the questions," he says, mixing my pale lavender cocktail.

"Very funny." I toss a nut at his head. "How's life? What's new? Dating anyone yet?" I ask again, lobbing another nut at his head.

Before I even have time to blink, Julian swipes the nut out of the air, pelts me with it and slides my drink across the bar, all in one lightning-fast motion.

"What the ...?" I'm laughing as I start throwing nuts at him, rapid fire. He does an impressive job of catching them in midair and sending them right back at me. "You have one heck of a reaction time," I say, protecting my drink and my face from the torrent of mixed nuts.

"You're lucky the bar is empty," Julian laughs. "I'm pretty sure employee food fights are frowned upon."

"Oh, that was fun," I say, taking a swig of my drink and helping Julian clean up the nuts. "You seriously have fast hands. Is that from drumming?"

"Maybe," Julian shrugs. "Never thought about it. Although my dad would say it's from all the Whack-a-Mole he made me play as a kid. He didn't want a musician, he wanted an athlete. He figured that stupid game would increase my reaction time."

I smile at this curious little piece of Julian's childhood revealed. "Well, perhaps he was right. Remind me to never get into a real food fight with you."

"How's the drink, by the way?"

"I like it," I say, taking another sip. "It's lemony."

"No pilot tonight?"

"Not unless you have a note for me," I say, sighing. "He's on a trip. The longest one since he left his wife."

"How's that all going?"

"Uh, uh," I say, shaking my head. "You need to answer some of my questions first."

Julian just looks at me, a smile playing at his lips. He's so good at saying nothing.

"Marcus moved to D.C.," I blurt out. "That's the latest and greatest. But enough, I want to hear about you."

"That sounds pretty serious, Q," he says, training his hazel eyes on mine. I notice that tonight, they are mostly gold with tiny flecks of green.

I nod. "It seems to be headed in that direction. Although he did say he would have moved out regardless of me, so that helps."

Julian cocks his head at me. "Helps how?"

"It makes me feel less like a homewrecker. I know I was probably the catalyst, but things were over before I ever came along."

Julian remains quiet. Once again, he reminds me of Alex.

"I also feel less pressure to make any big decisions," I say. "We can take things slow and let our relationship grow naturally."

"So, no big fat engagement ring anytime soon?" asks Julian, smiling at me.

"Absolutely not." I shake my head. "It's way too early for that. And he's still married."

"You sure about that?"

"What? Yes. Of course he's still married. Is a quickie divorce even a thing?"

Julian shrugs. "I guess it depends on the state. But I'd keep my eye on that one. Marcus does what Marcus wants."

"He does," I say, groaning. "And that's what makes him so unbelievably sexy. Among other things ..."

"Women," says Julian with a grumble.

"Yes! Speaking of. How did you get me so off track? You never answered any of my questions."

Julian smirks. "No, I'm not dating anyone. At least, not anyone worth mentioning."

"So you *are*, in fact, dating," I say, excitedly. "Who? Where? When?"

"Of course I'm dating. But like I said, not even worth talking about. So far, no second dates. Slim pickings."

"What are you looking for?"

"That's a big question."

"Top three."

"I need a woman who makes me smile. Who makes me think. A woman with some passion," he says.

"Passion for what?"

"For anything. For life. For work. For animals. For tattoos. Whatever. A woman with some guts and spirit."

I nod and stay quiet for once.

"A woman who brings joy with her."

"All great stuff," I say. "But a big ask."

"And you wonder why I'm still single," Julian says with a wry smile.

"Was that Violet? Was she all of that?"

Julian nods and starts folding bar towels into a neat stack. "I think she was."

"Julian. What happened between you two?"

"Q, that is a very long story."

"I have nowhere I need to be," I reply, settling into my seat.

"Someday, Q. Someday. But it appears you have a visitor," he says, grinning and glancing over my shoulder.

"Oh stop. You're just trying to get out of telling me your love story. Now spill it."

"I'm not kidding, Q. See for yourself," he says, gesturing behind me.

Oh for crying out loud. Who could this possibly be? I slowly turn around, bracing myself for crazy.

It's a woman. She looks vaguely familiar. Why do I know her?

Wait a minute. I recognize that shiny, perfectly straight, sheet of honey-colored hair.

Juliette.

Why is Juliette in my restaurant? This is so not cool.

I want her out of here. There is only one reason she's here.

Marcus.

Fuck that.

She's not getting him back.

CHAPTER 44

Rule #6: Never, ever, ever fall in love.

"Julian. Quick," I hiss. "That's Marcus's wife. Do I pretend I don't know her? What do I do?"

"Oh boy," he says, his hazel eyes suddenly turning a deep, dark, forest green. "I would go with honesty here. But you had better decide quick."

I watch as Juliette scans the restaurant. I can feel my pulse galloping and sweat trickling between my breasts. Fantastic. I'm so happy I chose tonight, the night I come face-to-face with Juliette, to whip off my bra and go swinging free.

I take a deep breath. You know what? She's in *my* restaurant. In *my* space. She's going to have to come to me.

Maybe she'll chicken out and leave.

Quinn, I reprimand myself. *Get a grip. She threw Marcus away and now he wants you. He chose YOU.*

Juliette locks eyes with me from across the room.

Here we go.

"Quinn?" she asks as she approaches the bar.

I nod. "Juliette."

She looks surprised that I know who she is. Damn, she's even lovelier up close. She has high cheekbones and full lips and wide-set, brown eyes the color of toffee. I am gearing up for a fight until I notice her lips are trembling. I was hoping for angry, spurned wife, not weepy wife.

"You're the one sleeping with my husband," she says quietly. "He left me for you."

I decide to employ the Alex-Julian technique and just shut up. I have nothing to say. And I really need to stop thinking of her as his wife. This woman is Juliette. And she didn't take care of her man.

And now he's mine. MINE.

She stares at me with those melted toffee eyeballs.

Nope. I am not backing down. I have nothing to say.

"What kind of person messes with another woman's marriage?" she asks. "Why would you do that? Isn't there some kind of code?"

I continue to look Juliette in the eye. It's getting a bit weird.

"What's wrong with you?" she asks, her voice starting to rise. "Marcus is MY husband. My man. Get. Your. Own."

"I'm going to have to ask you to leave now," I say calmly. "The restaurant is closing."

"Are you kidding me? I'm not going anywhere. Not until I get some answers. You owe me that much."

"I don't owe you a damn thing," I say, glaring at her. "Marcus has left. You two are over and we are in love. If you have any other questions, I suggest you take it up with him."

"We are not over," she says, practically growling at me. "I didn't even get a chance to fight."

I take a few deep breaths as I don't want this to escalate. Juliette needs to calm down. I need to calm down. I can see Julian keeping tabs on us from behind the bar. I swear, it's only his steady, soothing presence that's keeping me from totally wigging out right now.

"You never gave me the chance," she says, scowling at me. "One day we were celebrating our anniversary and practically the next, he's gone. He's already filed for divorce."

Divorce? Divorce? Did she just say he officially filed for divorce? I feel the wind knocked out of me. *Relax Quinn. Calm down. You knew this was coming. You're good. You can power through this.*

I take a sip from my water glass and try to gather my jumble of thoughts.

"You need to back off," she says, straightening her spine and squaring her shoulders.

I shake my head. "I can't do that. It's too late."

"Yes, you can," she says fiercely now, almost spitting at me. "He's mine."

"Not anymore," I say, drawing myself up to my full height and looking down at her. *I will take this woman out. Good god what is wrong with me?*

"Stay away from my husband," she shouts. "Please. Just go away."

"You bailed out a long time ago," I say quietly. "You did that. You turned your back on him." As I say this, I really don't know how much of it is true. I believe what Marcus told me about Jett and Juliette's subsequent downward spiral, but I also know there are two people in a marriage. Two sides to every story.

I'm not stupid. Just very much in love.

"You're right, I did," says Juliette, her pretty face crumpling. It's like all the air rushing out of a balloon, she simply collapses and deflates. "I drove him away," she whispers. "I did that."

I sigh. "Juliette ..."

"No. Stop," she says, cutting me off. "I take some responsibility here, but I don't want to lose my husband. We have a long history together and I deserve the chance to win him back. I do."

I don't know what to say. I am not backing down and I am not handing over Marcus. No way. And unless she's totally clueless about him, she knows this will not fly with Marcus. He does what he wants.

And he doesn't want her. He wants me. And I now know I want him too. And everything that comes along with that. *Wow. Oh wow.* I am ready to fight for my man.

I am ready to rumble.

Juliette starts to cry. Not just sniffling tears, but gasping, little-girl sobs. She puts her head in her hands, her shoulders shaking as the tears stream down her cheeks and drip onto the marble bar.

"Please, Quinn," she whispers, grasping at my hands. "I am begging you. Woman to woman. Please stay away from my husband."

Okay. I've had enough of this nonsense. I feel bad. I do. But Marcus doesn't want to be married to her anymore. And I'm certainly not going to bow to her demands.

"Marcus left you, Juliette. I'm sorry, but it's true. I did not take him away. He left."

Juliette is quiet, spent. Her face is pale and streaked with tears.

"Why do you even want him back?"

She ignores my question. "May I use the bathroom before I leave?" she asks, her voice barely audible.

I nod and point towards the restrooms. This just plain sucks. I know I have a role to play in all of this, but it's not like we're sneaking around anymore. Marcus came clean and moved out and lives near me now. He loves *me*.

It's just too late for Juliette. And I think she needs to hear it from him.

"Hey, Q, you okay?" asks Julian, rubbing my shoulders. "You handled that as well as could be expected, I think."

"Thanks," I say, smiling weakly. "That was hell. But hearing you say that helps. There is no manual for this."

"Is she coming back? Do you need me to do anything?"

"I don't know," I say, keeping an eye on the bathroom door. "Just being here is enough Julian, thank you."

We both watch as Juliette starts heading back toward us. I blow out a sigh. Really? I can't take anymore tonight.

"I'm leaving," she says quietly. "But I think you should know that I'm pregnant."

I stare at her, my jaw falling open.

"It's a miracle, really," she says, placing a hand on her still-flat stomach. "But I am. And I want to give this baby a chance at a family."

Anniversary sex, I think. *God damn that anniversary sex.*

I feel woozy. The room is spinning as if I just drank a half bottle of wine with zero food.

"And before you even ask, yes. Yes, he knows," says Juliette, her toffee-colored eyes huge and brimming with tears. "He knows. And he wants a divorce anyway."

I can't speak. I can't think straight. I'm afraid if I stand up I might pitch forward onto the floor, arms and legs akimbo.

Once again, I feel like a giant ass. A dinosaur ass, if you will.

"You don't have to say anything," says Juliette softly. "I wasn't going to tell you, but then, well ... I don't know. I'm desperate I guess," she says, her eyes pleading.

"Oh Juliette," I say, sucking in a deep breath.

"Don't. Please don't say anything," she says. "Just promise me you'll think about it."

I stay quiet. I know what she's asking and I don't want to hear it. I want to clamp my hands over my ears like a toddler and scream.

"Think about letting him go," she says, turning to leave. "Please. Think about giving this baby a father. Giving this baby a real family."

CHAPTER 45

Rule #1: Rules are meant to be broken.

If it wasn't for Julian, I'm not sure I would have made it home last night. I may very well have curled up under the bar and cried myself to sleep. I don't remember much after Juliette's revelation except Julian's solid arms around me. He scooped me up, put me in his car and somehow got me home and tucked into bed with a mug of hot tea and a glass of whiskey. Homewrecker's choice.

I owe that man a huge thank you.

I want to talk to Marcus. I need to talk to Marcus. But he's up in the air somewhere and literally unreachable. I also think this needs to be a face-to-face conversation.

I need to think. I need to run.

Within minutes I am out the door and flying down my usual jogging route, trying to clear my head. Trying to outrun this sticky, whopping mess.

I did the opposite of what I set out to do. The complete reverse. I wanted a casual, flirty fling with a man in a floundering marriage. I wanted fun and freedom and mind-blowing sex. Instead, I have commitment, a pending divorce I may have triggered and a desperate wife clawing at me. And now a baby in the middle of everything. A baby.

But I also have love. For the first time in my life, I have found a love I didn't know existed. A love I've always yearned for, but have been hiding from ever since Liam and Chris. A love that, for once, feels mutual.

And I have joy.

Had. I had joy. And I want it back.

I hate Juliette. I hate Juliette. I hate Juliette. It's my mantra with each step as my running shoes connect with the sidewalk. Bam, bam, bam. Hate, hate, hate.

I keep going until I wind up at Dezi's front door, sweaty and wild-eyed.

"Quinn, honey, what's going on?" she asks, pulling me inside and wrapping her bathrobe tightly around her waist. "What's wrong? Are you okay?"

I see Elliot coming out of her bedroom, hair tousled and yawning. I don't even know what time it is.

I put my hands on my knees, trying to catch my breath from that fast-paced run.

"Sorry to bother you," I say between gulps of air. "I didn't know where else to go."

"Hey, it's okay," she says. "We were awake. Did you run here?"

I nod as she gets me a glass of water.

I chug it gratefully as I try to sift through the words ricocheting around my brain — divorce, baby, father, stepmother, love, loathing, tramp, homewrecker.

I take a deep breath.

"Juliette is pregnant," I blurt out. "She found me at Persimmon and begged me to leave Marcus alone."

Dezi calmly hands me a towel and gently steers me towards her bathroom. "You, hot shower," she says to me. "I think you have an old pair of clean sweats here. I'll set them out." She then points to Elliot. "Will you go out for coffee and bagels please?"

"Already on it," he says, grabbing his jacket and rushing out the door.

I'm warm, clean and cozy on Dezi's couch as she hands me a mug of hot tea. The steamy shower and all of Dezi's lavender scented products did wonders to calm me down.

Dezi looks at me expectantly with what I can only imagine is her therapist face. But behind it, I see the clouded look of worry in her deep blue eyes.

She listens patiently as I give her the blow-by-blow details of Juliette's surprise visit, including my fierce and nearly uncontrollable reaction to do whatever it takes to fight for Marcus.

"You're angry," Dezi says softly.

"I know," I say. "I am. I do feel sorry for her. I really do. But for the most part, I'm just so mad at her. It's absurd, but I feel this rush of violence whenever I think of her. I can only imagine it's like what athletes feel when they're all hopped up on steroids."

"Why do you think you're so mad at her, Quinn?" Dezi asks.

I sigh. I know why. I know exactly why.

"Because things were going so well in my life," I say. "I let myself fall in love. Really topple into it. I was finally climbing out of the hole I had dug for myself after getting it so impossibly wrong with Chris. And Liam."

Dezi nods. "I know."

"And then she waltzes in and craps all over everything," I say. "Just blows up my world."

"Don't you think she feels the same way about you?" Dezi asks softly. "You know I love you Quinn, but you messed with a married man. That rarely ends well."

"But he left. Marcus left," I say, my voice starting to sound hysterical. "He doesn't want to be married to Juliette anymore. He left her, Dezi. He chose me."

"I know honey," she says, pulling me into a hug. "I know he did. But it doesn't seem like a clean break."

"Fucking anniversary sex," I say through gritted teeth. "One time a year. ONE TIME and the woman who can't get pregnant gets pregnant."

We are quiet for a few minutes, sipping our tea and coffee and picking at an array of bagels Elliot set out for us. I cannot believe this mess. I'm finally ready to commit. To give up my married man habit and now this. I am desperate to talk to Marcus but it's going to have to wait. I think about my encounter with Juliette and how we're fighting over him as if he were an object with no say in the matter.

I shake my head and sigh. "This whole thing is nuts. It's not as if Juliette has any control over Marcus. I know I sure don't. Everything has been his decision, his choice, done at his own pace. Hell, I didn't even know he moved out until after the fact."

Dezi nods. "He knows what he wants."

"Yes. He always has."

"Quinn, what would you say to Juliette if she wasn't pregnant?"

"Easy. I'd tell her to go pound sand. And if she wants Marcus back, she's going to have to win him back."

"So you'd fight for him," says Dezi, more of a statement than a question.

"Without question."

"And now? With a child on the way?"

I am quiet. I want to forget this part and just focus on Juliette, the checked-out wife who ignored Marcus for years. The wife who chucked her husband and essentially threw him in my path. Juliette just pisses me off. But the baby makes my heart catch in my throat. It's a feeling I want to outrun but can't. Scrub away, but there isn't enough hot water or soap. Breaking up a family counters one of my cardinal tenants of infidelity. But then again, I already smashed most of those rules the moment I met Marcus.

Marcus. I need to see Marcus. Can I break up a family that's already broken? Does that count?

I look over at Dezi. "I can't force him to go back to Juliette," I say, cringing somewhat at my own words. They sound so lame.

I can see Dezi fighting the urge to roll her eyes. "Of course not," she says, shaking her head. "But without obstacles, he may find his way back."

I stare at her. "Are you suggesting what I think you're suggesting?"

"I'm just saying you have a lot to think about, Quinn. You have some power here. How are you going to use it?"

"I love him, Dezi," I say, tears starting to well. "I didn't know someone like him was out there for me."

"I know. I know."

"I don't think I can do it."

"Do what?" Dezi asks.

"Let him go. I don't think I can let him go. Oh my god, Dezi. I am in this now. I am all in."

Dezi nods and just watches me.

"What would you do?" I ask. She's about to speak but I cut her off. "What would you do, right this moment, if you found out Elliot had an ex-girlfriend or wife who was pregnant and wanted him back? Wanted you to give him up?"

Dezi stares at me, clearly horrified at the thought.

"That's totally different," she says, waving at the air as if to blow away the offensive question.

"It isn't, though. It's you, loving a man, yet finding yourself in an untenable situation that's wholly out of your control."

Dezi shakes her head. "I know you're upset, but it would be a completely different situation."

"How you got there, sure. But the end is the same. We both found love. And your love for Elliot is no greater or less than my love for Marcus."

I watch as Dezi looks down at her hands, folded in her lap.

"Would you give up Elliot? Could you give up Elliot?"

Dezi rubs her face with her hands. "No," she whispers. "I don't think I could. Jesus Quinn, what are you going to do?"

"I'm going to fight for Marcus," I say, standing up. "There was never really another option."

CHAPTER 46

Rule #10: Yes, he's still having sex with his wife.

I step into Marcus's apartment and take a deep breath, inhaling the scent of rosemary, garlic and browned butter. It's comforting and solid, just like him.

"Come and get it gorgeous," he says, putting down his chef knife and opening his arms wide for a hug. I dive in, throwing my arms around him and wrapping my legs around his waist. I notice he's set the table with long-stemmed wineglasses, flowers and candles. And it appears he's warming up fresh bread, roasting potatoes and sautéing mushrooms in hot butter.

"It looks beautiful in here and it smells so good," I say, burying my face in his neck. I'm trying not to cry. I don't want to lead with Juliette, but it seems as if my heart isn't following my head.

Marcus wraps his arms around me tightly and whispers, "My god woman have I missed you. I don't want to let you go."

With that, the tears start to seep from underneath my eyelashes, creating a slick of makeup and salt down my cheeks. There goes my carefully applied mascara.

"Hey, hey, hey, sweetheart, what's going on?" Marcus asks, peering at my face and gently brushing back my hair. He sets me on his countertop next to a huge hunk of pepper-crusted beef. "What's wrong babe?"

I take a deep breath and wipe at my wet cheeks. "Marcus," I say, looking into those blue eyes. "It's Juliette," I say, my lips trembling. "She came to Persimmon last night."

Marcus sighs and pulls me in for a hug. "I'm sorry she did that."

"When were you going to tell me?" I whisper.

"Tonight." He takes my hands in his. "I was planning to tell you tonight. Hence, all of this," he gestures to the wine and candles and all the makings of a romantic dinner. "I thought in some sense, it could be a bit of a celebration."

"A celebration?" I ask, incredulous.

"Quinn, I'm getting a divorce," he says, scooping me up and spinning me around the kitchen. "Nothing can hold us back now. I'm free. And I'm all yours."

Marcus leads me to the table and pours me a glass of red wine. He pulls out a plate of warm, bacon-wrapped dates stuffed with cheese and sets it in front of me.

"Marcus. Is there anything else you want to tell me?"

He sighs and sits down next to me. "Juliette told you she's pregnant, didn't she?"

I nod.

Marcus shakes his head. "I was going to tell you about that tonight as well. I just found out myself and I wanted to tell you in person. I'm still wrapping my head around it."

"Was it the anniversary sex?" I blurt out. "I'm sorry. I'm sorry. I shouldn't have asked that, it's none of my business."

"Hey, it's okay. I want to be honest with you. Yes, it must have been because we hadn't had sex in months. Not since before Paris. It was our anniversary. It was rote. And truthfully, it felt like a duty more than anything," he rubs a hand over his face. "I'm sorry Quinn. I don't know what I was thinking except I figured it was our last time."

I don't know what to say. I think I am ready for him. Ready for us. *Finally.* But a baby?

He pulls me onto his lap. "Quinn, I love you more than anything. More than I ever loved Juliette. And a baby doesn't change that."

"But ..."

"Wait," says Marcus, taking my face in his hands. "Do you love me, Quinn?"

"You know I do," I whisper. "More than I ever thought possible."

"Then we can do this," he says. "What we have is worth it. It's worth everything."

"But a baby," I say, trailing off.

He nods. "I know. It's huge. So yes, I'm going to be a father. But I can be this baby's dad and not be Juliette's husband. I can't go back to that again. Not since I found you," he says, kissing me softly on the lips.

"You're going to be a father, Marcus. A *father*. Are you happy? Excited?"

He nods. "I am. I think. But I know this also complicates things. And I've been down this road with Juliette before ..." he trails off. "I guess it just doesn't seem real yet."

I push away the horrifying thought that comes to my mind. *Maybe she'll miscarry again. Maybe it's not Marcus's baby.*

I shake my head in a furious attempt to loosen those ugly thoughts and send them spinning away from me. I do not want to be a monster. Messing with a woman's wandering husband is entirely different from messing with a baby's dad.

"Marcus, I don't want to be the woman who breaks up a family," I say quietly.

He tips my chin up so I am looking directly into his inky blue eyes.

"You did not, have not and will not break up a family," he says firmly. "There is not a family to break up, Quinn. I am not going back to Juliette."

"Even if I was out of the picture?"

"Even if," he says, leaning down to touch his forehead to mine. "Even if."

We are quiet. The rhythms of our breath in sync. Our foreheads are still together and I can feel my eyelashes brush against his cheeks.

"Quinn," he whispers. "I am a different man now since you came along. I can't undo that now, even if I wanted to."

I nod, relieved but wholly overwhelmed. I want to speak but can't. I am soaked with emotion and can't seem to formulate a sentence. It's all too much. Everything feels so heavy now. And not just the pregnancy, but our relationship. I wanted a fling. A fling.

What have I done?

Marcus is getting a divorce. Marcus is going to be a father. He'll never be rid of Juliette. I'll forever be judged.

But Marcus is getting a divorce. A divorce!

Once again, my head and my heart are at war.

"Quinn, you are starting to scare me," says Marcus, gently kissing my cheeks. "Please, please tell me you aren't going to let this come between us. Quinn, don't walk away from us. We're too good. This is too rare."

"I know. And I won't," I say, putting my lips to his and kissing him deeply. "I can't. You're impossible to stay away from. Like it or not, you're stuck with me."

Did I just say that?

"Now that's what I want to hear," says Marcus, grinning at me and kissing me right back, gently parting my lips with his tongue. "So, bed or beef?" he asks, starting to slide his hands up my sweater.

"Beef! Definitely beef," I say, just as his hands slip inside my bra and find my nipples. "Ohhhh, forget it. Bed! Definitely bed!"

Two hours later I am well sexed, well fed and happily tucked into Marcus's powerful arms. He made me sigh with pleasure both in the bedroom and at the dinner table. Talented man, that one. Right now, at this moment, it seems unfathomable that I even entertained the idea of giving him up. I know, in my heart, that Marcus is a wholly different man from those of my past. And I am now a different woman. *I can do this*, I think. I can love this man. With all my heart.

We are spooning in his bed and playing a half-hearted game of Scrabble, which, for the record, I almost always win.

A baby, a baby, a baby. My mind keeps turning it over. It's like an itch I cannot scratch. A hangnail I keep picking at. A hunk of meat wedged in my teeth I can't dislodge. But then I look at Marcus and I know I need him in my life. And if a baby is part of the package, along with an ex-wife, so be it. I wouldn't be the first.

"Your turn," Marcus says, spelling out the word cheese on the board.

"Cheese? Really?" I smile.

"Anything to make you smile," he says, looking at me with those twinkling blue eyes. "Beat that my love. I'll be right back."

I'm fiddling with my letters and eyeing the board when Marcus slides a long, black velvet box in front of me.

"What's this?" I ask, my eyes going wide as my stomach pitches into that familiar Tilt-a-Whirl lurch. *It can't be an engagement ring, can it? The box is too big. And he's still married. And it's too soon.*

But oh how I would love to be his wife.

I clap my hand over my mouth as I fear I just said that aloud. I didn't even know I felt that way.

"Open it you nut," he says, nuzzling my neck. "Here, there's even a card."

Your hair is red.
Your lips are red.
We both like cheese.
Your hair, your lips, my love for you — still red, red and red.
Cheese.

I laugh and topple into Marcus. "You are terrible at these," I say, kissing every part of his face.

"You started it." He grins at me. "Now open it! Open, open, open," he chants.

I pry open the lid and find a stunning emerald tennis bracelet nestled in black velvet. It's breathtaking, the emeralds that perfect, unmatchable, shimmering shade of green.

"Oh Marcus," I say, staring at the piece of jewelry, almost afraid to touch it. "It's beautiful. I've never seen anything like it."

"It's just like you," he says softly, lifting out the bracelet and clasping it around my wrist. "The moment I saw it, it reminded me of you."

CHAPTER 47

Rule #15: Beware of the wives you could be friends with.

I'm sitting in my kitchen, admiring my emerald bracelet as the brilliant green gems glint in the winter sunshine. Marcus put it on my wrist several weeks ago now and I have yet to take it off. No matter where he is in the world, it's a constant reminder of him. Of us. Of our love. And that goofy poem, which always makes me smile.

He has officially filed for divorce. Juliette has left me alone. And my best friend is over the moon planning her blue wedding. Oh, and my mother is out of her mind with glee over the bracelet gift. She still doesn't know Marcus is married, but that's a conversation for another day.

Things are good.

Marcus and I have yet to take a deep dive into Juliette, the baby and how this is all going to work, but we'll get there. We have to, I suppose. I am the queen of looking no further than tomorrow, but I know I will have to come to terms with a new reality eventually. It's the only blemish on an otherwise rapidly blooming relationship. Although it's hard to think of a baby as a blemish. And it's hard not to think about Juliette. Pregnant.

I get the feeling that in a different life, under different circumstances, we might be friends.

I blow out a big sigh. Leave it to me to fall in love with a married man who then dumps his wife right at the time he gets her pregnant. I twirl the delicate bracelet around my wrist and glance at the time on my phone. Cindy will be here soon for her "lesson," but I have time to ping Dezi.

Me: Hey bride-to-be, busy?

Dezi: Was just thinking about you! Nah, just reviewing some client charts for tomorrow.

Me: I'm waiting for Cindy ...

Dezi: Ha ha ha! What's the lesson plan today?

Me: Hmmm. You ask as if I actually plan these out ...

Dezi: You should. You need a theme.

Me: How about this — fighting with your man? Show him your can. Or better yet, fighting with your dude? Flash him your boob.

My phone starts ringing. It's Dezi. I pick it up and all I hear is her musical, tinkling laugh.

"I love that," she says. "And the funny thing is, it probably would work."

I smile. "I try. I'm also hoping this is going to be the final lesson."

"I don't know. You seem pretty good at this. Plus, if you keep it going, maybe she'll forget about testing Zack."

"Good god I hope so," I say, picturing the naked, dancing surprise Cindy keeps threatening. "I want to ask her about it, but I also don't want to remind her in case it's off her radar screen."

"Look," says Dezi. "I'm actually calling to check in on you. See how you're processing everything ..." she trails off for a moment. "You're going to have a lot coming your way soon."

"I'm okay. I mean, things are great with Marcus. Really great."

"Quinn, it's not just going to be you and Marcus."

"Believe me, I know that. And I'm okay with that. There are worse things."

"Of course there are. But have you two discussed this yet? Do you have some sort of plan?"

I start to feel annoyed. I know she's just looking out for me, but not everything has to be planned down to the minutia. I'm confident we'll work things out. But Dezi knows me well, and she's homed in on my buried feelings of unease. Will Marcus dump me once he lays eyes on that baby? Will he still have room for me in his life?

Will he move back to New York? Will I give up my job and go with him? Would he even ask me to?

Would I make an okay stepmother? Do I even want to be a stepmother?

I sigh into the phone. I can always count on Dezi to hold up a mirror. "I don't know the exact plan yet, Dez. I just don't know how this is all going to work. And I'm worried."

"Maybe it won't be as complicated as you think," she says. "And perhaps having an actual plan, at least a tentative one, will make you feel better. More in control. The not knowing is sometimes worse."

"As usual, I know you're right." I nod into the phone. "I'll probably feel better. And sleep better too," I say, thinking of all my restless nights the past few weeks. And strange dreams that always end the same — me walking down the aisle in a wedding dress and unable to see the face of my groom.

"You okay?" asks Dezi.

"I am. I'm just tired of feeling on edge."

"What worries you the most?"

I know the answer in an instant. Knew it the moment I found out Juliette was pregnant. It's been burrowing inside my gut like a parasite, constantly there. Constantly gnawing.

But I can't tell Dezi. I can't even say it aloud to myself. I can only think it right now.

How long will this child hate me?

Forever. The answer to that is forever.

My thoughts are interrupted, thankfully, by a knock at my door. Cindy.

"Oops, my student has arrived," I say to Dezi. "Gotta run, but we'll talk later."

"Uh huh. Saved by the bell, literally. Have fun with the lesson. Love the theme."

I smile at that as I answer the door.

Cindy comes bustling in, all wrapped up in her winter gear. She sheds what appears to be several pounds of mittens, scarves, wooly things and a bright orange puffy coat.

"Wow the temperature is dropping fast," she says, pulling off a knit cap and shaking her hair out.

"Hot tea?" I offer.

She nods and gets settled on my sofa. I still can't believe I got myself into this. I actually like Cindy quite a bit. But I'd rather we were simply friends and hung out like normal women instead of gathering for these weird, antiquated lessons. I'm hopeful we are about to wrap them up for good as I'm running out of things to say. And honestly, for the most part, she just talks and I listen.

I have touched on the giant ass rule, but that really doesn't apply to Cindy and Zack. I still believe Zack is genuinely a good, decent human being. And Cindy is a loyal and kind, albeit pushy, woman.

The other biggie is just as straightforward — sometimes, it's simply too late. No matter how wonderful the two people are, no matter how much history they have, sometimes, the damage is just too great. The crevasse too wide. And that sucks.

But I'm optimistic that Cindy and Zack have not crashed into that wall of finality. I think they are going to be just fine. With or without me.

Now if only I can convince Cindy of that.

"So, how's Zack?" I ask. "Bring me up to speed."

"Good, I guess. Although we've been arguing a lot lately."

"That doesn't sound good at all. What about?"

"We're just picking at each other. It's annoying. I can't even remember what we've been fighting about."

I'm no counselor, nor do I want to be, but I've somewhat grown into the role Cindy has forced upon me. She has made me think about how I choose my married men, why I home in on certain husbands and how I set myself apart from their wives. Often, it's done more subconsciously than with true intent, but as I scrutinize my past, patterns do emerge.

I don't know what it is about long-term marriages, but most of my husbands have said the same thing — they fight with their wives about nothing and about everything, but none of it remotely meaningful. They feel as if they are getting chipped away at for no real reason. I recall my second affair with Nathan, a hunky gym owner and personal trainer. A few months into our affair he said to me, "she keeps hacking away at me. It's all pesky, nonsense stuff. Eventually, she's going to whittle me down and you know what's going to be left? A sharp spike. Why doesn't she see that?"

At the time, I was just annoyed that we were sucking up precious moments together talking about his wife. But, in retrospect, it was rather insightful of him. I'm pretty sure nobody goes into marriage wanting to turn their sweet, loving spouse into a sharp spike.

I glance at my student and decide to test out my extemporaneous theme for the day's lesson.

"Cindy. Now pay close attention. You may want to write this down."

She looks at me somewhat suspiciously and cocks her head.

"I have a rule for you. Two rules, actually."

"Yes?" she says, sitting up straight like a grade-school student expecting an award for good merit. I know she's excited about this as I never actually give her any rules, much to her dismay.

"Rule number one. Don't fight about small stuff. Save the aggravation and the headache for the big stuff. Otherwise, you'll wear each other out."

Cindy rolls her eyes. "That's stupid. We all know that."

I laugh. "Still always honest, I see."

"Come on Quinn, we all know not to fight about dumb stuff. That's not exactly a revelation."

"I wasn't done yet," I say. "I know inevitably you will argue about the little things. We all do. So, rule number two; when you're fighting with your dude, flash him your boob."

Cindy's freckles almost dance across her cheeks as she breaks into a smile. "That is insane advice but so simple. And I bet it would work."

I nod. "Think of how quickly you'll disarm Zack if you flash some cleavage. Or even give him a nipple shot."

"Or the whole boob, depending on how stupid the fight is," she says, laughing. "Are men that easy, do you think?"

I shrug. "I don't know, but it seems worth a shot. I figure it can't hurt, but then again, I'm no expert."

"But you've had experience with married men in a way most women haven't."

I nod. I suppose that's true.

"How many?" she asks.

"What?"

"How many married men have you slept with?"

I shake my head. "Oh I don't know …" I say, trailing off.

"Yes you do," she replies. "I know Zack wasn't your first."

"I never slept with Zack."

"I know, I know, so you say," she says, training her blue eyes on my face.

"Four. I've had flings with four married men. Zack would have made five, but we never got that far," I say, returning her gaze.

"Why?"

"Because Zack loves you," I say, omitting a few choice details.

"No, why married men at all?"

"Ah. Well, that is a long story. And you're not here to learn my life history."

"You can give me the short version."

"My, you are persistent," I say, suddenly thinking of Julian and how I insist on constantly quizzing him.

"Well?" she asks.

"Let's just say that marriage didn't agree with me. And I found I love being a mistress. As the other woman, you're always the sexy, fun one. The one being pursued."

Cindy just looks at me. It's hard to discern whether she likes me or really, really hates me. I get the feeling she's trying to figure that out for herself.

"Okay, let's get back to the rules," I say, trying to change the subject. Although I have no clue where to go from here. I tend to wing these encounters.

"Yes," says Cindy, clapping her hands together. "Go."

I'm trying to think of something to say when I hear a gentle knock at my door.

Yes! Saved!

I excuse myself and head toward my entryway. My mind wanders. I'm thinking about how to get Cindy out and what I should eat for dinner tonight when I open the door.

Juliette.

How does this woman keep finding me?

We stare at each other. She's as lovely as ever, her cheeks a little fuller, perhaps and bright pink from the cold. It's hard to tell if she's showing at all yet under the winter layers, but she's got that unmistakable pregnancy stance — feet planted wide, hips tilted, hands clasped across her stomach.

"Come in Juliette," I say, not sure what else to do. "It's freezing out here."

"Oh, I'm sorry, you have company," she says, glancing at Cindy as she wraps her coat around herself tightly. "I can come back."

"No, no, no, it's fine," I say tightly. I wish she wasn't here, but I certainly don't want her coming back. I just want to get this over with, whatever it is.

"You're sure?" she asks again, looking at Cindy.

"Oh, don't worry about me," says Cindy, smiling up at Juliette. "Come sit. I'm just here for my lessons."

"Lessons?" asks Juliette.

"Just ignore her please," I say briskly. "May I take your coat? Get you some water or tea?"

Juliette shakes her head. "I won't stay long."

"What can I do for you, Juliette?" I ask.

She looks at me, then at Cindy. "Can we talk somewhere in private?" she asks quietly.

"I can leave," says Cindy, jumping up from the sofa. "We can pick up later, Quinn."

"No. You stay," I say to Cindy, more brusquely than I intended. I had wanted her to leave, but that was before Juliette showed up. Surprising me at my place of work is one thing, but then showing up at my home, uninvited, with expectations to clear out my house? Uh uh. No way.

"Cindy, please continue to make yourself at home. This won't take long. Juliette, let's go into the kitchen."

Cindy nods and picks up my discarded newspaper while Juliette follows me out of the living room, still clutching her coat.

We stand there, staring at each other. It feels like a dodgeball face-off just before the referee signals the ball is in play.

"Did you think about what I said?" asks Juliette, quietly.

"I did," I say, nodding. "But you're not going to like my answer."

She nods and looks up at my ceiling, sighing.

"Juliette, I love Marcus. I'm not leaving him. And I have no control over him and what he wants and who he decides to be with. You must know that."

"I do," she says. "And I figured you were going to say that."

The kitchen is warm and I start to sweat. I can see a sheen building on Juliette's forehead as she finally starts peeling off her coat. I don't want to look, but I have to. She sees me staring.

"I'm not showing too much yet," she says, rubbing her stomach through her bulky sweater. "You could probably tell in tighter clothes though."

I sigh. "I know this sucks. I do. But I can't give you what you want."

"You're the only one who can," she says.

"Come on Juliette, you know that's not true," I shake my head. "This isn't about me. It's about you and Marcus."

"It is about you," she says, her voice starting to rise. "You meddled in my marriage. You did that. And now he doesn't want me back. It's most definitely about you."

We stare at each other. Her eyes are bright with tears and I can feel hot, salty drops starting to collect in the corners of my own eyes. I am trying desperately to extinguish that gnawing parasite in my gut, telling me that she's right.

"Don't you dare cry," she says to me. "You have no right."

I nod, blinking back the tears and willing myself not to cry. As usual, I oscillate between guilt and anguish for Juliette or pure rage.

"Look, Juliette. I think you should talk to Marcus. I don't want to be in the middle of this."

"Are you fucking crazy?" she shouts at me. "YOU put yourself in the middle of this. You will ALWAYS be in the middle. How do you think this is going to play out, huh? You think this baby is going to love you like a mother? You think you're just going to slide into our lives easily as the other woman? You think our families are going to welcome you, my husband's mistress, with open arms?" screams Juliette, her face turning bright red, her fists balled at her sides. "Heartless bitch," she says, seething.

"Please," I say, "Take a breath. Sit down."

"You can't just make me disappear," she says, her voice still raised. "That may have worked before, if I wasn't having Marcus's child. HIS child," she says, shooting eyeball daggers at me.

"Juliette, please calm down," I say, trying to ratchet down her anger. "This can't be good for the baby."

Juliette starts laughing like a lunatic. It's creepy. "Like you care at all what's good for this baby," she says. "You STOLE my husband. You lured him away from his family. Have you no shame? No humility?"

I suck in a deep breath. Where the hell is Marcus? I feel like he really needs to be here for these outbursts.

I'm about to speak when Cindy comes barreling into the kitchen. "Everything okay in here? There's a lot of yelling going on."

"We're fine," Juliette hisses through gritted teeth. "I was just telling your friend here to back the fuck away from my husband."

Oh boy.

Cindy's eyes go wide at that as she turns to look at me, eyebrows raised. I ignore her. I can only handle one crazed woman at a time.

"Juliette, Marcus was married to you. He's the one who took vows. You need to deal with him, not me."

"Is. Is married to me," Juliette says, widening her stance and crossing her arms defiantly. "He's still married to me. And we're having a baby."

"I know," I whisper, my intestines churning. I hear Cindy suck in a breath. I can't look at her. At either one of them. I look at the floor and then at my beautiful emerald bracelet encircling my wrist, the weight of all those green gemstones suddenly feeling heavy and burdensome.

How do I keep Marcus and not destroy this child's chance at a family? How can I hold on to the love of my life and still look at myself in the mirror every morning? There has to be a way.

There has to be.

"Quinn, I wouldn't be here if it wasn't for the baby. I'd let Marcus go. I really would."

I can't speak. I can't look forward into the future and I can't seem to look backward, either. I am here, in the moment, feeling smothered by Juliette's pain and the weight of my role in this mess. It doesn't help that Cindy is witness to this nightmare, either.

Juliette slumps against the counter, clearly drained. "What am I supposed to tell this child?"

I have no answers. I squeeze my eyes shut and try to block out Juliette for a moment. And Cindy. And that terrible mantra in my head — *this kid will hate you, hate you, hate you.*

"You're not going to back off, are you?" Juliette asks softly.

"There's no guarantee, you know," I whisper. "Even if I backed off, you still might not get him back."

Juliette nods. "I know that. I just want the chance. And you're in my way."

"Do you really expect me to give up the love of my life?"

"Yes. I'm banking on your decency," says Juliette. "It's not my fault you chose a married man. You could have picked a single one."

"She has you there," says Cindy, piping up from the corner of the kitchen. "You kinda made your bed."

"Seriously Cindy?" I ask, staring at her. "You really don't want to get involved in this."

"Okay, okay," says Cindy, backing out of the kitchen. "It's Juliette, yes?" she says, addressing Marcus's wife. "I get it. Quinn dated my husband for a while too."

Juliette stares at Cindy and then back at me.

"You've got to be kidding me," she says. "And now you're friends?"

Cindy shrugs. "I guess we are now. But that's only because she left him alone and decided to help me win him back."

"Okay," I say, feeling Juliette's incredulity shrouding the room like a wet storm cloud. "Enough. I'm done. Everybody out of my house."

"I'm just saying, I like you now," says Cindy. "You did have the decency to bow out. Zack and I are good now. Great, in fact," she says, smiling at both of us.

"Out. Please," I say. "I can't handle anymore today."

"I'll go, but we're not finished yet," says Juliette, putting on her jacket.

"Of course not," I say, exhausted.

I watch as the two of them start the winter bundling process.

How did I get myself into this? Will my life ever just be normal?

"You know, Quinn could help you win your husband back, too," I hear Cindy saying to Juliette.

I roll my eyes, too tired to respond.

"She'll do the right thing," says Cindy as they walk out my door. "Just give her time."

I close the door behind them and lean against it, too drained to move. I press my forehead into the cool fiberglass only to have my head rattled by a rap at the door.

Now what?

Cindy.

She stares at me with those perfectly round, navy blue eyes.

"Quinn, you cannot come between that family."

"It's really none of your business."

"But it is. We women have to stick together."

I rub my hands over my face. "It's complicated, Cindy. Way more complicated than it was with Zack."

"And you think throwing a baby in the middle is going to uncomplicate things?"

"I know. I know," I say, throwing up my hands. "It's a terrible situation."

"It is, but you're not a terrible person, Quinn," she says softly. "I know you're not. And you have the power to make a difference here."

"What am I supposed to do?"

"Use it," she says as she turns to go. "You're better than this. Let that woman have her family back."

I sigh as I watch Cindy walk away.

She looks over her shoulder at me one last time. "That kid is going to hate your guts."

CHAPTER 48

Daily Special

Roasted cauliflower soup with Parmesan cheese crisps
House-made tagliatelle with prosciutto, brown butter and fried sage

I'm late getting to Persimmon, so I hustle past the kitchen and make quick work of my wine selections. I've had a few days off, which has been mentally torturous since Juliette's visit, so I am glad to be back. I've been skulking around my apartment, ruminating and eating ricotta cheese sandwiches. I didn't even have the heart to tell Dezi yet about Juliette's latest visit as I didn't want to dampen her sheer, bride-to-be joy.

And Marcus is still on a trip, so I haven't had the chance to talk to him yet either. My plan is to be honest and direct as he needs to know what Juliette is doing and we need to figure out a plan. I can't keep fighting her. This is his battle and he needs to take over.

I make my first pass through the dining room to get my early birds squared away. I need three bottles of Crémant, an Italian primitivo, a half dozen cocktails and two bottles of sauvignon blanc that "don't smell like cat pee."

"Q," says Julian as I head to the bar to put in my cocktail orders. "Are you okay?" he asks, looking intently at my face.

"Not really. Don't quite have my usual mojo."

"Anything I can do?"

I shake my head. "It's been a rough few days. I'll get through it."

"Well, you know where to find me. My ears are always open."

I smile at that. "Thanks Julian. I plan to take full advantage."

"Glad to hear it," he says, winking at me as he starts filling my orders. "Happy to help."

The rest of the evening goes by in a blur of customers and wine orders and Chef barking at me about refilling the cheese cart. I happily take care of everyone and everything, grateful for the distraction from my internal war. The term cognitive dissonance pops into my head from my eons ago psychology 101 class when I was a college freshman. My head and my heart want different things. How do you reconcile that?

The evening crush is over, so I take advantage of the lull to take a quick break and check my phone. I really want to hear from Marcus. I have three text messages:

Marcus: How's my green-eyed girl? I love you. I miss you. I'm thinking about you.

I smile at that. I'm thinking about him too. Always.

The next two are from Alex. Uh oh. I've been ignoring him a bit since I found out Juliette is pregnant. I don't know how to tell him.

Alex: Yo. Quinn. What's up?

Alex: Are you alive? Are you avoiding me? I thought we were supposed to get together soon.

I shoot Alex a quick text just to tide him over while I think things through.

Me: Ha ha! I'm good. Just crazy busy. At work now. Talk soon?

I tell Marcus I love him and miss him too and then put my phone away and head back into the dining room. I can't wait to see him. Every time I do it affirms how much I adore him and renders all this other nonsense inconsequential. He's a part of me now, almost like an appendage or a vital organ. I need him. And he needs me.

I do a table sweep, pouring more wine and offering additional suggestions and pairings. I get my six-top a few more bottles — two reds and a white — but everyone else is now content, happily slurping shallow bowls of pasta or slicing through slabs of meat or Chef's eggplant Parmigiana.

I see Julian out of the corner of my eye, trying to get my attention.

"What's up?" I ask, making my way over.

"Somebody is asking for you at the bar," he says. "And before you even ask. It's a man. Never seen him before."

I sigh. At least it's not Juliette, I suppose.

I walk into the bar and see Alex sitting on a stool. I let out a whoosh of air in relief.

"Alex," I say, giving him a hug. "What are you doing here?"

"I'm working on a story and had to come to D.C. Your text said you were at work. Thought I'd come say hello."

"I'm glad you did. Hungry?"

He nods, "Starving. I keep seeing these giant bowls of pasta come out. Can you set me up with that?"

I nod. "Absolutely. It's tagliatelle and it's delicious. Chef's special tonight."

I get Alex squared away with his dinner and introduce him to Julian. They start yapping almost immediately — I knew they would get along great — so I leave him to his dinner and his new friend while I wrap up with my tables for the evening.

Twenty minutes later I'm done for the night, so I flop down next to Alex at the bar.

"What's new little brother?" I ask. "What story are you working on?"

"Can't say yet," he says, shrugging. "But what's new with you? You seem out of sorts."

"What is it with you two?" I ask, looking from Julian to Alex. "Do I look that horrid?"

"You just aren't your usual, joyful self," says Alex. "And you've been ignoring my texts. Spill it Quinn. I know you. Something is going on."

I sigh and fiddle with my emerald bracelet. Julian slides a Cognac in my direction.

"Quinn, you aren't getting scared off because of the divorce, are you?" Alex asks. "Please tell me you aren't going back to dating married men."

I shake my head and take a sip of my drink.

"Whew. You had me worried there. Marcus is a good guy. I like him. You two are great together."

I nod. "We are."

"So, what is it?" he asks, turning my barstool toward him and searching my face for clues.

"Juliette is pregnant," I say slowly. "She keeps badgering me to leave Marcus alone and give them a chance."

"I wasn't expecting you to say that," he says, shaking his head. "Wow."

"You're telling me."

I relay all the pertinent details — Juliette's two visits, the yelling, the begging, the name calling and Marcus telling me it wouldn't matter. He's leaving Juliette regardless.

Alex stays quiet and just listens.

"So that, dear brother, is what's new," I say with a half-hearted flourish.

He does his usual thing and remains silent.

"I love him so much," I whisper.

"I know you do," Alex says. "You finally turned a corner."

"Alex. What do I do?"

"I can't tell you that. Nobody can."

I sigh and take a long sip of my Cognac.

"Quinn, there will be regrets either way. But only you can decide what you can live with," Alex says. "And what you can live without."

CHAPTER 49

Rule #17: Never underestimate the bond of family.

"Q. Tell me why I'm coming with you again?" asks Julian as we start the drive to Baltimore to have dinner with my family.

"Because Marcus likes you, Alex likes you, I adore you and you need a solid, home-cooked meal," I say, smiling at him. "And my mother is making a stupid amount of food."

"And ...?" he asks, looking at me suspiciously.

"And I hate the drive by myself."

And I want to pick your brain. And I need some extra distraction from my love triangle. And if Marcus and I actually get engaged someday, I'd like you in the wedding party. So it's about time you met my parents.

We are off to Baltimore for an early dinner. Alex is coming, of course, and Marcus is meeting us there as he has a flight later. Dezi was supposed to come as well, but apparently there's some crisis with Emma and Greg, so she's sticking around to help Elliot with the girls. Greg, I'm told, is still trying to win Emma back, but she's having none of it. I guess she reached the limit of her patience.

"Please tell me you aren't trying to set me up," says Julian warily. "You promised you wouldn't."

"I'm not, I swear. I wouldn't try to pull a stunt like that on you. I know better. You'd never talk to me again."

"You got that right," he says, leaning back in his seat. "Okay then. I'm game for a good meal. And I dig your brother. He's a good guy."

"And Marcus?"

Julian sighs. "Q. I have always liked Marcus."

"But ...?"

"But cheating on your wife and then leaving her when she's pregnant? I'm not so sure he falls into the good guy category."

"It's more complicated than that," I whisper. "They were over long before he met me, but he couldn't just leave at the time. She was fragile. If anything, doing the right thing back then sort of screwed things up for him now."

Julian nods. I can feel him looking at my profile as I watch the road.

"I trust your judgement, Q," he says. "You know him better than I do. And I don't claim to have any clue as to what goes on inside another person's marriage."

"You think I'm doing the wrong thing," I say.

"Only you know what that is. Don't let anyone tell you different."

"Not even you?" I ask, smiling and playfully punching him in the arm.

"Especially not me," he says with a wink.

•　　•　　•　　•　　•

We are the last to arrive at my mom and dad's place. Marcus comes out of nowhere and is on me in a flash. I melt into him as he pulls me in for a tight hug, burying his face in my hair. I sigh and just breathe him in. It's been a few days so I can't get close enough.

"Oh, look at the lovebirds," says my mother, coming over to pry my cheeks away from Marcus for a quick kiss. "Okay, you can have her back now," she says, grinning up at him. We break apart and I'm about to introduce Julian, but find he's already settled with a beer and is busy chatting with Alex and my dad.

How long were Marcus and I entangled? This is embarrassing.

My mom hands me a glass of wine, refills Marcus's sparkling water and ushers us into the kitchen. The island is covered with all things Italian.

There are several types of cured meats, hard cheeses, gooey cheeses, roasted peppers, pickled vegetables, olives, whole walnuts for cracking and three types of dried figs. My mother also baked taralli, which are crunchy, ring-shaped, black pepper biscuits.

"You weren't kidding about the amount of food," says Julian, eyeing the spread and filling up a plate. "Everything looks delicious."

"I'm addicted to these," says Marcus, crunching through a pepper biscuit and spraying crumbs down his sweater. "It's like Italian crack."

I smile and reach up to kiss him on the lips. "I'll make sure to pack a bag for you for your flight."

I leave those two to try and make a dent in the food while I go say hello to my dad and Alex, both of whom are now lounging on the sofa and looking out at the city skyline. I plunk down between them and put my feet up on the coffee table. I feel like a kid again, safe and warm between my dad and brother. Only my sister, Reese, is missing. I wish she'd leave California and join us all on the East Coast.

"Hey sweetheart," my dad says, kissing me on the cheek.

"Yo, Quinn," says Alex, punching me in the arm.

"Carry on," I say, leaning back and closing my eyes. "I'm just going to rest here for a moment and listen."

I sink into the sofa and enjoy their warm, familiar voices discussing sports and politics and Alex's latest story. I open my eyes and take a sip of my wine, watching the city lights twinkling in the evening sky. My gaze wanders and then rests on a framed family photo perched on the fireplace mantle. It's the five of us. And it's an old one. Reese is probably about ten and I can't be more than five. Alex is just a toddler, perched on my mother's hip. Reese and I are sporting matching pigtails and patent leather shoes with ruffled ankle socks. Her socks are neatly folded over as they should be, whereas I've pulled mine up high instead. I remember liking them hiked up that way, oblivious to how ridiculous it looked. My tiny hand is tucked inside my father's and we are all grinning at the camera. Even Alex. You can see his smile around his thumb, which he has jammed in his mouth.

My heart lurches.

Family.

I look around the condo at my mom, dad and brother. All of us together.

Family.

And then I see Marcus, lively and charming and lighting up the room. Lighting up my life.

Family. He already feels like family.

My head is spinning again and it has nothing to do with wine. I am dizzy with desire for Marcus. Marcus. Marcus. My heart stops beating for an instant and then gallops like a crazed horse when I think of saying goodbye to him.

But I can't breathe when I think about cracking a family in two.

Where would I be today without my family, intact and whole?

But where will I be without Marcus?

I can imagine a future with an ex-wife and a stepchild. But right now, when I try to picture a life without Marcus, the screen of my mind turns to static like an old television set with wonky antennae.

Nothing.

I just want to stay wedged between my brother and father where I feel safe and taken care of. Where I don't have to make any decisions.

"Hey beautiful, I'm stealing you for a bit," says Marcus as he reaches for my hands and pulls me up off the sofa and into his arms. "I haven't seen enough of you lately," he smiles down at me.

I snuggle into his arms gratefully. My anxiety seems to vanish whenever he's near.

"I know. I wish you didn't have to fly out tonight," I say, wrapping my arms around his waist and looking up into his jewel-blue eyes.

Marcus leads me outside onto the balcony and wraps his enormous jacket around me.

"Are you okay babe?" he asks softly. "You just seem a bit off tonight. You've barely touched your wine and you haven't even taken a bite of cheese."

I smile at that. He does know me well.

"It's just all of this is weighing on me. Juliette. The baby. It's a lot."

He nods. "I thought that may be what was going on. I know this can't be easy for you."

I shake my head. "It's not. And Marcus, Juliette showed up at my house. *My house.*"

Marcus's eyebrows go up at that. "She did what? When? What did she want?"

I look at him, somewhat exasperated. "What do you mean what did she want? What she always wants. You. She wants me to leave you. She says you would take her back if I let you go."

"Oh sweetheart," he says, gathering me up into his arms. "She is sorely mistaken. Our marriage could not have been saved even a year ago and I'm so far beyond that now. You know that, right?"

"I do," I nod. "I really do. And I've told her that. But she doesn't seem to believe me."

"Quinn," he says, tipping my head back so I can look directly into his eyes. "I want to marry you someday. And I will not have her badgering my future wife."

My heart flips with joy at this. *His future wife.*

"Juliette will not bother you again," he says firmly.

I smile and wrap my arms around his neck. *His future wife.*

"I know we still have a lot to figure out. And I know it's going to get crazy, fast, but we can do this," he says, kissing my cheeks and the tip of my nose.

"You're going to be a father, Marcus. A father."

"I know," he says, smiling down at me. "It's wild. And scary. But you're going to be a part of this kid's life too and we are going to tackle this together. We'll build our own unique little family."

Family, I think. I guess it does come in all shapes and sizes.

•　　•　　•　　•　　•

As we head back inside, I realize I don't even know what my mother is serving for dinner. My brain is addled. I *always* know what's for dinner. She calls us all into the dining room and starts scooping out piles of her gooey, cheesy stuffed shells smothered in homemade marinara sauce. Yes! One of my favorites.

I'm seated between Marcus and Julian with Alex across from me. I'm inside a triangle of my three favorite men. Lucky me. I'm starting to feel better already.

We fall silent as we all tuck into the ricotta and meat-filled pasta. It's that good. Pure Italian comfort food. But soon the compliments are flying, second helpings are passed around and the chatter and banter strike up again.

Before I know it, Marcus has to leave to catch his flight and it feels like a punch in the gut. His leaving deflates me. He says his goodbyes to everyone and I walk him out.

"Quinn, my gorgeous redhead, I will miss you," he says, taking my face in his hands.

"Me too," I sigh, pressing myself against him. "I just can't get enough of you. You're like man crack."

Marcus laughs at that. "Well, if that's a thing, then you're my woman crack. I'll be back for my fix as soon as humanly possible."

"We can do this, right?" I ask softly. "You won't regret choosing me?"

"Never," he says, holding me tight. "My only regret would be letting you go."

After a long, deep, brain discombobulating kiss, we finally part and say goodbye.

"I love you," we say in unison.

I find my mother eagerly waiting for me back inside the house.

"He's just a dream," she says, beaming at me. "Just simply a dream. I cannot wait to help you plan your wedding."

"Whoa. Slow down, mom, let's not get ahead of ourselves. We're new and I don't know where this is going yet."

"Well I do. It's clear he's utterly besotted with you," she says, picking up my emerald-clad wrist. "And no man gives a gift like this without thinking you're wife material. Not a chance."

"Maybe," I say, trying not to break into a huge smile. "But it will be a while yet."

"Don't wait too long. You don't want to let this one get away. He's terrific Quinn. And he adores you. Your father and I couldn't be happier."

I am going to have to explain this new baby to my parents. To MY FATHER. How am I supposed to do that? They can do the math.

I don't know why this realization suddenly dawns on me. It's as if my brain is still stuck in infidelity mode and I need to shift gears into real relationship mode. I can't keep everything separate and clean anymore. My relationship with Marcus, and all the baggage that comes with it, will have to be woven into my life. My family. My friends. They will all know.

I am the other woman. I will always be the other woman.

•   •   •   •   •

Julian and I say goodbye to Alex and my parents and then we bundle up and head for home. He offers to drive and I gratefully accept.

"Well, you were right, that was a stupid amount of food," Julian says with a smile. "But so good. Thanks for including me. I love your family."

Family. There's that word again. Why does it keep catching in my throat?

"See? I told you it would be a good time," I say. "I'm so glad you finally met everyone. And they had the chance to meet you."

We drive in silence for a while, Julian tapping out a drumbeat on the steering wheel with his thumbs.

"How long have they been married?" he asks. "Your parents."

"Oh man, approaching 50 years I think. Something absurd like that. So crazy to think about."

"Wow. It is. My parents were only married a few years."

"Really? I didn't know they divorced."

"Yup," Julian says, nodding. "My dad left when I was six."

Ohhh, that hurts.

"I'm sorry," I say. "Was this the Whack-a-Mole dad who wasn't into having a musician for a son?"

Julian laughs. "The very one. I still saw him obviously, but it was different. It's nice to see people like your parents, together forever."

"Yeah, I hope to have that someday. It is pretty amazing. I just never thought it was in the cards for me."

"Well, you better get after it," he says, smirking. "You're not getting any younger."

"Hey! Look who's talking," I say, smacking him in the arm.

"I'm not the one interested in getting married," he says. "Speaking of, you and Marcus seem happy. Stupid happy, in fact."

"We are," I say, blowing out a sigh and running my fingers through my hair.

"I know, Q," he says softly, glancing at me. "It's great and it sucks. I've been watching you struggle."

I nod and stare out the window.

"I want him, Julian. At any cost."

"Any?"

I nod. "Does that make me a monster?"

"No, Q, it doesn't. Honestly, I felt the same about Violet."

"But you don't have her."

"She didn't want me. She wasn't for sale," he says with a wry smile.

"Her loss," I say, trying to lighten the mood.

I feel like a monster.

When Julian speaks again it's as if he's reading my mind.

"Evil doesn't have a conscience, Q. If you were a monster, you wouldn't feel so torn up about this."

"So maybe I'm just a giant ass, then?"

Julian smiles at this. "I can get on board with that," he says, laughing.

I smack him again, but just a teensy bit harder. "That's it, my friend. No leftovers for you," I say, gesturing towards the back seat, which is piled high with containers of stuffed shells and antipasto.

"Thanks for listening, Julian. I think I'm going to be okay."

"I know you are," he says gently. "Just remember, it doesn't matter what anyone else thinks."

"Is that true? It's hard to untangle myself from that."

"Absolutely true, Q. You're the one who has to live with your decision. You're the one who has to answer, every day, to your own heart and mind."

•   •   •   •   •

My heart and mind want Marcus, I think, as I crawl into bed with a glass of milk and two Nutter Butter cookies. I don't just love him, I feel consumed by him. It's as if he's wrapped his heart and soul around me and has simply absorbed me into his being. I know, in the deepest, darkest caverns of my mind and gut, that I will never love another the way I love him.

No regrets, Quinn. No regrets.

I'm dunking a cookie in milk when my phone pings. It's either Marcus or an emergency, as nobody else would be texting me this late.

It's Cindy. What the …?

Cindy: Hey. Juliette wants lessons.

You have got to be kidding me. I know I should just ignore this, but I can't. It will keep me up and I really need to sleep tonight.

Me: Nope.

Cindy: Oh hey, you're awake! Come on, why not? I told her I'd ask.

Me: When hell freezes over. That's beyond absurd. I am not giving up Marcus, so no way am I giving her lessons.

Cindy: Oh. So you're not leaving him?

Me: I'm not.

Cindy: Wow. Okay. I was so certain you would …

Me: You were wrong.

Cindy: Well, you should.

Me: This has nothing to do with you. Don't make me regret ever starting your lessons.

Cindy: I sort of told Juliette you would probably dump him and give her lessons.

This makes me laugh out loud. Cindy is a piece of work. Even if I were to let Marcus go, I wouldn't dream of helping Juliette win him back. It's a preposterous notion.

Me: Wrong! Good night Cindy. And please don't ask again.

Cindy: Roger that. One last thing. Zack and I were arguing. I brandished a boob! It worked!

I laugh again, almost spitting out a chunk of cookie. I'm happy those two are working things out. They are a good team and I'm sorry I ever messed with Zack. But Zack was never Marcus. With Zack, I always knew

I could walk away, intact and whole. With Marcus? Not a chance. I'd feel blown apart. Even more so than I did after Liam dumped me.

Liam.

I haven't thought about him in a long time. His timing was atrocious but, in the end, he did the right thing, the hard thing and I'm now grateful he had the gumption to call off the wedding. What if he hadn't? We might be married now. Married and miserable. Liam, stuck with a wife he doesn't love and me, running around like a lunatic just trying to make him happy. To make him stay.

I shudder at the thought.

What's the right thing now? For me? For Marcus?

I finish my late-night snack and head to the bathroom to brush my teeth. I look at myself in the mirror. Really look. Without the benefit of makeup, I look wan and worn and well, sad.

I am okay, I think, staring at my reflection as tears start to fall.

At least, I'm going to be. I have to be.

I flop into bed hoping for sleep to come quickly when my phone lights up with a final text.

Cindy: She's having a boy!

CHAPTER 50

Rule #3: No men with young children.

Marcus,

You have brought magic into my life. I feel you pounding in my heart. Swirling in my head. And electrifying every bit of me, from the inside out, whenever you're near.

I know, in the marrow of my bones, that I will never, ever, find another love like you.

I could find a different kind of love. Someday. Maybe.

But your baby can never find a different kind of father. You're it.

Marcus, I cannot be the kind of woman who stands between a father and son. I can't be the ongoing, daily cause of this little boy's pain.

Marcus, my love, I am sorry. I need to let you go and there's no way I could survive doing this in person.

I am dissolving now, as I write this.

You will forever have my heart. And I hope I will forever be a part of yours.

I will love you for the rest of my life.

Quinn

P.S.

Your eyes are blue
This is one lucky baby
He'll have the love of you. And maybe the love of cheese, too.
Your eyes are still the bluest of blues
Cheese

CHAPTER 51

Comfort Food Menu

Wine, a lot of wine
Cheese. An entire wheel if you will
Coconut cake. Extra frosting
Repeat.

I pick my head up off my kitchen counter and push away the cake, the wine and yes, even the cheese. Nothing tastes the same anymore anyway. I'm done. It's been a month and I'm over my pity party. I'm done with the tears and the raggedy ass sweatpants. I'm done feeling as if I can't breathe.

I want my life back. I want to savor wine again and laugh with my brother and throw cocktail olives at Julian and share in Dezi's bride-to-be joy.

Screw my dumbass rules. When I fell in love with Marcus the game changed.

I. Want. Him. Back. More than anything.

But that baby boy?

I pick up my phone and stare at it, scrolling to find Marcus's last text.

Marcus: Quinn. You are the queen of my heart. Always you. Only you. Forever you.

Damn him. His words on the screen start to blur as my eyes fill with tears yet again. I keep staring, watching my tears splatter all over his profile picture, obscuring his dimples and softening his edges.

Maybe, with time, that's how he'll take shape in my heart. Soft and hazy and out of focus. A distant memory.

I can survive this. And I can do it without cake and cheese and endless bottles of wine.

Right?

I swear that giant hunk of Parmesan is calling my name. I'm about to chuck it out my window when I hear a soft rap at my door.

My heart soars. *Marcus?*

I just want to be folded in his arms one last time. Because the last time, well, I didn't know that was it. I didn't know our story was about to end. I would have held on tighter. Longer. I would have memorized his scent and the feel of his arms wrapped around me. And the weight of his chin resting on the top of my head.

I open my door and am instantly engulfed by Dezi. Her might is surprising, given her tiny stature.

"I'm so glad you're here," I say, whispering into her hair. "I was about to do something really stupid."

I was about to call Marcus.

Dezi pulls back and looks at me with a hint of a smile. "You? Do something stupid? No way."

"Funny. Smart ass," I say, smiling through my tears. "I was about to hurl a whopping hunk of cheese out my window. I'm certain it would have conked somebody in the head. And then I'd be dealing with a lawsuit *and* a broken heart."

We are quiet for a moment as we flop on my sofa.

"Talk to me Quinn. How are you holding up?"

I shrug. "I'm sad. I'm exhausted. My insides feel crushed."

Dezi nods, squeezing my hand.

"I miss him. I feel, I don't know, lopsided somehow. And empty. Christ, here come the tears again."

"It's okay, Quinn. Just let it out."

"That's all I've been doing, Dezi. I'm over it. I have good stuff in my life. I love my job, I adore my family and you're getting married! I need to focus on that or I'll go crazy."

"Quinn, honey. Give yourself a break. You are allowed to grieve. You *need* to grieve."

"I know, I know," I say, running my hands through my hair. "Dezi, why did I let myself fall in love? Why?"

"You can't control who you love, Quinn. You know that."

"I didn't know that. I thought I could. But I don't know what happened."

"Quinn, you let Marcus in. That's a good thing. It's a great thing."

"It doesn't feel so great," I say, grumbling.

"Doesn't it, though?"

"You're such a therapist," I say, whacking her with a sofa pillow. "And no, it doesn't feel great at the moment. It feels as though someone died. And as though the world ran out of cheese. And decent red wine."

Dezi giggles. "I'm happy to see your sense of humor is intact."

I sigh. "I'm trying here."

Dezi hugs me tight. "You did the right thing."

Did I?

"And you're going to be okay."

"I know," I say. "I can survive love. And I can survive losing Marcus. I have to."

But I don't want to.

We are quiet. I can feel Dezi's eyes on me and I don't want to return her gaze. I'm about to cave and bring in the coconut cake when there's a knock at my door.

My heart soars. Again. Damn it.

"Dezi?"

"I'm on it," she says, heading to answer the door.

I put my head in my hands and wait for her to shoo away whoever it is. I *know* it's not Marcus. I can always *feel* Marcus.

"Quinn," Dezi says softly. "There's someone here to see you."

I drag my hands down my face as I slowly look up.

Julian.

CHAPTER 52

Rule #11: Nothing lasts forever.
Epilogue: Three years later

"Sometimes, you just need a good lawyer," I lean over and whisper to my student about her philandering, perpetually out-of-work husband. The woman, Jessica, is relatively new to my women's wine class, but has vented repeatedly about her husband's multiple affairs and penchant for lounging in their basement, smoking grass and playing video games.

"Sometimes, all the sweetness and flirting and glimpses of cleavage you dish up won't get you anywhere," I say.

Jessica twirls the stem of her wineglass and looks at me, somewhat bewildered. She's one of a dozen women today attending the Grape Ladies class I host regularly at a local wine shop. I glance around the tasting room and see all the women are in various stages of swirling, sipping and chatting.

"What she's trying to say," says Cindy, plunging her nose deep in her wineglass, "is that once a giant ass, always a giant ass."

I roll my eyes and shake my head at Cindy. And then tell her to pull her nose out of the glass. She's not supposed to blow bubbles in the wine.

Jessica turns toward Cindy, eyebrows raised. "Did you just call my husband a giant ass?"

"You tell me," says Cindy. "*Is* your husband a giant ass?"

The woman stares into her wineglass, then looks at Cindy and then back to me. Her gaze cannot seem to settle in one place. Cindy distracts me by holding up her hands about three feet apart and mouthing, "Giant ass," while this poor woman absentmindedly sloshes her wine.

"Quinn, tell her," says Cindy, looking to me for help.

"Cindy, pay attention to your wine and take a sip. Tell me what you taste." I then lower my voice and whisper, "And please, for the love of god, stop saying the word ass."

I turn to Jessica and pour her a bit more wine. "Do you want to hear this? We can just shut up and talk grapes instead."

She's quiet for a moment, then looks up at me and nods.

"Often, marriages can be salvaged. But sometimes, the guy is simply a jerk and there's no hope. It's just time to get out. But only you can make that decision."

She fiddles with the stem of her glass and starts breaking her cheese into bits. I turn to the rest of my students and ask about what they see, smell and taste in their glasses. I hear descriptions such as black pepper, mushrooms, violets and pipe smoke.

I smile and nod encouragingly, all the while watching Jessica out of the corner of my eye as she destroys her cheese and shreds her napkin. I'm also trying to keep Cindy distracted so that she gives the poor woman some space.

"I'm getting cherry coke out of this," exclaims Cindy, finally focusing on her wine. "It tastes and smells like a soda."

"Yes, definitely," I say. "That can be typical of this grape. Good nose, Cindy. Anyone else?"

"I'm not crazy about it," pipes up Jessica. "It's flat and sort of flabby. And boring. And look at that hoity toity label," she says, starting to get excited. "It's just like my stupid, life-sucking husband."

Wow. Okay. She's getting a hell of a lot out of this pinot noir.

"It's certainly good to know what you don't like," I say, watching her carefully as a smile slowly spreads across her face.

"You're right," she says enthusiastically. "It is. And I honestly don't like my husband. He IS a giant ass. And he always has been. God, what a jerk. What have I been thinking all these years? I've wasted so much time."

She examines the cabernet franc I just poured and takes a delicate whiff of the wine.

"Green bell pepper. I'm literally smelling bell peppers in this," she exclaims, taking a sip. "Now this is good," she says, smiling at me. "I like this one."

I love it when they finally get it.

And I really love teaching my Grape Ladies classes. I started this casual wine series for women a couple of years ago and it's been a surprising success. I found I prefer the combination of working at Persimmon and teaching classes on the side rather than owning my own boutique wine shop. At least for now, anyway.

So I'm still at Persimmon, working side-by-side with Chef and slowly convincing him to divulge more of his cooking secrets. But my Grape Ladies classes have been a rather fun and rewarding little side gig. We meet monthly and I plan classes based on a chosen theme. Sometimes I focus on a particular country, wine region or simply a type of grape. I tend to set up seasonal wine classes around holidays and often put together food and wine pairings for the women, which is always a hit. Regardless of the monthly theme, the classes roughly follow the same format — I chat for a bit, pour several different wines and the women get the chance to taste, compare wines and essentially discuss the contents of their glasses, and often, their lives. It's quite a social group.

Cindy frequently shows up and pretends to be interested in oenology, but really, she usually brings somebody she thinks needs a little marital help. She tried desperately to get me to hold group "Love Lessons" for jilted women, but I flat-out refused. I maxed out teaching those absurd lessons for her. But I did find that I genuinely enjoy teaching, which eventually led me to start this wine series. I am weirdly grateful for that, so I don't mind Cindy bringing along a friend from time to time. I think the women she brings just need a bit of girl-time and camaraderie to help them navigate their troubled relationships. It's not about lessons, it's about perspective and friendship and not feeling quite so alone.

But, of course, sometimes it's clear there is a giant ass in the room, so to speak. And if I don't say it, Cindy certainly will.

I'm embarrassed to admit that, very occasionally, I will agree to help out a friend or acquaintance of Cindy's. I don't give lessons, per se, but I will offer up my perspective as a mistress if it seems appropriate. And let's face it, Cindy can be insanely persistent. She also credits me for saving her marriage to Zack. It's sweet, but definitely not true, which I have told her repeatedly. But she remains wildly enthusiastic about my ability to help other women in similar situations, despite my pleas to the contrary. So, I acquiesce from time to time.

I suppose it's my way of using my days of dating married men for good, rather than destruction. I know Dezi sees it that way. I also know I'm not a counselor and I don't pretend to be, but it seems the women who wind up under my tutelage are looking for something a little less conventional. And, as some have pointed out, my experience dating married men puts me in a unique position to offer front row insight. For now, it just plain feels good to help other women for once rather than steal their husbands.

•   •   •   •   •

My wine class is almost over for today. I reveal the theme for next month and review my recommended homework wines. Some of the women like to come fully prepared, while others just enjoy showing up and chugging wine. It doesn't matter to me, everyone is welcome.

I answer a few final wine questions and then we all walk out the door together, spilling onto the sidewalk and into the late afternoon sunshine.

"Hey Quinn, did you just get engaged?" asks one of my students, grabbing my left hand. I nod and smile.

I am engaged. Engaged! And I'm over the moon. My days of dating married men are so over. As are my days of hardening my heart to love. We haven't planned anything yet as he just recently proposed, much to my surprise and delight. I wouldn't mind a simple wedding with just a handful of friends, but somewhere spectacular, like Italy or France. Somewhere with food and wine pairings to make us all swoon. But no big plans yet. It's so new my engagement ring still feels foreign.

"I did. Just last week," I say, feeling my cheeks heat up with pleasure as I display my hand.

"Wow, that is a beautiful ring," she says, admiring my diamond solitaire, which is flanked by two stunning, shimmering green emeralds. "I've never seen anything like it."

"Just like my bride-to-be," says my fiancé, coming up behind us and wrapping his arms around my waist, nuzzling my neck. "It's one of a kind. And green. Just like her eyes."

THE END

ACKNOWLEDGEMENTS

Writing a novel is not the solo endeavor I had imagined. It truly takes a team and I am eternally grateful for the talented crew who turned my dream into a book.

A huge thank you to the team at Black Rose Writing for their dedication, hard work and their belief in me and my vision for *Infidelity Rules.*

I certainly couldn't have done this without the steady support of my friends, my family, my comrades at the Women's Fiction Writers Association and all of my early readers. The book is infinitely better because of you all. Thank you to my insightful and sharp-eyed beta reading team — Audrey Ingram, Jessica Stevens and Jo Ann Mathews. To my mentor through the WFWA, Samantha Skal, I was unbelievably lucky to get paired with you. You never lost faith. A big thanks to all my friends who took the time to read this novel and provide feedback in its early stages. To my mother-in-law, Tikva Butler, for your unwavering strength, support and love. And a special thanks to Christina Rutheiser, Barbara Lakis, Pam Connolly, Kristen Flank, Karen Southern, Princess Hester and Michael Ryan Wright for reading multiple iterations of the manuscript and listening to me endlessly yap about my dreams. All of you unfailingly championed this novel, fell in love with my characters and told me repeatedly, do not give up. I am beyond grateful for that kind of support.

To my rockstar mom, Karen Babula, you've always been my biggest cheerleader. You loved the idea of this book from its inception and have applauded it every step of the way. And to my late father, William, the first author of the family and forever an inspiration.

And finally, a King Kong-sized thank you to my husband, John. Your ferocious support and utter delight in watching me find such joy in this process was nothing short of magical. *Infidelity Rules* would not be in the world today without you. Thank you for fighting for this book. For fighting for my dreams. And for always, always, being up for cheese.

ABOUT THE AUTHOR

Joelle Babula is an award-winning former journalist and columnist and currently a nurse practitioner. A graduate of Johns Hopkins University School of Nursing, she now lives in the Baltimore area with her husband and two ridiculous lap cats. *Infidelity Rules* is her debut novel. When not writing or taking care of patients, she can be found exploring Baltimore's fabulous restaurant scene, playing outside, or cooking for friends and family. Often, she's traversing the Eastern Seaboard in search of her next great food moan. She and her husband enjoy traveling, outdoor adventures, and all manner of ballroom, swing, and disco dancing. She is currently drinking wine and working on her next novel. Or eating cheese.

NOTE FROM JOELLE BABULA

Word-of-mouth is crucial for any author to succeed. If you enjoyed *Infidelity Rules*, please leave a review online—anywhere you are able. Even if it's just a sentence or two. It would make all the difference and would be very much appreciated.

Thanks!
Joelle Babula

We hope you enjoyed reading this title from:

www.blackrosewriting.com

Subscribe to our mailing list – *The Rosevine* – and receive **FREE** books, daily
deals, and stay current with news about upcoming
releases and our hottest authors.
Scan the QR code below to sign up.

Already a subscriber? Please accept a sincere thank you for being a fan of
Black Rose Writing authors.

View other Black Rose Writing titles at
www.blackrosewriting.com/books and use promo code
PRINT to receive a **20% discount** when purchasing.